Praise for Kerrigan Byrne and her captivating novels

"The dark, violent side of the Victorian era blazes to life as a caring, competent heroine living under the radar is abducted by a notorious crime lord with wonderfully gratifying results in this exceptional and compelling vengeance-driven romantic adventure."
—*Library Journal* (starred review) on *The Highwayman*

"The romance is raw, edgy, and explosive . . . the path they take through adversity makes the triumph of love deeply satisfying."   —*Publishers Weekly* on *The Highwayman*

"A truly mesmerizing series that highlights dangerous heroes who flout the law and the women who love them."
—*Library Journal* (starred review) on *The Hunter*

"Dramatic, romantic, and utterly lovely."   —*BookPage*

"Byrne is a force in the genre."
—*RT Book Reviews* (Top Pick!) on *The Highwayman*

"Romantic, lush, and suspenseful."
—Suzanne Enoch, *New York Times* bestselling author

"A passionate, lyrical romance that takes your breath away."
—Elizabeth Boyle, *New York Times* bestselling author

"Beautifully written, intensely suspenseful, and deliciously sensual." —Amelia Grey, *New York Times* bestselling author

Also by
Kerrigan Byrne

The Highwayman
The Hunter
The Highlander
The Duke

The Scot Beds His Wife

KERRIGAN BYRNE

St. Martin's Paperbacks

This is a work of fiction. All of the characters, organizations, and events portrayed in this novel are either products of the author's imagination or are used fictitiously.

THE SCOT BEDS HIS WIFE

Copyright © 2017 by Kerrigan Byrne.
Excerpt from *The Duke with the Dragon Tattoo* copyright © 2017 by Kerrigan Byrne.
Excerpt from *The Highwayman* copyright © 2015 by Kerrigan Byrne.

For information address St. Martin's Press, 175 Fifth Avenue, New York, NY 10010.

ISBN: 978-1-250-12254-4

Our books may be purchased in bulk for promotional, educational, or business use. Please contact your local bookseller or the Macmillan Corporate and Premium Sales Department at 1-800-221-7945, ext. 5442, or by e-mail at MacmillanSpecialMarkets@macmillan.com.

Printed in the United States of America

St. Martin's Paperbacks edition / October 2017

St. Martin's Paperbacks are published by St. Martin's Press, 175 Fifth Avenue, New York, NY 10010.

10 9 8 7 6 5 4 3 2 1

To R.L. Merrill and Ellay Branton
What would this book be without yous twos?

ᴀCKNOWLEDGMENTS

As always, my editor knows just what to say to encourage me and in what direction to point when I get lost. Thank you, Monique and Alex, for all your work, support, and communication. Justine, Marissa, their marketing team, the SMP design team, Jon Paul, and my copy editor—I don't know your name, but I'm in love with your red pencil—and everyone who touches these books who I never get to thank in person, are a tribe I'm grateful for every single day.

My agent, Christine, is the woman I don't know how to be, and admire constantly from a safe distance. She fights my battles for me, even the ones I don't know I'm fighting, and her warrior spirit is second to none.

Cynthia St. Aubin, there's not enough room on this page to sing your accolades, but congratulations a million times. Cynthia and Tiffinie Helmer, this book would not have happened without you. I have the best critique partners in the world.

Also for my love. You're the strongest person I know. Thank you for all the memories.

And all the coffee.

PROLOGUE

The boy they called Thorne lost his virginity at almost sixteen years of age. He'd lost his innocence long before that. So young, in fact, it never occurred to him to miss it.

It was the night his father had bought the bawd Tessa McGrath and brought her to Ravencroft Keep. He'd not have been the first man to purchase a prostitute for the purpose of turning his boys into men. But Thorne had been too young to guess, at the time, that Hamish Mackenzie never intended for his sons to learn to be lovers.

Only monsters, like himself.

The lass had been famous in the Highlands for specializing in the darker side of eroticism, but when she'd accepted the proposition of the Laird Mackenzie, she'd not realized the fathomless depths of his cruelty.

She'd thoughtfully brought her own satchel of playthings. Soft whips, buttery-leather straps for binding or lashing, and other creative and clever devices that even a randy boy of Thorne's age couldn't imagine the applications thereof.

He'd tried, as he'd stood next to his elder brothers and looked on in petrified fascination as his father had tied the purring, naked whore to the bed. He'd glanced up at Liam and Hamish, looking for cues as to how he should feel or what to expect.

Hamish the younger, his father's bastard namesake, had a predatory gleam in his onyx eyes. A malevolent anticipation that puzzled and confused Thorne. He knew that Hamish was no virgin. At twenty, the man had already boasted of a great deal of conquests, willing and otherwise.

Liam, the Ravencroft heir, barely spared the naked woman a glance. He, instead, regarded their father with a grim sort of misgiving. Liam had been born in the middle of Hamish and Thorne, but his mother was Laird Mackenzie's first wife. The one who died.

The one everyone said their father had killed.

Thorne's gaze bounced between Liam and the Laird. Their features almost identical. Long hair as black as a raven's wing. Midnight eyes. Hard, brutal features. He was surprised to note that Liam was almost as tall as Father now. To Thorne's reckoning, they stood as big as one of the oaks lording over Inverthorne Forest. He didn't know if Liam had a woman . . . or women. They didn't speak much anymore. But Thorne loved his brother with all the gentle ferocity his young body could contain.

Liam was brave. He was strong and stern and protective. Sometimes, when Thorne had been very young, Liam had shown him where to hide when the Laird had been on one of his violent rampages. He'd taken a few lashes or blows that had rightly belonged to Thorne.

And for that, he'd forever love his brother. No matter what.

Thorne wasn't small enough to fit in the nooks and crannies of Ravencroft anymore, which was why he now sought refuge in the outdoors whenever possible.

Tessa McGrath had been lovely that night. Lithe, with smooth, pale skin and intriguing beauty marks in places he'd never really glimpsed before, but had always fantasized about seeing. The underside of her generous breast. The inside of her thigh. Right above the soft tuft of hair between her legs.

The whore had aroused him. Excited him. She'd writhed and begged, she'd said the things ladies only did in his fantasies, but *out loud*.

He'd have to tell his closest mate, Callum, about this tomorrow, he thought. The stable master's boy was a year or two younger than he, but they had spent years romping about Wester Ross and galloping their horses over Gresham Peak to the freedom of the Erradale Moors. Lately, they'd taken to pinching a bit of fragrant tobacco from Callum's father's tin, and smoking it behind the Rosses' cattle pastures. They'd watch the waves bash against the black cliffs, and laugh at the antics of fluffy red Highland calves while speculating at length on just this very thing.

What a naked woman looked like. What she'd feel like. What they someday wanted to do to her. Or what they hoped she'd do to them. They'd spy on Mrs. Ross. A pretty, young, dark-haired lass with sparkling blue eyes and a way to her walk that endlessly enticed them both. She was a strong and shapely woman, with a laugh that carried over the moors and drew answering smiles from the boys. Though she was a cattle rancher's wife, she always dressed like a fine lady.

On a particularly sunny day, they'd peeked over one of the craggy stones at the base of Gresham Peak in open-mouthed stupefaction as James Ross had tupped his pretty wife against the barn in front of God and all the cattle. With her dress on and everything, much to the disappointment of the boys, as the particulars of the act had been hidden in endless petticoats. The entire affair had been fast and loud and the couple had sighed and laughed afterward.

"I could marry a woman like that," Callum announced in his brash Irish brogue.

"Aye," Thorne had readily agreed. Though he wasn't so sure . . . maybe he wanted a woman more like his own mother. Soft-spoken, elegant, and unfailingly kind. Mrs. Ross sometimes yelled at her husband, and once, they'd seen her throw a shoe at him.

Hit him right in the arse.

What kind of woman did something like that?

His mother would *ne-ver.*

His father would certainly kill her if she so much as raised her voice to him, let alone her shoe.

God, but he despised his father. Almost as much as he feared him.

Why couldn't he have been born to people like the Rosses? Simple, happy people. Wealthy in land and holdings, or so he heard tell, but not noble in the least. They lived in their own verdant kingdom, one Thorne visited as often as he could escape his own.

Well, the next time he and Callum slipped away, he'd get to boast that he'd become a man this night. That he'd done all the things they'd held in the scope of their boyish conjecture. And other things, besides.

Sometimes he hated Callum. Envied him his gruff but fair and kind father and endless days of freedom to hunt and haver like a bloody savage. Thorne had been an earl since his seventh year, as his mother's uncle had died, and he'd been the next male heir in the St. James line. Inverthorne Keep to the north belonged to him now, though his father claimed it in trust and held it as his troth.

Thorne's title meant nothing to him. He was only glad to be clever, that he'd a wit for words, as he'd lock away every detail of his experience with Tessa McGrath to describe in graphic, envy-inducing detail on the morn.

That was the last thought he'd spare for Callum until much, much later.

Who could focus on aught but the encompassing sight of the willing lass splayed before him?

Then, the Laird produced *the* whip, and Thorne's anticipation and arousal withered like a salted snail.

Hamish's favorite instrument of pain and terror had been a Mackenzie acquisition from the Roman era. Legend had it one of their Pictish ancestors had ripped it out of the hands of a Legionnaire and beaten him to death with it.

Thorne didn't know if the story was true. But he knew the pain of its kiss, and missed the flesh it had torn from his back upon occasion.

A desperate "no" tripped from his lips as the Laird ran the whip over the purring whore's back. She'd arched and gasped in anticipation . . .

Until the first two lashes had bit into her own perfect flesh.

Thorne shrank away as his father stalked to their side of the bed and held the detested whip's pommel out to his sons.

"Two lashes from each of ye," he'd ordered.

"She'll not survive that," Thorne had protested against his better judgment. He hated the crack in his high voice, and the slight pitch of hysteria at the sight of the blood welling on the woman's soft back.

He'd not seen the blow coming from his father, though he should have, he reflected wryly, as he blinked away stars from the flat of his back and swallowed a mouth full of blood.

"Two. Lashes. Each," the Laird repeated. "I doona care which of ye gives how many, but she'll not be released until she's been whipped six more times."

None of the Mackenzie lads spoke. They barely breathed. Though Thorne looked to Liam who glared at their father with a hatred that seemed to match his own.

"Ye do it," the Laird ordered with an evil smile. "Or I'll do it *myself*."

Hamish the younger had reached out for the whip, a frightening anticipation building beneath the apprehension on his less-compelling features.

"Nay." Liam had stepped forward, wrenching the whip out of his father's hand before Hamish could take the chance to. "*I'll* do it."

Six lashes. Six long, hellish, screaming eternities.

Thorne's cheeks were gritty from the salt of his tears by the time it was over. He wept not only for the poor lass, but also because of the darkness gathered on his brother's features. Liam. His hero. His savior. The brawniest of them all wielding the one instrument of wrath they'd all come to fear. He looked like a demon there in the candlelight, conducting violence upon a defenseless woman.

He looked exactly like their father.

It was a sight Thorne knew he would never forget.

Deep down, he understood Liam had no choice. That his brother didn't hurt the lass like their father would have. That maybe he didn't want Hamish and Thorne to have to do such a dreadful thing.

But that night, the pain writhing on that woman's face

would paint his nightmares for the entirety of his life. Because that night had changed everything.

It hadn't ended with the whipping.

It hadn't ended with the hour of unspeakable things the Laird had forced them to do to Tessa McGrath.

Nor had it ended when she'd been released.

Nay, for Thorne, the terror had just begun.

A dark pride and a sick relish glinted in the Mackenzie Laird's eyes as Liam bore the woman out. She couldn't walk correctly, but, to her credit, she spit and fought and vowed retribution.

"A rare lass, that," Hamish considered. "Never submitted her will . . ."

The Laird turned his cold notice to Thorne, who'd lost his ability to cry somewhere in the middle of it all.

Shame washed him in layer of filth and self-hatred.

Thorne looked down at his hands and wanted to cut them off. To keep himself from doing something unutterably foolish, he crossed his arms in front of him and gripped each of his skinny biceps, wishing with everything he possessed that he had a fraction of Liam's corded brawn. Or even Hamish's doughy bulk.

He was still a boy. He knew that. Nothing he'd done tonight made him feel like a man. No actions recounted to Callum would induce anything but disgust. Or worse, pity.

"Weakness is tedious and disappointing." The Laird sneered at Thorne. "Like yer mother. Like ye. At least I have two strong sons." He clapped Hamish on the shoulder.

"The whore is going to talk, Father," Hamish the younger had warned. "She might make trouble for us."

"Nay. There are ways to ensure her silence."

A soul-deep tremble racked Thorne's entire frame at the way his father spoke. He wanted to rip his flesh from his own sullied body. He wanted to flee this room and never return. He burned to take the dirk from his father's boot and shove it through his cruel, dark eye, ending both Thorne's misery, and his mother's.

But he couldn't reach that high. Not without his father cutting him down first.

Not yet. The thought snarled through him.

"There's a social in Gairloch tonight, and my blood is still up." The Laird yawned. "I think I'll wander there for some further sport."

"Can I come with ye, Father?" Hamish queried.

"Aye, there's a woman I've been after a long time, and tonight she willna tell me nay."

Then Thorne was alone. Naked but for his kilt and one wool stocking.

He didn't know how long he stood there in the dark and watched the candles flicker, the shadows performing a nightmarish reenactment of the horrors this room had been privy to. His gorge rose at the sight of the bed. There was blood on the sheets. Oh God, he couldn't look any more.

Eventually, his legs moved, and he wound his way through the corridors of Ravencroft Keep until he found himself in his mother's chamber. The slide of the lock roused her from her slumber, and the next thing Thorne knew, he'd collapsed against her, dry-eyed, and confessed everything. He wondered, rather numbly, if she could smell the sex and disgrace on him. If she'd stop loving him now. If she'd fear him like she did his father.

When he finished his tale, she just held him in the darkness for a long while, her hot tears dripping into his hair. "I'm sorry," she whispered piteously. "I'm sorry that he's your father. I wish I'd known. I'd have run to the ends of the earth rather than married him. You have to understand, I was only sixteen. He and my father had business and . . .

well, I was very innocent. I didn't know what he was like. I would have chosen for you a different father if I could reach through time and change it all."

Thorne's guilt doubled for distressing her. For laying his sins at her feet. He just didn't know where else to go.

"He wants to turn us into him," he whispered, despair threatening to drown him in the absolute darkness of her chamber. "What do I do?"

His mother's small hands, so prone to trembling, gripped the sides of his face with surprising strength and held him aloft in front of her. He could feel the warmth of her breath on his face. It was almost as though she could somehow make out more than his outline in the heavily draped room.

"Do *not* be his son. Do not be a Mackenzie," she pleaded with a whispered fervency he'd never before heard from her. "Hamish is his son. Liam is his son and heir. But you, dear heart, are *mine*. I am sorry I cannot protect you from him, but remember this in the years to come. You are the Earl of Thorne. Lord of Inverthorne Keep. You are beautiful and you are clever and you are good. *Promise me* to remain good. To never touch a woman but sweetly. To never delight in cruelty. To make your own way in this world, apart from this accursed keep and clan and your father's tainted legacy most of all."

"I swear it." Thorne felt the vow solidify in his chest, hardening his heart, nurturing the seed of cold darkness that had been planted this night. "I am *not* his son. I am no Mackenzie."

Thorne allowed his mother to cling to him, to wash away his sins with her tears. It felt unmanly to do so, but he didn't care. Tonight made up for all the nights he'd tried to save her from his father's attentions, and was thwarted by size and age. For all the tears she'd valiantly tried and failed to hide from him. They were equals now. Burdened by the same pain.

And the same name.

He did not have to be Hamish Mackenzie's son.

The Celts were matrilineal before. He didn't need the Mackenzie name to make his way. He'd establish his own name. His own land. His own legacy.

For he'd sire children with a woman he loved. And he'd hold them. And protect them.

They'd be safe. They'd never know fear, or hate, or this soul-crushing ignominy.

They'd be proud of their name.

His name.

Thorne must have nodded off, because he woke to a desperate shake and a sound like thunder.

"You have to hide." His mother was sobbing. "He's going to break the door."

"Eleanor!" One of the hinges gave beneath the Laird's mighty boot. "Ye would dare lock me out of a room in my own home? Do I have to remind ye what happened last time?"

Ye gods, he was drunk. They could hear it in the slur of his words.

"Hide," his mother begged again, creating a protective shield with her body.

"Nay." Thorne, nearly as tall as his petite mother now, vowed that he was never hiding again. He could protect her now that he was a man, or die trying.

The first thing he saw when the Laird finally splintered the hinges was the whip.

He'd never forget how his father looked that night. Not enraged, nor the least bit angry. He wasn't even breathing hard for all the evil he'd wrought. Some of which would remain unknown to anyone until decades later.

It was a cruel sort of triumphant mirth that sparkled in his coal-black eyes. He appeared very much the barbarian marauder, fresh from sacking an entire village, drunk on plunder and bloodlust and his own ruthlessness.

"Goddamn the two of ye." He staggered into the darkness with them, leaving the door open so his bulk was backlit by dim hall lights. "Know what I think?" he asked, seizing Thorne by the arm in a grip so strong, he feared his bones might crumble. "Ye're too pretty to be my son. I'd believe it if ye were my daughter, but all my sons are dark and braw, like me. Ye're no bigger than a toad, and if ye donned a dress, everyone would think ye a cunt."

"Leave him be," his mother pleaded. "Hamish, please. Of course he's your son."

"Did ye take a pretty lover, Eleanor?" Thorne could hear the smile in his father's voice. He knew the terror his question incited, and he reveled in it.

"Never." His mother sobbed. "I'd never dare be unfaithful to you."

"I believe ye," he scoffed. "Ye've not the spirit for such things, and neither does yer git. I'm going to make a man out of this prissy whelp."

Hamish started whipping then. Whipping and whipping and whipping, his arm falling with unnatural precision, even in the dark.

Thorne knew better than to cry out, but he couldn't stop himself. Once the whip was wet with his blood, the bite became an unimaginable agony. The open skin of his back was a queer and terrible sensation he'd not soon forget. After a while, he dimly wondered if the high-pitched cries belonged to him or his mother. Either way, they needed to stop.

Now.

Something dark and preternatural rose within him, and

in one fell move, Thorne turned, caught the whip on the next down stroke, and wrenched it from his father's hand. Driven by madness and instinct, he struck back. A stunned sort of triumphant pleasure swathed him as the whip made contact with his father's skin.

His absurd sense of victory was cut tragically short as his father yanked him off his feet, wrenched the casement open, and tossed him out the second-story chamber window.

The fall didn't last long enough for Thorne to fear his own death. It was just beginning to occur to him when impact with the frosty ground surrounding Ravencroft stole his ability to breathe. Fire lanced from his shoulder into his neck, and any kind of auditory stimuli disappeared, cocooning him in a shroud of silence and pain and biting cold.

His mother's screams ripped through the night like a claymore through chain mail.

It cut him with just as jarring a wound.

When Thorne tried to push himself from where he landed, the burn in his shoulder intensified with such astonishing profundity, he didn't know which impending reaction to fight off first, retching or fainting.

His arm, he could not move it.

Gritting his teeth until he felt they would crack, he gripped the moss embankment with his one good hand, and pulled himself to his knees, still fighting to fill his lungs.

A crash broke the stillness of the night, and then the split of a shriek was cut abnormally short.

"Mother?" he gasped.

Nothing.

"*Mother?* Mother? Answer me!"

"Survived that, did ye?" His father's head appeared from two stories above. "Ye're a damn sight tougher than I thought. Though crying for yer mother ruins the effect."

"What did ye do?" Thorne demanded.

"I shut her up." The Laird's slur intensified. "I didna notice the trunk until her head cracked on it."

"I'll kill ye," Thorne vowed to the night, cursing the break in his adolescent voice. "I'll kill ye, do ye hear me? If she's dead, I swear to Christ and all the old gods, ye're a dead man."

The Laird laughed, and what was left of Thorne's soul bled out of him. "Ye're no killer." The prospect seemed to cause the man no end of amusement. "In fact, ye'll not be allowed back into this keep until ye are. Next time ye see me, little cunt, ye'd better be ready to challenge me."

Not even an entire English regiment could have lain the siege Thorne had to Ravencroft Keep that night. He hurled himself like an animal at every barred door. He broke a window with a heavy rock, but merely succeeded in peeling off more skin in the thorny hedgerows beneath, only to find that he couldn't climb the casement with one hand.

Thorne never knew what brought Callum to his side, or how many hours he spent screaming incoherent curses beneath his mother's window before his small, wild friend pulled his frozen body from the ice-brittle ground. He was dimly aware that dawn had begun to outline the Kinross Mountains to the far east in silver.

Though the cold had stolen his ability to move, and his voice had been lost hours before, he still screamed.

His soul screamed.

And he vowed before he lost consciousness that he'd return a killer.

That wasn't the last night Thorne saw his mother, but it *was* the last night she ever saw him.

CHAPTER ONE

Gairloch, Wester Ross, Scotland, Autumn 1880
Twenty years later

"So, it's true. The Earl of Thorne made a deal with the devil." The unique Scots-Irish brogue slid through the night like a sharp dirk through supple skin.

Even on the Sannda Mhòr, the wide swath of beach leading down to Strath Bay, Gavin St. James recognized the deceptively light footfalls of the large man behind him before he'd spoken.

"Wouldna be the first time," he retorted mildly as he clasped Callum Monahan's sturdy forearm in welcome. "Willna be the last. The devil has been many men to me. Here is only one more."

Even by the dim light of the fire, Callum's swarthy, sun-weathered skin contrasted with eyes so golden, they shone with an otherworldly luminescence. They matched the irises of the falcon perched on his left forearm as they studied him from beneath a woolen cowl. "Despite every-thing we've been through, you've not the look of a man who's dealt with many demons."

"And yet . . ." Gavin summoned his signature rakish

grin, letting his insinuation drift into the shadows. Callum knew Gavin's demons were darker than the black waters between Isle of Longa and the shores of the Sannda Mhòr. That Gavin's immediate family—all half brothers—consisted of a hanged traitor, the king of the London Underworld, and a certain Mackenzie Laird all the empire had literally termed the Demon Highlander.

"Ravencroft might *actually* see you hanged this time, if he discovers us." The man the locals christened the Mac Tíre joined Gavin in scanning the moonless night for a sign of the incoming cargo. Mac Tíre in the old language meant Son of the Earth. Master of Beasts.

Gavin thought of his brother. Liam. Now the Laird Ravencroft. He'd not only inherited their father's title, but his temper and proclivity for violence, as well. "One of us is like to kill the other before long. Seems to be the fate of the Mackenzie men." Gavin made an ironic sound, and crouched to add another log to the fire. He idly wondered what it would do to the Demon Highlander to have to witness one more brother kicking at the end of a rope. "Ravencroft never ventures this far north. He gives Inverthorne Keep, the village of Gairloch, and all of Strath Bay a wide berth. He may be the Mackenzie Laird, but this is *my* land. And well he knows it."

"Which makes it a perfect cove for smuggling." Callum's raptorlike eyes shone with the gleam of a man looking forward to the sin he was about to commit.

"Aye," Gavin agreed. "So it does."

In the unnatural stillness of the night, the unmistakable sound of oars sluicing through water announced the arrival of a longboat.

"Speak of the very devil." Callum strode to the edge of the tide, nearly beyond the glow of the fire. A gentle wind stirred his dark cloak and kilt like shadows around his body until he seemed more specter than man. "The Rook approaches."

"How he can navigate this craggy cove in such darkness boggles the mind," Gavin remarked. "Most use a lantern, at least."

Callum slid him a mysterious look over his shoulder. "The land has its demons, and so does the sea." The Mac Tíre whispered something to the falcon, and released it into the air with several powerful beats of its wings. "I trust that Sannda Mhòr is secure, but Manannan Mac Lir will alert us to an unwelcome presence all the same."

Gavin nodded and drew up next to his oldest friend as the gentle surf stole some of the sand from beneath his boots. He lifted the lantern he'd been holding, and signaled a welcome in the direction of the approaching vessel. "What I canna ken, is why a hermit who lives in a cave and sleeps with sheep has a connection to the most notorious pirate since Sir Francis Drake."

"It's more a *shieling* hut than a cave," Callum protested. "And I defy you to tell Angus and Fergus to sleep outside." At Gavin's droll glance, he continued. "I met the Rook some time ago in Tangier. I assisted him with the movement of some exotic animals for a wealthy local warlord, and in return he . . . helped me recover something I'd had taken from me."

" 'Tis a good thing ye're not vague," Gavin muttered.

" 'Tis a good thing you're not your brother." Callum chucked him on the shoulder.

"Amen to that."

Callum took a flask from his cloak and knocked it back before offering it to Gavin. "To Gavin St. James, Earl of Thorne. The profligate black sheep of the Mackenzie Clan."

Gavin drank deeply, welcoming the burn of the Irish

whiskey Callum favored to ward off the chill seeping in from the sea. He silently thanked the gods that it wasn't Ravencroft Scotch. He'd had enough of that to last a lifetime. Returning the flask to the man he'd known since they'd romped about the Highland moors of Wester Ross as wild children, he said, "It occurs to me that to be labeled a black sheep in *my* family, ye'd ironically have to be a good man."

"I see no good men here." A dark, cultured English voice, more menacing than the night surrounding them, hailed over the sound of the lapping water as the tide delivered the boat onto the Sannda Mhòr.

"And ye'll find none," Gavin replied.

"This pleases me, as I have no use for them."

A shadow in a long black coat jumped from the bow with a handful of men, and assisted Gavin and Callum as they dragged the burdened boat farther onto dry sand. That accomplished, they gathered at the fire to conduct their business.

As the son of a notoriously violent man, Gavin had perfected the skills of observation and obfuscation well and early. He could read any man in a matter of seconds. He could tell if they were dangerous, armed, afraid, or compensating, and just how much rope he had to hang himself with. He knew which buttons to press to cause a volcanic eruption, or which levers to pull to release steam and defuse a situation.

As he studied their conclave of criminals, his entire being focused on only one man.

The Rook.

Here stood the kind of chap that sent Gavin's hand inching toward his dirk. It wasn't the Rook's size or height that put him off, as Gavin sensed he easily matched him in strength and stature. Nor was it his menacing scars or the palpable vibrations of danger seeming to throw shadows over the firelight.

It was his eyes. His eerie black eyes.

They were not wild like Callum's, nor skillfully indolent and impassive, like his own. They conveyed no greed, no rage, no approbation, nor scrutiny. They held neither devilish gleam nor demonic malevolence. And what Gavin could read in the pirate's eyes had him reassessing his dealings with the man.

Nothing.

They were dead.

Gavin stood convinced they were not the eyes of a man, but a shark.

The Rook was a creature of the sea, after all. A consummate killer known for his powerful, lethal precision and no natural predators. All the armadas of all the governments in the world had tried to best him.

Yet here he was.

Gavin could tell any that stood before him were not men, only meat.

I see who ye are, he thought. *I have yer measure. But ye doona see me.*

No one did. No one ever saw him. Never knew him. Not his fears or his flaws. His thoughts or his needs. Not his motivations or desires.

And they were legion.

Though the Rook's empty, unblinking stare disturbed Gavin, his own gaze never wavered. He knew the pirate caught his meaning before any word was exchanged between them.

This is dry land, my *land, and ye're not alpha predator here.*

I am.

After a moment spent taking the other's measure like titans on an ancient Olympian battlefield, the Rook finally addressed him. "The Earl of Thorne, I presume?"

"Aye." Gavin nodded. "Welcome to Gairloch."

"You've pretty features, for a barbarian lord."

"I wish I could return the compliment." Gavin smirked at Callum's hastily indrawn breath. The Rook was obviously not a vain man, and so this was neither censure nor challenge. It was a language men like him spoke fluently. Quid pro quo.

Gavin wouldn't have called the pirate unsightly, per se. The strange disfigurement reaching from beneath his collar marred a great deal of the right side of his face, but didn't hide his strong, broad features bladed by sharper, almost aristocratic lines. The Rook had midnight hair and eyes to match.

In fact, he reminded Gavin of a Mackenzie.

Though where Gavin was handsome, and Callum savage, the Rook was nothing more than arresting. Striking. Remarkably so, and the scars surely added to his menace, and thereby his appeal as *the* terror of the high seas.

The corner of the Rook's mouth twitched with the ghost of amusement. "I must say, noblemen rarely rouse themselves to meet me during nocturnal escapades. They generally send a servant to collect their thirty pieces of silver."

"What happens on my land is my responsibility. Also, I require proof the cargo is not human as I'll have no part in that."

The Rook pulled back the heavy canvas to reveal several stacked, unmarked square crates, each too small to hide a person, even a child.

Appeased, Gavin nodded. "This way."

Loading the cargo into the carts was backbreaking work, and it impressed Gavin that the Rook matched him burden for burden, load for load. The dark silence of the moonless Highland night pressed upon them like a shroud as they took the old road along low sea cliffs to Inverthorne, and stored the crates in the old Jesuit caves beneath the keep.

This finished, the Rook declined Gavin's offer of a conveyance for his men back to the beach. He made a gesture, and one of his crew stepped forward with a bag of coins for Callum, and a larger one for Gavin, as the cargo was to be stored on his land for a very specific amount of time.

"I'm rather new to pirating, but is the exchange still the doubloon? I'd assumed currency had changed since the eighteenth century." Gavin shook the heavy bag of coins, wondering if the Rook was unaware of the rather less weighty pound paper note.

The Rook seemed neither perturbed nor entertained. "In your hands is pure undetectable gold coin. It can be claimed by no government, trade organization, nor even traced to a mine. It is not bound to any certain economy, nor do you have to worry about an exchange rate."

"In that case, it's a pleasure doing business with ye." Gavin nodded.

"I'll return in one year's time to collect my cargo."

Calum turned to Gavin. "What are you going to do with your share, I wonder?"

A blood-chilling cry sounded from above, before Manannan Mac Lir dove to reclaim his place on Callum's forearm.

"We're not alone." Callum pulled a pistol from beneath his woolen cloak just as a copse of elms and ash trees rattled nearby.

Gavin counted the clicks of seven gun hammers behind him, each pulled a hair slower than his own. He hoped to be spared the indignity of a death in the dark by friendly fire.

"Show yerself," he commanded the interloper, and was instantly obeyed.

By a brindled long-haired Highland heifer who noisily waded from the underbrush to nose at some tender clover.

A release of the instant tension was followed by a discharge of pistol hammers and a few relieved grunts and chuckles.

"There's yer answer." Gavin smiled. "That's what I'm doing with my share."

"Highland cattle?" Callum snorted. "Tell me you're joking."

"Nay. I'm going to sell my part of Ravencroft Distillery to my brother, and buy the abandoned Erradale Estate and its bounty of cattle from the late Mrs. Ross's daughter, the one raised in America."

"Alison Ross, ye mean?" Gavin could feel more than see Callum's dumbfounded expression in the darkness. "It'll be the greatest land acquisition the Highlands have seen in centuries."

"That's rather the point."

"But . . . the Mackenzie have never been cattle folk."

Gavin noted that the Rook and his men had already melted into the night, and his hand tightened around the gold in his grasp.

"Nay," he agreed. "The Mackenzie have never been cattle folk."

But as soon as he could, he'd no longer be a Mackenzie. Not only would he have the St. James surname, a non-Mackenzie title, and an income all his own, but after the crown granted the emancipation he'd requested, the bulk of his land would no longer be considered the purview of Laird Mackenzie of Wester Ross.

He'd be free of the Mackenzie clan once and for all. Among all his numerous desires, that one burned the brightest.

CHAPTER TWO

Union Pacific Railway, Wyoming Territory, Fall 1880

Samantha Masters squeezed the trigger, planting a bullet between her husband's beautiful brown eyes.

She whispered his name. *Bennett.* Then screamed it.

But it was the woman in his grasp she reached for as he fell to the ground.

Though they'd known each other all of twenty minutes, she clung to Alison Ross as though the younger woman were the most precious soul in the entire world, and they sank to their knees as their strength gave out.

Alison's hold was just as tight around her, and their sobs burst against each other's in a symphony of terror, shock, and abject relief.

What in the hell just happened?

Not twenty minutes ago, Samantha and Alison had been no more to each other than amiable fellow passengers on an eastbound train, chugging across the wintry landscape of the Wyoming Territory.

What were they now? Enemies? Survivors?

"I'm sorry. I'm sorry. I'm sorry." Samantha repeated the

words with every short, sobbing exhale. Though she couldn't have said who the apology was to, exactly. To Alison? To Bennett? To whoever had been shot on the other railcars?

To God?

This morning she'd been the irate, disillusioned wife of a charming and dangerous man. An insignificant and unwilling member of the outlaw Masters Gang.

This afternoon, she'd been the new acquaintance and confidant to Alison Ross, commiserating over childhoods spent on secluded cattle ranches.

This evening, because of what she'd just done, of what they'd all just done . . . chances were good that she'd be hanged.

This train job was supposed to be like any other. Each of the Masters boarded on the last platform for miles and miles. To avoid detection or suspicion, Bennett, Boyd, and Bradley Masters would each take a seat in separate passenger cars.

Samantha would be placed in the least populated car, usually first class, as it was also the least dangerous. Once civilization completely fell away, the signal was given, and the men would strike, rounding up all passengers into one car.

This was done for the safety of the passengers as much as the Masters brothers themselves, as the gang didn't generally rob *people*. Cash, jewelry, and personal items were never as valuable as actual cargo. The Union Pacific Railway didn't only deliver citizens across the vast American continent. It delivered goods, sundries, and often . . . federal funds.

Even in these modern times, when it seemed all the gold had been mined from the rich hills of California, American currency was still minted in the east. Which meant everything from company payrolls, to government bonds, to cash and precious metals were transported by transcontinental railways.

And the Masters brothers, aspiring entrepreneurs, had decided that if the government wouldn't allow them land, nor the banks grant them loans . . .

Then they'd take what they needed.

This was supposed to have been their fifth and final train job. It was supposed to have gone like the others.

No one harmed or robbed. Merely a bit inconvenienced and perhaps a little shaken. The Masters brothers would escape with a few bags of money that the government could simply print again, a "frightened" female hostage as played by Samantha herself, and the papers would have an exciting story to publish in the morning.

The signal, both to each other and to the passengers, was one shot, fired at the ceiling, and then a command to disarm, get moving, and a gentle promise that all this would be over before they knew it. Samantha's job was to act like any other passenger, and incite them to obey. Then, if necessary, act as the hostage to force compliance.

"People are sheep," Boyd had always said. "They'll follow a sweet thing like you to their doom."

On this job, Samantha had been more comfortable than any other. At this time in October, with winter settling in but Christmas still a ways off, travel wasn't foremost on the mind of the average American.

Her railcar had only two occupants other than herself. Alison Ross, a lively, bright-eyed San Franciscan socialite, and a well-dressed businessman more interested in his paper than conversation.

At first, Alison's friendly overtures had vexed Samantha, as she found it hard to concentrate on responses when her blood sang with equal parts anticipation and anxiety. But, she realized, to not engage would be suspicious, and before long she'd found herself enjoying Alison's company.

She'd not known many women her own age, least of all friendly ones.

Samantha imagined that in another life, she and Alison could have, indeed, been friends.

Had she not been about to rob the train.

Had there not been more gunshots than were agreed upon . . .

Had Boyd and Bradley not bailed with the money, leaving Bennett to come after his wife, his white shirt and dark vest splattered with blood.

Oh God. What had they done?

Over the deafening beat of her heart, she'd heard Bennett say something about federal marshals. About someone taking a bullet in the shoulder. Boyd? And then a shootout.

Through vision blurred with tears, Samantha glanced at the businessman, dead-eyed and bleeding.

Her fault. *All* her fault.

Bennett had shot him without a word or warning. Then he'd grabbed Alison and put his pistol to her temple, because he'd *known.*

He'd known the second he'd seen the horror and denial on Samantha's face at the blood on his shirt, that she wouldn't have gone with him. That, while she'd have stayed married to an outlaw, she could *never* love a murderer.

"Come with me, Sam," he'd ordered tersely. "Come with me now, and we will go to Oregon."

It was in that moment Samantha had *known* he lied to her.

They'd fought about it the night before, when he'd said Boyd wanted to go south to Texas or the New Mexico Territory instead of north to Oregon like they'd planned. That oil towns were the new gold rush.

She'd railed at him. It wasn't the life he'd promised her. They were supposed to go to the sea to make their fortune in lumber. He was going to build her a grand house on a cliff and make love to her while serenaded by thunderstorms. They'd only *just* escaped their desolate life on a cattle ranch in the high desert. She didn't want to go *back* to bleak sweaty days beneath the harsh, unrelenting sunshine. She wanted pretty green hills, trees, and meadows. She wanted to live somewhere she could wrap a shawl about her and listen to sea storms toss rain against her windows.

Last night, she'd been shrill, and Bennett had been cruel.

But he'd awoken his charming self, randy as he ever was before a dangerous job. And she'd lain beneath his thrusting body, unable to relinquish the churning of her resentments and worries enough to appreciate his affections.

Then it was time to wash, and dress, and commit a crime.

Bennett had promised to revisit the issue. To make her smile again, to fulfill her dreams.

Problem was, Samantha had already lost faith in Bennett Masters's charming promises. A part of her had begun to accept what she'd long feared. Bennett would never go against his brothers, brutal and backward as they were. If Boyd decreed the family was going south to work in stinking, desolate oil towns, then there was no other option but to do exactly that.

Boyd had once whispered to her in secret that, while Bennett might love her, he feared him more, and fear was always more powerful than love.

"He'd let me fuck you, if I wanted," Boyd had threatened

once when she'd been mouthy. He'd grabbed her through her trousers, his fingers digging painfully against her sex. "You'd best keep that in mind."

She'd never forgotten that night five months ago. Because she'd told Bennett of Boyd's behavior.

And, as Boyd predicted, he'd done nothing.

Now, when Bennett held his pistol to this helpless woman's head, and ordered Samantha to open the door to the railcar, she'd looked into the eyes of her husband of four years.

And seen a stranger.

"You'll let her go," she'd reasoned evenly. "You'll let her go, and we'll get out of here."

She'd opened the door. Bradley had the horses keeping pace with the train as it slowed around the McCreary Pass bend. She motioned to him, and he spurred his ride faster. They'd get off the train, and she'd figure out just what the hell had happened before making any hasty decisions.

"She's seen us."

Bennett's words had frozen her blood as she realized that he wasn't wearing his bandana.

"People have seen us before," she'd said over her shoulder.

"Not like this, Sam. We can't leave witnesses. She has to die—"

Samantha had reached across her body, drawn her Colt single-action, turned, and shot him between the eyes in the time it took him to pull back the hammer of his higher-caliber, slower-action Smith & Wesson.

Only now, while clinging to a stranger on her knees, did she have time to think about what she'd just done.

She'd killed a man. Not just any man.

Her *husband*.

"Thank you," Alison said ardently against her ear.

"Thank you. I know he was your man, but I wasn't ready to die."

Pulling away from Alison, Samantha noted the mark that Bennett's recently used gun left on her pale temple. He had to have killed before, hadn't he? He just . . . murdered that innocent man like it was nothing to him. He didn't even hesitate. And then to even consider executing a slight and lovely girl like Alison?

Her husband of *four* years.

God, had she ever known him at all?

Wood paneling splintered above them as a bullet pierced the wall, and Alison screamed, lifting her arms to cover the green silk hat perched above a wealth of mahogany curls.

Bradley.

Samantha's head whipped around to see that he'd gained on their car, and had witnessed the entire thing. Luckily, of the four of them, Bradley was the weakest shot and only the second-best rider.

The distinction as the best, of course, belonged to her.

Boyd was the gunslinger.

Samantha dimly remembered Bennett saying that Boyd had been wounded, and with any luck, those wounds would be fatal.

Bradley's mount galloped closer, and Samantha realized that if he gained on the train, he'd be coming for her, and only one of them would survive the encounter.

She'd found her gun where she'd dropped it, but Alison stayed her hand. "I know a way to keep your neck out of a noose," she said, her blueberry gaze surprisingly steady through the tears. "But we'll have to . . . to get rid of the body."

Samantha's racing heart shriveled, but she and Alison stayed low as they rolled Bennett's limp body the few feet to the door.

"You're dead, Sam!" Bradley, unable to reload his pistol on horseback, was reaching across his saddle for his rifle. Which gave the women no time to pause. No time to hesitate.

Together, they pushed Bennett through the door, and the force of the train, the wind, and momentum pulled him sideways down the iron steps. The broken sounds his body made when he hit the earth nearly killed Samantha, but Alison slammed the door just as Bradley's rifle had found purchase on his shoulder.

Samantha could tell his shot went wild, and waited a few eternal seconds for another.

Alison gathered her wealth of skirts and knelt on a seat, peeking through the window. "He's stopped." She breathed in obvious relief. "He's stopped for your—for the body."

It was only then that Samantha began to shake. Great, bone-rattling tremors coursed through her. All warmth leached out of her, and she slumped into a seat knowing her freezing limbs wouldn't hold her weight for much longer.

Resolutely, Alison Ross claimed the seat across from her. A bone structure as sharp and perfect as hers was only accentuated by pink blush and rouged, full lips. Emeralds swayed and twinkled in her ears, catching the light as she leaned toward Samantha.

"He called you Sam," she noted in a sweet voice that contrasted with her sharp tone. "That's your name?"

"S-S-Samantha," she managed through rattling teeth. "H-his brothers. T-they're going to kill me. I'd rather hang."

"You told me you grew up on a cattle ranch. Was this the truth?"

Samantha nodded, wondering if she'd ever be able to breathe again. Assaulted by the picture of Bennett's handsome face marred by a perfectly round hole between his eyes.

"You can shoot, obviously. Can you ride, herd cattle, work figures?"

She nodded again, before the absurdity of Alison's question registered. "W-why are you being kind to me? My—my husband almost—" She couldn't bring herself to say it. It was too horrible.

In spite of everything, a corner of Alison's painted mouth lifted at Samantha's expression. "Where I come from, in my country, saving a life is no small debt. Also, in my savage part of the world, from the time we're very, *very* young one law is paramount to all others. *Tha an lagh comraich.*"

"*Comraich?*" Samantha blinked rapidly at the lovely, obviously wealthy woman. Either she'd gone mad, or Alison was speaking in tongues.

"It means *sanctuary.*"

Shaking her head, Samantha tried to understand the woman. That word had no meaning to her. What was Alison talking about, *her* country? She didn't look or sound at all like an immigrant. Was she not American? Had she not said she had a fiancé in San Francisco? That her family had been wealthy ranchers and she was forced to travel east to settle a land dispute?

"I don't know what you've been through, or what has happened to bring us to this place, but I think we can help each other," the elegant woman was saying.

"I'm lost" were the only words Samantha could conjure. Hopelessly, incredibly lost. Adrift. Misplaced. In every conceivable way.

Alison's gaze gentled. "Tell me, Samantha, have you ever been to Scotland?"

CHAPTER THREE

Wester Ross, Highlands, Scotland, November 1880

Of all the things Samantha feared after agreeing to this farce, finding herself in the arms of another man so soon after the death of her husband hadn't been one of them.

It really should have been, she thought, as she tried to gain her breath whilst crushed to a body hard as stone by arms as unyielding as the iron shackles she'd crossed an ocean to escape.

She should have dreaded this *very* thing, most of all. The wicked response of her traitorous body to the proximity of a strong and dangerous man.

She'd thought she'd prepared for every contingency, every dangerous pitfall.

Of course, in all the frenzy of the past few weeks, she'd never once considered the treachery of a proper woman's footwear.

High-heeled boots were the devil's contraptions . . . or perhaps one of the many punishments a wrathful God cursed upon modern descendants of Eve.

Either way, if Alison hadn't insisted she wear these

damned things upon disembarking onto the platform of Strathcarron Station in the Highlands, she'd have been sure-footed when the little urchin bastard had snatched her handbag.

It wouldn't have mattered that she'd been staring, open-mouthed, wondering—like a dim-witted idiot—just what a fierce Celtic barbarian was doing at a railway station at this hour.

Or, rather, in this modern day and age.

For hell's sake, she'd not even had a chance to step down from the steaming, wheezing train onto the platform when the handbag was wrenched from her grip by a sprinting little wretch. Which was why she'd toppled from the highest rung of unstable folding stairs with an indelicate shriek, and landed in the miraculously awaiting arms of said fierce barbarian.

A barbarian . . . dressed like a gentleman?

That couldn't be right, as he was no *gentle* man. The steady strength crushing the air from her lungs rendered that quite obvious.

"I've got ye, lass." Something about the way the Highlander uttered the word "lass" instantly turned her insides to liquid. Even in such a setting, his baritone was supple as silk against naked flesh.

Writhing in his grip, Samantha pulled away enough to look up at him and changed her mind, yet again.

He was no barbarian. And certainly no gentleman.

He had to be a Celtic god.

Men worshiped metal and money these days, and he was crafted of both in equal measure. Also, there was no denying that the suit stretched over shoulders as wide as the Rocky Mountains must have cost incomprehensible amounts of cash.

More than she'd ever . . .

"My handbag!" Reminded of money, she squirmed in his grip, surprised that he didn't set her down right away. All the cash she had in the world was contained in that lovely burgundy bag, along with other priceless documents.

Identity papers.

"Doona-fash, lass. Yer handbag will be recovered and returned to ye."

She'd have asked him what the hell "fash" meant, if his eyes hadn't stunned her mute. Samantha had never in her life seen anything so verdant or so shockingly, absorbingly beautiful. Not the quaking leaves of the sparse aspens on the Nevada homestead where she'd been raised, or the brief spring grasses that quickly faded to gold, then brown beneath the relentless desert sun.

Not even the apparent ever-lush landscape of her new country.

Scotland.

She could still scarce believe it.

How *did* a man come by eyes so impossibly green? Set like precious gems in features crafted by the same celestial hand that pulled the treacherous Sierra Nevada from the wild, willful earth.

It wasn't only his spectacular height and breadth that set him apart from the scant crowd—if one could call it a crowd after experiencing the crush of humanity at London's Charring Cross Station—it was his uncommon magnificence. Samantha tried to find a different word. Something less dramatic, less ostentatious, and simply couldn't.

He was, in a word . . . Magnificent.

Though his suit was the very picture of elegance, the shoulders barely contained within were anything but.

Having only just had her first gowns hand-altered for her in Chicago at Alison Ross's expense, Samantha wondered if his tailor made as much fuss over the girth of his arms as her seamstress did over her own extraordinary height?

Samantha had been raised around her share of rough-hewn men with muscles built by long days of labor, and she'd taken the time to appreciate them.

Hell, she'd been married to one.

Damn, but the Highlander holding her was born into the world with more than his fair share of physical allowances.

She'd never in her life seen his like.

"Thank you," she breathed, then cleared the detested note of feminine awe from her throat.

"American?" An expression of equal parts scorn and se-duction lurked beneath a haughty brow, and she had the sense he'd known that even before she'd articulated a word.

She nodded in confirmation. "You can set me down now."

To her chagrin, his hold tightened, the gleam in those unnatural eyes both appreciative and roguish. "I'd rather not. Ye're light as a wee baby bird, and about as stable on yer feet, it would seem. Perhaps it's safer I hold ye a while."

Samantha became instantly certain that every second in his brawny arms was more dangerous than the last. Had to be that *damned* accent. An unsightly cretin could se-duce a woman sounding like he did.

Shit, she realized. Her pistols were in her handbag, too.

Struck by the sudden intuition that she might have to shoot at this man someday, she decided she'd do her best to miss his attractive face.

"Put. Me. Down," she commanded. "Or I swear to Christ, I'll scream so loud, they'll hear it in London."

"That wouldna help ye in these parts, lass."

To avoid the equal shares of titillation and trepidation his words evoked, Samantha glanced around, noting that they'd already garnered rapt attention from the several evening travelers at the station, but none of them seemed inclined to offer her aid.

Hell, no one even batted an eye at his rank, inappropriate behavior. Though she took comfort in the fact that neither did they seem alarmed on her behalf.

Summoning her best glare, she directed it at him, opening her mouth to deliver a censure every bit as scathing as the unwanted heat prickling beneath the skin of her chest and throat and spreading south.

He interrupted her by bending to gently place her feet on the platform. "I've been the cause of many female screams, I'll admit, but never because of distress."

Any retort she could summon was lost to a gasp at the sudden clench below her belly button.

His reluctance to release her certainly seemed less practiced than his wicked humor, but he eventually did. Not before he took an unnecessarily long moment to steady her.

Samantha did her best to ignore the way his big hands left imprints of sensation on her corseted waist as she narrowly avoided tripping over the train of her skirts in her haste to put space between them.

The distance created an alarming new problem. It had been impossible to grasp the full magnitude of his beauty from so close.

It was enough to render her speechless.

Samantha slammed her eyes shut, grasping for an excuse for this inexcusable attraction. She was exhausted, hungry, and unutterably soul-weary.

And ultimately alone.

After an arduous rail journey across the entire United States, she'd embarked from the port of Philadelphia on a ship a great deal less crowded than it had been when it arrived. She'd filled the Atlantic with tears of grief and pain, along with the upheaval of nearly every delicious meal afforded to her as the first-class passenger and apparent Scottish heiress Alison Ross.

She had all the right papers and identification, along with a new trousseau, complete with a burgundy silk handbag in which to keep what few documents she had.

In her old life, she'd have found such an accessory quite silly.

Now it was the most precious thing in her possession.

So, of course, it had been taken . . .

She wanted to ask the gray skies what else could possibly go wrong, but knew better than to tempt the fates with such a question.

Now, not only were her identification papers missing, but she hadn't the relevant information with which to prove she was who she claimed to be.

Alison had promised to write all pertinent details in a letter, and assured her that other documents should be arriving by mail as soon as possible. During the frantic conversation on a very different train—through most of which Samantha had been in complete shock—she'd gleaned only what Alison had the time to impart to her.

Gavin St. James, the Earl of Thorne, was after the Ross family estate, Erradale.

Alison had ignored his numerous requests, until he filed papers with the British government to have Erradale deemed abandoned, as neither Mackenzie nor Ross had inhabited it for several years. In order not to forfeit her legacy, Alison was required to physically take custody of the land for a period of time and put it into proper working order. She'd had to postpone wedding plans to her wealthy fiancé in San Francisco to set it to rights.

"I'd rather eat my own hat than ever return to Scotland," the heiress had vowed. "I've not been there since I was a girl. After my father died, my mother married her American lover, a railroad man named Mr. Delmont, and I've lived happily here with them since childhood. We've always had so much money that my mother never gave a fig for Erradale. Like me, she didn't want to face the memories there. Unfortunately, she passed a couple of years ago, and all the responsibility falls to me, now."

"Why not just take the money, if you don't want the ranch?" Samantha had queried, breathless at the staggering amount this Earl of Thorne had offered.

"I would, if *anyone* else wanted it. But I made a vow to my father that, so long as an Erradale Ross still drew breath, no kin of Laird Mackenzie of Wester Ross would own our land. Laird Hamish Mackenzie killed my father, you see."

"I do see." It was a vow Samantha could understand. And so, before the train had reached the platform in Cheyenne—from which every available law enforcement agency would be called to investigate what would be later known as "the Masters Massacre"—Alison had shoved her identification papers and cash into Samantha's hands, and bade her to take a stagecoach from Cheyenne to Denver, to continue east on a different railway.

"No one in Wester Ross knows me from any other American girl," Alison had promised. "In the unlikely event anyone should still remain at Erradale who would remember me from a decade ago, they'd only recall a quiet thirteen-year-old child with darkish hair and blue eyes. We're like enough in age and coloring that it shouldn't present a problem in the least."

Samantha hadn't been as skeptical as she'd been desperate. As a known member of the Masters Gang, she'd be hunted in America by not only the federal marshals, but also Bradley and Boyd, should the latter survive his wound.

The remaining Masters brothers had their enormous take from the last five robberies.

It would be enough money to hunt her to the ends of the earth.

Samantha had had no money, no prospects, no family, and nowhere to go.

And that's why she now found herself on a chilly, mist-covered evening in the Scottish Highlands, staring dumbly up into the twinkling green eyes of the aforementioned magnificent male.

She'd first spied him on the platform through the frosty glass as the train pulled into the station. A head taller than any other, he ate up ground with loose, long-limbed strides, flanked by two other well-dressed men. One very thin with a garishly orange plaid cravat, and the other rather rotund with kind eyes beneath endearing round spectacles perched on his red nose.

A red-faced young footman jogged up to the tall, broad Highlander and placed *her* handbag into *his* hand. "Recovered it just in time, sir."

"Thank ye, Kevin." The Highlander gave the footman a conspiratorial wink.

"That doesn't belong to you," she snapped, reaching for it.

"Not exactly my color, is it, lass?" He pulled it just out of her reach under the guise of holding it up to his face for assessment.

Christ, but she'd had quite enough of charming, unspeakably handsome men who assumed they were hilarious. If she wasn't so damned tired, she'd be spitting mad. At the moment, all she could summon was rank irritation.

"Give it here," she demanded.

"Give it here . . .?" He drew out the last syllable.

"Please," she muttered, galled to the core that she was even having such a ridiculous interaction.

"Gladly." The beauty of his smile stunned her blind, which must have been how he was able to cup the back of her hand with his, in order to set her handbag in her open palm.

The tiny striations of her lace gloves became her only feeble defense against the feel of his coarse flesh against hers. The weight of her returned handbag drove her knuckles deeper against his palm.

A rough exhalation drew her notice. Nothing about his haughty, nonchalant expression had changed.

And yet . . . everything had.

The rim of his nostrils flared with quickening breath. His lids became heavier, drawing to half-mast. His sinfully full lower lip drew tight against his teeth before he consciously seemed to relax it.

Quickly, she pulled her hand from his, half expecting him not to allow it.

Half astonished when he did.

"I couldna help but notice ye're traveling alone, lass."

She clutched her bag to her body, trying to summon similar indifference in the wake of his troubling observation.

"I surely am." Exhausted beyond reason by what seemed like endless days of travel, Samantha daintily covered a feigned yawn with the back of her gloved hand.

The thin man gasped, reminding her that she and the haughty Highlander were, in fact, not alone. "Ye mean to say, ye voyaged all this way . . . *unaccompanied*?"

"I mean to say." She tried to keep her growing uncertainty out of her amiable smile. Who were these men to approach her like this? "Thank you for your help recovering my handbag, gentlemen. But I really must be on my way."

Feeling more unsteady on her heels than ever, she made

to totter around them, only to be foiled by their synchronized move to block her.

Anxiety flared. "Can I . . . help you?"

With a nervous gesture, the thin man passed a briefcase from one hand to the other. "Could you not have retained a suitable chaperone—er—companion for yer journey?"

This couldn't seriously be the reason they were detaining her, could it? Who were they, the constabulary of conduct? "Why bother? I keep my own company well enough." She scrutinized the three men blocking her path, especially Mr. Magnificent, with a growing sense of alarm.

He watched her alertly with that strange, vibrant gaze. She had the sense she'd pleased him.

A prickle of awareness washed over her, lifting each fine hair on her body. Tuning to something primal. A warning. Something like she imagined a deer in the woods felt when it seemed to sense the very breath of a nearby predator. "While I *am* alone, I am not, however, unarmed." She patted her silly handbag, in which her beloved Colts resided. "Now, if you'll excuse me, I've a ride to hitch."

"Well, arena ye bonny?" His brogue deepened immeasurably.

"No," she said warily, "I'm Alison. Alison Ross."

A chuckle she didn't understand rose from the men before her would-be savior said, "Then there's no need to . . . hitch a ride, as ye say, bonny. I've come to save ye the trouble."

"Oh! Are you my driver?" she asked hopefully, abashed at her unnecessary suspicion. And here she'd thought nothing could improve the breathtaking view of the Highlands.

Apparently, she'd been wrong, as he most certainly could. Though she'd never seen a coachman so expensively attired before. Perhaps things weren't as desolate at Erradale Estate as the real Alison Ross had assumed.

Samantha fished in her frilly purse for some coins she still barely recognized. What was considered generous gratuity in the Scottish Highlands? She hadn't the first idea. "I packed rather quickly, so I only brought the two trunks—"

She froze when he reached out and cupped her elbow. *Shit.* He was touching her again. He really needed to stop doing that.

Was it really necessary to wield a hand so incredibly large? An arm so thick and solid? Samantha fought the ridiculous urge to lean all her weight into the strength she sensed there.

"I occurs to me, Miss Ross, that we havena been properly introduced."

"Oh, right." Introductions were of some significance hereabouts, she'd noted. Annoyed with herself, she wondered how many times she'd break custom. Generally it would mean nothing to her. But this brawny stranger with features the perfect paradox of barbarian and aristocrat seemed to have her thoughts tumbling over each other like a litter of exuberant puppies.

And with her husband only weeks dead by her own fucking hand.

Lord, she really *was* going straight to hell.

"Alison Ross." She stuck out her hand for a shake, though the gesture just seemed superfluous now. "Pleased to make your acquaintance, Mr. . . ."

His hand engulfed hers, once again, and he pulled it toward him, looking like a man amused with a joke she was not a part of.

He was someone aware of his effect on women. On her, in particular.

Infuriating quality, that.

"When I offered to save ye trouble, I meant the trouble

of an arduous ride out to Erradale on such a frigid evening. Ye see, Miss Ross, I am quite sure ye've traveled all the way here on account of the documents of notice I sent ye, as I am Gavin St. James, the Earl of Thorne, and I'm here to take Erradale off yer lovely hands."

She snatched said hand away before he could press those full lips to her glove as he was about to do.

This was Gavin St. James? Alison's adversary. No, her *enemy?*

She couldn't think of a thing to say. She was so incredibly travel-weary, heartsick, seasick, and—if she were honest—more than a bit dazzled by the Earl of Thorne. Alison Ross hadn't exactly given her a physical account of the man. She hadn't expected someone so . . . so . . .

Words failed her, yet again. As did her body, which seemed to be calling for her to surrender her hand back into his so he could place the kiss on her knuckles she'd denied them both.

"If ye'd like, lass, I could conduct ye to Inverthorne Keep, my castle, where we could conclude our business in comfort for a few days . . ." His gaze traveled the length of her burgundy traveling gown. "And a few nights."

"I see," she clipped, crossing her arms over the heart pounding against her ribs. She'd been right when she'd sensed danger. "Well, while your offer is appreciated, it's pointless. If residence at Erradale is necessary to retain the land, as was mentioned in the documents, then Erradale is where I'll be spending my days . . . and also my *nights.*"

She turned toward the porter's station, praying to keep her balance on the blasted boots, when his wide shoulders blocked her. Yet again.

"Perhaps ye've not received my generous offer?" His alluring smile became strained, showing too many even, white teeth. "It's nearly twice what the land is worth."

"I received it, all right," she said mildly.

He took a full breath, waiting for her to elucidate.

When she didn't, he was forced to ask the implied question.

"Ye're not saying that ye're refusing the offer, are ye?"

"Well, I wasn't gonna put it like that, but I certainly didn't plan to accept."

"Yer family's had no interest in Erradale for several years. Why now?"

"Why not now?" She shrugged, then picked up her cumbersome skirts and set off for the porter's station, focusing extra hard on avoiding a stumble on the uneven planks of the platform.

She had a feeling he'd not catch her again should she fall.

He waited five entire astonished seconds before easily blocking her path once more, the two rather unobtrusive men taking up their respective posts behind him.

"Did you bring these fellows to intimidate me into compliance?" she quipped, forcing irritation above the unease in her voice. "Because you've obviously never been to Reno."

His haughty brow wrinkled. "I ken nothing about this Reno."

"Well, I do, which is why I'm not impressed." As unimpressed as she was, she still slid her hand into the bag, comforting herself with the feel of her pistol.

The earl stepped forward, and Samantha forgot what she'd been taught over the years. *Never* yield ground to the aggressor.

She yielded to *him,* stepping back to maintain their distance, to avoid his touch. His proximity. His earthy, intoxicating scent. Something that reminded her of a loamy forest and cedar soap.

"I brought these men to *pay* ye, lass." He gestured behind him with measured movements. "This is my solicitor, Mr. Roy Mackenzie." He pointed at the kind-faced, rotund man, who nodded and blushed. "And my banker, John Douglass."

The thin man sniffed his disdain.

She sniffed hers right back. "I apologize for your wasted trip, gentlemen."

She would have taken her leave had the Earl of Thorne not gripped her elbow once again. "If my aim was to frighten ye, bonny, ye'd be terrified." He sneered, and then gentled his grip, as though his behavior had shocked himself more than it had her. "I'll do whatever it takes to convince ye to yield. Ye'll be *pleased* to find, Miss Ross, that I do nothing by half measures." The gleam in his eyes was now decidedly more sensual than sinister.

"How nice for you." She flashed him a taut smile. He might be handsome as the devil, but she'd be damned before she'd let him charm her.

She knew better.

And that knowledge was hard-won.

"Coincidentally, *you'll* find, Mr. St. James that—"

"*Lord* Thorne is the correct way to address me."

Thorne, she thought wryly. How apropos. "If you say so. You'll find that—"

"The queen says so."

She snorted. "Not *my* queen."

Both men behind him gasped in audible distress, and even *Lord* Thorne dropped her elbow in dismay.

"My dear Miss Ross." The solicitor—another Mackenzie, she hadn't been remiss in noticing—gently stepped in front of the flummoxed lord and said in a careful, if nasal, voice, "I ken ye've lived a great deal of yer life in the American West, and that country is rather . . . infamous for its lack of . . . governance." He cast furtive glances at the mildly interested passersby, and then lowered his voice further. "However, I'd beg ye to keep in mind that so long as ye're a citizen of this empire, and yer feet are on this soil, ye're indeed governed by our queen, Parliament, and her appointed agents. Even in these modern times, to declare otherwise is still considered treason by those subject to Her Majesty's crown. Which ye are."

Well. Shit. Not two minutes off the train and she'd already stepped in a steaming pile of sedition.

She decided to blame Lord Thorne-in-her-side.

Samantha had never really considered the consequences of relocating from a democratic republic to a monarchy. No Constitution. No Bill of Rights. She'd do well to remember that.

"Understood." She gave a noncommittal shrug, not willing to either excuse or apologize for her behavior to self-important men. "I'm also given to understand that you English folks pride yourselves on custom, tradition, and upholding a certain code of gentlemanly conduct."

"Aye, that we do, lass." The solicitor nodded congenially.

"Wouldn't an agreed-upon appointment in an office or my home be considered more appropriate for business dealings such as this? Rather than an ambush on a train platform, I mean."

The two businessmen glanced at each other uneasily, while Lord Thorne concealed an increasingly malevolent expression behind a charming one. "Well, it's the Highlands, lass, we're only barely less barbaric than the Americans, all told."

That had to be the first honest statement he'd uttered thus far.

"Well, since we're being forthright and all, we Americans are also notorious for fighting to keep what's ours."

"Not to mention violently taking what isn't," he muttered.

"Let's not measure the sins of our respective empires on *that* score."

Though his features remained impassive, Samantha recognized the familiar set of his perfect jaw, and the corresponding tic at his temple.

Her husband had been afflicted with the selfsame expression when they were about to row. This time, she realized with relish, she didn't have to stick around for the event. She didn't have to deal with the aftermath. Gavin St. James wasn't *her* man, which meant his displeasure wasn't *her* problem.

And didn't she have enough of those? Problems. Not men. Thank the Almighty.

"Erradale Estate is *mine,*" she said firmly. "And I plan to keep it."

"To do what, exactly?" Thorne asked mockingly. "Ye'll find Erradale neither properly staffed, secured, nor well kept. The cattle have spread for miles with hardly anyone to herd them, and it hasn't turned a profit or annuity in nearly a decade. No one in yer family has much bothered with it for twice that long. So I'll ask ye again, lass. *Why now?*"

She stepped up to him, uncomfortably close. Face tilted to meet the jade fire in his eyes, simmering behind his deceptively relaxed façade. Nose to perfect, aquiline nose. "Because, Gavin St. James, *Lord* Thorne. No matter what you call yourself, I *know* you're still a Mackenzie. Which means your father killed my father, and I'll see you in *hell* before I let anyone in your family have what is rightly mine."

She turned and did her best to stalk away, painfully aware how ridiculous she looked in her tottering heels.

A low growl drifted from behind her and she thought she heard, "I'm no Mackenzie."

She didn't look back as she silently answered, *And I'm no fool.*

CHAPTER FOUR

If Alison Ross planned to stand in his way, then Gavin decided he'd do whatever it took to get her on her back. Beneath him.

In his infamously extensive experience with women, he'd found that denial of desire, more often than not, increased the pleasure of the final effect.

Not, however, in this *fucking* case.

Acquiring Erradale wasn't merely his pleasure, nor was it a flippant desire, it was a necessity.

Which was why he didn't consider himself above orchestrating what should have been a simple gambit on a persistent interloper. He and his footman had planned Miss Ross's arrival and *immediate* departure over a shared snifter of brandy, drunkenly naming their maneuver "the swoon and scoop."

Had everything gone according to plan, the spoiled socialite would have arrived at the tiny station on what must seem to her the edge of the civilized world—a place she'd previously insisted she had no desire to visit—and she'd instantly be robbed. The little scamp would grab a bit of her hand, along with the bag or valise or whatever she used for her feminine incidentals, and tug hard enough to topple her into Gavin's strong, waiting arms.

Thus terrorized, the poor lass would decide the Highlands were too desolate and too dangerous for a young, lonely city dweller such as herself, and she'd be a great deal more susceptible to her handsome white knight's tremendously generous offer.

He'd rescue her from a millstone property, and she'd be the grateful damsel.

Well, he was certainly paying the price for one gigantic assumption.

The lass was no damsel.

He'd prepared himself for a hard sell, one that might require a few extra knee-weakening smiles, perhaps so much as a seduction, but he'd never in a million years expected the disaster that landed his arms.

The disaster named Alison Ross. Light as a feather, she was, and devastating as a tornado. All long limbs and electric eyes.

The moment his arms surrounded her, his body had responded in a way completely antithetical to his purpose. And suddenly, all his hands could do was find ways to keep themselves attached to her.

He was supposed to be seducing *her* with all the practiced calculation he'd garnered over decades. So . . . why in the name of all the bloody Scottish saints had he been the one with the unsteady knees?

Because he wanted her—no, *Erradale*—he wanted Erradale. So fucking much.

That had to be it.

Once, whilst traveling in the Orient, Gavin had supped

with a monk who'd told him that desire was at the root of all suffering.

Gavin had scoffed at the idea at the time.

Now, with his every desire within reach, yet thwarted by a smart-mouthed American chit, he was beginning to believe the monk had the right of it.

After the infuriating encounter at Strathcarron Station, it had taken him only two minutes of exasperated calculation to concoct a stratagem as to how, exactly, he'd approach his erstwhile neighbor to the north.

The two days in which he'd deemed it essential to wait passed with all the alacrity of eternity.

But certainly not because he wanted to see her again.

Miss Ross, tiny as she was tempestuous, would be hungry by now, he surmised as he allowed Demetrius, his shire steed, to pick his own lazy way along the Alt Bànghorm, the river separating Inverthorne lands from Erradale. The shallow tributary's name literally translated to Light Blue River, thus deemed for the uniquely colored stones beneath the crystal stream.

Gavin found himself appreciating the shade in a way he'd not done before, as it conjured to mind the singular hue of Alison Ross's clear, impertinent gaze. An unbidden smile touched his lips as he pictured the brash American heiress losing a great deal of her self-assurance once she'd crested Gresham Peak, as he did now, and truly beheld her legacy.

He'd have given his eyeteeth to carry the treasured memory of her distress.

Erradale Estate was little more than an aged, one-story manor home amid a gathering of crofter's cottages and a lone, dilapidated stable. The buildings were scattered like chaotic white marbles on a lush carpet of wintry, amber-green grass. Aside from Gresham Peak, only very gentle hills interrupted the wide swaths of open moors stretching west and north until black stone cliffs abruptly crumbled into the sea. Ominous clouds, pregnant with a looming storm, huddled together over the distant Hebrides, and made their leisurely way toward the mainland on a biting breeze.

To a spoiled American raised in the garish and gold-rich city of San Francisco, California, it must have seemed like the loneliest, chilliest corner of perdition.

To Gavin, it was paradise.

It was home.

However, the only places to find markets or supplies were at the Rua Reidh fishing village to the north, or Gairloch to the south. No fishmongers or butchers lined this abandoned stretch of coast, and there was no staff to send on supply errands. Alison would have found the fireplaces cold and the woodstores and larders long empty.

She'd not been to Gairloch to collect supplies—he'd have heard about it—and he highly doubted she could navigate Rua Reidh, as the people of that village held fast to their ancient Pictish ways and were still famous for summarily refusing to speak English.

Even Callum—widely considered a local despite his Irish father—rarely ventured there.

As far as Gavin knew, two old ranch hands named Calybrid and Locryn occupied one of the dilapidated cottages. Then there was Callum, who tended to lurk by the Dubh Gorm Caves, where the cliffs gave way to a very narrow beach carved by the crystalline river.

These notably reclusive men made up the sum of society for miles in any direction. They hunted, trapped, or fished their food, and it wasn't bloody likely the lass was equipped for any such deed.

Wee Alison Ross didn't have an extra store of healthy weight anywhere on her scrawny frame. She'd waste away if she missed so much as a meal. Lord, he remembered thinking he'd not seen a lass so thin since he'd been to London. So delicate. Nay, maybe not delicate, but he'd spent more time than he'd like to admit wondering how such a large force of will could be contained by such a weak frame.

He'd had the ridiculous urge to measure the circumference of her arm against his wrist. One angry Highland sea gale and she'd be tossed into the ocean like a leaf torn free of its branch.

Were all her limbs so long and delicate as her arms and swanlike neck? As she'd stood against him, casting aspersions in front of God and all Highland travelers, he'd realized his one hand could completely span that elegant throat.

Meeting her at the train station dressed in his finery and accompanied by those who could facilitate their trade had been considered a courtesy on his part.

One extended at great expense.

Apparently, what the lass lacked in brawn she more than made up for in pluck. That, added to the ax her family had to grind with his, made for a shocking failure of negotiation.

Gavin had long since given up cursing his father. The man had been dead nigh as long as hers. Besides, he'd learned long ago that if he took his hatred out to examine it, it wanted to smother every façade Gavin had worked so hard to construct.

And that just wouldn't do.

Not when he was so close to getting what he wanted.

As he descended into Erradale, Gavin murmured a line from Shakespeare that had stayed with him since the dark winter days he'd spent hiding from his father in the library. "'Tis best to weight the enemy more mighty than he seems."

Or *she,* as was this particular case.

He'd underestimated Alison Ross. Though she'd been draped very well, he'd noted her dress had been premade and altered, rather than sewn for her distinctive measurements. Tall, she was. And slim, but not without the distinctive curves branding her a woman.

He might be a Scot, but he was no philistine.

Perhaps she hadn't the wealth he'd been led to believe. He'd have to look into that. Fiscal desperation could be a weapon added to his arsenal.

Also, he'd not been too astonished by her uncouth vitriol to notice the dark smudges painted by exhaustion beneath her startlingly large eyes. Or the pallor of her skin beneath golden freckles. When she'd not been angrily squaring off with him, her shoulders tended to curl forward, as though burdened beneath a Sisyphean weight.

That had to be why she'd seemed inured to his charm. Hadn't it? Every woman from eight to eighty, even the happily married ones, took a very obvious moment to simply appreciate his pulchritude in one way or another. They'd cast him furtive glances beneath coy lashes when they didn't think he'd notice. Or they'd stare outright, their appreciative gazes roving from his lush hair and sculpted features, to every one of his thick bones upon which the famous Mackenzie brawn bunched and bulged in ways that sent their fans to fluttering.

Alison Ross . . . She only ever looked him in the eyes. Like he was more than his uncommonly well-made parts.

Like she considered him as a man, not merely a conquest or lover.

Had he been mistaken when he'd interpreted a spark of appreciation beneath her scorn?

When the uncouth lady had all but stumbled away from him, Gavin calculated that he'd have to use a completely different advance to achieve his aspiration.

As a slight and fragile woman, her tattered condition certainly wouldn't improve upon her arrival at Erradale. He'd warned her that she'd be afforded no staff, servants, or creature comforts to speak of in her father's abandoned home.

According to Callum, to whom he'd spoken yesterday, she'd barely left the manor for nigh on two days, and had made no move to acquire aid.

She had to be starving and desperate, subsisting on whatever tins she might find in a cupboard, or the dubious survival skills of two harmless but essentially useless old goats.

Which is where *he* came in.

Instead of the illustrious Earl of Thorne, handsome, charming, and intimidating in both stature and symmetry, he'd approach Miss Ross as simply Gavin. Handsome, charming, and solicitous neighbor, paying a call to deliver both contrition and sustenance.

He'd eschewed a waistcoat or cravat, deciding instead to dress informally in only trousers, riding boots, his shirtsleeves—purposely left open a few rebellious buttons—and a vest beneath his long wool coat.

He'd brought Trixie along as an emissary, his adorable and endlessly friendly—if a bit daft—sheepdog, and a basket of perishables that would keep the starving woman fed.

But not for long enough to stay.

"Och, poor lass," he'd say upon finding her listless, cold, and beleaguered.

The scent of Cook's fresh bread and flaky sausage box-ties would tantalize her into allowing him in—as he couldn't very well rely on any well-bred manners where she was concerned—and once he'd crossed the threshold . . .

She didn't stand a chance.

He almost felt sorry for her. Almost.

Like most Highlanders, Gavin had tended to admire and bed lasses with feminine curves and soft, secret places. Alison Ross seemed all bones and bawd. Though he couldn't deny a passing curiosity about kissing a tall woman he wouldn't have to bend in half to reach.

And, if he recalled correctly, her lips might have been soft, if she'd not been pursing them with distaste at him.

Nay, she was not his typical mistress, but neither could he say that any part of her was unattractive.

So, he could fuck her if he had to.

He'd do what it took to get the papers signed.

He'd be whatever she needed, savior, father, brother, friend, or, hopefully, lover.

Nothing would get in the way of what he wanted.

Not that revealing her intriguing daintiness would be much of a chore. Gavin had bedded every different sort of woman he could think of in his six and thirty years. A few of them had been slender, or tall, or brash. But none had been her particular blend of all three. Somehow, that particular blend had kept him up the past few nights, riddled with curious heat.

Better to work that out of his system with a good tup before he charmed her into doing what he wanted and sent her on her merry way.

As he ventured closer to Erradale, Gavin surreptitiously checked the fences and corrals he'd mended over the summer in anticipation of their belonging to him. Once he gathered the cattle against the harsh winter, they'd need a place to be kept. Inverthorne, his land on the south of the peninsula, was covered in a lush forest interrupted by celestial meadows. To call Erradale's single copse of trees to the immediate north of the estate grounds a forest would be kind. The rest was prime grazing land as far as the scope of a lens could capture.

Gavin scanned the planes of lush greenery, carefully schooling the hunger from his gaze. Perhaps out of practiced habit. Or perhaps because, even when alone, he dare not allow his desire to show, lest someone see it, and know how to punish him.

All was quiet in Erradale, though smoke did drift from the south chimney of the manor, which meant Calybrid or Locryn must have put down their pipes long enough to light her a fire.

No matter, he thought. Firelight was ultimately flattering, and daylight had begun to fade. All the better to seduce her by.

At the sight of movement from the northern tree line, Gavin kicked Demetrius into a canter as more than a dozen rangy, red, long-haired beasts spilled onto the Erradale grounds.

Trixie went mad at the sight, streaking across the lawns in a ball of black and brown frenzy. She vaulted through two corral fences, and barked up to what must have been, to the dog, a congregation of very strange creatures.

Gavin tried to call her back, but she'd never really been smart enough to train.

A confusion of whistles and yells filtered through the trunks of the ancient oaks as startled, hesitant cattle began to balk at the noisy dog, and turn back toward the trees.

Not all of the irate voices were male.

What the devil?

"Hey!" The screamed censure whipped from inside the tree line. "Quit that racket, mongrel!"

If the voice hadn't identified her, the American accent certainly would have.

Alison?

Stymied, Gavin spurred his horse faster. He'd never heard a woman's voice so loud and demanding before.

Not outside his bedroom, in any case.

"I said, shut it!" The earsplitting volume intensified as two of the cattle broke from the rest, veering to the west toward the sea cliff. "I'm warning you."

The ruckus seemed to spur Trixie on, and she made chase after the two wayward cattle, driving them faster in the direction of the cliffs.

The gunshot startled every living creature in Erradale.

Birds broke from the trees with panicked, percussive wing beats. The mangy Highland cattle started, and then trotted forward with renewed vigor, deciding the wee sheepdog was less of a danger than whatever had created such an explosive sound.

Gavin's own heart stopped beating and his lungs froze.

Had she just . . . shot his dog?

Trixie gave one astonished yip, then jumped around and barreled back toward him.

A gray horse plunged from the trees. Astride it, a lanky man with a tam-o'-shanter cap covering his mostly bald pate rode for the errant beasts. Calybrid cut them off from their certain demise and steered them back toward the herd.

Gavin cursed every god he could name as shorter, stockier Locryn also emerged from beneath the grasping elms, and joined Calybrid, whooping and hollering as he drove the cattle east toward the makeshift corral.

His fucking corral. The one he'd fucking built with his own fucking hands.

The number of cattle had to be in the twenties now, Gavin marveled as he thundered closer.

Nay. The word repeated through his thoughts in rapid-fire bursts of denial. *She couldna possibly have—*

All life-giving breath deserted his lungs in a painful *whoosh* as Alison broke from the tree line.

Astride an impressive dark thoroughbred, she loped behind the jostling herd, pacing back and forth and creating the strangest ruckus he'd ever heard, presumably to keep the stupid beasts moving forward.

Gavin's brain processed the vision before him with stupefied sluggishness. One detail filled his recently evacuated lungs with thick, sea-salted air as he sucked in an uncharacteristic gasp.

She rode astride. And clad in incredibly strange, incredibly *tight* blue trousers.

His own trousers tightened, as with each distinctive detail he processed, Gavin marked a lamentable redirection of blood from his head.

By the time his gaze traversed her surprisingly shapely calves, to the intriguing way she seemed to be maintaining her mount with her knees, and along the astonishing length of her slim thigh, his mouth was devoid of moisture.

Jesus kilt-lifting Christ. She might not have made the most pleasant of first impressions upon him, but astride a horse?

She was, in a word, magnificent.

Never in his life could Gavin say he'd witnessed such grace. Alison Ross moved like woman and beast were one.

Bent low over her horse, her long dark braid matching the mane she'd clutched in her fingers, she veered from the herd and gave chase after Trixie, who sprinted straight for him, her master.

Och, right. She'd just shot at his dog. If he'd not been so entranced, he'd be furious. Calybrid also cantered toward them, as though he'd only just noticed Alison hadn't quite holstered her gun.

Bewildered, Gavin slowed as she approached. This was certainly not the wilted lass he'd expected to find. This was . . . someone else entirely.

Eyes blazing like a Baltic tempest, she let her mount dance beneath her as she drew up in front of him, upsetting Demetrius.

Calybrid approached them, placing his steed between Gavin's and Alison's like an intercepting arbiter.

"Whit like, Lord Thorne?" he hailed. "What brings ye to Erradale? Are ye after Callum? He's in the trees somewhere, helping gather a pregnant heifer."

Gavin struggled to maintain his nonchalant expression. How in the name of King *bloody* James had this prickly lass managed to recruit Callum Monahan of all people to do ranch labor?

"Nay," he replied with a friendly smile. "I'm here to check on my new neighbor."

From a not-too-distant rise, Callum appeared astride his own black steed, and ambled toward them, tapping at a cow's rump with a long swish of a willow's tail.

"She has us well in hand." Calybrid's smile revealed several missing teeth as he tapped the wee ball of fluff atop his cap. "Woke us up well and early with fish, potatoes, and leeks torn from the ground over there, and told us she'd give us each a ha'penny for every head of her cattle we help her to scavenge."

"Did she now?" Gavin lifted a brow that he was pretty certain conveyed that he was impressed rather than surprised. At least, he hoped he did.

She regarded him stonily, allowing the prancing of her horse to convey her tumultuous opinion of him.

The mist had gathered in her lashes, and they clung together in dark spikes. The chill painted her cheeks with color beneath the dim frosting of freckles. Her mouth, tightened into a furious line, quivered slightly, though from chill or temper, it was impossible to tell.

With tendrils of her dark hair escaping the braid and wildly floating about her fierce expression, she could have been the Celtic Queen Bouddica facing General Suetonius.

Gavin had never tried harder in his life not to be impressed.

The sight of her limbs, all but exposed, created a strange, tingling burn behind his eyes that spread to his skull, his neck, trickled down his spine, and landed in his cock.

A drop of sweat beaded from her hairline and trickled down her jaw and neck, running into the open collar of the button-down shirt she'd tucked into those incomprehensively tight trousers.

Gavin swallowed as moisture flooded his mouth.

Adjusting himself in the saddle, he decided her pistol was the safest point of focus, and the smartest, come to think of it.

Finally, she opened that distracting mouth to, no doubt, deliver a scathing censure. But Gavin knew it was prudent to not only have the last word, but to gain the first whenever possible.

"I'd take it as a kindness, Miss Ross, if ye didna shoot at my dog." He forced all the possible teasing levity he could into his smile, so as to crowd out the ire.

He'd had to learn how to smile, so many years ago. He'd never quite been able to manage it until he realized he could use it as a weapon.

As currency.

Then smiles had come easy, followed by charm, and finally the powers of temptation.

Her blueberry eyes narrowed. "I'd take it as a kindness if you and your mutt would get the fuck off my land."

The profanity should have shocked him. The disrespect should have angered him. But all he could think was that this had to be the first time he'd ever heard *that* word from a woman he was not, himself, about to mount. Also, the word seemed to have the same effect on his cock out here on the wintry moors as it did in the bedchamber.

He covered his heart, as though she'd wounded him gravely. "And to think I'd come here with peace offerings to keep ye fed and warm. I suppose I should just count myself lucky that yer shot missed. Are ye hungry, bonny?"

"I neither want nor need a damn thing from you." Her cool expression turned decidedly arctic, her eyes like chips of ice. "I rarely miss. I didn't shoot at your dog, I shot *over* her. While we're on the subject, you should be glad this isn't America . . . I could shoot *you* for trespassing."

"Ye can do that here, too," Calybrid supplied helpfully, the wrinkles branching from his eyes crinkling further with mischief.

She grinned and nodded to him. "Good to know, Cal."

Cal? Gavin made a face.

Alison pulled back the hammer of her pistol, and aimed it dead center of Gavin's chest. "I've always wondered, do you lordlings bleed as blue as you think?"

Fighting equal measures of arousal and antipathy, he summoned his most charming smirk. "I yield, lass, I yield." He chuckled. "Since we're to be neighbors, I come bearing a white flag of . . . surrender." He let that insinuation sink in, and noted that her eyes flickered over him for the briefest of moments. She'd caught the seductive double entendre.

And was not immune to it.

Excellent.

"Maybe I can be recruited to help ye gather yer herd." *My herd,* he added silently. "And after we'll share a drink and repast by a fire."

"What do you know about herding cattle?" she scoffed.

Now that he thought about it . . . not much. But if she could do it, how hard could it be?

"It would behoove us to get to know each other better, bonny."

"You'll call me Miss Ross, or nothing at all," she spat. "And make no mistake; I know all I need to know about you, *Lord* Thorne." The scorn she injected into the word was unmistakable.

Gavin had to fight to keep from squirming. He did have a certain . . . reputation where women were concerned that certainly wouldn't help ingratiate him to her. Though how she could have gleaned that information out here in the wilderness was beyond him. It wasn't like Calybrid and Locryn kept up on gossip, and Callum would never repeat an ill word against him.

"Do ye?" he challenged.

"Sure do. You're a famously unscrupulous man. A notorious womanizer. A rake who thinks nothing of seducing other men's wives."

Gavin surmised this woman was no fool, and to deny it would be folly. Instead, he chose to own his reputation, adopting a look of mischievous contrition. "Well, some-one has to, do they not? I doona know many men who seduce their *own* wives."

A momentary bleakness crossed her features, a reaction he catalogued and stored for later analysis.

She continued as though he hadn't spoken. "A jealous second son who's forced to work at his elder brother's distillery in order to keep his castle from crumbling around his ears."

Gavin had to actually stop himself from flinching, as her barb hit a little too close to the mark. He remained studiously impassive. "Ye forgot to mention all the virgins I've debauched," he supplied helpfully.

"Don't think I don't know exactly why you want my land," she forged on, unamused. "But you're not going to get it. So you can fuck away off any time."

Her unflinching use of vulgarity struck a chord of endless hilarity in their audience. Gavin had to fight the tremor of amusement that toyed with his own mouth once he recovered from the initial shock.

"Why do ye believe that is, lass?"

"You're a Mackenzie. They've wanted to take this land from the Ross family for generations."

"What if I told ye I'm no Mackenzie."

She snorted. "I know better. *Everyone* knows better."

"I mean, my father was one," he admitted. "The Mackenzie Laird, as ye say, and so is my brother, Liam. But I'm in the process of officially emancipating myself from the Mackenzie clan, if that means anything to ye."

She cast him a wary, bewildered look, her pistol finally wavering beneath the weight of her obvious curiosity. "Why would you do that?"

"The reasons are numerous, and they remain my own, but know that the death of yer father is among them."

"Oh." She concealed a flicker of doubt with a blink, but it was the sign of weakness Gavin had been waiting for. And he pounced.

"And so ye see, Miss Ross, selling me Erradale wouldna be giving it over to a foe, but to the enemy of yer enemy . . . and doesna that make us friends?"

He knew he'd made an error in judgment even before she pointed the pistol in his direction and pulled the trigger.

Calybrid, the old coot, lost control of his mare and she leaped away from them, bolting and bucking a little before he subdued her.

Again, the gunshot shocked everyone. Even Callum, who galloped toward them.

Gavin froze for an unerringly tense moment, searching his body for pain, for a trickle of blood. Remembering to breathe when he encountered neither.

The woman was daft. Mad. A trigger-happy harpy without a lick of sense.

"*That* time I missed." She pulled back the hammer. "It won't happen twice. Now get. The fuck. Off. *My.* Land."

Gavin had never heard the voice of a woman carry such hard, caustic gravity. "Careful, lass," he said over the sound of a pulse thundering with the fury that chased away the initial astonishment. "I'm not an enemy ye want to make."

"I've had enemies before." Her pistol remained locked level with his heart. "And you know what I've learned, *Lord* Thorne?"

He was beginning to hate the way she said his name.

"That it's those closest to you that you have to beware of," she continued. "Along with those looking to be your friend when they have no cause but their own."

Gavin's eyes met hers and they held. Never once did she look away. Her breath was steady and her gaze clear as Loch Lomond and just as cold.

For once in his life, he had no comeback. No witty retort.

Because the lass was right. He'd learned that selfsame lesson in the most terrible ways possible.

Who'd taught it to her? he wondered. The same person who'd conjured the pain beneath the chill in her glare.

Callum sidled up to them, strategically placing himself in front of her pistol. Beneath his beard, it was hard to tell if he smiled or frowned, but his eerie eyes crinkled a bit at the corners. "'Tis wicked work digging a grave in the Highlands after the night frosts have already set in," he said mildly, his voice heavy with a disarming Irish lilt.

"Good point," Alison agreed without inflection. "We'll just toss him into the sea, then."

This time, Gavin recognized his oldest friend's amusement, and his own eyes narrowed.

Callum pretended to weigh the idea. "While your logic is sound, you forget the man is an earl. He'll be missed."

"You sure about that?" She cocked a brow.

"Well, by his mother, anyway. She lives with him in yon Inverthorne Castle where my father is stable master." Callum rolled his broad shoulders hidden beneath an ancient cloak made of sealskin.

She wrinkled her nose and lowered the brow. "You still live with your ma?"

"*She* resides with *me*," Gavin snarled. "In *my* castle." Why was he explaining himself to this scrawny, loony, altogether vicious wench? He couldn't remember the last time anyone had angered him like this since . . .

Well, since his brother.

"Why don't you let me conduct him back to Inverthorne?" Callum suggested.

"*Let ye?*" Gavin repeated, aghast.

The Mac Tíre shrugged again. "I've been meaning to pay a call to my father."

Nodding, Alison returned her pistol to its holster. "I

catch you on my land again, Thorne, even your mother won't recognize your corpse."

She rode away before Gavin's usually glib, biting wit could summon a retort.

"Ill-tempered wench," he spat, though he knew the retreating woman couldn't hear him. Turning, he rode abreast of the Mac Tíre, his mind spinning with new calculations. Never before had he met someone like Alison Ross.

"She's all right." His friend waved him off.

"*Et tu,* Callum?" he admonished.

The enigmatic hermit shrugged. "She made me breakfast," he said by way of explanation. Gavin studied his friend for a moment, noting the way his golden gaze avoided him. There was something the Mac Tíre wasn't telling him, and he was certain it had to do with the disagreeable Alison Ross.

"One way or another, Erradale will be mine," he vowed, spurring Demetrius into a gallop. Now was not the time to act rashly, which is what Miss Ross seemed to goad him to do. He needed to think, to scheme, to bide his time because, though bonny Alison Ross had learned to keep both friends and enemies at bay, she'd likely not lived long enough to learn an even more valuable lesson.

To never underestimate the long-suffering fury of a patient man.

CHAPTER FIVE

Dear Alison,
Enclosed are the documents from your solicitor re-
quired for your appearance in front of the magis-
trate. According to them, you must maintain
residence at Erradale for no less than one year. I
hope that is agreeable to you. I've heard tell that the
place has become a bit ramshackle in the absence
of a Ross caretaker, but I daresay it's better than
the American alternative at this point. Most espe-
cially since what they have come to refer to as "the
Masters Massacre."

Since you've been away from Scotland for so
long, I thought I'd remind you a little of your
family's history, so you might use it against our ad-
versaries. Though Highlanders are notoriously a
clannish people, the name of the Mackenzie family
of Wester Ross was tainted by the previous Laird,
Hamish Mackenzie. You know, of course, that he
defeated your father in a duel. Unlike the American

West, dueling has been illegal in England some forty years, but Highlanders tend to keep to their own traditions.

Gavin St. James, Lord Thorne, was born Gavin Mackenzie. He is the son of Laird Hamish Mackenzie's second wife, Eleanor. He didn't come by his earldom through the Mackenzie line, but through his mother's family, the St. Jameses, as his great-uncle died childless and Inverthorne passed through Eleanor to her firstborn son. It is widely known that Hamish Mackenzie married Eleanor to gain control of Inverthorne, and then he turned his eye to Erradale.

Lord Thorne isn't known for violence or cruelty like his father, but he's a notoriously unscrupulous rake. After a poorly concealed affair with his elder brother Liam Mackenzie's first wife ended in her suicide, Lord Thorne philandered his way across most of the empire, and some of the Continent, in a hedonistic frenzy unrivaled since the days of Caligula. Though he and Laird Mackenzie—also known as the Marquess Ravencroft—are infamously at odds, he works as the Ravencroft Distillery foreman, as barely less than half of the operation was left to him upon their father's mysterious death. This is why, I think, he shares his father's lust for Erradale.

Your presence on the land should render his claim moot altogether, so stay at Erradale as long as you like. Indefinitely, if you wish. We can write to each other, you and I, though I very much doubt you'll ever see me set foot in the Highlands. I hope you understand. Do with it what you wish. Should you turn enough profit to buy the land, I am open to your offer above all others.

Laird Mackenzie has recently retired from a long military career, whereupon he gained his moniker, the Demon Highlander, through unparalleled brutality. In the few short years since he's reclaimed his seat as Laird of Wester Ross, he hasn't shown any interest in Inverthorne or Erradale so I don't think you are in danger from him on that score.

But I caution you, Alison, for your own safety never to set foot inside Ravencroft Keep. Your mother told me it's an unspeakably dangerous place.

I will write more soon, dear friend.

Yours,
Mrs. Grant Rollins
(Or I will be once this reaches you, God willing)

If Samantha were to compile a list of things she hated, riding a horse in a skirt was only *just* beneath rapists, people who were cruel to children and animals, and handsome, arrogant Highland lords.

Murderers used to be higher on that list . . . but, she supposed, she'd need to ponder that a bit.

Seeing as how she was one.

And she only hated herself a little.

Instead of riding bareback, she chose a saddle this time to keep her skirts from gathering dust from her horse's hide. She picked her way through the Erradale moors atop the bay gelding she'd come to favor, all the while practicing what she'd say when called in front of the magistrate.

This morning, she'd dressed in her finest blue silk-lined wool frock, arranged her heavy hair into a neatly braided knot at the nape of her neck, and had done some damage to her scalp trying to pin her best hat in place. The clouded mirror atop an ancient bureau had confirmed what she knew all along, that she'd never resemble a regal lady.

Alison Ross—the *real* Alison Ross—had been confident and lovely in a way Samantha could never hope to be. Sure, she could shoot a bull's-eye at a full gallop, mend a fence, help brand a herd, and whelp a calf. But she'd never glide across the floor in that way that made a person wonder if a lady's feet even moved beneath the ruffles of her skirts. She wasn't made to sparkle brighter than the gems gifted by scores of admiring suitors. She wasn't elegant, fashionable, or refined.

She was just skinny Samantha Masters.

I like my women plump, pleasant, and pretty, or slim, smart, and sassy, Bennett used to say with that crooked half-smile of his.

Well, she'd definitely been the latter, Samantha thought as the familiar breath-stealing pang sliced through her at the thought of her late husband.

There'd never been enough food for her to get plump. Being pleasant got her exactly nowhere in Nevada. And as for pretty . . . She'd heard the word to describe her before, but not as often as other descriptions.

Like capable, for instance. Or smart. Diligent. Hardworking. Agile. Men were more likely to praise the way she sat a horse or lifted a hay bale than the way she filled out a dress.

Mostly because she didn't.

Bennett hadn't seemed to mind too much. He'd said her sweet face was enough to make up for her bony hips.

It had been the nicest thing she'd ever heard anyone say.

He'd praise the length and weight of her hair, always requesting that she let it loose when she was naked. He'd drag it over her breasts and nuzzle his face into it when he was above her.

She'd been so desperate to get away from the ranch where she'd been raised—from the Smith family—that she'd believed every word that ever left his charming mouth was intended to praise her.

Now . . . dark and hateful suspicions and insecurities shadowed every one of the good memories she had of him.

Had he used her long, thick hair to cover a body that didn't please him?

I like lookin' into your beautiful blue eyes while we fuck, he'd say. *Why would I look anywhere else?*

All she'd taken from that was he thought her eyes were pretty.

Now she was certain he'd meant that there wasn't much else to look at.

Cresting Gresham Peak, Samantha found the road that led between her lands and Inverthorne. She wished it was only the view of such untamed beauty that took her breath. Or the blue-gray stones of the castle spires in the distance jutting over the ancient forest that put the ache in her chest.

But during moments like this, when she wasn't working, her mind ceaselessly churned with a thousand disturbing unknowns.

And every one of them hurt.

During her engagement, Bennett had come home with Boyd and Bradley a week late from selling the Smiths' herd with extra cash in hand. Had he really stayed to help with the slaughter of the herd, as he claimed? Was the blood she'd washed from their clothes even bovine?

Or had their butchery been more insidious?

The prior night, Samantha had lain awake and thought of the day she'd shoved her husband's shirt, reeking of perfume, beneath his nose and demanded answers. They'd been married four months at the time. He'd laughed at her, and then praised her possessiveness. He'd explained patiently that she was well aware that every hotel in Reno supplied whores, and that whores all drenched themselves in perfume.

Can't walk down Main Street without coming out the other side smelling like a French dandy. He'd laughed, picked her up, and tossed her onto the bed. *Can't all women smell as sweet and clean as you do, darlin'.*

Another time, when she'd found the smears of what she knew to be rouge on his collar, he'd admitted sheepishly that he'd lent his best shirt to Bradley so he could go to a saloon and have his pick of the working women.

It had never occurred to her that he was a liar.

When he'd convinced her to elope on her twentieth birthday, she'd only seen him as her knight in shining armor, saving her from becoming the third wife to a disgraced Mormon elder.

When he'd stolen the Smiths' cattle, she'd helped him, thinking they'd deserved it for working her fingers to the bone since she was seven only to sell her to an old, lecherous man.

When he'd become an outlaw, forcing her to do the same, she'd truly believed it was because the cattle business was overrun by government-subsidized land barons, and there was no more work left for men like them. The Masters brothers had claimed that their way of life was not only threatened, it was dead. She'd believed them when they spoke of tyranny. That they were like Robin Hood taking their oppressors' ill-gotten gains to start something that would employ displaced homesteaders, and people whose jobs were now done by machines.

"You might be slim and sassy, Sam," she muttered to herself. "But you're none too smart."

An intelligent woman wouldn't have landed herself in this unholy mess.

"Who's Sam?"

"Jesus Jehoshaphat Christ," she gasped, pulling her pistol and aiming it at the interloper before the curse had completely escaped her.

Down the sight of her gun, Callum put up his hands. "Sorry to startle you, lassie," he said with a conciliatory grimace. "I thought an entire regiment could have heard me canter up here, but I didn't notice that you were conversing with your ghosts until I got closer."

Not for the first time, Samantha was struck by the chilling perception in his golden eyes. She found herself wondering if, beneath the layer of black sand on his face that he claimed protected him from the sun and cold, he was a young man. A handsome man, even. Beneath those skins and furs, she knew he had a lean, predatory ranginess to him that indicated a long life. His gaze held a haunted, secret pain that suggested the soul beneath had witnessed all there was, and wanted to see no more. However, something about him seemed so . . . vital, for lack of a better word. Perhaps the way he moved? With the loose-limbed ease of a man in his prime.

"Ghosts?" she queried, looking at him askance as she holstered her pistol.

"You were talking to someone named Sam," he reminded her simply.

Was she a ghost? Had Sam also died when she'd pulled that trigger?

No.

"No," she repeated out loud with confidence. "I *am* Sam. It's what I'm called back in America." She smirked. "I was talking to myself."

"Sam?" he repeated skeptically. "How do you get Sam from Alison?"

"How do you get Bill from William?" she volleyed back. "Or Dick from Richard?"

"Fair point." His eyes traveled the length of her dress with more curiosity than masculine notice.

Typical.

"Thank you for the fish you left." She remembered her manners. "I'd have to slaughter a cow to survive without your little deliveries, and I'd like to avoid that."

He nodded, and she got the sense that he understood her meaning as well as her words. She appreciated the offer of sustenance that appeared on her doorstep in the morning, but would not be beholden to him for any favors he might ask in return.

"I was on my way to Inverthorne to visit my da, and noticed you were traveling toward Gairloch dressed for church . . . or a wedding?"

Samantha found that she liked this lonely man. He had more social graces than one would expect from your typical hermit. She liked the way he communicated. If he wanted to know something, he outright asked it. If he thought you might want to be left alone, he'd open a door and let you decide if you wanted to walk through it.

"I'm off to see the magistrate," she offered. "Do you remember the letters and documents that you kindly delivered from Gairloch the day before our little . . . encounter with Lord Thorne?"

"Aye." Though he said the word with ease, Samantha read tension in the wide shoulders beneath his ever-present cloak. And maybe a sharpening of his intense regard.

"Well . . ." She hesitated, but decided she was giving away no great secret. "Those were the documents I'm required to present to the magistrate in order to retain Erradale."

"I see." He looked over to Inverthorne. "There was a letter from a friend, as well, I think," he prodded lightly.

"Yes," she said brightly. "I miss my American friends, and they promised to write so I wouldn't get lonely."

After reading the letter from Alison Ross, Samantha had congratulated herself, once again, that she'd had the restraint to keep herself from shooting Lord Thorne when he'd trespassed.

Maybe she'd be lucky enough to get another chance.

But first, she had a promise to fulfill. If Alison was kind enough to lend her the land, then she had a duty to protect it with her life . . . whatever that was worth.

"This magistrate an acquaintance of yours, Callum?" she asked.

The Mac Tíre turned back to her and nodded. "I was raised as a lad with him."

She smiled, considering this encouraging news. "Any advice on how to proceed?"

He thought for only a beat before answering. "Keep your wits about you. Some people have a hard time with that around the magistrate. And remember this above all. Though you are meeting in an office, in a civilized place, we men, especially Highlanders, are little better than beasts. Appeal to our baser natures, and you're likely to get a more predictable response."

Samantha thought on this a moment, wondering if he'd been a fantastic help or none at all as he steered his mount in the direction of Inverthorne. "Why help me, Callum? Aren't you and Thorne friends?"

Instead of looking at her, he glanced west, out across the Atlantic. His expression would have been cryptic even without the sand and shadow of his hat. "Aye, we are. We always will be. But I believe this land belongs to Alison Ross. And I'll help you fight to keep it."

"Thank you." Samantha welled with more gratitude than she thought herself capable of.

His only reply was a nod as the dark horse disappeared into the Inverthorne woods.

Every friendly feeling Samantha harbored for the hermit disappeared the moment she arrived at the Wester Ross magistrate's office in Gairloch and saw the name on the placard.

Magistrate and Justice of the Peace. Lord Gavin St. James, Earl of Thorne.

CHAPTER SIX

Gavin didn't so much as glance up when someone punched his door open with such force, it crashed off the wall.

He knew who it was. He'd been expecting her.

His blood quickened in time with his breath, and he had to set his pen down for fear of a slight tremor in his hand revealing his reaction.

Alison Ross charged into his office with all the subtle, ladylike remonstration of a rutting stag charging his opponent.

It surprised Gavin how much he'd been looking forward to locking horns, as it were.

From the moment he'd spied her name on the docket he'd been, for all intents and purposes, utterly useless. He'd heard a few cases, rescheduled most of them, and directed his clerk to clear the rest of his afternoon until the lass was scheduled to appear before him at half past two o'clock.

It'd taken him until about lunchtime to identify the disquieting sensation plaguing him in regard to bonny Alison Ross. It started with a vague, nagging discomfort, and graduated to something altogether more consuming.

Hunger.

In the space of two very intense interactions with the woman, he'd gone from being willing to fuck her to get what he wanted, to wanting to fuck her above all else.

Above all else, that was, but Erradale.

"What in the ninth level of hell is the meaning of this pile of horse shit?" she demanded, tossing the document he'd instructed his clerk to give her on his desk with a flick of her ungloved hand.

"Ah, bonny," he greeted with the warmth he'd afford his cherished niece or beloved mother, knowing it would irk her beyond her apparently limited capacity for self-containment. "Still pleasant as a cornered hedgehog, and as well mannered as a badger, I see."

"I've told you not to call me that," she hissed. "My name is—is—" Her voice died away as he rose from his desk chair.

Gavin knew the moment the glacial ice of her eyes became liquid pools of azure heat . . .

That she wanted to fuck him, too.

He read desire in her body's every slight reaction to him before she violently rejected it. Her pupils darkened and dilated before she slammed her lids shut. Her lush lips parted and her jaw slackened before she clacked her teeth together and pressed her mouth into a furious hyphen.

Good. He'd begun to fear he was losing his touch.

Her delicate nose flared but, come to think of it, that could be as much irritation as arousal.

With bonny wee Alison Ross, it seemed the two went hand in hand.

"Did ye forget yer own name, bonny?" he rumbled. "Doona fash yerself, happens more often than not when a foreign lass first sets eyes on a Highlander in his native garb." He gestured to his sporran, kilt, and tunic. "Do ye recognize the plaid, lass? Ye should."

He'd expected a reaction of fury in response to his brandishing her Ross colors. Instead, she glanced away. "I—I thought I'd be appearing in front of the magistrate in court—with witnesses—not in his—*your*—office."

Gavin's eyes narrowed. Was the lass truly so Americanized that she'd not even recognized her own clan colors?

That couldn't be so. Though his cynical mind whispered 'twas more likely the canny lass was less easily manipulated than he thought. Did she want him to underestimate her? Was she hiding her true intentions behind a veneer of artless vehemence?

"I thought it would serve us both better if we were to meet in private to discuss this new . . . evidence I've uncovered." He didn't miss her retreat as he stepped around the desk, splaying his hand on the documents she'd thrown down like the proverbial gauntlet.

"It seems there is some dispute to the claim that yer great-grandfather Sir James Ross bought Erradale. These papers maintain that he leased it from the Mackenzie clan for ninety and nine years. Come January 1, 1881, yer payment of a thousand pounds is due if ye want to keep the land out of Mackenzie hands for another century."

"And if I don't pay?" she demanded, her shoulders squaring beneath the puffed sleeves of her handsome pelisse.

"If payment isna received, ye'll forfeit Erradale to Laird Mackenzie."

"Fuck. Fuck. *Fuck*." Vibrations of her muttered expletives shimmered over his skin until his cock twitched in response.

"Are all American women so vulgar, or is it just ye?"

he queried shortly, bemoaning the husky note that crept into his sleek voice.

She ignored the question. "But that doesn't help you at all," she reasoned aloud. "You said yourself that you're no longer a Mackenzie, and so the land will not be forfeit to you, but your brother."

Gavin leaned on the front of his desk, studying the delicate woman as she stood against him. He'd dubbed her a shrew. Perhaps *shrewd* was the more appropriate word.

She might not be a lady, but neither was she a fool.

"The emancipation proceedings will take a great deal longer than these." He shrugged. "So technically, I'm still part of the Mackenzie clan. Despite our differences, Liam has no use for, or interest in, the upkeep of Erradale, nor will he want to pay the estate taxes owed on the land. He'll be happy to accept my offer to surrender my shares in his distillery. He'd be rid of two millstones from his neck for the price of one."

An unwanted parcel of land, and an unwanted brother, he thought bitterly.

"I have a bill of sale that directly disputes this so-called lease." She brandished it at him, but snatched it away from his hand when he reached for it. "I'll fight you in court, tell me when and where."

His smile felt as sweet as warm honey and spread just as easily. "Ye produce all evidence to the contrary, and plead yer case to the Bench of the Magistrate."

Her brows slammed together in a rather adorable show of bedevilment. "But . . . but you're the magistrate."

"Och," he said in mock surprise. "So I am."

As he watched color rise from beneath her collar, Gavin wondered just how far down her lithe body the delightful pink spread.

"You dirty, low-life crook!" she huffed, the papers in

her grasp loudly protesting her fingers' propensity to curl when angry.

"I am a servant of the law, not its master." He bowed for effect.

"That's a conflict of interest, and you *know* it!"

"We're not as worried about such things here as Americans are. Servants of the crown are most often served by it, as well."

Her superbly squared shoulders slumped, and he glimpsed a flare of panic beneath her expression of defeat. "There has to be something I can do," she said, more to herself than to him, he surmised.

The hollow exhaustion he'd initially recognized created a twitch and a tug in an altogether more dormant organ than the one that had taken to responding to her presence. One Gavin had long since deemed infinitely less reliable.

He idly rubbed at his chest as he asked, "Were ye not a Ross, and I not a Mackenzie, would my offer to buy Erradale tempt ye?"

She eyed him warily. "I—I couldn't say."

He took a careful step forward, and then another when she didn't shy away. "Just because our fathers were enemies, doesna mean we have to be," he reasoned, reaching out to tuck one silken strand of hair behind the shell of her ear. The motion was astonishingly familiar . . . almost . . . natural. "Ye can still sell to me, bonny, walk away a wealthy woman instead of a ruined one."

Her lower lip disappeared into her mouth as she seemed to consider his words very carefully. Then, it slowly reemerged glossed and plump.

Lord, but he wanted a taste of it, as well.

"This isn't fair . . . or right . . ." she murmured weakly. "You have me bent over a barrel, here."

"Not yet," he breathed against her ear. "But if it would

convince ye to sell, I might be persuaded to bend ye over and—"

"I'm not falling for your wicked, arrogant attempt at seduction." She enunciated every word with clarity. Jerking away from him, she leaped for the paper they'd both abandoned to the desk, and brandished it at him like a hatchet poised for the death strike. "You can shove this up your ass, you son of a bitch."

"'Tis proper to address the magistrate as 'Yer Worship,'" he corrected, crossing his arms so they didn't feel so empty.

"All right then . . ." She took a centering breath. "You can shove this up your ass, Your Worship. You'll not get Erradale through some closed-door deal or by treating me like a back-alley whore. I'll make you fight for it."

All the while she said this, he stalked her until she landed with her back to the office door.

"Perhaps," he said, feeling like a lion about to pounce on a gazelle. "It seems, bonny, that neither of us are inclined to back down from a fight."

His hand grazed her hip as he reached for the door and pulled it open, crowding her toward him. She ducked beneath his arm and sidled out of his reach but not before losing her hat.

"You are *such* a bastard," she accused, swiping the frilly thing out of his offered hand after he'd bent to retrieve it.

"For a legitimate son, ye'd be surprised how often I hear that."

"No," she spat, "I wouldn't." She whirled on her boot and stalked past his slack-jawed clerk.

Gavin suppressed the disquieting urge to call her back by watching the furious sway of her skirts. All he could think as he adjusted himself and reclaimed his seat was that he missed whatever those blue trousers were she'd been riding in the other day. The ones that had appeared to be painted on like a second skin.

Blue, like the fire in her eyes.

It occurred to him just then that blue fire burned the hottest.

"I'm not speaking to you." Samantha slammed the door, opened it, swiped the offering of plucked grouse from Callum's hand, and then slammed it once again.

"I brought salt," he called through the keyhole. "And some fresh rosemary and fennel that grows wild by the cliffs. But it only comes in if I do."

Her mouth salivated at the thought of succulent salted fowl, but she didn't make up her mind to invite Callum out of the driving rain until poor Calybrid's quivering voice replaced his at the keyhole.

"Ye're not sore at *us,* are ye? Because I canna quite stomach another winter of Loc's potted meat stew. I'll go daffy."

Samantha couldn't quite catch Locryn's low-registered reply, but it sounded something like "Then cook for yerself, ye tarty invert."

With a put-upon sigh she only half meant, Samantha released the latch and stepped aside, allowing the small parade of misfits to drip bog mud and freezing sleet onto the ancient entry.

By means of sharp elbows and tenacity, Calybrid scrambled in first, his knobby knees fairly knocking together beneath a kilt of red and gold. Wild wisps of white hair poked out from beneath his trusty wool tam-o'-shanter cap, and the lone strip of his chin beard dripped water onto his wool sweater. That, along with his bristly, overgrown eyebrows, lent a more literal meaning to the term "old goat."

Locryn, on the other hand, boasted legs just as skinny,

but they bowed beneath a jolly apple-shaped torso and strong, heavy shoulders. Samantha thought he had the kindest, most handsome pudgy face she'd ever seen, which was why his finicky surliness always surprised and delighted her. He eyed her with such rank skepticism, one russet brow dropped so low, it forced the lid to close.

"Preparing grouse is no mean feat," he announced. "Perhaps I should do it meself."

Calybrid set his hands on Locryn's shoulders and steered him toward the blazing fire in the great-room hearth over which Samantha had erected a spit. "Why doona ye put the peat and cedar chips o'er the fire and get a nice smoke going?"

Distracted by the prospect of lingering near the fire after a tromp through the winter storm, Locryn grunted "Aye," and ambled toward the blaze.

Thus had become their supper routine. After a long day of herding cattle, the men dispersed, only to reappear after dark when smoke from the great-hall chimney beckoned.

Aside to Callum and Samantha, Calybrid muttered, "Last time he prepared a bird, my body violently expelled it for a week, if ye ken my meaning." With an overdramatic shudder, Calybrid's lanky saunter was only interrupted by the slap of his wet outer clothes hitting the flagstones of the great hall. First his scarf, then his sweater, beneath which was another sweater, and then one of each of his boots discarded five steps apart.

"Ye can eat outside with the cattle if ye're just going to leave shite all over the ground as they do," Locryn bellowed.

"I always pick it up on my way out, do I not, Sam?" Calybrid didn't wait for her answer. "So shove one of those peat bricks in yer mouth, if ye're planning on being peaky nag all night."

"Why do ye pick up for Sam and not for me?" Locryn planted plaintive fists on his hips, looking like a red-bearded matron with shockingly hairy knees. "She doesna do half of what I do to deserve the courtesy."

"Oh, stop yer havering, Loc, or Sam'll force ye to sleep in the coop with the rest of the pecking hens."

Both amused and bemused, Samantha leaned over to Callum, whispering out of the side of her mouth, "They bicker like an old married couple."

"'Tis widely thought that's what they are," Callum whispered back.

"Oh?" Samatha curled her lip as though it would help her decode his insinuation, then her eyes peeled wide. "Ohhhhhh," she drawled more meaningfully. Looking back at the squabbling fellows, she fought both a grimace and a giggle as their relationship, their lifestyle, and their seclusion here at Erradale made a great deal more sense. "Which one's the husband, and which one is the wife?"

Callum's chuckle was a deep, pleasant rumble, not unlike the thunder over the distant Hebrides. "'Tis been the cause of much speculation between Thorne and me over the years."

At the mention of her nemesis, Samantha was reminded of her ire with the handsome hermit, who met her frown with a look of contrition.

"I assumed you knew who the magistrate was." His beard parted in a penitent smile, and Samantha caught herself noting that the silver peppered into his beard hadn't quite reached his shaggy hair yet.

"Yes, well, we have a saying about assumptions in America," she muttered, accepting his peace offerings of herbs and salt before bustling over to skewer the little bird carcasses over the warm fire.

"What's that?" Callum queried, his golden eyes sparkling with mirth and intellect. He was familiar with the saying, and they both knew it.

"That they make an ass out of you and . . . well, in this case just you."

"Granted, lass. Granted." His laugh was a low harmony to the melody of hers, and it did as much to warm Samantha, as did the firewood she'd finished chopping just in time for the storm to reach them.

It had helped her to imagine that each one of the logs was Lord Thorne's smirking face.

The ax had split them with the most satisfying ease.

Damn his perfect, dimpled chin and his stupid, rolling burr. The arrogant bastard knew the effect he had on women. He understood just exactly how to artfully use his lean, predatory body and wicked, crooked grin to steal a woman's wits from her.

Not this woman, Samantha thought darkly as she roasted supper. *Not this time.*

"I gather your meeting with Thorne didn't at all go well?" Callum correctly guessed the direction of her meandering attention.

"He supposedly found a hundred-year-old lease that contradicts the bill of sale. Though which is the forgery is anyone's guess. They both look legitimate to me."

"Perhaps 'tis time to employ a solicitor of your own," Callum suggested.

Samantha nodded. She'd considered doing just that, but being unfamiliar with the British economy, she wasn't sure if the money Alison had sent her was generous or a pittance.

"Callum," she ventured. "If I were to go over the head of the magistrate to argue my case, where would I go?"

"To the Queen's High Court, I suppose."

"It says in this summons here that I have to first argue

in front of the Magistrate's Bench that the Ross bill of sale trumps the lease Thorne found. But the magistrate *is* Thorne. How is that just or fair?"

"Did you say the Magistrate's Bench?"

Samantha looked up from her rotisserie at the note of disbelief that crept into Callum's tone.

"Yes."

His genuine smile crinkled the corners of his eyes and flashed shockingly clean teeth. "What Thorne neglected to tell you is that though he's the main justice of the peace, three men sit the quarterly Magistrate's Bench, and their jurisdiction reaches from the Isle of Mull all the way north to Lochinver."

"What does that mean?"

"It means that the majority rules. You only need two out of three of the magistrates to rule in your favor."

The breath rushed from her. "Who else sits the bench?"

"An English earl who replaced Hamish, the younger, after he was killed for treason. The Earl of Northwalk, I believe?"

"The Blackheart of Ben More, ye mean," Locryn corrected, adding another peat brick to the fire.

"'The Blackheart of Ben More'?" she echoed. "That doesn't sound very promising."

"He owns yon Ben More Castle on the Isle of Mull. Don't worry, lass. He's known to be a reasonable justice," Callum soothed. "If a bit unscrupulous. 'Tis rumored he's a Mackenzie bastard; however, he generally takes his cues from the Laird."

"The Laird?" Samantha was beginning to feel like a rather traumatized parrot. "You don't mean . . ."

"The Demon Highlander," Locryn announced dramatically.

"The Laird Mackenzie." Callum shot him a censuring

look while Calybrid simultaneously elbowed him in the guts. "Also known as the Marquess Ravencroft. He's claimed the third seat since his return from his adventures abroad."

Sam's flying hopes plummeted. "Then we're well and truly buggered." She blew a lock of hair away that had fallen in front of her eye.

"Not necessarily," Callum supplied. "Ravencroft and Thorne rarely agree on anything."

"Because Thorne slept with his first wife?"

The Mac Tíre shifted away from the uncomfortable subject, and Samantha was again reminded that he did owe his friend, Lord Thorne, more fealty than to herself. "Well . . . I'm sure that didn't help," he muttered.

Something the scoundrel Thorne had said against her ear produced unwelcome waves of gooseflesh, despite the heat of the cook fire.

Isna the enemy of my enemy my friend?

"Do you think this Laird Mackenzie would be swayed by my plight?" she fretted. "Do you know him very well?"

Calybrid peeled a charred piece of skin from one of the grouse and crunched it before Samantha could swat his hand away. "Everyone from Dorset to Cape Wrath knows if ye want in good with the Demon Highlander, ye'll get his wife to champion ye," the old ranch hand stated sagely.

"Aye," Locryn readily agreed. "If ye want my opinion, it's on account of her large—" He held his arms away from his chest, curving them as though to support a hefty bosom.

"Heart." Calybrid seized Locryn's wrists and pulled them down. "She's reputed to be unceasingly kind."

"Aye, that she is." Locryn attempted to grapple his wrists away from his wiry counterpart. "But also, she is blessed with an uncommonly generous—"

Calybrid slapped his hand over Locryn's mouth.

"Spirit," he crowed. "Ye'd like her, generous as *ye* are with yer home and land and supper and whatnot."

"Nay!" Locryn succeeded in peeling Calybrid's hand from his beard while simultaneously shimmying his shoulders like a bawdy saloon dancer. "I'm referring to her big—"

Abandoning all pretense, Calybrid just slapped him upside the head.

"Ye'll answer for that," Locryn threatened.

Unceasingly amused, Samantha guessed, "You're referring to her tits, right?"

"Nay," said Calybrid only a beat faster than Locryn's "Aye."

"You know you can be frank around me."

"Who's this Frank?" Locryn scratched his russet hair.

"It means candid." Samantha laughed. "You don't have to mince words just because I'm a woman."

"We ken that," Calybrid said sheepishly. "It's just . . ."

"I think Cal didna want ye to feel slighted because ye doona have any breasts," Locryn said.

"I do too have breasts," Samantha argued, then crossed her arms over her conspicuously flat chest when three pairs of eyes skeptically surveyed the unimpressive topography.

"Doona fash, Sam." Calybrid, spying her scowl, hurried to balm the wound. "Ye're plenty fair."

"Aye," Locryn agreed.

"With eyes the color of the Alt Dubh Gorm."

"Sure, that too."

"Just . . . no one will write odes to yer breasts is all."

"On account of ye not having any," Locryn supplied, rather unnecessarily, in Samantha's opinion.

Calybrid knocked Locryn again. "It's like ye doona even want supper, ye daft ox."

"Well, I know who's not getting the grouse breasts, anyhow," she teased, winking her forgiveness at the odd, elderly pair.

When Samantha summoned the courage to glance over at Callum, she noted a bit of pink had crawled from beneath his collar and disappeared beneath his beard. His eyes gleamed like amber in the sun, though, with good humor and perhaps something else.

Something that made her look away.

While her little operation of outcasts ate grouse, wild greens, and gravy she made with the drippings, in companionable silence, Samantha considered her position.

Despite her promise to Alison, she realized that she truly didn't want to lose this place. In the week she'd been here at Erradale, she'd fallen in love. The manor house itself was a rather labyrinthine, rambling estate that seemed to have been added onto by each generation. This main hall, its windows rippled with age and thick wood and mortar walls, was bigger than any cabin she'd ever lived in. The structure itself older than her entire country.

Because she spent her days rounding up cattle spread for miles across bog-riddled moors dappled with splendid lochs, she was left with no time for the care and upkeep of the house. Nor could she split wood for a fireplace in both the spacious master suite and the great hall. And so each night, she rolled a plethora of soft furs onto the giant flagstones of the great hearth, and let the dancing ghosts cast by the firelight on the blue stones lull her exhausted body to sleep. Sometimes, she'd wake with a start and the shadows created by nothing but dying embers would loom over her.

Sometimes they wore the faces of her demons. Of her sins.

Of the man she'd murdered. The man she'd loved.

At least she thought she'd loved him.

However, Samantha had begun to wonder, if she'd truly

loved Bennett, would she not mourn him more deeply? Would she not remember him more fondly?

Would she have been unable to pull the trigger, in spite of everything he'd done? Of everything he was threatening to do . . .

Troubled, she felt the hairs at the nape of her neck prickle with awareness, and she looked up to find Callum silently studying her with the steady gaze of an cartographer deciphering a foreign map.

Unwilling to be caught in a brood, she ran a tongue over her teeth to clear any remnants of her supper and flashed him an unrepentant grin, which he blithely returned.

"Callum," she ventured, having dispensed with proprieties almost immediately after they'd become acquainted. "Have you always lived here . . . in the Highlands, I mean?"

To her surprise, his smile disappeared. "Nay," he answered carefully. "I've traveled to every place you can imagine. From the Orient to Argentina. Even to America. I only returned here recently."

Flushing, Samantha changed the subject, dearly hoping he hadn't been to San Francisco in his travels. "It makes sense that you chose this place to settle," she said, gesturing to encompass the storm, the sea, the high beams of the ceiling, and the grandness of the stone hearth. "I wonder, though, why the Dubh Gorm Caves? Why not settle somewhere . . . more comfortable?"

Something dire surfaced from the depths of his eyes, something ancient, and hollow, and infinitely sad. "I've seen all there is of humanity, and you know what I learned?" he asked.

"What's that?" she breathed.

Locryn cut in, his voice warm and tongue heavy with Scotch. "It's better . . . to just live alone in a cave."

Calybrid reached out and rested his hand on the portly man's knee in a gesture so tender, Samantha's eyes stung.

Not wanting to cry, she blinked and shifted her focus back to Callum, who still watched her with those eerily perceptive eyes. "That it's better to just live alone in a cave," he murmured in agreement.

A fraught melancholy threatened to swallow the room, and Samantha refused to let it take her. Rising to her knees, she swiped the bottle of Scotch and topped off everyone's drink in turn. "Except on nights like this one," she said, lifting her glass a little. "To warm hearths and full bellies, which is more than some have."

"Aye." Callum's sharp eyes softened a little as he drank to that.

"To Sam." Calybrid lifted his Scotch. "The best cook in Erradale."

"To Sam!" the drunk Locryn echoed. "The only cook in Erradale."

"To Alison Ross," Callum said, casting her one of his speaking glances.

Samantha blanched as she made an intense study of his shuttered features. This was the second time he'd referred to Alison Ross as though she were someone not present.

It was as though the enigmatic man was trying to tell her he knew who she was.

Or . . . at least . . . that he knew who she wasn't.

CHAPTER SEVEN

For your own safety . . . never set foot in Ravencroft Keep.

Alison Ross's dire warning ricocheted in Samantha's thoughts, drowning out the more pleasant sounds of soft rain against glass and the metronomic tick of a grandfather clock.

She hadn't just crossed the threshold of the red stone keep on Ravencroft lands, she'd climbed two flights of stairs and navigated three lush hallways, only to be shown into a receiving room done in dark greens contrasted with spun gold and burgundy.

The burgundy matched both the port wine in her glass and the Marchioness of Ravencroft's wealth of upswept hair.

"I'm thoroughly glad you've called on me." Mena Mackenzie's genuine smile was possibly the warmest, most lovely expression Samantha had witnessed in her entire twenty and four years. "I've been expecting an announcement card from Erradale, and it only just occurred to me that you might not have that custom in American society." Lady

Ravencroft's grace both put her at ease and made her supremely uncomfortable. How could this gently bred and unmistakably noble English lady be married to a violent laird whom all of Europe knew as the Demon Highlander?

Samantha carefully forced herself to focus on Lady Ravencroft's regal features, instead of her form, as she worried that one glance below the neck would send her into a fit of nervous giggles.

Locryn hadn't been wrong. The voluptuous woman was blessed with a luxurious abundance of curves. There was a great probability that someone, somewhere, had written odes to her incomparable tits.

Fighting the urge to cover her bust, or lack thereof, Samantha took another sip of the port offered by Lady Ravencroft in lieu of tea after she'd appeared on the castle's grand doorstep, drenched from riding through the icy November drizzle.

As the Laird Ravencroft had been temporarily detained at his distillery, the lady of the manor had agreed to visit with her while they waited.

Next to the elegant, stunning, and—she assumed—stylishly clad noblewoman, Samantha felt both conspicuous and dowdy. She fought not to squirm beneath Lady Ravencroft's curious jade gaze as she groped for a reply.

"I—I've never had much use for calling cards," she stated honestly, spreading a restless hand over the garnet and butter-yellow stripes of her finest wool skirt and failing in her efforts not to measure it against Lady Ravencroft's imported violet silk gown. In quality and voice, Samantha very much compared the two of them to their skirts. One coarse, ordinary, and practical, the other smooth, stunning, and majestic.

"I can't imagine what's keeping my husband." Lady Ravencroft cast a glance at the clock. "But I'm very glad that I get this opportunity to know you. It isn't every day one meets an American railway heiress. You can regale me about the American West. Is it truly as wild as we tedious Brits are led to believe?"

"It sure can be," Samantha hedged, finishing off the syrupy port in two nervous gulps.

"Are you a . . . connoisseur of port?" Lady Ravencroft asked alertly.

Samantha shrugged. "If 'connoisseur' means I like it, then I surely am. Though I confess this is the first time I've ever tried it."

Lady Ravencroft's husky, melodious laugh washed her with pleasure, though Samantha suspected it was a little at her expense. "Please, have some more, then." She gestured to a servant with skin the color of dark exotic pine, clad in an outfit so startlingly vibrant, she'd have said he was wearing a desert sunset if she didn't know any better.

"I, um, did try some Ravencroft Scotch the other night. It was mighty good."

"Won't Laird Ravencroft be glad to hear it?" There was that smile again, one completely charming, but lacking in any amount of artifice. "Pray, tell me about yourself, Miss Ross. What are your interests and accomplishments?"

Samantha froze. Perhaps she'd made a gigantic mistake coming here. She'd already known passing herself off as a San Franciscan socialite was a stretch, but thus far, she'd only had to convince a bunch of unobservant men who would barely know silk from wool unless they had to wipe their asses with it.

A lady, though . . . would see through her in a New York minute.

She should have anticipated that.

"I . . . can't say I've accomplished much of anything to speak of, yet, my lady," she answered vaguely.

"Call me Mena, please. We are neighbors, after all," Mena admonished through another good-natured laugh. "What I meant to ask was, what is it that you do in America, Miss Ross? Do you paint, stitch, or study anything in particular?"

Stymied, Samantha shook her head.

Mena's smile lost a bit of its sparkle. "Do you sing, perhaps, or play an instrument?"

"Not where people can see or hear me."

They each took another drink before the marchioness tried again.

"I've heard that Americans are also very fond of the waltz . . ."

Samantha knew she'd failed to keep her panicked expression from her features when Mena's sentence trailed away. The Smiths, who'd raised her, believed dancing was of the devil. She'd never so much as been to a barnyard reel.

"Do you favor more physical pursuits, I wonder?" Mena persisted, abandoning her wine to a delicate table at her elbow. "I enjoy all things equestrian, and we host a fantastic stag hunt in the summer."

The gold velvet of her delicate settee abraded the wool of her jacket as Samantha straightened. "I can ride, it's about all I'm good at." She nodded a bit too enthusiastically, she feared. "And I can shoot."

"Wonderful!" Mena clapped two delighted hands together and leaned forward, as well. "I was raised on a small baronetcy in the southwest of England. I've always counted riding among my favorite pastimes. We simply *must* schedule a riding afternoon."

Delighted that she shared common ground with a marchioness, Samantha almost blurted that she, too, had been raised in the southwest. But she swallowed the admission just in time.

"Every afternoon is a riding afternoon for me," Samantha explained. "I spend my time with a few hired hands rounding up the herd that's taken a decade to scatter from here to perdition."

"Perhaps I can come visit you at Erradale, then," Mena suggested. "Come to think of it, with the harvest long over and the distillery rather quiet until spring, more than a few local men would enthusiastically accept an offer of employment at Erradale, if you're in need of extra help gathering your cattle."

"I might just do." Samantha abandoned all sense of suspicion at this point, though whether because of the disarming Lady Ravencroft or the two glasses of port, she couldn't be certain.

Darting her gaze to the gilded framed canvases and delicately painted china, she asked, "Can you do all those other things you mentioned? Do you have those other . . . accomplishments?"

"Yes. Indeed, all of them." The grand lady had the grace to look discomfited at her admission of skill, and cast her gaze down at the lush carpets while stained with a soft peach blush. Suddenly she straightened, as though struck by an idea. "Are there any that interest you? The winter months can be lonely here in the Highlands, and we weren't exactly planning on going to London for Christmas, as my husband's duties tie him to Ravencroft this year. Perhaps when the weather permits, you can call and I could . . . tutor you in something? I was a governess for a while, before marrying Laird Ravencroft. Do you have a notion of what your proclivities would be?"

Not in the least. "Um—what's your favorite thing?"

"I've always adored dancing."

Shit. Samantha had to wipe suddenly clammy hands on her dress. She hadn't expected to be invited over on the regular. Besides, should she be dancing with the enemy? Weren't they enemies? Because right now, Mena Mackenzie looked very much like a friend.

But . . . so was Alison Ross. She had to remember that. She wasn't here to play like a princess, she was here to hide from her adversaries, from her sins, and look after Erradale.

She was saved from committing herself to anything when a footman informed them that the marquess would be much longer than expected, and certainly not back in time for Samantha to return to Erradale before dark.

"Oh dear, I'm terribly sorry your call was wasted," Mena lamented. "Is there any atonement I can offer? Sometimes, since I am the Lady of Clan Mackenzie, Laird Ravencroft asks me to hear certain matters and advise him in those respects. I'm especially familiar with civil disputes, if that is your particular need."

She gave Samantha a look that said she already knew it was.

Samantha decided she'd had all the niceties she could handle. "Lady Ravencroft—"

"Mena, please."

"Are you aware your husband's younger brother, the Earl of Thorne, is trying to steal my land from me?"

"Thorne?" The marchioness gasped, blinking rapidly. "That doesn't sound like him at all."

To Mena's credit, she listened very intently to Samantha's account of her plight, her winged auburn brows shifting lower and lower as a troubled expression overtook her pleasant one.

"I was aware he'd filed paperwork to claim the abandoned Erradale land," she conceded once Samantha had finished. "But now that its rightful owner is returned, it doesn't seem like he would persist in his pursuit of ownership. Especially not to the extent of harassment."

"He said I could take his deal or forfeit it to the Laird, from whom he'd buy it for cents on the dollar."

The marchioness frowned. "Forgive me, but I'm not familiar with that expression."

"Um . . . pennies instead of pounds," Samantha converted.

"I see. Correct me if I'm wrong, but didn't he offer you a great deal of money for it?"

"A fair bit." More like a staggering amount.

"And you don't want to stay here for the long term, nor do you want to sell it to him? May I ask why?"

Once again, Samantha shifted, not wanting to cede diplomatic ground on enemy territory. Despite herself, she liked the statuesque Mena Mackenize. She wasn't the anticipated old, stodgy matron, but someone not a great deal older than herself. Though the lady was fine and far more worldly, she had an approachable kindness that opened up a sort of void in Samantha that she hadn't known was there.

Finishing her port with the queasy feeling that it would be her last for a good, long time, she decided to tell the truth. "No offense meant, Lady Ravencroft—Mena—but I promised my father that no son of Hamish Mackenzie would ever own Erradale . . ."

Regret lined Mena's otherwise smooth ivory skin as she offered her a sad smile. "There's none taken, my dear. I do not begrudge you the sentiment, and neither will my husband. He's well acquainted with his father's crimes against his own people."

Stunned, Samantha groped for something else to say. She hadn't exactly expected such a delicate and understanding reply. In fact, she'd gripped her pelisse in anticipation of being tossed out by the tall East Indian listening intently from the corner.

"I'll discuss it with Lord Ravencroft, and he with Lord Northwalk and Lord Thorne before the Magistrate's Bench convenes. We shall see what can be done for you and your family's honor."

"That's mighty kind of you . . ." Samantha offered her halting gratitude. Unsure of what to do next, she stood abruptly, which seemed to oblige the marchioness to do the same.

"My previous offer is still extended, of course." Mena took Samantha's rough hand with gloves as soft as goose down. "I'll personally deliver you an army of amateur cattlemen to gather your herd should you need it."

"I'd—be obliged." Samantha gave the lady something like a bow or a curtsy, but ultimately less graceful, and turned to follow the footman out when she paused, remembering something.

"May I ask you something else, Lady Ravencroft?"

"Of course." The question seemed to please her.

"Do you know the meaning of the Gaelic insult 'bonny'? Lord Thorne insists on using it to address me, and I'd like to find a comparable offense."

It was Mena's turn to be astonished, as it took her a full minute to recover her wits. "Well, Miss Ross, 'bonny' is certainly a Scottish word, but it is more endearment than insult."

"You sure?"

"I'm quite positive," she insisted with a secret smile. "You see, 'bonny' is the Gaelic word for beauty."

Gavin had always been an excellent hunter. A consummate predator. From the Sahara Desert to the Black Forest to the most exclusive *salons* and royal boudoirs in the empire and beyond, he'd been known to stalk his prey with unsurpassed mastery. The trick, he'd learned, was to know your quarry. To get close enough to expose their weaknesses, and to strike with perfect, lethal efficiency.

Sometimes that meant making oneself unassuming . . . donning the sheep's clothing and waltzing among the bleating herd like one of their own. Other times, it meant becoming the lion, parting the tall grasses with wide shoulders and a broad chest, prowling the landscape secure in the knowledge of his dominance over all territory in his scope. There were moments that absolute stealth was required. He'd make no sound. He'd leave no footprint. Naught but shadows and vapor. There, and yet intangible.

Until it was too late.

His favorite was pretending to be the prey. Allowing himself to be stalked, to be desired, pursued. Then, just as the predator thought him ripe for the picking, he'd turn and strike, savoring the openmouthed, confounded astonishment of his opponent.

This tended to be just as efficient with women as with wolves.

There was something more than a little satisfying about ripping the heart out of someone the moment before they expected to do the same to you.

Perhaps his enjoyment of that made him a monster.

But the blood of monsters ran in the Mackenzie family, did it not? He'd been sired by one. His body sullied. His name tainted.

His mother ruined.

He'd initially thought that if he learned to be something else, anything else, his family curse wouldn't touch him. He'd taught himself to be everything. The poet and the prince. The lordling and the lion. The lover and the hunter. What were the Scots before steam and smoke and English money?

They were hunters.

He'd learned his artful skills from observation, experience, and the most remarkable tutors of all . . .

Pain. Hunger. Failure.

He'd been a fool to assume this new venture at ranching would be any different. That it wouldn't be one more thing that would chip away at his soul before he mastered it. He'd thought he could study enough books, discuss it with enough experts, that he'd slide into it as easily as he did a lathered countess's quim.

Why, he wondered with an expelled breath, must *everything* be such an arduous battle? Why did all he sought come at such a price to his very being? When so many seemed to hack their bloody way through life, heedless of the devastation left in their wake, and still the heavens poured bounteous blessings on their undeserving heads. While *he* was left in the mire with no choice but the difficult, undesired one.

Cocking his rifle, Gavin watched the prey he'd hunted by way of small puddles of blood and such flail about in piteous distress before relaxing back to its side.

"I'm sorry it had to come to this," he muttered.

The beast looked up at him with eyes both gentle and wary from beneath a fringe of ridiculously long russet hair.

There was pain in those eyes too, and fear.

Strange, he thought bitterly, how there's always a little more innocence left to lose.

The click of someone else's firearm froze the finger he'd inched toward the trigger. Gavin knew just who was behind him before she even opened her mouth.

He could sense her, somehow. In the way the hairs on his body seemed to lift and vibrate at her approach.

"Oh, it's you," she lamented.

"Aye, bonny . . . 'tis me." William Blake he was not, but

he'd not the temperament to cultivate a persona at the moment, as he was just about as happy to encounter her as she sounded to have happened upon him.

"Where I come from, butchering someone else's cattle is a hanging offense." Her threat was wry, if not subtle.

Gavin cursed every square inch of that capitalist mecca that turned what should have been a good Scottish girl into a goddamned, trigger-happy American.

"I'm not *butchering* anything," he replied from between clenched teeth. Fury at himself for allowing her to sneak up on him surpassed his ire at the strange anticipation that heated his blood as she nudged her horse nearer. "I'm putting it out of its misery."

"That right?" Her dismount from behind him was muffled by the soft ground cover. "She keel over from tedium after too long in your company? Can't be the first time that's ever happened. No reason to put a bullet in her head."

"If a woman loses consciousness in my company, it's generally due to a swoon. Or pleasurable exhaustion." As she drew abreast of him, Gavin looked down at her to weigh the effect of his innuendo and, once again, found himself enjoying that she was among only a handful of ladies he'd met in his life who were taller than his shoulders.

Because he wanted to smile at her, he frowned, sternly.

The sound she made was so unladylike, he couldn't tell if it was a snort or a laugh. "You saying that's what happened here? You tuckered her out with your lovemaking?"

Her cobalt eyes danced with self-satisfied mirth, and yet he found himself surveying their surface with the same appreciation he'd done for Loch Awe beneath the rare noonday sun.

"Nay." The droll syllable should have dried up the relentless rain. "Seamus McGrath said he spotted a rabid deerhound in these woods not three days ago." He gestured to the high canopy of ancient elms and beyond. "I think it got to one of yer beasties."

She returned her pistol, which she'd been aiming from close to her hip, to its holster before venturing ahead of him. "What makes you think that?"

Gavin tried not to notice how the fine cut of her serviceable dress exhibited the dramatic indent of her waist. How her nose and ears and the skin beneath her freckles was tinged pink with the same cold that painted her quivering lips a vibrant red.

Before he knew it, his own lip was caught between his teeth in a gesture of unwelcome deprivation.

She was his rival. His prey. He shouldn't be wondering where her cloak was in weather that could turn to ice and illness in her lungs. This was no time to follow the beads of moisture clinging to the damp curls not protected by her sopping hat, its once-proud feather now weighted and listless against butter-yellow felt. Her dark hair tumbled loose down her back, and bounced with her avid movements. Those curls, they beckoned to a man's hand. He wanted to stroke them. To test them. To wind his fingers in them until he could anchor her head back and lay siege to her impenitent mouth until she was—

"I don't see evidence of a bite or an attack," she reasoned. "Though with a coat this long, it's hard to tell."

"Look here." He pointed. "There's a bit of foam about her mouth, and she'll flail intermittently as though in immense pain. Also, see how bloated she is about the middle?"

"Hmmm." Ripping off her hat and discarding it to the moss, her delicate features pursed with scrutiny, she made to approach the animal. "I don't at all think it's rabies. It looks to me like she's just about to—"

Unaware of what he was doing, Gavin seized her arm, pulling her up short. "What do ye think ye're doing?" he demanded. "Did ye not mark the place where I told ye that large beast with sharp hooves and horns known to gouge a man clean through was prone to *flailing*?"

"You've obviously never wrangled Texas longhorns."

"Nay, but ye're daft if ye think I'm going to let ye go over there." The vehemence of his statement seemed to startle them both. He'd never thought himself as much of a hero, but a protective instinct welled in him from a place so deep, he'd thought it dormant.

She stared at him in wide-eyed wonderment for a rare, silent moment before her features hardened with stubborn defiance. "Let me go," she commanded, wrenching at her arm. "Don't you have someone else to cheat or hassle?"

"Ye seem to be the only woman alive to find my company a hassle," he countered.

"I doubt that very much."

He'd been right, Gavin noted, his hand did span the entirety of her arm so that his fingers touched when he encircled it. She was delicate, but not exactly frail. Sinew flexed with strength beneath the wool of her pelisse. Though her bones would disintegrate like spun sugar should he desire it.

The flash of fear in her eyes advertised the instant she read his thoughts.

In that moment, he recognized his prey. With her, he needed to be the lion. Maybe if she feared him, she would run. Leave Erradale to him. "It's a mystery to me how such a reckless woman born with an obvious lack of sense has lasted so long in this world without someone to protect her," he drawled.

"Protect me from who, you?" she retorted with false bravado. "Thanks, but better men than you have tried to break me." She reached for her pistol again, but he abandoned his rifle and caught her other arm. In no time, he had her pinned against the closest oak, her wrists caught between them.

Her words caught somewhere in the vicinity of his chest, and he had take in a breath of frigid air to remain cold. Calculating.

"Nay, bonny, not from me. From yerself."

Her nostrils flared and her eyes flashed like the sea goddess Li Ban, summoning her stormy wrath.

"Why worry about me?" she demanded, attempting to wrench her arm out of his grasp. "I get kicked in the head, or gored by old Bessie here, and your problems are solved. No one stands in the way of you getting everything you desire."

"What do ye know of my desires?" His blood ran through him like liquid heat, a startling sensation against the freezing rain. Every vein dilated, allowing the molten awareness of her to spill through him with confounding potency.

Uncertainty splashed across her features and, for once, her eyes darted away from his, only to snag on his lips, and then lower, to the white shirt the rain had painted onto his body. "I know you desire Erradale, and that's all I need to—"

Following a foreign and reckless impulse, Gavin stole her words with his mouth. Even as he made the conscious decision to kiss the soft lips that only uttered hard or foul words, he acknowledged the foolishness of the act.

She was right about Erradale. He desired it above all else, and he was beginning to realize that he desired to possess *everything* that went with it.

Including its current owner.

Even as he claimed her mouth, the urge to do so confounded him. She was nothing like the coy, buxom mistresses he usually coveted, or the unspoiled maidens he allowed to chase him. She was slight, crude, and prickly with all the erotic enticements of a willow switch.

But when he pressed his mouth to hers, more to shut her up than anything, he was distressed to find that years of intently practiced seduction abandoned him instantly.

Arousal lanced him with stomach-clenching swiftness, threatening to steal both his breath and his wits.

He couldn't afford to cede his wits. Not to her. She'd throw them in the tall grass and set them ablaze only to spite him. Yet here he was, hard as a diamond and uncertain as an untried whelp.

They stood there beneath the dripping oak, damp and frozen in more ways than one. Lips locked and still but for shared tremors that weren't entirely produced by the unrelenting cold.

Her eyes were closed, he noticed, squeezed shut in what he hoped wasn't a grimace, and her breath carried sweet notes of port wine and promises of wild, artless passion.

It was that promise that mystified him into stillness.

Life as the second son of Hamish Mackenzie, as brother to the Demon Highlander . . . as someone who'd loved and lost as profoundly as he had, had taught him a very important lesson.

Passion, in all its forms, was a man's undoing. Lust and hunger were permitted, of course, as these were functions of the body and instincts primordial.

But *passion*.

Passion was consuming. It painted everything with a pall of red, the only thing identifiable with any sort of clarity the object of the obsession. It was an ardent, zeal-provoking, violent mania, and it had no place in his heart, or in his life.

Best he feel nothing. That he remained composed. That he control all desire so that it didn't control him. Best he feed his hungers and lusts so that his passions remained eternally banked and his heart perpetually cold.

Like any muscle, the heart atrophied with disuse, and it was upon that fact he heavily relied. That he'd survived all this time. If one did not love, then one could not hate. For each emotion was equally consuming.

Equally passionate.

And, some-fucking-how, Gavin recognized that the woman in his arms was comprised mostly of untamed, unspent passion. Her very matter flooded with it. She tasted of it. Rich and spiced with exotic enticements. She would respond to his every maneuver with it. She would use it as a battering ram against the ramparts of the walls he'd fortified with cavalier mirth and selfish wickedness.

What if . . . what if passion was contagious?

With a stunned gasp, she turned her head, tearing her lips from his.

In the time it took for her to form the indignant words "What the fuck do you think—" Gavin's decision was made, and it no longer paralyzed him.

His fingers released her wrist and anchored in her hair, where they'd previously itched to be. His next kiss was so fierce, it drove her head against his palm, and the back of his hand against the tree.

Her lips were already parted, and he pressed them wider.

This wasn't a kiss, but a claiming.

The first stroke with his tongue tasted of rain and salt. The second, deeper plunge was flavored of fine, syrupy port and the hint of that uncultivated passion he both craved and feared.

His body followed close, aching for contact. Though her hands lifted, pressing feebly against the swells of his chest in weak resistance, he drove his other arm between her body and the tree, and pushed his weight against her, craving her nearness. Her vitality. The fire that always seemed to lick at him from behind her eyes.

She kissed him back, but not with the trained skill of a jaded noblewoman, or the unpracticed vehemence of a virgin. Her kiss resembled all his other interactions with her.

A battle.

One she had no intention of allowing him to win.

Her hands bunched in his lapels with aggression, her wee fists pulling him closer, into her. Though her muscles went rigid, her tongue sparred with his, as he might have guessed it would. Each lick and swirl, each plunge and retreat became a point counted for or against.

Gavin had never enjoyed a woman's mouth so much in his entire life.

And that was a powerful fact, as he'd tasted more than his share.

He knew the moment she'd stepped off the train that she was unlike his other conquests, but until he'd actually had her in his arms, he'd not known exactly *how* singular she was.

He'd thought, erroneously, that it was merely her unique imperfections that lent him a sense of fascination. Though he'd had just about every different flavor of woman imaginable, he'd begun to remember them with the exact same disillusioned ennui. His reminiscence of them became a forest where all the trees were the same size, shape, and color. All the husky moans and screams of pleasure the exact same melody. Perfect in their pitch and percussion.

And, as everyone who chased excellence came to eventually agree, perfection was *boring*. It was both predictable and insipid.

Generally, where women were concerned, it came at a great cost, one way or the other.

Nothing about Alison Ross was perfect. Her thick, heavy hair belonged to a woman with a much less elegant neck. Her eyes, too wide and shrewd for such a delicate chin and sharp nose, should not have been paired with a brow so prone to censure. She was too tall, too thin, too crass, and much too insolent.

All of that gave her a sort of uncultivated allure, a beauty much like the forest in which they stood, dappled with several genuses of trees and moss, grass and blossoms. Its own beauty cultivated by its rather random, untamed imperfection.

He could look at the unsophisticated topography for hours, and not think to move a single tree or replace a meadow.

These were the eyes with which he appreciated Alison Ross.

Though she often spoke, swore, and rode like a man, she felt like a woman against him, feminine and fragile.

She undeniably tasted like a woman.

And yet . . . so unlike any other women he'd sampled. To say she was sweeter missed the mark entirely. She was rather like strong Turkish coffee when one had only ever tasted multitudes of tea.

A shock.

A revelation.

As Gavin feasted on lips softened with a rare lack of ire, he realized what dangerous ground they both stood upon. Treacherous because it was terrain he'd promised never again to tread. Paved with sweet stones of consideration and vulnerability that—once outlived their usefulness— were always picked up and hurled at him.

Instead of taking from her, he was seized with the urge to give. He pressed against her because the desire to infuse her delicate bones with warmth overcame his need for self-preservation. He'd tupped a lass or two against a tree come Beltane or Samhain . . . and he'd allowed her back the abrasions of the bark to remember their pleasure by.

But this . . . this was no casual, alcohol-infused encounter. And it should have been. He'd meant to dominate her, hadn't he? To show her that he could leave her panting and boneless while he, the great seducer, could stow her convictions with a kiss.

Then, unaffected, he'd walk away and take her land.

Well . . . that simply could not happen now.

This kiss was a dynamic shift in the very stars that wrote their fates. It peeled back years from his soul somehow, took him back to before he'd become a hunter, and a traveler. Before Colleen had torn what was left of his heart from his chest and left him alone in the world, before his mother was blinded and his father killed.

Before Liam, his brother, left for the army, thus condemning Gavin's own childhood to death.

To when these woods were a haven to a kind, sensitive boy, and the open land of Erradale the only bit of freedom he'd ever tasted.

The only place his cruel father would never look for him.

Having Alison in his arms now, coaxing a response other than defiance from her, was a chance, a challenge. One he wanted to embrace.

One he wanted to reject.

And knew he could not.

He had to take care with her. To recognize her strength, but honor her softness. To shield her delicate skin from any abrasions but those caused by his own whiskers.

Or his teeth.

Fierce hunger reared in him at the thought of any part of her in his mouth. Now that he'd tasted her lips, he wanted a taste of it all. He wanted her writhing in capitulation as he supped on every part of her. The soft lobe of her ear, the taut arch of her neck, the turgid peak of her breast, and ultimately, her sweet, soft sex.

She broke the kiss only an intake of breath's time before the deafening report of her pistol shattered the peace of the forest, and drove their heated, straining bodies apart.

CHAPTER EIGHT

Samantha used the time it took the startled Lord Thorne to figure out that he hadn't been shot—once again—to sag against the tree and catch her breath.

Everything trembled. Her limbs, her bones, her lips, the leaves beneath the percussive rain. The earth beneath her feet.

Noting that her aim had not been true the first time, she lifted her pistol, aimed carefully, and shot again.

This galvanized the astonished lord, and he had her back against the tree and relieved her of her pistol before she had the chance to react.

God, he was strong. And fast.

She'd be afraid if she wasn't so aroused.

Goddammit.

"Have ye lost yer bloody *mind,* lass?" he hissed, his thunderous expression, along with the fingers digging into her upper arm, warned her that he was seconds away from shaking her senseless.

His was a relevant question, Samantha had to admit, though not in the context he'd meant it.

She had to be certifiably insane to have kissed him back.

Damn, but he was the devil. Temptation personified. The theoretical favored son of whichever God crafted such physical perfection. And, like the so-called star of the morning, he infamously used his powers for wicked, *wicked* ends.

He made the wrong choice feel so utterly right. In his arms, an immoral sin became heavenly bliss. But at what cost?

Her body? Her soul?

Samantha berated herself with a bleak and stolid self-loathing that reached into the very core of her being. She *should* have shot *him*. Put him out of her misery. Her favored Colt had protected her from more than a few drunken cowboys who'd mistaken her for an easy mark. Not that she'd ever actually had to pull the trigger.

Not until Bennett . . .

The moment Thorne had freed her wrists to tangle his fingers in her hair and better lay siege to her lips, she could have drawn and fired.

Had he treated her like the high-handed, dishonest, self-ish, entitled, arrogant bastard that he was, she probably would have.

But . . .

His kiss had conveyed a sentiment she'd thought him incapable of.

Tenderness.

And not that disingenuous, overwrought sort a man expressed when attempting a seduction. He'd been anything but romantic, in fact. But there had been something in the dichotomy of his hard kiss and his soft embrace that had captivated her. As mesmerizing as his lips had been, the hand cupping the back of her head had been equally so. As had the other strong arm gliding up her back to cushion her from the rough trunk of the tree. He'd not merely pressed his arousal against her, as Bennett was wont to do, grinding at her like a bull anticipating a rut.

He'd seemed to . . . curl around her. Like a warm, muscled shelter from the bite of the winter rain. Delicious, masculine heat had permeated her garments, singed her flesh, and culminated in a pool of aroused sensation between her legs.

Damn you, she thought up at him. *Damn you for making me weak.*

She wanted to snipe at him. To demand he let her go. To give him a tongue-lashing he'd never forget.

Best she not think of the word "tongue" just now. She winced.

Seeming to misread the glare and the gesture, his grip on her shoulders instantly gentled, though he didn't release her.

Had she been a worldly, witty woman she'd have said something coy and nonchalant. Something that both insulted his manhood and expressed a lack of affectation over what he'd just done to her.

What they'd just done together.

Instead, she muttered, "Your friend McGrath was right about the rabid deerhound."

Possibly the least provocative sentence uttered by a woman whose lips still tingled and burned from the abrasion of an unbelievably erotic Highlander's shadow beard.

God, she loathed him.

Didn't she?

She just couldn't yield her wits to another devastatingly handsome man with strong shoulders and a dimpled smile. Not again. Not after what happened last time.

The cold bit through the layers of her clothing more viciously now that the warmth he'd shared with her slid away like a careful thief into the storm.

She gestured with her chin behind him, and tried not to notice the coil and sinew of his muscular neck as he glanced over his shoulder to validate her claim.

The tall, emaciated silver hound lay crumpled on his side, bleeding from two wounds. Her first shot had broadsided him. The second one caught him behind the ears. The poor thing's death had been a mercy.

"I'd be obliged if you'd return my pistol, or is that something *else* you plan to steal from me?"

Her insult washed every last vestige of a smile from his sensual, kiss-warmed lips.

He dropped her arms and stepped back, as though he suspected she might draw her own weapon from where he'd stashed it in his waistband. "I might just hold on to it a while, until I know ye're sane enough to be armed."

"The hell you mean by that?" she demanded, her temper replacing the heat she'd lost when she'd lost his proximity.

He crossed his arms over his chest, mirroring her widelegged stance. It was impossible not to notice the bronze flesh molded to perfection beneath the cling of his soaked shirt. Nor the way it dipped and settled into the grooves created by the muscles in his arms. So, Samantha did what she always did when trying to ignore his damnable attractiveness.

She stared him right in the eyes.

Eyes darker than the most ancient evergreen tree, ringed with traces of amber—

Goddammit.

"Ye'll have to admit, bonny, that it *does* seem ye're mighty eager to use yer wee gun when in my company."

"That *can't* be a new phenomenon."

"And to be fair, this is the second time ye've shot in my general direction."

"I already told you." She locked her fingers around her biceps to keep from gesturing wildly. "If I was aiming at you, you'd be full of holes."

"It seems ye've something against dogs," he continued casually. "And everyone knows that only the troubled are cruel to animals."

"Look at it." She stabbed a finger at the poor animal. "It's emaciated, foaming at the mouth, and its hair is falling out. I just *saved* one of my herd."

"Which ye should have let me put down in the first place, as it has been suffering all this time."

"You mean all this time you've been molesting me against a tree?"

His jaw locked into a stubborn position, advertising his culpability.

The extent of his *wrongness* stole her capacity for speech for a full minute. "Oh, I get it. This is all because I'm a *woman*."

"That has nothing to do with—"

"Do you mean to tell me that if you were out here with Callum, and he'd put down a rabid animal, you'd treat him with this same ridiculous condescension? Relieve him of his weapon? Talk down to him like he was nothing more than bog mud beneath your boot when *you're* the one who's so mistaken it's almost laughable?"

His jaw now worked to the side in a gesture of unmitigated masculine gall, but after a bracing breath, he pulled her gun from where he'd stashed it in his waistband, and offered it to her.

"Pardon my reaction, lass. It isna every day a man's kiss is interrupted by gunshots."

Samantha took the weapon, checked it, and returned it to its holster before replying, "Had my aim not been obstructed by your . . . ironhanded, oafish ass grinding me into that tree, then I'd have only found it necessary to shoot once."

Ignoring her remark, he stepped over to the animal, inspecting it with a solemn nod. "I'll admit, ye're better than a fair shot, bonny."

Frowning, she eyed him warily, half wishing she was still ignorant as to the meaning of the word.

"Yeah . . . well . . . thanks." If she hadn't despised him, she'd have been flattered.

But she did. So she wasn't.

"Now, let's discuss what ye meant by laughably mistaken." He arched a dubious brow at her.

She should have been grateful that he'd given her a chance to correct him. At any other moment, she'd have pounced on it like an alley cat, claws extended.

But . . . he'd just ceded a point. He'd begged her pardon. Well, perhaps *begged* was a bit of a reach, but he'd returned her gun. In her experience, confronting a man while questioning his intentions was more likely to acquaint her with the back of his hand than his admission of fault.

In the West, to call a man's pride into account was to flirt with the business end of his pistol. Not the other way around.

"Look," she admonished softly. "The cow isn't rabid."

He turned and followed the direction of her finger to

where a little black nose and two ungainly hooves had already emerged from beneath the laboring heifer.

"Holy Christ," he marveled. He reached for her, gripping her elbow gently as though he'd forgotten himself. His focus never wavered from the spectacle. "What do we do? I read that ye can help by pulling the wee thing out . . . should we . . . ?"

It took Samantha longer than it should have to abandon her shock at his friendly hold on her elbow. People—men—just didn't touch her like this. Casually. Gently.

She . . . liked it.

Clearing her throat, she answered. "Unless she's in trouble, there's really no need. Best to let her do it on her own."

"Does she look like she's in trouble to ye? How do ye tell?" he queried, taking only a moment to check her expression for an answer before his notice was dragged back to the delivery.

The beast's great body was seized by another convulsion, and she instinctively pushed, and the little creature emerged to the shoulders.

"No trouble at all," she was glad to note. "She's doing beautifully."

"Aye. Aye, that's good." He squeezed her elbow in a kind, grateful gesture, a dimple of pleasure appearing in his cheek.

He didn't let go.

Instead of watching the quick, messy birth, Samantha observed the Earl of Thorne with something akin to open-mouthed incredulity.

An alert anxiety had transformed him from a haughty, cynical Highlander to someone much, much younger. He studied the event with an intent concentration colored with a bit of excited, almost . . . boyish wonder. On features so fiercely masculine as his, the expression was unrelentingly endearing.

In the moment of unguarded distraction, Samantha couldn't stop herself from laughing softly at his grimace of disgust as the new mother began to lick her newly emerged calf clean. Nudging it encouragingly with her nose.

"It's a wee bit . . . slimier than a litter of cats or pups, is it not?" he remarked with an impish curl of his nose.

"Don't tell me the great hunter Gavin St. James, Lord of Inverthorne, is squeamish," she teased. "What will the ladies say?"

His sheepish smile unleashed a swarm of butterflies low in her belly.

"Blood and offal is one thing, this is . . . something else." They fell silent, though Samantha thought she wasn't alone in cheering the little red creature to gain its feet. "Something better, I think. The giving of life, instead of the taking of it," he murmured many minutes later, in a voice so low, Samantha wondered if he'd realized he'd spoken out loud.

By now the cold and wet had become a part of them, seeping into their bones. Even through her layers, Samatha couldn't remember ever being consumed with such a pervasive chill. She couldn't imagine how he fared in only a shirt and trousers.

His focus drawn by a violent shiver she couldn't hide, he turned back to her. "Where's yer cloak, lass?"

"It was soiled so I washed it last night, and foolishly hung it somewhere beneath a leak in the roof I was not aware had sprung until the storm hit last night," she confessed with chagrin. "I thought the rain had passed when I left Erradale. I assumed my wool pelisse would be enough."

"Highland weather is as temperamental as a randy stallion," he remarked, striding past a few dark trees to an oak with low branches where he'd lashed his horse. He returned with a dry, folded length of cloak retrieved from his saddlebags. "Blue skies one moment, confounding mist the next, which might be chased away by a sea gale in an hour or so."

"What about you?" she protested as he unfurled the cloak and settled it around her shoulders.

"I've a woolen in my other bag. Besides, this stretch of road runs through Inverthorne land and . . ." Samantha watched in horrified fascination as his eyes narrowed in suspicion as they traveled the length of her best dress, darted to her discarded hat, and then followed her horses' damning tracks back toward Ravencroft.

"What have ye been up to, lass?" The mild note in his tone wouldn't have sounded false to an ear untrained in deception. "Had ye business in Strathcarron today?"

"No," she answered simply.

"Ravencroft, then?" He enunciated the syllables of his brother's title and keep very carefully.

"What if I did?" she queried, defensively. "What concern is it of yours?"

"If it concerns Erradale, it concerns me."

"Like hell it does," Samantha snapped, retreating a few strategic steps away so she wouldn't have to look up at him. "Erradale is and will *always* remain mine." Even as she said this, Samantha knew it rang false. Erradale no more belonged to her than it did to him. And yet, she was willing to fight to the death to keep it away from him. Because of the depths he seemed to be willing to sink to take what he thought was her home.

He gave her no quarter, matching her retreat with a relentless advance. "Ye're wasting yer time. I've already told ye, my brother is not my laird. He willna stop me from getting what I want."

"You said, yourself, that you are not yet emancipated from Ravencroft," she challenged.

"That'll have no bearing on the outcome." He shrugged.

"Won't it? You didn't want me to know that the Magistrate's Bench is comprised of three magistrates, did you? That there's still a chance you could be in the minority? What, did you not think I'd find out? That I wouldn't use every means at my disposal to fight you with everything I have?"

He didn't hide his displeasure quickly enough. The motions were almost imperceptible, but Samantha read them as easily as a child's primer. A twitch below his eye. A slight tightening at his hairline. A ripple in the extraordinary musculature of his torso. She'd been right. He'd not expected her to figure him out. He'd known of Alison Ross's enmity for Hamish Mackenzie's sons, and guessed that it would be intensified for his first-born, Liam.

Enough to keep her away from Ravencroft.

"You're not getting your way, this time," she declared. "Not while I draw breath."

A bit more of his impartial veneer slipped, and what she read in his eyes drove her back a few more steps.

"What is more important, lass? That ye win? Or that I lose?" A leashed aggression threaded into his brogue. A subtle warning, like the shift in the air before the carnage of a decisive battle.

Behind the charm and wit and seductive manipulation shimmering in his eyes' mercilessly beautiful depths, Samantha read something that sent her hand to rest on her pistol . . .

There was violence in those eyes.

He marked the subtle motion of her hand, the corners of his lips dipping in a poorly concealed frown. "Ye'll not need that, lass. I doona hurt women."

"Yes you do," she argued.

"Never." Tension gathered in his shoulders like thunderclouds building upon themselves and she noted that the rise and fall of his breaths hadn't slowed since their ill-conceived—admittedly unforgettable—kiss. "I've not raised my hand to a lass in the entirety of my life," he said in a voice laced with more sex than rage as he opened his palms to her. "These hands have done nothing but caress wanton flesh. Or produce shivers of pleasure. Women doona *fear* these hands, they crave them. They doona cringe from my strength, they beg for it. They drop their fans and handkerchiefs. They run into me on purpose, only to touch my body. They titter and wave and swoon and make themselves ridiculous. I have piles of perfumed letters and unanswered invitations from women I've bedded, beseeching me for one more night. One more whispered conversation. One more tender caress. So doona ye *dare* treat me like I'm a monster. That was my father. That *is* my brother. They are the Lairds of the Mackenzie of Wester Ross, bathed in blood, both male and female. My hands are soiled only by slick desire and sins ye canna even *begin* to imagine in yer most wicked dreams."

Samantha snorted. "You truly believe that, don't you?"

It wasn't the reply he'd expected, she could tell by the tightening of his lips. "I've heard the moans and cries of bliss, lass, which I ken are easily fabricated," he said drolly. "But the wet rush of ecstasy and the pulsing flesh around mine are unmistakable. Belief turns to knowledge with evidence."

She swallowed around a tongue gone suddenly dry at the pure, vulgar images his words evoked, but stepped forward fueled by principled, righteous indignation.

"Do you actually think your actions don't hurt women?"

The wicked gleam in his eyes darkened to a villainous one. "Not unless they ask for it.

"What about all those unanswered letters?" she challenged. "Do you suppose that the cold, selfish rejection of your former conquests doesn't cause intense pain? That it doesn't leave a deep wound?"

"Doona speak in metaphors, lass, it doesna suit the occasion. One blow from a man like me is like to leave a wound a wee lass would never recover from. Doona think I'm unaware of that. An unanswered letter is nothing like."

"But so does a broken promise," she insisted. "Rejection and dismissal are their own form of cruelty."

"What would ye have me do, offer to marry every woman who contrives her way into my bed?"

"Not at all, I wouldn't wish marriage to *you* on my worst enemy. No one deserves a lifetime of nothing but arduous lessons in disappointed expectations."

"Och, lass, ye'll have to admit that I'm not alone in my cruelty. Yer tongue scores through like a bayonet."

"The truth is rarely kind," she volleyed back. "And I highly doubt most of the scores of hapless women who find themselves swept into your abbreviated attentions are contrivers. You're a predator, Gavin St. James."

"That's Lord Thorne to ye," he reminded her with haughty vehemence.

"A Thorne, maybe, but you are not. My. Lord," she bit out. "If you refuse the Mackenzie as your laird, though he is thought to be by tradition and *law,* then I do not see fit to address you as mine as you are neither a gentle nor noble man. Where I come from, a man must earn an exalted title by way of education, merit, or endeavor. Call that barbaric if you like, but it makes a great deal of sense to me as I stand in front of a man who can only count his ac-

complishments as high as the number of women he's bedded. Or hearts he's broken."

"Do not speak to *me* of broken hearts," he warned, taking another dangerous step forward. "I've never led a
woman to believe she was anything more to me than a
passing fancy or a pleasant fuck. Should she build more
in her mind than what I promised, the fault is hers."

Samantha's eyes narrowed with such strain, his impossibly beautiful face blurred into nothing more than brutal
planes and sharp angles. "You *are* a monster. One more
dangerous than those who you would denounce. You're a
monster who believes himself other than he is."

He threw his hands up in a sweeping gesture of deri-
sion. "So tell me, Saint Ross, whatever shall I do to gain
yer condemnatory esteem? Is there no redemption in your
heart for a lowly fiend like myself?"

"I'm no saint." The fathomless void of shame swirled
beneath her temper, spiking it ever higher. "I've allowed
monsters to tempt me to do the devil's work. I've frightened and hurt people. Innocent people. I've watched beautiful, powerful men like you hold their actions up to true
evil and I found the *good* in the comparison. I excused who
they were right up until they crossed the line they promised never to even approach. You think you're the first wayward son or younger brother who vowed to be left
untouched by the sins of his elders? In the end, the past
will catch up with you, and men like you always pull the
trigger when they ought not to."

She raked him with a glare that told him she saw past
his untamed beauty, to the ugly violence that rippled beneath all his taut, bronzed flesh. "As much as you'd like
to think your hands are clean, we both know they're not.
They're stained with a million sins, with a thousand
tears, a hundred deceits, and maybe a little blood you pre-

tend isn't there. You may ignore it, but *I* see it. I see who you are."

"Then why did ye fucking kiss me back?" he snarled.

Samantha hid her gasp behind a shrug. "Because maybe I'm a monster, too."

They stared at each other, each shaking from the cold rain and icy rage.

From the electric passion arcing between them like currents of lightning, brewing a tempest each of them knew could sweep them away.

The forest darkened as the storm intensified, casting his bright eyes into shadow, and slicking his sand-colored hair a darker shade. The rivulets of water running down the grooves next to his sensual mouth, tracing the sinew of his neck, his clavicles, dripping from his hair, could have been the tears of angels who'd given up on his soul long ago.

He appeared to her a bleak pagan god, forsaken by time and progress to lurk alone in primeval forests that had once been considered his temples.

She didn't want to pity him, to feel any compassion . . .

But an ancient pain surfaced from beneath his hard fury like a long-forgotten corpse dredged from the bottom of a loch.

"Well then . . ." He reached down to retrieve his rifle, and Samantha's hold tightened on the butt of her gun. "May the best monster win."

Without another word, he gave her his back and stalked away, allowing both the forest and the storm to swathe him in shadows.

Samantha faced the new mother, who'd silently observed the spectacle with uneasy, exhausted curiosity while nursing the calf, who stood on quivering, unsteady legs.

For many reasons, both identifiable and befuddling, all Samantha wanted to do was cry. She fought it with deep, quivering breaths and lips pressed tight. Somehow, she was certain that the heathen Highlander still watched her from some dark vantage in the forest and she'd take a bullet from his rifle before he caught her crying.

The calf noisily detached from his mama upon her approach, and blinked at her in frozen uncertainty.

"It's all right," she crooned. "You can finish supper once we get you home." He only let out a *whuff* of protest as she wrapped her arms around his spindly legs and hefted him up against her chest.

For the first time in her life, Samantha bemoaned soiling what was her second nicest gown, but damned if she would leave one more of what was *her herd* on Inverthorne lands.

The mama made an anxious noise when Samantha heaved the little thing over her saddle and climbed in behind it.

"Well, come on then," she encouraged. "Follow me properly, and I'll give him back."

The urge to cry had morphed into more of a simmering snit by the time she reached Erradale and situated mother and calf into one of the deserted, ramshackle cottages.

She fought another, more insistent urge the entire way home, and lost the battle when the all-encompassing aroma of Callum's latest offering of fish assaulted her nose.

Doubling over on the porch, she retched and heaved into the undeserving flower beds.

CHAPTER NINE

Gavin approached Erradale with a great deal more caution this time, wary of the gunshots that ricocheted across the moors.

He'd already paused at the top of Gresham Peak and used a spyglass to scope possible danger in the form of a wiry beauty with a tongue every bit as treacherous as her trigger finger.

Callum had revealed Alison would be alone today, as the Mac Tire was at Inverthorne helping his father, Eammon, with some heavy lifting. Locryn and Calybrid took to Rua Reidh on Sundays, for drinking and trading.

And bonny? Well, she apparently used her day of rest to take potshots at a few tins she'd tied with twine to a fence. They danced, jumped, and swayed as holes ripped through them with each masterful aim of her pistol.

Christ. She impressed him. She intrigued him.

Hell, she *aroused* him. Especially in those astonishingly skintight blue trousers.

Just wasn't decent of a lass to wrap legs the length of a

long plummet into temptation with fabric that revealed just as much as it covered.

He wished he could rip out what he felt at the sight of her and trample it into the mud beneath Demetrius's feet. Every time he saw her, her indefinable allure grew stronger.

Every. Time.

As he drew closer, he dismounted, taking a moment to appreciate just how the pockets on the back of her trews would fit his fingers as he cupped her wee arse. Wasn't frequently a man chanced upon such a view of just exactly how much a lass had to fill his hands. She wore no strange contraptions, bustles, bows, or petticoats to hide or enhance a thing.

And she didn't have to in order to entice his absolute attention.

She boasted a heart-shaped arse, he noted.

His favorite kind, as it turned out.

After emptying her second pistol into the distance, she reached into the pocket of her men's chambray shirt and retrieved six bullets.

The sun had begun an eventual descent into the west behind gathering storm clouds, but for a moment, the afternoon burnished a rare and flattering gold.

"Well, if it isn't the infamous Lord Thorne-in-my-boot." She flipped the chamber to the side to reload.

"It's better to be infamous than invisible." He winked, expecting a flash of blue fury in return.

"Not necessarily," was all she muttered.

Though he'd come to throw down a white flag rather than a gauntlet, Gavin had found himself looking forward to their verbal dance.

Which was why the melancholy note in her reply threw him. Why hadn't she looked in his direction yet?

As he drew abreast of her, Gavin scanned the north fence where her tin targets swayed. "Who taught ye how to shoot like that?"

"My father." How her lithe fingers could make loading a pistol seem strangely erotic, he'd never know. Maybe it was her coaxing the rather phallic shafts into their chambers. The perfect fit.

The perfect weapon.

Wisely, he said nothing, but was unlucky enough to find that she'd glanced at him in time to catch his expression. "That surprises you?"

"A wee bit."

"Why, because your father killed mine with a ducling pistol?"

Unable to look her in the eyes, he watched the west wind toss the long hair she'd secured behind her with a leather thong, his fingers curling at the memory of threading through the silken strands. "Well . . . I wasna going to mention . . ."

"I imagine I practice more than he did," she remarked dispassionately.

He could understand why. If the past repeated itself, it made sense that she'd do what she could to fight. To win.

"Not to be rude or anything." She picked up the second pistol, her long fingers disappearing back into the same breast pocket. "But what the fuck are you doing on my land?"

God save him, she was lovely.

"I came to cry peace with ye, lass. And to . . ." Well, he'd meant to apologize for his high-handed behavior. For accosting her in the forest and stealing a kiss.

But he couldn't seem to. Because, dammit all to perdition, he couldn't conjure remorse.

The breeze turned from cold to bitter, and he detected a shudder start at her shoulders and roll down her lithe body.

Her nipples were puckered, he knew. And Lord, what he wouldn't give to warm them.

With his tongue.

"I came to talk sensibly. Perhaps without guns this time." He allowed irritation to edge the arousal out of his voice.

"If you're truly talking sense, you've nothing to worry about from my guns."

He opened his mouth to deliver a cautious and practiced apology, but what came out was, "Why are ye here, lass? It's cold and gray unforgiving. Yer family home is falling down around ye. It willna be easy to put this place back together."

She paused at the fourth bullet, but still didn't look at him. "Nothing that matters is easy," she said, continuing her reload.

For fuck's sake. He wasn't starting to . . . respect her, was he?

Fighting a shudder of his own, he turned away to collect himself.

"Regardless of what you've heard about me, I'm not a wealthy woman," she stunned him by admitting. "Once my mother died . . . I was disinherited by my stepfather. I truly have nothing left to my name but Erradale. I *need* this place. Do you understand? I need it to survive."

He whirled on her. "*Nay.* Nay, ye doona. Not when I'll pay ye an entire fortune for it. Enough to keep ye yer entire life. Anywhere ye want to go. In some places, even yer children could live like kings. Yer grandchildren could—"

Her big, wan eyes silenced him as they finally looked up into his. The indecision in her gaze did cause a bit of hope to flare somewhere south of his throat.

"Say I sell to you. What would I *do* then?"

"Anything ye wanted."

"But I'd be alone. I'd have no one."

"How is that different from now?" He regretted the question the moment it escaped him. She studied him with an exhaustion he hadn't before seen. A desolation he'd not known she'd hidden behind blue flames and a tarty vocabulary.

Suddenly he felt like the biggest shite to ever walk on two legs.

"I have Locryn and Calybrid," she said quietly.

"What about in ten years when they're gone?"

That brought a suggestion of the smirk he'd been missing back to the corners of her mouth. "I think you underestimate them."

"I'll give ye that." He chuckled.

"There's Callum." She shrugged. "Someone has to entice him out of the caves every now and again."

Gavin's smile died an instant, painful death. Was she implying that she had Callum . . . or that she'd *had* him? Just by what means did she entice him out of those caves? He'd known Callum a long time, and the man had never been much of a skirt chaser.

But Alison Ross wasn't wearing a skirt.

Had they . . . ?

A sick darkness curled deep in his gut, and he pressed his lips together so the question churning inside didn't escape as some covetous demand.

Oblivious to the direction of his thoughts, she surveyed the cattle lining the far pasture, and the new mother and calf in the round corral. "My entire life I've felt like I've been waiting for something to happen. I've been staring across the empty desert of the future with restless desperation, and never finding a path that was mine. Here, I have purpose. Something I'm good at. A safe home for . . ." She let the thought trail away.

"But what about the ghosts that haunt these moors? The reminders of all ye've lost." Of what his family did to her.

To his utter astonishment, she shrugged. "The past is a place that only gets bigger and farther away . . . it's not all darkness. Erradale doesn't have ghosts for me. It has potential. Possibilities for a life I really need right now. A life *you're* trying to take from me."

"To *buy* from ye. Goddammit. I'm not the villain here." He stabbed a thumb at his own chest. "That was my father. Do ye truly believe I should be punished for his sins?" Hadn't he been punished enough?

Listlessly, she shook her head. "I don't think I believe in villains. Heroes either. Just people. People with agendas and the things they're willing to do to get what they want."

Something else they had in common. Gavin's gaze charted the bruised exhaustion left beneath her eyes, and he suddenly longed to do something about it.

"Why do you want Erradale so specifically?" she queried. "You have a castle, a title, money, obviously. You have everything most men would kill for. You could buy land anywhere. Why do you want this broken-down old place?" She pointed with the barrel of her pistol at a sag in the eaves.

"Ye want the pure and simple truth?"

She made a caustic noise that tugged at his heart. "The truth is rarely pure and never simple. It's usually hard. I want the hard truth."

Christ. He'd known she was bonny. That she was small, strong, and spirited. What he hadn't known was that she was wise. A wisdom bordering on the cynical, he noted. Who'd caused such a tendency in a lass so young?

Gavin had tried every trick in the book to lure her to accept his offer.

All, that was, but honesty.

"The hard truth is, I detest running my brother's distillery. I loathe traveling there for the sowing every spring, and the reaping every autumn. Ravencroft Keep is where all *my* ghosts still live, and I yearn for the day I never have to see it again." He looked to the south, beyond which his childhood home hunched at the top of the Balach na ba pass. Red stones that seemed to run with blood upon a rainy day, blood spilled by the past Mackenzie Laird's infamous tempers. "I'll admit, it wasna so bad when my brother Liam was away at war all the time. But now that he's returned . . ."

Resolve hardened in his bones and tightened his jaw. "I am *not* a man who can be ruled. Not by him, not by anyone. I want my own trade. To make my own way. And Inverthorne's forests are too ancient and sacred to be cleared for timber. Her grounds too craggy for true agriculture. Erradale has the potential to provide me my own legacy. I roamed these moors endlessly as a boy. They've always . . . meant something to me."

Gavin thought the sound she made might have been one of distress, but when he looked back at her, it was appreciation he read in her eyes.

For once.

She'd really wanted the truth. She accepted that he'd given it. And, all told, it felt like his burden had been made a bit lighter in the telling of it.

"My brother. He's a true Mackenzie. A violent, high-handed lout. An arse, really. More like our father than he'd ever admit. I'm nothing like them. I would look after yer father's lands. Cherish them. I would—" God, he was perilously close to begging.

"It seems our only problem is . . . I want the same things from Erradale that you do." She said this with a conciliatory gesture. As though she regretted that fact. "They're not my father's lands anymore. They're mine."

"Not if Liam takes them from ye. Or did ye forget the lease?"

Her features hardened. "Well, that's up to you, isn't it? Lady Ravencroft said he wouldn't."

"Mena's not the Laird. She's a sweet English lass, but she underestimates her husband's ruthlessness. She doesna ken how to think like the Demon Highlander. Like I said, if ye sold Erradale to me, I'd fight Liam for it, should he lay claim to it, and I'd win."

"How do you know I wouldn't?" Her usual blue fire snapped back into her eyes, and Gavin hadn't been aware of how much he'd missed it until that moment.

"Ye underestimate my brother."

"Maybe *you* underestimate *me*." Turning, she lifted her arm, aimed, and nailed every one of the hanging targets all those yards away.

Ye gods, that was unexpectedly erotic.

"Perhaps ye're right," he agreed, suddenly distracted. "Ye know, bonny, I've hunted my whole life. Mostly with rifles and arrows, but I'll admit I'm only a passing fair hand with a pistol."

The look she leveled at him was knowing and sly, but she shrugged and handed him the spare gun. "Show me."

Challenge heated the cold autumn air.

Blood singing with it, Gavin took her gun, stepped his left foot back, canted, aimed, and hit two of the four remaining targets.

She assessed him for all of two seconds before she said, "The man who taught you to shoot was a small man, wasn't he?"

Her guess amused him, mostly because she was right. "Aye, lass, a slight Spaniard. How did ye know?"

"Because you cant your wrist to the inside at a fifteen-degree angle, which I do as well, to mitigate the recoil of the pistol." She wrapped her long, elegant fingers around his wrist, and twisted it until the pistol perched vertically. "Big as you are, I'd suggest that you're . . . er . . . strong enough to keep your wrist erect."

"I didna think ye noticed." He flashed her a flirtatious smile and fought the urge to adjust himself. Wishing she hadn't uttered the word "erect."

"Don't be cute. It's just the hard truth."

Aye. And the longer she touched him, the *harder* it truly was.

"Also," she continued. "Your aim is more accurate if you face what you're shooting at." She moved behind him and put her hands on his hips, nudging him to square off with the targets.

He pressed his lips together, staving off a groan. "I'm a big target, lass, I turn sideways to make myself smaller should someone be shooting at me."

"Anyone shooting at you now?" She released his hips and stepped around him, a level expression feathering her gaunt features.

"Nay, but I've learned to keep my watch up around ye in that regard." Dammit, why did she refuse to smile? He thought he'd die of old age before he saw her blush, and here she was pink as an autumn sunset, but still refusing to smile.

"Well, you have my gun so I'm trusting you to be a gentleman."

Big mistake.

"Show me how to stand, again? Like so?" he asked, all innocence and absorption. His forward direction purposely atrocious, his boots together. His arm bent at a shameful angle.

"You really are bad at this." There it was. At least the ghost of a smile. She adjusted his position again, this time from the front. Kicking her boot between his. "Part your legs," she ordered. "And bend your knees a little."

He swallowed around a tongue gone suddenly dry. "Generally speaking, bonny, those are commands given by me."

She snorted, but the unladylike sound was close enough to a laugh that he decided it counted. "Just when I was beginning to think you weren't as much of a pig as I'd initially assumed."

He grunted out a sound of amusement—for her benefit—as she moved out of the way and motioned to the targets. Concentrating, he inhaled, and squeezed the trigger four more times. Three of the four targets pinged his triumph.

He'd have hit the fourth one, if she hadn't bent over to pick up her bandana in those fucking trousers.

His dry mouth watered.

Turning around, she caught him staring, and slapped him on the arm with her dusty bandana. "You talk all this nonsense about separating yourself from a tainted Mackenzie legacy—"

"It's not nonsense."

"Then why insist on being such a hooligan?" she challenged. "I heard of your boudoir scandals and shenanigans long before I even made it to the Highlands. You're infamous in your own right."

He decided, now that he'd established a certain length of trust between them, he might give honesty a longer attempt. "I look at it this way . . . I'm adjusting my expectations for a satisfied life."

"How's that?" She reached for her pistol, and he caught her palm in his.

"If I put out my hand for a drink, a gun, or a woman to fuck, my hand is always full . . . my expectations always met and my life a merry one. But what do ye suppose happens when I reach for something more? For honor. For justice. For truth. For understanding or love . . ."

She only thought about it for a beat, examining her small fingers wrapped in his with undue exactitude. "You're always reaching."

"With an eternally empty hand." He opened her palm, and placed the handle of the pistol inside it.

She turned away, but not before he caught the bleakness twisting her features.

Wanting to fill the emptiness. *His. Hers.* Gavin reached for her, pulled her back against him, and brushed his cheek against the downy hair at the crown of her head.

"I am glad we made peace, bonny . . ."

"Just because we're not at war, doesn't mean we've made peace." As she said this she expelled a sigh that could have been composed of eternities and relaxed against his chest in slow, careful increments.

"If ye sell Erradale to me, ye'll not be breaking yer vow. I'll no longer be a Mackenzie. I swear it. Perhaps ye can stay here and—"

Her body made a heave, a little like a cough but not quite. She clamped her hands over her mouth, as though to hold in a sob.

"I've had *enough* of the empty promises of charming, beautiful men!" she hissed through her fingers. Wrenching out of his hold, she sprinted for the estate, her hand firmly holding back whatever wanted to escape her lips.

Gavin winced as the door slammed against him and the

bolt slid home. A strange and foreign ache settled in the emptiness of his arms.

So *that* was it . . . Someone had broken her heart and she was licking her wounds on the forlorn moors of Erradale.

Returning to his horse, he mounted and swung south toward Inverthorne, hoping to outrun the storm blowing in from the west.

The lass thought him charming and beautiful, did she? A slight warmth glowed in his chest where it ought not to have been.

That, at least, he could work with.

Because, God save him, he felt the same about her.

CHAPTER TEN

Five weeks.

The flames contained by cold stone mesmerized Samantha into an unblinking caricature of herself. Locryn and Calybrid's bickering had become something of a lullaby in her short time at Erradale, a sure sign that the day's hard work had ended and the evening's rest could commence. But tonight, she barely noted the musical cadence of their singular brand of Highland harassment.

Five weeks ago, almost to the day, she'd boarded that train in Wyoming. Five weeks ago she'd met Alison Ross.

Five weeks ago . . . she'd *killed* her husband.

That fateful morning, he'd moved between her legs. That afternoon, she'd shot him between the eyes.

She'd lived a lifetime in little more than a month. Any dream she'd had of the lush Oregon coast was as cold and dead as Bennett, himself. Where were his remains? she wondered. Had Bradley been forced to burn or bury two brothers that day? Or had Boyd survived? She still wasn't sure what all happened on that train. Who'd started the shooting, or how many people had been killed or injured.

A massacre, Alison had called it in her letter.

Dear God. What had they done? How many innocent people's lives had been ripped apart because of her outlaw family?

Best she kept an ocean between herself and what was left of the Masters brothers.

Alison had written that life on Erradale never had to end if Samantha didn't want it to.

Something about this land called to her. The wind sang over the moors, where it howled in the desert. The hills whispered ancient, lyrical words, where the sounds of the American West always seemed to be some sort of warning. The rattle of a copperhead. The screech of a buzzard. The yips of coyotes or the scream of a mountain lion. In Scotland, the sun became a warm, welcome, and occasional visitor, rather than a relentless nemesis. Heather and brine scented air free of dust or industry. And the water ran pure from springs with holy pagan names.

She loved it here. If only she could stay. If only . . . she knew what to do.

To Samantha, the future had become a nebulous uncertainty, something that barely mattered and might never arrive. She'd become incapable of seeing past tomorrow. For tomorrow, she'd wake, dress, gather cattle, see to the ranch, cook the food Callum or Locryn would bring her . . . And if her luck held, she'd get to do it again the next day.

But now . . . the future mattered, didn't it?

Five weeks.

Five weeks ago, she'd taken a life . . . on the same day she'd created one.

"Are ye going to finish that biscuit, lass?" Locryn eyed the pastry she clutched in her hand, unable to hide his chagrin at how her worrying fingers had begun to reduce the precious thing to crumbs in her lap.

"What?" She blinked at him, doing her best to rouse herself from her disquieting reverie.

"I mean, we're willing to look past ye devouring Callum's portion of the quail, as he no doubt dined at Inverthorne with his father," the gruff Highlander explained as though he'd reached the limits of his magnanimity. "But that'd be your fourth biscuit, while Cal and I have only had one, and if ye think I'm after splitting the last one down the middle with this idle goat, ye've gone daft."

"Oh, I—" After glancing down to find the offending biscuit in her clutches, she handed it across to Locryn, who snatched it up like a thief might the crown jewels. She tried to remember when she'd picked it up. Had she really devoured three biscuits?

"Are ye mad at us, Sam?" Calybrid asked carefully.

"I'm sorry if I've been quiet," she soothed. "I'm afraid I have a lot to . . ."

"It's just that ye used all the butter," he whined. "And I canna figure why ye'd do that unless ye're in some sort of wrathful feminine state or another."

Feminine state . . . that was one way to put it.

"Aye, even after we brought ye cheese from Rua Reidh," Locryn agreed with a solemn nod.

"Which ye ate for lunch without sharing," Calybrid grumbled under his breath.

Locryn's brow lowered over the one eye that tended to narrow as the other one bulged with observant suspicion. "Yer appetite shames that of the cattle, lass," he marveled. "Have ye as many stomachs as they? For I doona ken where ye keep all those biscuits."

Samantha rested her forehead in her hand, wondering if it was truly possible to expire from exhaustion. She'd have to tell them, she supposed. Not everything, of course, as her very existence depended on her deception. At least for the moment.

But she wouldn't be able to hide her pregnancy for long.

Strange, she thought, that it was better they think her a hussy than a liar.

"I have something of a confession to make . . . ," she began.

"Then find a vicar," Calybrid huffed as he hauled himself to his spindly legs and trudged toward the door with the uneven limp of an old man. "Or at least wait until I drain the cod."

The frigid November chill barged into the great room the moment Calybrid flung open the door.

"It's going to be the coldest night, yet." He shuddered. "It's stopped raining, but the dew on the grass has turned to ice."

"Do ye smell smoke?" Locryn queried, his bulbous nose twitching like that of a bloodhound testing the air.

"I used more peat in the fire than usual," she replied. Though it was hard to detect any scent past the pleasant aroma of fresh cedar and clean, loamy forest that seemed to envelop her at the moment.

Just as Thorne had done with his superlative body.

She should return his cloak, she supposed, drowsily. But that meant seeing him again. Besides, it was a great deal warmer and better made than the woolen or the pelisse she'd brought from America. It didn't carry with it the strength or the weight or the warmth that had beckoned to her when he'd wrapped his arms around her. But it was an admittedly lovely alternative.

An unmistakable crack resonated down to her bones, arousing her every nerve to instant vigilance.

Locryn's fretful gaze collided with hers.

"Was that . . . ?"

"A rifle shot," she finished. "And not far off, either."

"Poachers?" Locryn speculated.

Samantha sprang for the gun belt hanging from the antlers of a stag head some long-dead Ross had mounted close to the fireplace.

Another shot echoed over the moors, even closer this time, and a heart-rending call of torment instantly followed.

"Calybrid!" Samatha gasped, too frightened and astonished to note that old, top-heavy Locryn beat her in a race to the door, his own rifle in hand.

Shoving bare feet into her discarded boots, Samantha checked her pistol, testing its familiar weight in her hand. She looked up just in time to keep Locryn from charging out of the door like an ill-tempered bull.

The wool of his old sweater abraded her palm, already slick from fear, as she yanked him back behind the door. "We don't know who's out there, how many there are, or where the shots came from."

"I ken Calybrid is out there," Locryn snarled. "That's all I need to know."

"Wait!"

A sound from behind them turned Samantha's terror to anguish. A distinctive noise, like a gust of wind quickly ushering in a storm.

Writers often described the din of a large fire as a roar, a narrative she'd never before understood until this moment. She turned in time to see flames race along an invisible path toward the floor-to-ceiling window that overlooked the back pasture as it crawled to the sea.

Fire didn't move like that. Not without an accelerant of some kind.

Smoke had already begun to cloy against the ceiling, spilling in from down the hallway that led to the manor's deserted living quarters.

Dropping low, Samantha dragged Locryn down with her, but what she'd seen in the racing line of flames didn't leave her time to think.

Sparks.

Sparks meant gunpowder. And if her attackers had used that to hasten the fire, then they might have stowed some beneath the window, or even the house.

An explosion meant certain death. She had better chances with a rifleman in the dark.

"Go," she ordered. Pushing Locryn out into the night, she plunged after him, veering right along the house toward the stables and corrals. As much as she didn't want to, it would be easier to hide her movement in the herd that stood between her and the small copse of dilapidated cottages on the other side of the square.

Small fires surrounded her home, and seemed to be cropping up everywhere, impeding her ability to see past the smoke and flames.

Samantha bent as low as she could, keeping her head down and her body ensconced in what shadows she could find. Though her night rail was thin and white, Thorne's dark, heavy cloak aided her escape. Her unlaced boots encumbered her speed, but the grasses crunching beneath her footsteps and the cold seizing in her lungs kept her from abandoning them.

In her haste, she tripped over something warm, something that made a very recognizable, very welcome sound of indignation.

"Calybrid." She gasped her relief.

"Fucker bit me in the side," he groaned. "Knocked me down."

"Can you walk? We have to keep moving."

Locryn swooped in from behind her, and dove for Calybrid. In one shockingly graceful motion, he plowed his meaty arm beneath the prone body, and scooped the man onto his shoulders without seeming to miss a step.

At Calybrid's howl of pain, he hissed, "If ye doona stop yer havering, I'll drop ye in a bog."

An explosion shattered the unnatural quiet of the darkness, and wood splintered behind Samatha, cutting into her calf.

Locryn kept moving in front of her, Calybrid's thatch of white hair bouncing along with his unsteady lope. Good. The shooter had missed his mark.

And had given away his position.

The shot had come from behind them, back toward where smoke and flames now ate up half of the manor house.

Samantha dropped down to her belly and aimed, hoping to buy the old men some time to find cover.

There. The shadow of a man rushed toward the house, backlit by one of the fires. Samantha pointed her pistol toward the next fire he'd reach if he maintained his trajectory, and only had to wait the space of a breath before his silhouette flashed in front of it.

She squeezed the trigger. He fell. She shot again at the ground for good measure.

She blinked at the route she'd last seen Locryn and Calybrid going, but was unable to find them. The canny Scots were likely making for the dark ridge of the trees, beyond which they could skirt Loch Gorm on their way to Rua Reidh.

The fires had been lit in the direction of Inverthorne, so to attempt escape that way was nothing but folly as they'd be easy marks for any half-decent rifleman.

Had their attackers come from Inverthorne? Had the earl tired of her insolence and decided to lay claim to Erradale by turning it, and her, to ashes?

Her stomach churned at the thought, reminding her just what was at stake here.

Where were her cattle? They were no longer in the corrals. Also, the fire she'd seen rushing toward her back window had come from the direction of Rua Reidh.

Which meant they were surrounded.

Her best hope was to reach the corner of the manor and sprint along the tall grasses to the caved-in outbuilding built into a small knoll. There would be a good place to make a stand.

Surging to her feet, Samantha took off at a sprint.

And crumpled back to the freezing earth. *Her calf.* The moment she put weight on it, fire had skewered clean through it.

She wanted to scream, but knew it would bring whoever else lurked in the darkness.

A small pop permeated her shock at the pain, and she looked up to see flames licking at the roof. So, they'd not laid enough oil and gunpowder to make an explosion, but enough to devour the entire dwelling in a matter of minutes.

She had to get up. She had . . . to . . . keep . . . moving.

Gritting her teeth and pressing her tongue to the roof of her mouth to keep from making a noise, Samantha willed herself to stand. Dragging her lame leg behind her, she used the side of the house to support her weight as she made terrifyingly slow progress. How was it possible some shards of wood splinters from her house skewered through Thorne's thick cloak?

A shadow stepped from around the corner. A man. Tall, wide, and only as far from her as the barrel of his shotgun would allow.

"Hands up, or I'll—"

Samantha slapped the barrel away in time for the blast to deafen her, and shot him at such close range, his cowboy hat flew off his head, catching in the wind created by the gathering inferno that was her home.

Another fire crawled up the only building tall enough to rival that of the modest Erradale Manor.

The stables.

Smoke hung thick enough in the cold air that she had to squint against the burn in her eyes as she hobbled toward the burning structure.

The stable doors flew open, and Locryn emerged with their three horses and the gelding Callum stabled there against the cold.

Samantha tried to call out to him, but smoke invaded her throat, closing it with spasming coughs. Finding a wellspring of will she hadn't known she possessed, she reached Locryn right as he managed to help a sagging Calybrid onto the dappled pony's bare back.

Two of the horses broke away, racing for the Gresham Peak, their panicked equine screams an eerie cry against the night.

Callum's mount danced beside that of Locryn's in obvious eagerness to put as much distance between it and the flames as possible, but it stayed, as though obeying the Mac Tíre even in his absence.

"Can ye ride, lass?"

Samantha nodded. Though the Erradale horses remained bridled, Callum wasn't in the habit of bridling or saddling his steed, so Samantha had to use the gelding's mane to haul herself onto his back.

The last of her reserves depleted, she leaned low and held on for dear life, unable to use her leg to maintain a stable mount.

Locryn swung up behind Calybrid, and spurred his horse up Gresham Peak toward Inverthorne.

Samantha allowed her mount to follow, knowing for sure now that Lord Thorne, scheming as he was, could have had nothing to do with the devastation she left behind.

She knew this, because Highlanders didn't wear cowboy hats.

Chapter Eleven

I see who you are. Alison Ross's words echoed at Gavin with all the weight irony could wield.

Was that not *his* line? Was he not the cunning huntsman with the capricious veneer that no one had yet to permeate?

No one but a lass who'd spent less time in his company than almost anyone else, and somehow coaxed him to reveal more about himself than he'd ever intended.

The four stone walls of his chamber at Inverthorne had become a cage and he the lion pacing within. The tapestries padded his beloved prison and his bed was a snarled, empty study in discouraged restlessness.

Alison had gone to Ravencroft, to Liam, and made a case to his bleeding-heart marchioness, Mena. God love the dear woman, but she had a weakness for lost causes.

Look who she'd married.

And his love-addled brother followed the buxom British wench about like a daft spaniel. *Yes, Mena, mine. I like to kiss yer lips the most when they're smiling.*

It was enough to induce vomiting.

If Mena and Liam were in accord, then Lady Ravencroft would certainly contact her friend, coconspirator, and sister-in-law Farah Blackwell. Farah would ensure that Dorian Blackwell, Gavin's bastard half brother and the Blackheart of Ben More, would align with them.

Thus gathering the Magistrate's Bench against *him*. The bully who would steal Alison Ross's land from beneath her wee, stubborn arse.

Would they take into account that he offered her twice what it was worth? *Nay*. Because the truth was, if he pushed the document in his possession through to the Magistrate's Bench and Erradale did, indeed, revert to Liam, then the fucking Laird would probably just give it back to her by way of reparation for the hell their father had visited upon her family.

Fine time for the Demon Highlander to go all penitent and altruistic. Just in time to fuck Gavin up the arse with repentance.

To take away the one thing that could make him happy. The one thing he wanted.

Again.

Frustrated breath hissed through his throat as he balled his fists and . . . pressed his knuckles down very decisively on the writing desk adjacent to the mirror.

He didn't punch things. That was how his father dealt with obstacles. How Liam did.

He schemed. He used the wits, the strength, the intellect, and, granted, the looks God gave him to get what he wanted.

Glancing up, Gavin glowered at his reflection. These features, the perfect mix of his father's brutish, Pict ancestors and his mother's aristocratic breeding, served him well in all endeavors but this.

Had he been wrong about Alison Ross? When he thought he'd glimpsed lust in her eyes, could it have been something else? A mirror, perhaps, of his own desire . . . What about the kiss? He'd not imagined her response. The aggressiveness of it.

The passion.

It had set him on fire, and the blaze had yet to burn out. And after, they'd come to—well, if not a truce, at least a ceasefire. He'd held her for a moment and . . .

She'd let him.

He tried not to think of how many times he'd poured manipulation and skill into a seduction as a means to an end and winced. There had been more honesty and intimacy in that moment between them than he'd shared with a bevy of mistresses. Something had blossomed between them, hadn't it? Some new understanding, some sort of nebulous whisper toward a reconciliation of terms.

Why had she run from him?

What if she hadn't felt it?

Impossible.

A soft, familiar knock interrupted his reverie, and he rushed to open the chamber door.

"Mother?" he asked anxiously. "Are ye well?"

Eleanor Mackenzie, the dowager Marchioness of Ravencroft, had lived above five decades, and still her beauty remained unravaged by time. Her hair, once gold, fell in silver ringlets about a face nearly as smooth as that of a porcelain doll. Maybe the creases of her mouth had considerably deepened, and the skin beneath her chin was no longer as taut as it once was. When she walked, she made no sound. When she talked, her voice contained eternal apologies and shook with neurotic anxieties.

Even after all this time.

"Where is Alice?" Gavin took her hands in his, his

broken, beautiful mother, and restlessly checked the hall for her maid and caretaker.

Green eyes, identical to the ones he'd only just been studying in the mirror, found his general direction, but never landed on anything.

Because they couldn't.

"I—I'm sorry to disturb your sleep, my son," she stammered. "But Alice has already gone to bed, and I didn't think this was aught she could do something about."

"What's happened?" Wrapping an arm around her shoulders, Gavin gently nudged her toward the plush blue velvet chair by his fireplace.

"N-nay, take me to the window," she stated, then amended. "If you would."

Gavin led her there as she explained, "I—I opened my casement because the fire made my room a wee bit close, you see, and I thought I heard terrible echoes. A rifle shot, maybe. I was worried about poachers or . . . something worse. Perhaps we should call upon Mr. Monahan to look into it."

When she'd said "Mr. Monahan," she wasn't referring to Callum, but to his father, their stable master, Eammon.

Unlatching the window, Gavin pushed it outward, muscles instantly tensing against the bracing chill. He listened to the darkness, and didn't at all like the eerie silence that greeted him.

"There's smoke upon the north wind tonight," his mother fretted. "Do you smell it, son?"

Gavin didn't need his mother's keen senses, honed by her lack of sight, to catch the acrid smell of fire on the wind. "Aye." He scanned the darkness to the north and the west, but the lack of moon made the inky shadows absolute. There were very few times Gavin imagined he could understand his mother's plight, but tonight was one of them.

Something wasn't right out there. The smoke wasn't fed by peat or coal, this was something strange and unnatural.

If the smoke came from the north and west, that meant—

A powerful knock served to push his chamber door open, as he'd left it unlatched.

Callum burst in, grim-faced and wild-eyed, followed by his father, an older version of the Mac Tíre, with a thinner beard and a thicker waist.

His mother whimpered and clutched at him, ever sensitive to loud, abrupt sounds.

"Gunshots to the north," Callum informed him.

Careful not to grip his mother too tightly, though every muscle wanted to seize, he asked, "Do ye smell gunpowder on the wind?"

"Aye, but it would take two warring battalions to produce enough smoke to drift this far—"

Eammon's hand fell onto his son's shoulder, stopping his word with a meaningful grip. "You'll forgive us our intrusion, my lady," he enunciated gently, his County Claire accent always a melody with an upward inflection. "We mean to cause you no distress. We didn't realize you were in here with your son."

"Oh, Mr. Monahan." Eleanor's shaking hand lifted to clutch the collar of her robe closer to her high-necked gown. "I was—was just—I came to warn—I thought I heard . . ." Words failed her, as they often did in the company of men.

"Right you were, my lady, and so you did." Eammon Monahan praised her as though she'd accomplished a brilliant feat. "But never you fear, the blasts were too far away to pose any threat on Inverthorne lands. Though they'd carry over Gresham Loch well enough." He cast a meaningful, golden-eyed look at Gavin.

His breath tripping over a sudden weight in his chest, he had to force out the question. "Erradale?"

"Could be." Callum nodded shortly.

Alison.

Even the trigger-happy lass wasn't likely to be honing her skills at this time of night.

"The horses are ready," Callum stated shortly.

"Mother, let me take ye back to yer room." Gavin struggled to keep his impatience out of his voice, wrestling with it like an unexpected foe as he shuffled her forward.

To the wood and peat dwellings of Erradale, a fire would mean instantaneous disaster. And who would be shooting rifles in the middle of such a frigid bastard of an evening? A man would no more like to be outside than he would be caught beneath the ice forming on the loch.

"You young bucks can tear out of here after the wee Miss Ross," Eammon offered. "If her ladyship would permit me to escort her back to her quarters, I'll be along after seeing to her safety."

Both Callum and Gavin took a moment to gape at Eammon. Never in their lives had they heard the grizzled man speak with such gentility of phrase.

Unperturbed, he stared right back at them.

"A-alone?" Eleanor croaked, her fist tightening on Gavin's sleeve.

"I'll fetch Alice," Gavin offered.

"Nay." A swallow heralded a polite smile perfected for a long-ago presentation to the queen. "Nay, you go, son. I can find my way on my own. 'Tis only three doors. I do it all the time."

Kissing his mother's forehead, Gavin launched himself toward the doorway with Callum close on his heels, as it had always been. They reached the end of the stone hall before they realized one set of footsteps was missing.

Gavin took a precious moment to look back.

Eammon stood at his door, holding it open. His chest

held tight beneath his vest as though the older man wasn't allowing himself to breathe. The fist curled at his side shook with the burden of restraint as he watched Gavin's ethereal mother tiptoe back to her own chamber.

Retrieving his own rifle from the armory, Gavin tossed Callum his bow and quiver, and they each stowed their dirks and hatchets with the practiced alacrity of Highlanders who'd comfortably hunted together for the better part of a quarter century.

Demetrius's hooves clattered over the stones of the ancient Inverthorne Bridge that arced over the McRae Burn. Just as soon as Gavin heard the ground soften beneath his tread, he swung immediately to the north. The pace he set surpassed foolhardy to downright reckless on a night with no moon.

Callum had thought to bring a lantern but sensitive creature that Demetrius was, he seemed to recognize Gavin's almost desperate haste. He leaned his neck into a gallop, his long stride eating up a road that had become a ribbon of ink barely distinguishable from the shadows.

Gavin kept his head down and his breath steady, forcing himself to exhale to the cadence of her name.

Alison.

He barely knew the woman. Hell, he couldn't even claim to be overfond of her. She was little better than a banshee with a sidearm.

And yet . . . anxiety pounded through his veins with an intensity he'd thought himself incapable of. What could possibly be amiss at Erradale? As far as he knew, Calybrid and Locryn had no enemies to speak of. The Ross and the Mackenzie had been at peace for generations.

If one didn't count Hamish Mackenzie and James Ross. His father and hers.

He supposed the backward folk from the Rua Reidh

could have started trouble. The year had been lean, and some of them had come to Liam looking for work in the barley fields before Samhain to help with the harvest to get them through winter. Perhaps they'd been driven to poaching, and the lass's itchy trigger finger and apparent distrust of strangers would be tinder for an altercation.

Just as the ancient Erradale manor house would be easy tinder for an arsonist with a vendetta.

Gavin flinched as a stab of worry for the cargo hidden beneath his own keep pierced him. Though Inverthorne was a drafty stone castle, it now sat on a literal powder keg.

Fat lot of good that deal with the Rook had done him. He now possessed his own staggering fortune, and still he was perpetually denied.

Gavin took two miles to convince himself the sick, desperate feeling lodged in the pit of his stomach was for Erradale, and not its heiress. As she'd so inelegantly put it, if something were to happen to her, no one stood in the way of him getting everything he desired.

The land would be there even if the structures were not. The full herd of several hundred had yet to be gathered, and any losses garnered by poachers could easily be gained back in a spring or two of calving.

So, why was he risking a broken neck racing to her—to Erradale's—rescue in the middle of the night?

It wasn't because the thought of Alison, as fierce as she was tiny, in any danger made his chest burn as though he'd swallowed an ember of coal. It wasn't the panicked, macabre thoughts stabbing at him with all the savagery of a thousand native spears . . .

All that luxurious hair of hers would burn first.

He kicked Demetrius to go faster.

Callum and my mother had heard rifle shots. Alison Ross didn't use a rifle.

The Mac Tíre in question called after him, both a warning and an entreaty to slow down. To take care.

I willna reach her in time. Not if she's been shot.

It didn't matter, he told himself. It shouldn't matter. *She* shouldn't matter.

Not this much.

But it did. *She did.* Because he was not his father. He was not his brother. He didn't litter the path to his legacy with violence. He didn't create blood feuds that lasted generations. He didn't take a little girl's father from her so that he might possess her land.

And he didn't . . . he *couldn't* stomach the idea of her being hurt.

Or worse.

Goddammit. If the stubborn lass would have stayed in America, if she would have taken his offer, she'd be safe and he'd be ignorant that Alison Ross was anything but some name he'd once written on a transfer of funds.

He'd never have known that a woman could shoot just as well as a man, maybe better. He'd never have considered the amusement and arousal feminine profanity could provoke in him. Nor would he have known that a battle could be waged with a kiss, the casualties of his power and pride a small price to pay for the rare sensation of being truly alive.

For Gavin had never met anyone with more life and vitality than Alison Ross.

And now . . .

He spurred Demetrius with a merciless kick. At a dead run in the middle of the day, it took the better part of an hour to reach Erradale. Time became a nebulous thing as Gavin raced through the darkness. It was impossible to tell if minutes or an eternity had passed before he nearly collided with a traveler galloping with identical recklessness in the direction of Inverthorne.

"Callum? Callum, is that ye?" Locryn's grizzled voice contained an altitude to its register that had Gavin swallowing his own unruly heart. He could barely make out the outline of a horse and what appeared to be two riders bundled against the cold.

Panicked words tumbled out of the infamously terse Locryn with heart-rending speed. "Sam. Ye have to help Sam. I couldna keep her on her mount and I have nothing to lash her down. She bathed before supper. Her hair was still wet. I doona ken if it's the cold, or if she's wounded, but she willna wake. They came for us. Two of them, and if it wasna for Sam they'd have . . . Well, she killed them both. A right terror with that pistol she is. And now she willna wake. Oh God. And Calybrid's guts is pouring out of him and the surgeon is miles away and I had to leave her—"

"What do ye mean, she willna wake?" Gavin demanded. "Where is she? What the fuck did ye allow to happen to her?"

"Lord Thorne?" Locryn gasped.

"My guts are all where they're supposed to be, ye oaf, now just tell him where Sam is," Calybrid's voice admonished weakly.

The light from Callum's lantern reached them, illuminating the pair of old men, hunched against the cold. Locryn sat mounted behind Calybrid, pressing a bundled-up plaid to his side with one hand, and clutching at the reins with the other. Even in the golden light, poor Calybrid's pallor was startling.

"Who the fuck is Sam?" Gavin demanded. "Where is Alison?"

"In America, she is called Sam," Callum explained, entirely too calmly for Gavin's liking.

"Where is she?" Gavin roared, a murderous ire snarling forth from a dank, forgotten place. The place with the Mackenzie name. "How could ye leave her?"

"She is maybe half a mile down the way." Locryn pointed, his rheumy dark eyes gleaming with moisture. "Around Brollachan Bend. Rowan is lashed by her on the left."

With a savage curse, Gavin spurred Demetrius with such strength, the stallion leaped forward.

"I couldna carry them both so I came for help!" Locryn called after him. "She's bundled in a fine cloak, and . . ."

The rest of the old man's words were frozen into the air, lost to the frantic pounding of Demetrius's hooves and Gavin's heart.

Gavin knew this road as well as he knew the slopes and planes of his own body. He could have counted the strides to Brollachan Bend were he as blind as his mother. He knew every bog, every meadow. He'd memorized this land as though it'd become a part of him.

Once he reached the bend, Gavin leaped from Demetrius's back before he'd completely come to a stop. He bellowed for her, for Alison, for Sam, and the answering silence ripped away a small part of his humanity.

Then he heard it, a rustle in the bushes. The soft, welcoming nicker of a horse left alone in the darkness.

There. There she was, curled beneath an ancient elm and, indeed, wrapped in a very fine cloak.

In *his* cloak.

Gavin scrambled to her, slipping on dead leaves made brittle by frost. The night had grown cold enough that he could barely feel his own hands in their fine gloves.

"Alison," he called, snatching her into his arms, giving her a shake when she didn't respond. "Alison. Wake up, lass."

Running on naught but primitive instinct, he ripped his

cloak open and his gloves off, passing his trembling hands over her face, her neck, her arms, and torso. Nothing. No wound.

Had she hit her head? he wondered as he spanned her thighs and lower. Had she—

The slick moisture instantly cooled on his palm when he pulled it away from her calf. Callum approached with his lantern just in time to illuminate what Gavin already knew would be coating his hand, the crimson horror of it signifying that they were running out of time . . .

Or might be too late.

CHAPTER TWELVE

Pain filtered through the darkness first, and Samantha desperately tried to retreat into the warm void of oblivion in which she'd been drifting. It was too cold out there in the world. Cold enough to lock her muscles tight and stiffen her bones. Too cold to survive. Too bitter.

Too lonely.

She understood now what Locryn and Callum had meant. This was better, this dark, safe cave. One of her own making. Where she didn't have to be afraid of her world rupturing apart at any moment.

Could she not just remain here? Here in the safe, velvet darkness where the ground was feather-soft and the walls were solid, impenetrable, and radiated with fragrant warmth that reminded her of both the forest and the sea. Of Wester Ross. The Scottish Highlands.

Of her new home.

Of something—someone?—both disquieting and captivating.

Samantha fought the pain with all her might as it tried

to pull her away from her cave. First, when pressure winched at her thigh and liquid lightning had lanced through her calf with indescribable pain. She'd struggled and sobbed until her body had been seized by bands of iron, and crushed into stillness by warm, iron shackles.

The void had reclaimed her for a time, until she'd surfaced with her muscles seized in great, bone-rattling tremors. Her core had become ice, and her skin pricked with fire laced with a thousand needles. And still, her arms remained secured to her sides, her body locked against a hard, blazing heat.

It had frightened her at first, being unable to move, unable to speak through a jaw incapable of doing anything but grinding her teeth with involuntary shivers.

But she'd had no strength left to struggle, and moving had become an agony that began in her calf and radiated up her leg. Finally, she'd given in. The fear and fight drained out of her, and she'd sagged against the hard walls of her cave, allowing them to curl around her. To pull her in with warm rumbles of strange masculine whispers that reminded her of ancient prayers.

A gentle rhythm vibrated against her ear, like the sound of hoofbeats on the marshy earth of Erradale. A rhythmic lullaby punctuated by a warm breeze tickling errant hairs at the top of her head.

She should have known she'd not be allowed to stay here. That the dark wouldn't remain peaceful, that demons and memories would find her and yank her back to face the cold light of day.

For this place—this cave—was not somewhere she belonged, nor did she deserve to remain. It was safe here. A place where she wasn't a liar. Where she wasn't a murderer.

Where she wasn't a mother.

The word "mother" pulled her from where she'd floated

in weightless obscurity, and dropped her into her body with jarring, unceremonious brutality. This new place met her with a plethora of merciless particulars. Her left calf throbbed. Her mouth tasted of the sun-baked desert. Her bones seemed to have melted, no more able to lift her limbs than she could a one-ton cow.

But she was finally warm. Utterly, deliciously, languorously warm, and . . . oddly comfortable.

Unable—or unwilling—to return to the land of the living just yet, she sank into the heat, luxuriated in the cocoonlike sheath that seemed to coil around her in just the right places.

But for the dull ache in her leg, she'd have thought it all a nightmare. Some drink-addled dream she'd regale Bennett with upon waking. About the train robbery gone wrong, forcing her to shoot him. About a harrowing journey across the Atlantic, and a slice of land that might as well be heaven but for the treacherous cold. A cold Samantha hadn't known existed until now. A cold that reached through the layers of her clothing, through her flesh and sinew and bone, until it chilled even her marrow.

Even her soul.

His coffee-colored eyes would crinkle, and he'd quirk that half-smile which seemed to have vanished once they'd married. He'd tease her like he used to, in the early days, saying that a girl so small shouldn't drink bourbon before bed.

Squeezing her eyes tighter, she sniffed at the sting of tears searing across the seam of her lids and escaping down her temple into her hair.

The rasp of a thumb against her skin, smudging the damp path of her tear, both soothed and vexed her. She turned her face toward the sensation, her thoughts swimming in nebulous clouds just beyond her reach.

"Why do ye weep, bonny, are ye in pain?" The concerned question filtered through the distance in dim echoes, as though reaching her from above the surface of a bath in which she remained emerged. "Do ye need another dose of laudanum?"

Bonny. "Bonny" meant beauty.

How did she know that?

"I—I deserve . . . pain," she rasped through a throat made of sandpaper and blocked by tears. "I shot him. I *killed* him." Maybe it was best her eyes never opened. That she joined her degenerate late husband in hell.

Except . . . she had more to consider now than just her own sins.

"Nay, lass, doona fash yerself over what ye had to do. Ye did what ye must to protect what was yers. No man could have done better." A gentle hand settled in her hair and stroked through the strands with a tender strength that opened an aching void in her chest. "Had ye not shot them, a quick death would not have been a mercy I granted them."

Who was this being with a fierce, beautiful voice? An avenging angel, perhaps?

"You don't understand," she whispered. How could he? She wasn't talking about the men who'd burned down Erradale and wounded Calybrid. She'd killed them both and she'd do it again. She'd been referring to her husband, the man she'd shot little more than a month ago. How could she recount the strange and terrible decisions that brought her to this moment, to the burly angel with the lovely voice and brogue both foreign and familiar?

She'd have to start at the beginning, with the death of both of her parents. Smallpox. She'd had it too, and had recovered. The Smiths, ousted Mormon ranchers who'd maintained the outlawed practice of polygamy, had taken her in as an orphan under the guise of good, Christian duty.

They'd worked a seven-year-old girl as hard as any ranch hand. Though, she had to admit, it hadn't been because she was not their own. They'd treated their thirteen natural children—born of the three various Smith wives—with the same expectations of strenuous duty.

Idle hands were the devil's workshop, and bleeding hands reminded you of the divinity and sacrifice of the Lord.

By the time Samantha had turned sixteen, she could ride, shoot, herd, rope, and brand cattle just as well as any of the Smith boys.

She'd casually thought she'd marry one of them, as well, though they'd grown up close as siblings. Northern Nevada wasn't exactly known for its populace, and she'd been one of the only girls within a day's ride that didn't share the last name of Smith.

Bennett Masters and his brothers, Boyd and Bradley, had showed up at the Smith ranch looking for work the year she'd turned seventeen. They'd been a lean, masculine trio with excellent demeanors and good teeth. Both of those virtues were in short supply thereabouts.

That Bennett Masters could charm a serpent out of his skin, Ada Smith, the second wife, had warned the girls. *You avoid temptation, you mark me.*

Samantha had listened to Ada, and really, she'd *tried* to avoid temptation . . . but when the Masters brothers had returned the next year with the seasonal ranch hands, along with a balding man named Ezekiel, and a few gauchos from Mexico, Sam hadn't been inured to the sparkle of mischief in Bennett's eyes. Or the wickedness in his smile.

And when Mr. Smith informed her of God's revelation that the sour, solemn, pious Ezekiel was to take her back to his cabin for his second wife, she'd run into Bennett's open arms sobbing and panicked.

He'd offered her escape. Excitement. He'd plied her with all the foreign emotions never afforded her since her parents had died, and then some. Affection. Validation. Anticipation of a different fate. One that wasn't breaking her back beneath the desert sun until exhaustion, illness, or injury put her in an early grave.

Samantha had always known she didn't have the heart of a pioneer.

What she hadn't realized was that her new husband and his family were not only orphans, they were outlaws, and the next four years had been a slow decline into infamy. She'd fought it, at first, like a weak child swimming upstream. She'd done her best to change him, to transform them all into honest men. But eventually an empty stomach, the fear of Boyd's brutality, and the relentless desperate hope for a better life overcame her scruples.

That was, until she'd met Alison Ross.

Her conscience had settled for a thief as a husband, but never a cold-blooded killer.

Oh God, how could she have been so senseless? How could she have been so blind? She'd thought that shooting Bennett would be the absolute worst thing she'd ever done. The worst tragedy she'd have to survive. It would be the stain on her conscience she'd forever have to live with, but on the same hand, she'd thought the nightmare was over.

She'd assumed they wouldn't find her here, perched on what had seemed to be the wild, untamed edge of the world.

She'd been a damned fool.

Now she knew the remaining Masters brothers had used their fortune to find her. That they'd sent those men after her, and once word reached them that they'd failed to do her in, they'd come for her again.

Boyd and Bradley wouldn't stop sending people after

her until she'd paid for what she'd done to Bennett. She knew this with a zealous fervency.

"Shhhhh." A soft croon whispered through her, vibrating in her ear and rippling down her flesh, creating goose pimples with a pleasant shudder. "Doona cry, bonny, I have ye. Ye're safe."

Would she ever be safe again? Who could protect her from vicious Boyd and his dead-eyed aim? Or cruel, simple Bradley with his heavy fists? Who would stand against men known to massacre an entire train car of innocent people?

Who would . . . *wait* . . . whose bed was she in right now?

Her eyes flew open, and the lone flame of a lantern assaulted her with light she'd not been prepared for.

Moaning her disapproval, she wrenched her neck to the side, and instantly realized her angel was not that of the avenging cast. Neither was he celestial in the least. Oh no. The handsome features hovering above hers knew nothing of grace, sacrifice, or piety.

This man had surely fallen from heavenly favor eons ago. His soul besmirched with sin, self-indulgence, and unrepentant wickedness.

Lord, but he was beautiful, though. She could imagine him a fallen angel, perhaps, with a span of long, powerful wings.

Never a halo, though. Never that.

Thorne. Her deluded memory whispered to her. He was Thorne. Or . . . a thorn . . . Was that what prodded against her backside even now? No . . . it was too blunt, too hot.

"Welcome back, bonny."

Samantha blinked rapidly against the overwhelming devastation wrought within her by that smile, trying to regain her scattered wits. Everything was so muddled. It was as though the earth had sped in its orbit and she could not catch it up. Her tongue was heavy and useless in her mouth. She wriggled her fingers, only to establish that they remained attached to her hands.

"Wh-where am I?"

That smile again. It dazzled and infuriated her at the same time.

"Ye are in my bed at Inverthorne Keep, lass. A position coveted by untold throngs of women."

Inverthorne Keep. Certainty permeated her untidy consciousness, dawning with slow degrees of mounting horror on the heels of each revelation.

The feather-soft floor of her cave had been the Earl of Thorne's *mattress.* The hard, warm, unyielding walls were, in fact, the lean muscles of his incomparable body, honed to obdurate swells by long months spent toiling in his brother's barley fields.

She lay positioned on her left side, and Thorne had curled his body against hers from behind, fitting himself into every curve and bend.

Jesus Jehosephat Christ. She'd not been safe in *the least.* In fact, other than the clutches of Boyd Masters, himself, she couldn't think of a more perilous place to be than *this* bed with *this* particular Highlander.

Instinctively, she reached for her pistol at her side, and only found her bare hip.

That fact was enough to lance whatever had drugged her wits with a lightning bolt of sobriety. But it didn't last. Her muscles remained weighted down like wool cast into a loch. Full and slow and heavy.

Crisp hairs tickled her shoulder blades each time the swells of his chest rose and fell with even, cavernous breaths. The rippled definition of his stomach rolled against her spine.

The *thing* pressing against her backside with hot, insistent flexes was, in fact, *not* a thorn, but could prick her just as easily.

Could wound her much more seriously.

Because, she realized, he was as naked as she beneath the heavy covers.

He'd lifted onto his elbow and now smiled indulgently down at her. His arm, which had been casually draped over her middle, belonged to the gentle fingers wiping at the tears still leaking from eyes peeled wide with astonished panic.

"Doona worry, bonny," he soothed, though a gleam of something dangerous shone beneath the concern in his verdant eyes. "Ye've nothing to fear from me. Though, I'll warn ye that ye're not leaving this bed until ye've revealed to me yer dangerous secrets . . . beginning with just who is after ye, and why they burned Erradale to the ground."

CHAPTER THIRTEEN

Sometimes Gavin would take someone, *anyone,* to bed and pleasure them into oblivion for the sole purpose of having a person to press his body against in the night. It was a raison d'être he never admitted or expressed. At the end of any given night, form and feature held little sway over his decision, and he didn't especially pick a woman whom he might want to invite back or form an attachment to.

Because he didn't want them to guess his motives. He didn't want them to recognize him for what he truly was.

A boy who'd spent too many nights hiding in a closet, or huddled in the hollowed-out tree trunk of the ancient oak he and Callum had claimed as their own domain next to Bryneloch Bog.

On those nights, he'd crafted his hatred very carefully. He'd covered his bruises, his lashes, and his pain with the balm of cold calculation. Until he'd nearly forgotten what it was to feel.

What it was to live.

It wasn't until he'd met Colleen as a boy on the cusp of

manhood that he'd realized what would keep him human. The primal and instinctive necessity of physical contact. Of pleasure, or pain. It was both a palliative and a compulsion. When his thoughts would race, when his gorge would rise, when his mind seemed to want to disconnect from his body and lose itself into the vast emptiness that yawned inside of him, only the touch of another would anchor him to reality. He'd reach for someone in the night, whoever it was, and offer pleasure, his only intention to hide the endless, cavernous need inside of him.

It had made him a legend, this fiction, which had not been his initial intention. The women he'd taken assumed that his voracious need had been more erotic than emotional.

And he'd let them.

Because life had taught him, with few exceptions, that once a person discovered your true desire, it was in their nature to deny you. It's not that he blamed anyone, exactly. Power was a heady thing, and having your fingers clenched around the pulse of someone else's greatest ambitions, or their driving force, meant you owned them.

Body and soul.

He'd never allow someone that sort of power over him. Never again.

Now, pressed against his petite nemesis, he was stunned to discover that his motives had somewhat realigned from their usual arrangement. Certainly the obvious difference had been she was no lover or companion.

Indeed, neither was she even a willing occupant of his bed.

The slim, fragile body against his offered him nothing, and yet provided what others could not, despite their best efforts.

He'd like to call it distraction, but in reality it was

something else. Something that felt like purpose. Something akin to contentment. Relief. Peace.

But . . . that couldn't be right, could it? Not with Alison Ross. The lass was anything but peaceful. Indeed, she was chaos personified. Since her appearance in his life, she'd been a disruption at best. A nuisance, more like.

An obstacle.

One he was beginning to enjoy coming up against.

Verbally. And now . . . physically.

It occurred to him to resent her. In fact, he had at first, for the sole reason that she'd kept Erradale from him. Now his motivation for umbrage had just become a great deal stronger. It wasn't that he no longer desired Erradale; he did. More than ever. But now he desired something else.

Someone else.

And this yearning certainly complicated things. Convoluted his intentions. It made him analyze his own needs. Question everything he knew about himself.

Such as, why should he be more distressed over the near loss of his *obstacle,* Alison Ross, than the loss of his *desire,* Erradale?

She'd said that her demise would remove his last impediment to claiming Erradale as his own, and he'd objectively acknowledged the veracity of her statement.

But the moment he'd thought her lost to him, the moment he'd tried to wake her with no success, all thoughts of Erradale had vanished like wisps of vapor before the sun.

All that had mattered was that she survived. Because without her, Erradale would be . . . empty. Like his bed.

Like his heart.

As he stared down into Alison's eyes the color of the summer sky, both anxious and unfocused by the opium syrup Eammon had administered to her, the well of fathomless emptiness inside him seemed to abate.

She was awake, and despite everything, it felt like a miracle.

The bullet that had torn into her calf had been little more than a flesh wound. Callum had bound it on the roadside while Gavin had winched a tourniquet below her knee that lasted through the frantic ride back to Inverthorne.

It had been the cold that had almost taken her, and Gavin had warmed her by using the oldest and most effective method he knew.

Body heat.

It had taken him all of three seconds to consider his options in that regard, as he'd held her unresponsive body against him while Eammon quickly and expertly sterilized and stitched her leg.

Drawing a hot bath would take too long, and a fresh wound rarely fared well in tepid water. Infection was a risk he wasn't willing to take.

So he'd ignored Callum's protests, and Eammon's raised eyebrows, and swept her up the spiral staircase to Inverthorne's tower. He made short work of stripping his cloak and her night rail off her. That accomplished, he divested himself of his clothing, and climbed into bed.

Relief seemed too insubstantial a word for the all-encompassing feeling that had taken him once she'd begun to shiver and struggle. After what seemed like an eternity, she'd exhausted her strength, and instead of fighting his hold, she'd relaxed into it. Instinct drove her naked flesh against his, seeking the heat he provided.

Which had aroused, for lack of a better word, another persistent dilemma.

Gavin had always been a clever liar, but he'd never truly been able to deceive himself. He'd known that he wanted Alison Ross for some time now. But it wasn't until he had her here in his bed, soft, pliant, and tantalizingly nude, that he realized just how desperate his carnal need for her had become.

He wanted her beside him. Beneath him. Above him.

He wanted her in his bed . . . in his arms . . . for longer than just one night.

All he had to do was figure out how to convince her to remain.

It wasn't that he was by any means grateful that she'd been attacked, that she'd been in danger, but he was never one to let an opportunity pass him by.

He smudged at her tears with his thumb. Thinking that it was certainly difficult to maintain his wits when they leaked from her eyes in soft rivulets of pain. Instead of kissing them away, as was his first instinct, he capitulated to better sense, driven by the confusion and fear he read in her rare, unguarded expression.

It was the look of a fox caught in a snare laid out for rabbits.

He watched her grope around for fabrications made less accessible in her mind by the opium tincture and exhaustion.

When it became obvious that she wasn't going to answer his question about her attackers, he changed tactics.

"How do ye fare, lass?" he murmured gently, surprised by how much he really wanted to know. "Does yer leg pain ye overmuch?"

Wordlessly, she shook her head.

"Then I need to know who hurt ye and ye must tell me the truth," he prodded. "Once dawn breaks, there's no stopping me from riding to Erradale and finding out myself."

He tracked her dilated eyes as they chased erstwhile thoughts, ignoring the strange, wondrous liquid thaw in the vicinity of his chest. She was concocting something, he surmised. Which meant she believed the truth still posed a threat, despite the men she'd killed.

"Someone's after ye?" he queried. "Ye landed yerself in a ripe bit of danger in America, and part of the reason ye've come back to Erradale is that ye're no longer safe in yer adopted country."

Her gaze darted away.

He'd hit the mark.

"Why—why are we naked?" she mumbled as if retraining her tongue to form language. "Did you . . . did we . . . ?"

"We didna," he soothed, painfully aware of the pulsing arousal resting against her hip. "But we *could,* if ye think it would help."

Her eyes rolled in a reaction to his repartee so indiscreet and honest, a delighted laugh escaped him, surprising them both. "Doona fash. If I'd ravished ye, bonny, ye'd be certain to remember the deed."

"Then why . . ."

"Hypothermia. Ye were in the cold in naught but yer nightgown and my cloak for longer than was safe, it seems. I saved yer life. Och, nay, lass—" He held his hand up to cut off a profusion of gratitude that was obviously not forthcoming. "No need to thank me. Ye may, instead, answer my question."

Her brows attempted a scowl, but didn't quite hit the mark. "It's hard to think with your . . . with *that* pressed against me," she muttered, attempting to angle her hip away from his aroused body.

"How do ye think I feel?" he teased. "I deserve a medal of gentlemanly conduct for honorable restraint in the face of unmitigated temptation. How many men do ye know that would have yer fine, naked body in their arms and allow ye to maintain yer virginity?"

"I'm no virgin," she snorted, artlessly squirming a bit

to escape their intimate proximity. "And you're no gentleman."

Her confession shouldn't have shocked him. It shouldn't have aroused his jealousy, but it did.

On both accounts.

"Aye," he admitted, artfully keeping the strange possessiveness growling through his muscles from seeping into his tone. "Ye've caught me. I'm no gentleman, but ye could use that to yer advantage at *any* time." He allowed her a measured retreat, but he did not let her go.

Could not let her go.

She made an excellent point, he ceded, that conversation became futile with his insistent cock pressed against her skin.

That particular part of his anatomy wanted to make no discoveries tonight past what it felt like to be buried deep inside of her.

But his soul . . . his soul couldn't rest unless he knew who else might pose a threat to her survival.

Who else might be hunting her? For there he would find a predator worth turning into prey.

Despite the wrath churning in his gut, he reached down and smoothed a lock of her uncommonly lovely hair away from her face. He'd known she was young, as no lines branched from her eyes or bracketed her lips, but she looked like a girl rather than a woman curled as she was against him.

Lost. Alone. Afraid. All her impetuous bravado melted beneath the pinch of pain between her brows and the strain of trepidation pursing those soft lips together.

"What happened in America, lass?" He murmured the question, allowing his fingers to brush over the arch of her dark brow, smoothing the crease of tension he found there. Then he followed the hollow of her temple, still damp with recent tears, circling the tender place in a light, kneading motion. "Maybe I can help."

"Why would you help me?" she asked drowsily, her eyes fluttering closed beneath his ministrations.

"It is ye who decided we must be enemies, not I," he reminded her. "I may not be a gentleman, but I'm a Highlander, and we protect our own."

"I'm not a Highlander. I'm nobody." Her lamented whisper tugged at his heart.

"Yes ye are, bonny. This remains yer home, even though ye left."

She was quiet a moment as his fingers traced and massaged, learning the lovely regions of her features. The knots of her jaw, which he coaxed to unclench. The downy skin beneath her chin. The pronounced outline of her plump lips. The four and twenty golden freckles he counted on her uncommonly high cheekbones.

After a while, her breath had become so even, he thought he'd put her to sleep.

"I killed Bennett." Her monotone admission stalled time itself.

Gavin's hand froze, cupped against her chin. Her eyes remained closed, her lashes fanned against her cheek. Neither of them breathed for what seemed like an eternity.

A thousand questions swarmed into his throat, and Gavin had to press his lips together to keep them at bay. Confessions, once they began, traveled at their own pace.

"It was on the train toward Cheyenne, on my way here," she continued on a swift exhale. "The Masters Gang went after some government bonds and payroll. Something happened in a different car. I heard that federal marshals were shot. And then . . . Bennett burst in and killed a man in my railcar, then pointed a gun at . . . And I . . . And I shot him. I shot him right between the eyes."

Hot tears began to flow again, and Gavin caught them, his own throat aching on her behalf.

"Ye did well, lass. Maybe even saved lives."

"Only one life." She sighed.

"Is it his brothers who are after ye, do ye think?"

"His brothers," she whimpered in bleak response.

"Aye, what are their names?"

"Boyd and Bradley. Bradley saw me do it. I didn't think that they would find me here. They somehow figured out that Alison Ross was on the train, and where she—I was going. Then they used their stolen fortune to send those men to Erradale. For revenge, I think." She hiccupped around a sob; her limbs began to tremble once again as she valiantly fought the rattles of grief and fear in her chest.

Gavin gathered her to him, astonished when she clutched at his shoulders as though he were her bulwark against a battalion of sorrows.

"Shh, bonny, shh," he soothed, attempting to comfort her with a bit of levity. "Ye doona mean for me to believe that ye've only shot *one* man before today, do ye? For as many times as ye've nearly shot me, I was certain that America had turned ye into some sort of bloodthirsty Yankee gunslinger."

To his delight, it worked. A burp of laughter interrupted her sobs, and she pushed at his shoulder with a self-conscious sniff that he found unutterably adorable.

"That's only because all of this is your fault," she accused with a slurring sort of churlishness. "If I'd never been on that train, maybe none of this would have happened. I could have gone to Oregon, like I'd planned. I would be married when—"

"Married?" The word hit him in the chest with all the power of a draft horse's kick. "Married to whom?"

Her gaze sought to escape his again. "That isn't the point."

He caught her chin in a gentle grip, firm enough to force her to look at him. "Married. To. *Whom*?"

"You've never heard of him."

"Try me."

She wrinkled her brow again, as though sifting through elusive memories. "Grant . . . a . . . a banker."

"I'll be honest, bonny, I have a hard time picturing ye settled with a banker."

Thunder gathered in her watery eyes. "What of it? He's a gentleman. A self-made man with a fortune all his own. He's honest and kind and virtuous. All the things you're not. He keeps his word and he—"

"Oh?" Gavin interrupted, unwilling to hear anything else about this Grant bastard. "Then, pray, where is this paragon of honor, that I may kiss his boot?" She hadn't, he noticed, mentioned the word "handsome" among her intended's myriad of virtues.

"Back in San Francisco," she hedged.

"He doesna write ye? He willna join ye, even after all ye've been through?"

Her lashes fluttered down again. "Circumstances don't permit . . ."

"Fuck circumstances," Gavin snarled, startling them both with the ferocity of his vehemence. "If he loved ye, he'd not let ye face yer enemies alone. He'd have learned of the robbery and have hunted every single one of the so-called Masters brothers to the edge of perdition. He'd have marched them to the gates of hell and handed them over to the devil, himself. Then, he'd return for ye. Claim every part of ye, with his hands, with his mouth, and not allow ye out of his sight again."

She blinked up at him for several astonished minutes. "Is—is that what you would do?"

"Och, nay, lass, I'd do one better. If a man touched my beloved in violence, I'd tear off his limbs with my bare hands and beat him to death with them. Slowly. And I'd receive a pardon for it, as well, as it would be no less than he deserved." His hand curled into a fist as he relished the idea. "While we're at it, let's hope I never meet this Grant—this *self-made* man—for I'd take him back apart again. I'd break his body first, then his will, and then I'd make him watch as I took ye, just to show him how a *man* does it."

He blinked down at her for a silent moment, the ferocity melting into bewildered displeasure. Where had this barbaric vehemence come from? This simmer of violence and wrath in his blood?

That place. The one he named Mackenzie. The one he'd shoved into the void and locked behind vaults comprised of dispassionate nonchalance and cold calculations painted with a veneer of charm.

Would that he could cut it out of himself.

He didn't want to feel like this about her.

He didn't want to feel . . .

"I—I don't think I ever was his beloved," she whispered, biting her lower lip to still a dreadful wobble in her chin.

"I should think not," Gavin muttered. "And neither should ye love him."

"I thought I did . . . but after everything . . . I knew it could not be so. Or losing him would have broken me."

Struck with an encompassing tenderness, Gavin looked down at the woman in his bed with a new and genuine respect. He knew a thing or two about loss.

About a broken heart.

"I'm becoming convinced that there's nothing in this world that could break ye, bonny."

Suddenly, a path revealed itself. One better than any he'd yet been presented with. One where both of his desires were bundled into a tidy package and delivered into his anxious, enterprising hands.

"Ye're certain it was these fuckers, these Masters brothers, who sent those men after ye?" he pressed, his heart accelerating with the weightiness of what he was about to propose.

"I know they are. There's no one else."

"Then I can help ye, lass, I can help keep ye and, more importantly, Erradale safe from yer enemies."

"How?" she whispered, then stronger, said, "I mean, *why*? Why would you?"

"Because if we married, both ye *and Erradale* would be mine. And I fight to the death to protect what's mine."

CHAPTER FOURTEEN

"Marry you?" Samantha wheezed around the heart that had begun to leap into her throat. Was she still dreaming? Dear God, let her still be dreaming. "What makes you think I'd even consider it? We can't stand each other."

That devastating dimple indented the groove next to his cheek. "I'll give ye that, bonny, but what I have in mind doesna involve a great deal of standing."

"Be serious," she hissed. "That may be the worst idea anyone's ever spoken aloud."

"I'm not asking ye to like me, lass, only to marry me."

"Is this some kind of cruel fucking joke?" she gasped.

"Do ye mean to tell me there's no such thing as a convenient marriage where ye come from?" He twisted his lips into an expression of doubt.

"'Convenient'?" she echoed. "I very much assume that if you considered marriage *a convenience,* you'd have done it once or twice by now."

He had the temerity to laugh, the rich sound producing

the usual explosion of moths inside of her belly. "Do ye know what I like about ye, bonny?"

"I really wish you'd stop calling me—"

"It's that ye say what ye mean. Ye doona care what I think. Ye're an honest woman who isna afraid of her own capability. Also, ye're cleverer than most, which I wouldna have guessed about ye right away, I'm ashamed to admit."

An unexpected burst of pleasure at the compliment stole her capacity for speech. An honest woman? Lord, was he ever mistaken. She wondered if he'd realize just how much he'd missed the mark in his estimation of her . . . She was neither honest nor predominantly clever, though she wished to be both. At the moment, neither was she particularly capable of much, since her leg was out of commission.

Also, to make his compliment false in the absolute, she was beginning to realize that she *did* care what he thought . . .

Not that she'd ever admit it to a soul. Especially to him.

"To keep Erradale, ye'll have to stay on the land, lass," he pointed out. "And it sounds to me like going back to America with these Masters brothers after ye is out of the question."

"I'm not safe from them here, either, apparently," she lamented.

"Ye'd be safe from them at Inverthorne." His levity disappeared, and his jaw tightened with absolute solemnity. "As my wife, ye'd be a countess. The walls of Inverthorne withstood English sieges and battles. They can certainly keep out a few American train burglars."

"Train burglars?" It could have been his earnest distaste for the word, or the ridiculousness of the phrase, but Samantha caught a gasp of a giggle, even as she groped for reasons to refuse him.

At least, ones she could repeat out loud.

She wasn't really Alison Ross. Erradale was not actually hers to grant to anyone. She couldn't betray Alison's wishes after the woman had provided her sanctuary. She'd been Bennett Master's wife little more than a month ago.

She was pregnant with a murderer's child.

"I *can't* marry a Mackenzie," she said lamely. "I swore an oath."

"Consider this, bonny, if ye married me, ye'd technically not be surrendering Erradale to a Mackenzie, as I technically willna be one for long. Or so I keep having to remind ye."

She had to admit, that seemed a more salient point in this moment than it had before.

"Besides, this blood feud is a bit too Shakespearean, if ye want the truth. I'm no Montague, and ye're no Capulet. We're naught but the victims of the circumstances of our births. Think on it, lass, would not joining our families do more good than harm? Would it not put the matter of our parents to rest for generations that come after?"

"I'd fight to the death to protect what's mine." His proposal echoed through her addled mind clearer than the screech of an eagle over the stark plains of Wyoming.

Samantha's hand drifted up to rest on her stomach, still flat and toned by arduous years of work.

Five weeks—nigh to six now—since she'd boarded that train. Since she'd last lain with her husband.

And almost three weeks late.

What if . . . what if she confessed? What if she told him she *wasn't* Alison Ross, but Samantha Masters, and that she was likely carrying her deceased husband's baby? Oh, and also that the fact that she'd shot said husband between the eyes was the reason for the vacancy of said position in her life at present?

Would he still want to protect her then?

Likely not.

Would the next hired guns Boyd and Bradley sent give a care that she might be pregnant with the Masterses' niece or nephew and spare her?

Not a chance.

"Mutually beneficial marriages have been little better than land contracts for millennia," the Earl of Thorne continued with infuriating rationality for someone so astoundingly nude. "Think on it, lass. I'll not stop until I get what I want, so ye might as well give in and save us both a great deal of effort. I doona see what other choice ye have. What with yer estate burned to the ground, yer herd scattered, yer homeland crawling with yer enemies, and a pending appearance in front of the Magistrate's Bench . . ."

He let his list trail off, and Samantha filled in a few points of her own. Any cash or paperwork with the claim to Erradale she'd had from Alison blew away with the ashes of Erradale. She'd a leg that would be useless for a month or longer, which left her little more than helpless.

And a child on the way with no father.

God, she wasn't really allowing for his absolutely naked, utterly unromantic proposal, was she? How much of that tincture of opium had she been given?

"I'd be a very good, somewhat faithful husband to ye, lass," he vowed, plying her with his most charming smile.

"Somewhat faithful?" she echoed.

"Well, as we established, I'm no saint, and neither, by yer own admission, are ye. I see no reason a marriage between us should be a prison sentence."

"You're saying . . . you don't expect fidelity . . . ?" she clarified carefully.

"I suppose not," he said lightly, then he frowned. "But perhaps we should wait to take lovers until our familial duties are carried out. We'll need a St. James heir, or both Inverthorne and Erradale would just go to my nephew, Andrew, upon my demise and, seeing as he's Liam's son, that would deliver Erradale right into the hands of a Mackenzie Laird, which supplants our purposes outright."

There's a chance that shouldn't be a problem, Samantha thought, curling the fingers of her hand that rested over her belly into a fist.

"So, lass, what do ye say we put our differences aside, and rewrite the ending to *Romeo and Juliet*?"

"You're certainly no lovelorn Romeo, promising me the moon," she muttered.

"Aye, and ye're no maidenly Juliette," he volleyed back. "Besides, it looks to me like the moon appears to have enough holes in it. And ye'd just use it for target practice, anyway."

The smile he directed down at her summoned an unbidden answer from her own lips.

"I just . . . *can't* imagine myself as a countess." She chuckled.

"Me neither, bonny, and willna *that* be half the fun?" When his eyes sparkled just so, and his lips quirked in that way that caused his dimple to appear, Samantha thought it made him look very young and devastatingly handsome.

How was she supposed to think straight? This wasn't fair.

"What—what does a countess even do?" she wondered aloud.

"Whatever she likes, so long as she breeds the next generation of nobility," he answered with a passionless nonchalance that drew her brows into a grimace.

"That can't be," she argued. "Isn't a wife beholden to her husband? Doesn't she have to obey him? Where would she get the money to do what she likes, if everything she owns goes to him? I don't think England and America are very different in that regard."

"Well . . . nay," he admitted. "But in noble marriages, it is standard practice for the woman to have a certain allowance settled upon her, usually provided by a dowry."

"But . . . I have no dowry."

"Aye, but I'm no pauper, and I plan to vastly improve my fortune with the help of Erradale, which is sort of the same thing, is it not? If ye were to marry me, bonny, ye'd have your own annuity. Above that, once ye provided an heir, it is custom that a large sum is bestowed upon ye, as well. Ye could do with it what ye like. Travel the world, shop, rent yer own residency if Inverthorne isna to yer liking." His features dropped, suddenly very solemn. "Ye'd have freedom, lass, once yer duty was done. And a lifetime of protection once the vows were spoken."

Suddenly breathing as though she'd run a long way, Samantha squeezed her eyes shut once again, not wanting the otherworldly sight of him to hold sway over her decision. She'd been staring at him with wide, unbelieving eyes for so long, the details of his face followed her into the darkness behind her lids, lingering in every possible color of shadow.

Was she truly considering this? This madness, this lunacy?

Not only was she considering it . . . there was really only one impediment to her acceptance.

Alison. The real Alison Ross. She'd said in her letter that Samantha could remain as long as she liked at Erradale. That she planned to never return. She'd even offered to sell it to Samantha once the herd had turned enough profit to pay her with.

I never want to see Erradale again. Do with it what you wish. Those had been her exact words.

So long as it remains out of Mackenzie hands.

A multitude of scenarios danced behind the words flowing through her mind as clearly as though Alison had spoken them into her ear.

Had Samatha any of the cash left that Alison had given her, she'd consider running. This world was big and wide, and there had to be a place where Boyd and Bradley couldn't reach her, right?

Or would she, an excessively tall, exceedingly thin American woman stick out like a pervasive weed in a field of flowers no matter where she tried to hide herself?

It didn't matter now, she supposed. The money was gone.

She was left with nothing but a false name, a wounded leg, and a child to care for and protect.

And a choice.

A frightening choice that could end in absolute disaster.

What if she married Gavin, and Alison changed her mind and came back? What if Boyd and Bradley learned of her survival and came after her, themselves? Her ruse would be uncovered . . .

Would Gavin still march them to the devil like he'd so passionately threatened to do?

Both scenarios were unlikely, but not impossible. She knew the sum of money Boyd and Bradley had at their disposal and, while it was grand, it wasn't enough to sustain a vendetta for long. Especially not if they needed to use it to escape the law. The Masters brothers were wanted criminals, their names and likenesses posted at ports and railway stations across the country.

And Alison would be happily married by now.

What would the young and lovely Alison Ross say if she knew of Samantha's latest plight? What would she tell her to do if she knew she'd found herself both with child and in mortal danger? What if she knew Gavin no longer wished to be a Mackenzie? That he hated his father for what he'd done?

Samantha had told a great many lies in her lifetime. She'd done so many dishonorable things.

But could she really lead a man to believe that she bore him a child that wasn't his, all for the sake of an annuity? For security?

Once upon a time, she would have said no.

Never.

This decision, though, was about more than just security now. It was about survival . . . And should the worst happen, and Gavin learn of her deception, she could at least take what money the marriage afforded her and run.

His heart wouldn't be broken to see her go, and he'd still get what he wanted.

Erradale.

His hot breath fanned across her temple as he leaned to croon in her ear. "Doona tell me ye're not tempted by my offer, bonny. That ye're not tempted by *me*."

He silenced her sound of protest with a long, agile finger on her lips. "That kiss we shared proves our compatibility. At least here in bed. I'll apply myself to my husbandly duties with singular focus. I'll not let ye sleep until ye beg, limp with pleasure . . . I'll fill you so often, ye'll be with child in a week's time. I'll—"

"All right!" she cried, only to stop the torrent of whispered words wreaking havoc on her insides and making her thighs clench together, which set her injured leg to throbbing. "I'll marry you. But . . . I want the annuity in advance."

"Done," he said without a breath of hesitation, his eyes gleaming with almost malevolent triumph.

"Also," she continued. "I'd like to be on with the

wedding as soon as possible, if it's all the same to you. Tomorrow wouldn't be too soon."

A devilish grin spread across lips made for sin. "If I'd known it was bed play that would sway ye, I'd have opened negotiations with that."

"That wasn't—I didn't—*no!*—I just wanted you to stop talking." It had been her delicate situation, not her desire, that had prompted her plea for expediency.

Hadn't it?

"Whatever ye say, bonny, but I'll do what I can to accommodate yer demands for an expedient claim to my name . . . and my body." This he said in a tone that mocked her protestations.

"Don't flatter yourself," she insisted. "My haste has nothing to do with your dirty insinuations and everything to do with the fact that living at Inverthorne without marrying you first would ruin my reputation."

He cast her a skeptical look. "Ye doona seem the type to worry overmuch about reputation, lass."

He had her there. "Well . . . no . . . but what would your mother think?"

He frowned. "Ye raise an excellent point."

"Not to mention Callum and Locryn and . . . *Calybrid!*" The memory of her injured friend jolted her to her elbows, followed by the burn of guilt that she'd not given him a thought until now. Another fault she could possibly place at the feet of the unabashedly nude male trying to coax her back down.

"Calybrid is resting comfortably, lass. Never ye worry," Gavin soothed. "Eammon is trained to doctor animals, but around these parts he tends to stitch up us folks just as often."

She relaxed back to the bed, fighting lids made heavy with equal parts relief, exhaustion, and trepidation. Her mind felt as though it wanted to race, but could only swim through a convoluted stew that was her muddled thoughts.

"Ye get some sleep, bonny." His warm mouth covered hers in a remarkably chaste kiss that felt anything but. "I'll make arrangements. I imagine we can have papers signed in a few days' time."

Sleep *did* sound like heaven. Her leg was beginning to ache, and oblivion called her down to a soft escape from the magnitude of her situation. Of what she'd just agreed to.

A great weight shifted beside her, and she lifted a lid to watch him roll away from her and sit on the opposite edge of the bed.

The unexpected sight peeled her eyes wide with dismay.

Gavin St. James, the ever-smiling jackanapes, the notorious rake and infamous seducer, carried upon his shoulders and back the weight of unimaginably deep scars. Lashes, it looked like, stretched across his topography of bunched sinew and strength. They didn't seem as though they'd been created by a whip. At least, not all of them. The lines of long-ago wounds were long, but blunted on the ends. Or angled just so. In the shape of a buckle or a belt.

Breath escaped her at the sight. She imagined the lashes fresh and open, the skin flayed apart by vicious, repetitive violence.

Drawn by a well of sympathy so deep it threatened to drown her, Samantha's hand drifted up from the bed with dreamlike sluggishness, and reached for him. She felt driven to trace the strange, exacting angles, and smooth the offending scars away.

How had he come by these? His hated father? Were they the reason for his—

The moment her fingertips found the ridge of one scar close to his spine, her wrist was caught in a painful grip, the spell of compassion broken.

Startled, she blinked up at Lord Thorne . . .

And found someone else.

Someone fierce and wild and violent. His green eyes burned down at her, his nostrils flared, and his shoulders—his broad, disfigured shoulders—heaved with the rhythm of furious breaths.

She wanted to tell him to unhand her, almost as badly as she wanted to apologize. She hadn't been thinking when she'd reached for him.

Only feeling.

What she read behind the verdant inferno in his eyes caught any breath that would feed her voice behind a lump in her throat. The pain was as naked as the rest of him. And wariness resided there, too. Along with a strange vulnerability behind the hostility that would be easy to miss if one didn't look closely enough.

"Do. Not." His words were enunciated with a low, muttered exactitude that reverberated through her entire being.

He didn't say more. He didn't need to. She knew exactly what he meant.

Do not touch. Do not ask. Do not mention.

This was a wound he didn't share, an experience he didn't discuss.

She had a few of those, herself.

"I won't," she said evenly, having learned long ago that the best way to avoid a topic was to redirect it. "Is there a church close by? I haven't really seen one since I've been here."

"There's a chapel at Ravencroft." The sardonic twist of his lips took on a cruel cast, but he released her. "My father ran off the priest before I was born, but we only need a justice of the peace to make our nuptials official."

"But you're the . . ."

"That's right, though Liam will have to perform the ceremony, as I canna perform my own." An unholy darkness cooled the heat in his eyes.

"Are you sure that's wise? Would he even agree to it?"

"He has to." He shrugged shoulders that she made a very concerted effort not to even glance at. "It's his responsibility as Laird and as one of the magistrates. He canna very well refuse."

"But . . . I mean . . . there's bad blood between you, isn't there? You're emancipating yourself from him, after all."

"Aye, there's bad blood, Mackenzie blood, but that willna stop Liam from doing what has to be done. I'll say that much for my brother." Pausing, he scrutinized her from beneath a suspicious brow. "What do ye ken of it, lass? Ye went to Ravencroft. What did ye learn of the bad Mackenzie blood?"

She didn't know what compelled her to be honest. The challenge she read in the set of his jaw, or the anxiety beneath the dark anticipation in his eyes.

"I—I heard you had an affair with his late wife, Colleen."

She didn't miss that he visibly flinched when she said the name.

"Is it true?"

"Aye," he clipped.

"Was it because you loved her? Or because you hated him?" The question escaped her before she could call it back. And oh, how she wished to when the darkness he'd summoned to his features became absolute.

"If we are to marry, ye'll have to accept that there are three things I will never discuss with ye. My scars, my father, and Colleen Mackenzie. Do ye understand?"

"I understand." She had her own terrible secrets; she

could leave him his, safe and somehow comforted with the knowledge that both of their souls were stained with sins.

Maybe they were both beyond forgiveness.

Maybe . . . they deserved each other.

CHAPTER FIFTEEN

Gavin didn't stay and hold her precisely because he wanted to do just that.

And because . . . the lass saw too much.

It struck him anew, while he'd subdued Alison's wildly trembling body, how intensely vulnerable someone was whilst asleep.

How strange, then, that he'd invite so many into his bed, or join them in theirs. Perhaps because he didn't see women as a threat.

Or hadn't, until recently.

After dressing with all haste, Gavin made for the stables, looking forward to another hard ride with which to work away whatever seemed to be searing and fizzing in his blood.

It didn't surprise him to find Callum there, seeing to the faithful horse, Rowan, that'd conveyed Alison as far as she could go, and then did not desert her once she fell.

"Yer beast can have his pick of oats, barley, and grain,"

Gavin said as Callum glanced at him over the slight curve of the horse's back. "He deserves the best."

"I'm grateful to you," the Mac Tíre replied, not missing one rhythmic stroke of his brush across the glossy coat. "Are you after investigating Erradale at dawn?" he asked mildly. "Is that where you're off to at this ungodly hour?"

"I'll go to Erradale directly after Ravencroft," Gavin said shortly. "Is Eammon abed?"

"Aye, me old man had a dram or three after doing what he could to sew Calybrid's guts together and is snoring in his chair." Flicking Gavin a look of speaking curiosity, Callum asked, "Why are you going to Ravencroft an hour before dawn?"

"I told Alison that Calybrid was going to be all right . . ." Gavin let his silence ask the question, even as he evaded Callum's.

"Aye, he'll live, so long as the stitches hold and don't turn putrid."

"Good."

Callum patted his steed on the withers and stepped out of the stall, brushing dust and hair from his old, fingerless gloves. "I've cooled Demetrius down, but I'll saddle ye another to take to Ravencroft."

"I can do it." Gavin turned away from his friend's eerily perceptive gaze to gather saddle and tack, and worked alongside his friend as dim striations of gray began to filter into the open stable doors.

Lifting his saddle onto a light-footed Arabian-thoroughbred mix, Gavin suddenly remembered something he'd long forgotten. "Callum." He turned to his friend. "Didna ye know Alison Ross well when she was a wee girl at Erradale?"

His friend's impassivity slipped for only a moment, one too quick to read what emotion filtered through.

"Aye. I knew her."

Were the Mac Tíre's lips tighter than usual, or was that his imagination? Damn the man's unruly beard.

"Ye used to complain about the lass ceaselessly bothering ye. In fact, ye'd come to Ravencroft to escape her, did ye not?"

"I did."

"Is she at all like ye remember?"

Had Gavin been paying closer attention to his friend, instead of cinching the saddle, he'd have noticed Callum took longer than necessary to reply. "The woman you know is nothing like the Alison Ross who left Erradale all those years ago."

A thoughtful sound escaped on a long breath. "Life has a way of turning us into strangers, even to ourselves."

"Aye, that it does."

Gavin broke a long, inexplicably glum moment by swinging into the saddle. "I've found a way to gain Erradale," he announced.

"Oh?" Callum's brows lifted. "And just how will ye convince Sam not to shoot ye, first?"

"Easy." Gavin bared his teeth in what was supposed to be a grin, but felt a little too wild to maintain the distinction. "I convinced her to marry me, instead."

With a swift kick, he shot into the bracing predawn chill, leaving his friend gaping after him in an openmouthed stupor. The ground crunched beneath his mount's hooves, the winter path kissed by delicate frost. It would sparkle when the sun rose, clinging to the winter foliage and turning Wester Ross into something out of a Faerie Tale.

Except he was no Prince Charming. No Romeo.

And Alison Ross was certainly no damsel.

The past chased him all the way to Ravencroft. How

many times had he made this trip in the middle of the night? How many times had he been summoned to the secret door off the north wing, and fought not to answer?

As many times as he'd given in.

It was in front of that door, they'd found Colleen's body, when she'd thrown herself from the ramparts rather than run away with him.

He thought about the wild, torturous ride he'd taken to Ravencroft a decade ago when word had reached him. He thought about it every time he took this road.

This time, though, different tragedies tore after him.

All of them linked to the place where Alison Ross's fingertips still seared the uneven flesh of his back.

Of course, she wasn't the first to see his scars. One couldn't bed so many women without baring one's skin. Sometimes, if he was feeling unwilling to discuss it, he'd leave off the lights, leave on his shirt, or blindfold the lass. Other times, when he was less brittle, he'd concoct a wild story, one just farfetched enough to be believable.

Pirates had overtaken him and Callum in Borneo. He'd done time in a foreign prison during his youthful travels. Or, his favorite, he'd made a pilgrimage to a zealous monastery; doing his best to cure himself of his wicked, salacious need for fornication through self-flagellation.

Anything but the truth.

Oh, how their legs would part, their fingers smoothing over the groves and welts, right before their nails scored them.

So why did her single, curious touch evoke such a violent reaction?

Perhaps because . . . he'd forgotten about them for a precious moment. He'd not been in control of the narrative, and realized suddenly that if he asked a woman to share his life, all the pleasant fictions he'd created for himself would not last for long.

It had also been what he'd sensed behind her touch, what he'd seen in the eyes that'd stared up at him with astonishment, but not fear.

She wanted to pity him.

She needed a reason to think him better than he was. An excuse for his wicked ways.

Well, he had none. His scars were given to him by the same man who'd shot and killed her father, and if he was going to wed and bed her, that was a conversation best left alone.

Forever.

Samantha had done a few perilous things in her life, but this had to be among the worst. One misstep could mean an absolute, humiliating disaster.

Just what in the nine levels of hell had she gotten herself into?

She made slow progress toward the Earl of Thorne's window, half hobbling, half hopping with the chamber pot she'd retched into that morning clutched carefully in both hands. She had the bed sheets wrapped around her, and it was as difficult trying not to trip over them as it was not to spill the disgusting contents of the pot. Putting any weight on her leg hurt enough to evoke beads of sweat on her brow and upper lip. Tears stung her eyes, but she gritted her teeth and persevered, because the alternative was unthinkable.

The thought of the Earl of Thorne, her fiancé, catching her thus not only mortified her.

It terrified her.

What if she repulsed him? Or worse, what if he guessed her condition?

Dear God, she'd pulled a few stunts in her day, but this . . . this beat them all.

Reaching the wall, she leaned heavily upon it, muttering a rare request to heaven in hopes that no one lingered beneath the window. She used her elbow for leverage, and set the chamber pot on the stone ledge as she opened the casement and peeked down to the grounds of Inverthorne to check for any unsuspecting victims below.

What she found was paradise.

Had she not known better, she'd have thought Inverthorne a castle in the clouds. Indeed, dense swirls of silver and white mist as thick as bales of lamb's wool hovered over both the forest to the north, and the moors to the south below the window. A pale, brilliant sky met the darker blue of the ocean on a distant horizon to the west, beyond which Samantha understood were the Hebrides. The wild green isles were visible from Ravencroft, but not from the long shores of Gairloch and Inverthorne lands.

Winter scented the air with frost and evergreens and juniper. The camphorlike essence mixed with the damp chill, and miraculously stilled her unsettled stomach. Closing her eyes, she inhaled what felt like the first deep breath she'd taken in years.

This. This place. This handsome castle in the clouds. Its towers of gray stone had lorded over the Highland mist for longer than the country in which she was born ever existed. It had withstood epic sea gales, invasions, and brutal sieges.

That had to count for something, didn't it? Maybe . . . maybe she could find sanctuary here. What had Alison called it?

Comraich.

What a lovely word. She wondered if it would be

extended to someone like her. Not Alison Ross, an orphaned Scottish heiress, but Samantha Masters, an orphaned nobody.

No, worse than that. A thief. A liar.

A murderer.

As she stared, unblinking, down into the vapor, Samantha had never in her life wished harder to be someone else. Not somewhere else, living another life. But here. Now. In this chamber belonging to quite possibly the most arrogant, most beautiful man ever created of the earth and mist and fortified by fire.

But not as Samantha Masters. As someone elegant and graceful, ladylike and seductive with buckets of—what was the word Mena Mackenzie had used?—ah, yes. Accomplishments. What if she were someone who could entice a man such as Gavin St. James to be more than *somewhat faithful*?

Emitting a self-loathing sound, she scowled down at the covered chamber pot, gripping the handles in preparation to empty it, keenly aware of a few calluses on the pads of her palms pressed against the smooth porcelain.

Christ, when had she become so sentimental and foolish? Marriage to Lord Thorne was a very unlikely long-term solution. It was a means to an end, a desperate grasp for survival. She knew next to nothing about him, only that he was an unscrupulous scoundrel, a notorious rake, a relentless rival, and . . . a man of his word.

She didn't understand exactly how she knew that. She just did. She felt it in that place unpolluted by desire or distrust. That place that recognized the verisimilitude in his vow to protect her once she belonged to him.

She muttered a low curse every time she was forced to accept that she needed protection at the moment. That her child needed it. Needed *him*. But only for now. Once she healed. Once the baby arrived. Once she was paid her first and maybe her second annuity.

Once Gavin had tired of her . . . which he undoubtably would.

She could consider her choices.

The ancient hinges of the chamber door protested movement in the late morning chill. In a thoughtless panic, Samantha shoved the entire chamber pot out the window, simultaneously allowing the sheet to drop from her body.

"Shit," she cussed. "Goddammit." She watched the pot disappear into the mist with something akin to fascinated horror, before whirling to face Gavin and groping for a viable reason to be up and about on her screaming leg just as desperately as she groped for the bedclothes.

First, she'd need to gauge just how much he'd seen of—

The figure framed in the stone arch stymied her speechless. A woman. A small, delicately beautiful woman with lush hair the precise color of the sand about eighty miles east of where she'd grown up. The place where the sun-baked Nevada desert met the stretch of salt flats.

A melange of dark gold, laced with striations of white was styled and coiffed to perfection. The woman stood still and straight as a china doll, and she gave Samantha the impression of similar fragility. Her skin had surely never touched the sun, and when she drifted into the chamber, her feet didn't seem to touch the ground.

"Is everything all right, Miss Ross?" Her accent was a softer version than that of the Highlands men Samantha was used to, laced with touching feminine concern.

No. She couldn't think of one thing about this situation that even approached the realm of all right.

But she was alive. She'd survived. And that was a place to start.

"I'm just fine, thank you." Samantha lied carefully.

"That surprises me. I can't imagine that any woman who'd fought off malefactors almost entirely on her own, was shot in the process, and then proposed to all in the course of one night could resemble anything close to fine." The lady's delicate nose twitched a little, and she turned her face to the window. "Are you ill, Miss Ross?"

Two things became very apparent to Samantha the moment the elegant woman turned her face toward the window, revealing stunning eyes the color of dappled oak leaves. First, that the woman was blind.

And second, that she was Gavin St. James's mother.

They didn't resemble each other in the least. Gavin was sculpted of steel and sin, and this woman was naught but an ethereal whisper. But those eyes. Those unbelievably green eyes. They were unmistakable.

"No . . . I . . . um . . ." Samantha turned, and then gripped the ledge with gritted teeth at the stab of pain the movement caused. When she could breathe again, she closed the windows with the hand she wasn't using to clutch the sheets to her, secured the latch, and contemplated closing the shutters, as well. Immediately she felt foolish, the lighting wouldn't matter, not to her guest.

And, thankfully, neither would her nudity.

"There was a draft," she finished lamely, cursing the obvious tension that escaped on the words.

Her visitor's face remained placid as she took three more steps and reached out for the high back of a chair, one of a handsome set arranged artfully by the fireplace that could have comfortably housed a small family.

"Worry not, dear. It's always a bit blustery out to the west. 'Tis why all the outbuildings are over on the other side of Inverthorne, so they can be protected by the structure and its high walls from the buffeting of the sea. Nothing but the moors and bogs out this side of the tower all the way down to the beach. Though that makes the view bonnier, does it not?"

There was that word again, "bonny."

"Sure." Samantha had the idea that the woman was babbling, though why the fine lady had reason to be nervous was beyond comprehension. She breathed a sigh of relief, confident her erstwhile chamber pot had a good chance of remaining hidden in the bogs. Thus encouraged, she began the painful journey back over the cold stones toward the bed. "Are you—are you looking for Lord Thorne?" she asked through teeth clenched with pain. "I'm not sure where he's gone off to."

God, she was ridiculous. Caught out half naked in her fiancé's room by his sweet, blind mother while trying to rid herself of the evidence of a most terrible deceit.

Dear Christ, what if the woman thought they were in love?

"I didn't come to see my son. I came to meet the woman he's about to make his wife." The lady smiled at where Samantha had been three hobbles ago.

"Oh! My God—I mean gosh—*goodness*. Of course. He must have told you before he left." Shit, had she just cussed in front of a marchioness? "I'm . . . Alison Ross, but my friends call me Sam." She felt like she should do something. Curtsy?

No, not to a blind woman! Christ. What was the matter with her? She should probably go shake her hand or . . . kiss it or something, but walking the span of the grand master suite might as well have been paddling across the Atlantic. Her leg was going to give out any moment now. And all she needed to do was reach that damn bed. Suddenly she changed her mind about the laudanum. She'd give her right arm for a healthy dose right about now.

"And I am Lady Eleanor Megan Mackenzie." Running her hand along the chair, Lady Eleanor drifted forward, reaching out for the next chair, finding it, and letting it guide her toward the bed, as well. "But you can call me Mother, if you'd like. That is, if your mother wouldn't object."

Samantha suddenly ached to aid the poor woman, but as close as she was to collapse, she'd rather make it to safety.

Mother. She'd never called anyone that before.

"My mother passed," Samantha explained simply, knowing it was true of Alison, as well.

"I knew her," Lady Eleanor said, her lashes sweeping down. "I was always so sorry . . ." She let that thought trail away, before picking up another thread of their previous conversation. "Gavin didn't tell me he was considering a match between the two of you, but there's little in this castle that a blind woman doesn't hear."

Reaching the bed, Samantha collapsed onto it with a sigh that quickly became a moan as she scooted toward the headboard with only the strength of her arms. The bedclothes were in complete disarray, but she was covered and warm enough, so she couldn't summon the strength to care as she lay there, panting and hurting, wishing the kind woman would leave and alternately not wanting to be alone.

"You're . . . a Mackenzie, not a St. James?" she queried, plucking the first question out of the nebulous of them drifting just beyond her pain and mortification.

Samantha had the impression that Lady Eleanor was counting as she took measured steps toward the bed, her silvery, diaphanous gown magically insinuating that she was some sort of floating angel.

Once she reached the bed, she perched on the edge ever

so delicately before answering. "St. James was my maiden name. I'm unable to extract myself from the Mackenzie as Gavin has done. I am the dowager Marchioness of Ravencroft, after all. A distinction I cannot escape, I'm afraid."

"I'm sorry." It was all Samantha could think to say.

"I feel as though I rather earned the title." Lady Eleanor smothered a bleak expression with another of her soft, polite smiles.

"Oh."

They were both silent an uncomfortable moment.

"It is no secret why Gavin should like to so suddenly marry you, Miss Ross," Lady Eleanor began. "You are from an old and respected family, and we both understand how desperately he desires Erradale."

Good, so she knew it was a marriage of convenience. That uncomplicated things a great deal.

"The question is, why would you agree to marry my son? Has he . . . gotten you into trouble?" she asked meaningfully. "Does it have anything to do with what you tossed out the window?"

"Well . . . er . . ." Dammit. Was this some kind of a nightmare?

"Are you in love with him?" The dowager hurried on, blessedly saving her from the previous question.

Samantha agonized over what to tell her. Ultimately, she chose the truth, as she could really only stand so many lies at once.

"No. I do not love him." Hell, she barely liked him. "But I . . . but we need each other."

"I believe that's for the best."

Samantha gaped at the woman, thinking she couldn't be more shocked if God reached down and miraculously restored her sight.

"Don't misunderstand me, Sam—I hope I may call you Sam, as I dearly wish that we will be friends—but while my son is an unfailingly good man, he'll make a terrible husband if you expect love, devotion, or forgive me, fidelity from him."

"I don't," Samantha whispered.

Lady Eleanor nodded her approval. "It isn't his fault, you know." She invoked the chorus of many a mother with a roguish son. "It's not that he has his father in him. I don't believe that he'll ever harm you physically. But . . . he was—is—such a sweet boy. And his tender heart has been broken simply too many times, you see, there are too many pieces for him to give away."

The expression on Lady Eleanor's face was so painfully earnest, Samantha forgot herself for a moment and reached for the woman's hand. "I understand, Lady Eleanor— Mother—Gavin and I have an arrangement, nothing more. In truth, if he gave me his heart I—I don't know if I'd have anything to give back."

"For that I am both sorry and grateful." Lady Eleanor smiled forlornly.

Samantha couldn't remember ever having such a candid discussion with a friend, let alone a veritable stranger. It was both unsettling and wondrous and unspeakably sad.

"I'll admit to some excitement when Alice told me we were welcoming a gunslinger into the family," the dowager continued. "What an ordeal you've suffered. I'd be nigh catatonic in your place."

"I was lucky your son found me when he did." Samantha was glad Lady Eleanor couldn't see her flush of pleasure at the rare compliment. "Who is Alice?" she asked, never truly comfortable at being the subject of a conversation.

"She's my companion and maid. For a woman with my

particular ailment, she's no less than invaluable. She's my eyes and sometimes my ears, and she's heard a great deal about you."

"Like what?" Samantha asked nervously.

"Like that you're clever and capable and brave. That you're an unparalleled horsewoman and—apparently—a crack shot. That my son finds you infuriating, but that he calls you bonny."

"Oh . . ." Samantha brought a hand to her burning cheeks, wishing she could be just a tiny bit more verbose and erudite than one of the gutted fish Callum was in the habit of leaving for her.

"I wish we'd met back when . . ." Lady Eleanor's eyes closed and remained that way, as though hiding a secret pain. "As a girl I was considered the best horsewoman from Cape Wrath to Argyll. But that was before . . . before I married Laird Ravencroft. I'd have showed you the very best riding paths along the moors, and taken you to the highest point of Gresham Peak, where it seems that you could almost see across the whole of the Highlands, all the way to Inverness."

So Lady Eleanor hadn't always been blind. Samantha burned to ask her what happened, but something told her she would regret the answer the moment she learned it.

A door bounded against the stone, announcing an interloper, and Samantha jumped just as violently as Lady Eleanor did.

"It has been always said the women of Wester Ross are the most beautiful outside of Tyr na Nog, and here be the evidence right in front of me, not that I doubted it." The years Eammon Monahan had spent in Scotland did next to nothing to change his Irish brogue, and Sam was very glad. For he was as lyrically jovial as his son, Callum, was enigmatic. It was obvious that the lines at his eyes had been grooved by smiles rather than scowls. Unlike Callum, his beard was more gray than red, and matched his darker hair not at all. He was like his voice, big, merry, and approachably handsome.

"Beauty i-is not a-always a blessing, Mr. Monahan." Eleanor's grip tightened to crushing around Samantha's fingers, though she kept her features and voice schooled into the very picture of passivity.

Strange, the woman hadn't struggled with a stutter before.

"And beauty is not always encompassed by the scope of what the eye can perceive, is it, my lady?" He addressed the dowager marchioness, but winked at Samantha, who pulled the counterpane up to cover her bare shoulders.

Lady Eleanor fell silent, her shoulders curling forward, and her sternum doing its best to kiss her spine as she seemed to deflate. It was a protective gesture. A way of making herself seem smaller, unthreatening.

Eammon regarded the woman for a silent, compelling moment. His familiar golden eyes moved over her elegant frame as though reading her like the page of a book he couldn't put down.

Samantha saw Callum in his father's look. The long-denied yearning. The unbreachable loneliness. What did Callum long for? she wondered. Or who? Because with Eammon, the answer was readily apparent.

"I'm after checking on my patient," the Irishman sang. "Someone tried to poke holes in all of you at Erradale, and I did my best to sew you back together. 'Tis a wonder they missed Locryn if you ask me, as you'd think he'd be the easiest target." He patted his own belly beneath his vest, only a mild testament to a love of evening ale and sweet rolls.

Despite her pain, Samantha joined him in a short laugh.

"You should have seen him, Mr. Monahan. For a man so short and round, he sure can move."

"Aye, well. Desperation makes us do all sorts of things we'd not thought ourselves capable of," he stated blithely, blinking quizzically when Samantha's smile disappeared.

"I—I'll be going." Lady Eleanor stood, the once graceful lady moving as though her bones and joints were trying to remember how.

"And leave this one with a strange man in a bedroom with no chaperone?" Eammon teased, his tone a strange mixture of aghast levity.

"You're hardly a stranger, Mr. Monahan," Lady Eleanor said patiently, inching along the wall.

"I am to the lass," Eammon argued merrily. "And I'll have to lift her nightgown to the knee to check the stitches. If that's not enough to cause a scandal, I can't think of what is, can you? What would your son say? Better yet, what would the queen say?"

"I'm not wearing a night—" Sam clamped her lips shut the moment Eammon's pleading eyes met hers.

Eleanor hesitated. "I—I could get Alice . . ."

The man's brawny shoulders deflated much in the way Eleanor's had done only moments before. "It's all right, my lady," he crooned softly, as though speaking to a skittish filly. "I'll fetch her for you. She's all the way down in the kitchens, and . . . that's a lot of stairs for you to navigate on your own."

He set the bag in his hand down at the foot of the bed and turned to leave.

"Will it take you long?" Samantha queried, allowing more of the pain she was in slip into her voice than was strictly necessary. "I foolishly tried to walk on my leg this morning, and now it feels like a fire poker ran it clean through."

"Och, nay." Lady Eleanor made an exquisitely feminine sound of distress and returned to the bed, groping for her hand and clutching it when she found it. "I didn't ken you were in such pain, lass. Mr. Monahan, Eammon, you must see what is wrong immediately. Do you think it's infection? Are you feverish, Sam?"

Samantha flashed a conspiratorial look at Eammon, who squinted at her with a skeptical glance of which she'd seen the identical like in the eyes of his son.

A soft, motherly hand traced from her wrist, up her arm, her shoulder, and found her forehead, checking for a rise in temperature and finding none.

"I don't think so," Samantha said pathetically. "It just . . . hurts. Will you stay and hold my hand?"

"Oh, aye, lass. I'd not leave you in pain." She clucked again before asking anxiously, "Is there aught you can do, Eammon?"

Samantha didn't miss that Eleanor had forgotten to address the stable master as "Mr. Monahan" twice now.

"Aye," Eammon said slowly as Samantha fought a smile and tugged the blanket above her knee, revealing her bandages. Scandal be damned, it really *did* hurt, but not as bad as that time she'd tripped and fallen on the red branding iron when she'd been naught more than a gangly girl of fifteen who hadn't yet learned to control her long limbs. Now she sported a Circle T branded sideways on her hip as an eternal reminder of what pain really was.

"How is Calybrid?" she asked as a gentle hand with rough skin held her ankle still while the other undid her bandages.

"He was awake and thirsty this morning, and bleating curses at Locryn like an ornery old ewe," Eammon answered. "I don't at all think this is the end of that old bas—" He stiffened, catching himself in time. "Bloke," he finished lamely, glancing up at Eleanor, who still smoothed over Samantha's brow.

"I'm glad," Samantha answered. "He's become a friend." She hissed in a breath of true pain when Eammon's fingers tested the skin around the stitches.

"There's no swelling or redness," Eammon remarked with satisfaction. "'Tis a good sign, lass. Would ye like any more laudanum before I reapply the salve?"

Samantha shook her head, making a face. "I think it made me sick this morning." Not a complete lie, but she knew it was now time to keep her wits about her. Pain or no pain.

"Aye, it'll do that to some. Best to avoid it if you can, lest you develop a taste for the stuff."

Another word he'd said struck her. "Salve?"

"Just something I concocted to use on the horses when they're injured. Keeps them from going lame. Miracle stuff, this." He fetched a tub of a repulsive-looking gelatinous substance the color of bog mud, and dipped his fingers into it.

"What's in it?" Both Samantha and Eleanor wrinkled their noses at the smell.

"Just some garlic, lavender, honey, blessed thistle, and . . ." He squinted a little, as though debating something. "A few things you need not worry about overmuch."

"But—"

Samantha hissed as he plopped a generous portion of it onto her wound, and then glared at him as though he'd betrayed her, promising retribution. And after she'd guilted Eleanor into sticking around and everything!

White teeth flashed at her from behind his beard, and his big shoulders lifted as though to say, the damage had already been done, she might as well allow it.

Samantha had to admit, after the first initial shock,

some of the throbbing in her calf did abate after the application of the dubious substance.

"Worry not, lass, the wound isn't as deep as we feared. The bullet grazed you by instead of poked you through. More a cut than a hole, which will heal faster, and did less damage to the muscle."

"Oh, that's excellent news," Eleanor breathed, patting Samantha's hand.

That it was, Samantha agreed. Being helpless was bound to make her mad. If she couldn't walk, then she couldn't run.

And something told her she'd need to run before long. Because if her lies didn't catch up with her, the Masters brothers might. As much as she relied on Gavin's offer of protection, she didn't want to bank on it for longer than she had to.

Just in case . . .

In case her instincts about him turned out to be as terrible as they had about the first charming, beautiful man she'd married.

Samantha decided to save a brood for a more private time, as Eammon's attempt to charm Lady Eleanor distracted her.

"Did ye know, my lady, that Great Scot sired another foal?"

Samantha suspected Eleanor had carefully constructed her placid façade during her years as the wife of the dreaded Laird Hamish Mackenzie.

"That is welcome news," Eleanor said politely.

"They named him Great Scot's Ghost, and what do you think of that?"

"How clever."

"And . . . uh . . . he's a bright lad. Friendly, too. Softest ears I ever stroked, like those fine velvet chairs I carried to your solarium a few months ago. Might welcome an apple or some sugar cubes if you and Alice are ever inclined to come by the stables during your three o'clock walk."

"I don't much have use for the stables anymore, Mr. Monahan," Lady Eleanor murmured.

Eammon nodded, swallowing loudly enough to be heard as his large, meaty hands deftly dressed Samantha's leg with a fresh bandage.

"Aye, well . . . your son's fiancée rides astride, I've heard tell."

Lady Eleanor's winged brows lowered. "Is that true, Sam?"

Samantha nodded, feeling like an outsider in this interaction. "Might not be proper, but it's safer," she offered by way of explanation.

"It is, at that," Eammon agreed. "Just about anyone could stay aloft, if they had the right mount."

"I would never have been allowed to . . ." Lady Eleanor trailed off.

"Well, you are mistress of your own mind now," Eammon said softly. "You could do what you like."

"So I am." Eleanor thought on that for a moment as Eammon finished his work and retrieved his bag.

"I think you can keep your leg, young lady."

"Praise be." She returned his cheeky smile with one of her own.

"I'm leaving you a dollop of this sleeping drought for tonight if the pain gets to you. And I hear congratulations are in order. Never thought our Lord Thorne would be enticed to the altar."

"Not so much enticed as contracted," she clarified with a look that assured him that she was more a coconspirator than coerced.

"Even so. Let me know if there is aught I can do." He

stood to take his leave, reaching down to take her hand in a firm shake. "Miss Ross."

"Mr. Monahan."

He hesitated about what he did next, and then his jaw set behind his beard in firm resolve. "My Lady." Before Lady Eleanor could protest, he caught her hand in his and bent to press a lingering kiss to her pale, delicate knuckle.

She gasped, but didn't move, her sightless eyes round as jade tea saucers.

Samantha enjoyed the look of pleasure on his face so intensely, that she couldn't stop herself from saying, "Mr. Monahan, if Alice is downstairs, would you very much mind escorting my mother-in-law down to her?"

"Oh no!" Eleanor surged to her feet. "That is, I couldn't impose upon Mr. Monahan's precious time."

"I would be delighted." Eammon recovered his wits faster than she'd thought he would after such a shock.

"As he said, Mother, that's a lot of stairs," Samantha reasoned innocently. "And it's been so long since I've eaten . . . maybe you could ask the kitchen to send me something to settle my stomach?"

"Yes, but—I could wait for . . ." Eleanor folded her hands in front of her, and Samantha didn't miss that she covered the hand that had been kissed with the other, not as though to scrub the kiss away, but to protect it.

Eammon took her delicate hand once more, and tucked it into the crook of his arm, gallant as any lordly gentleman, even in his workshirt and vest. "Haven't you waited long enough?"

It was Eleanor's turn to audibly swallow, but after a breathless moment, she took her first hesitant step forward, the long-legged Eammon allowing her to lead the way.

"Thank you, Mr. Monahan, for everything," Samantha called.

Eammon looked back at her from the doorway, regarding her as though she'd worked a miracle. "Thank *you*," he said softly.

Samantha settled back into pillows soft as down clouds and breathed in the scent of the man to whom they belonged as she listened to the couple make their way down the echoing halls of Inverthorne.

"Tell me, Mr. Monahan, was Great Scot's foal as dark a gold as he is?" the dowager asked, politeness overtaking her terror.

"That's just it, my lady," came the husky, delighted reply. "He's more white than gold, but for a bit at the mane and tail."

"Which is why they named him Ghost?"

"Aye, you have the right of it."

"I believe I like that name . . ." Their voices faded with distance.

Samantha looked around her, at the chamber in which the legendary Earl of Thorne took his legions of lovers to this very bed. It was different than she'd suspected it would be. No silks or velvets or draperies done in lascivious colors.

His chamber was a testament to a restless, masculine hunter. Furs stretched beneath the chair by the fire in place of a carpet. Various landscape tapestries insulated what would have been cold stone walls. Strange and foreign figurines, sculptures, and sketches littered the surfaces of very simple but finely crafted furniture. From Africa, she wondered, or India, perhaps?

She couldn't believe Gavin St. James slept here. She'd expected something fit for Casanova or King Louis XIV or some other famous libertine.

Inverthorne was very different than she'd been led to believe.

Much like its lord.

Sure, he was a selfish opportunist. A charming schemer. An enterprising rake. A beautiful fallen angel. But he was also just a man. A man with a family who loved him.

A man with a broken heart.

CHAPTER SIXTEEN

Samantha should have known the moment she'd woken the next morning to the rain, that her wedding would be a disaster. Wasn't it supposed to be a bad omen to have rain on one's wedding day?

Of course, it had been relentlessly sunny when she'd signed papers and spoken vows with Bennett, so there went the omen theory. Maybe the curse belonged to her, and had nothing at all to do with the weather.

Certainly seemed more likely.

Upon waking, she was again examined by Eammon, who announced her on the mend and had left her a cane should she attempt to walk. Immediately, she had left to seek out a washroom and toss the contents of her stomach into that, like proper folk.

She found that the cane worked passably well. In fact, she'd been able to hobble back to her breakfast tray and keep down a slice of toast spread with Devonshire cream and preserves, drink an entire pot of scalding tea, and clean her teeth before collapsing into a chair with exhaustion.

God, but she was glad there was no long walk up the aisle; she probably wouldn't make it.

She'd seen neither hide nor hair of her husband-to-be since he'd returned the previous afternoon to inform her that his brother, the Marquess of Ravencroft, would arrive this evening to officiate their marriage.

She attempted to read near the fire for a while, and then tried to nap, as she seemed to tire more easily than usual. After a couple of hours, a lonely restlessness drove her to her feet.

Using a throw blanket as a shawl, she limped to the door, pulled it open on hinges that had probably needed oiling since the Jacobite rebellion, and peeked her head around the corner. Finding the hall empty, she ventured forth, teeth gritted against the pain in her leg, as well as the cold of the stones on her bare feet.

Luckily, she was a woman used to discomfort.

Inverthorne's west tower only sported three doors, and then a short hall that led to stairs that spiraled below. Using the wall to help support her descent, she marveled at the feel of the ancient stone abrading her fingertips. She wondered if any of the chinks and groves had been made by implements of war.

Sweat slicked her palms and upper lip by the time she'd descended three stories. Her leg felt like a few scorpions were taking their wrath out on it, but the sight she found when she reached the ground floor of Inverthorne rooted her like a hundred-year-old tree.

Gavin stood in profile, framed by the arch of the great entry. He was dressed in the most dapper, expensive-looking suit she'd ever clapped her eyes on, staring intently at whatever was in front of him, which was blocked from her vantage on the stairs by a half-wall.

Breath escaped her in a swift whoosh that left her jaw gaping open.

The rain made more sense now, as his beauty was such to make the angels weep. In a dark suit and trousers, his neck swathed in white-tie finery, his magnificence was impossibly elevated from untried and untamed to no less than diabolical.

His lambent hair had been trimmed and shaped with just the right amount of pomade. The ever-present stubble removed from his sharp jaw revealed his dimpled chin with even more stark, cruel precision.

Had she not been leaning heavily on the stones, she would have fallen.

Falling for Gavin St. James. Just like legions of women had before her, and many women would hereafter.

She'd do well to remember that. To remember it was not her right to ask him where he'd slept last night, because that wasn't part of the bargain. If he promised to be only somewhat faithful after they were married, then what did that mean the night before?

And why would she care?

She didn't, of course.

She cared about nothing but safety for her and for the child that grew inside her.

A few immaculately dressed footmen bustled about. The butler, too, approached from the west hall and nodded to his lord before disappearing behind the half-wall.

Samantha studied him for an unguarded moment, a motionless mountain amid a sea of vibrant energy, as still as the suit of armor that stood to attention behind him. He looked more serious than she'd ever seen him. More sinister. Cruel even, a dark sort of anticipation—or apprehension? Dread?—holding dangerous tension in the broad shoulders that bunched high enough, his neck all but disappeared.

The muscles of his jaw flexed ever so slightly, and a vein pulsed at his temple. His mouth, that sinful mouth so often curled in a lazy, sensual smirk, twitched as though holding back words that battled to be free of him.

A strange, feminine part of her ached to call out to him, to go to him and shape her hand to his jaw, to coax it to relax.

To tell him that whatever furrowed his perfect brow would be all right.

What a fool she was, not because of the impulse, but because she almost did it, but what stopped her, surprisingly, was his name.

What did she call him now? Certainly not Lord Thorne, she'd die before calling him lord again. But Gavin? Were they on those terms? They'd have to be after tonight, she supposed.

After they consummated their marriage.

The sound of a heavy, antique bolt-lock being thrown aside interrupted an impending collapse at the thought of sharing a bed with him.

Samantha watched in astounded fascination as the brooding, savage Highlander she'd been spying on transformed in front of her eyes. His smile appeared first, and then he remembered to unclench his jaw and peel his shoulders away from his ears. He rolled them a few times and shook out his white-gloved hands that she just realized had been clenched into fists at his sides.

His brow released last, drawing a smile from a scowl.

He was like an actor about to step on the stage. His every movement practiced and meaningful, his every line memorized for the greatest effect.

For a terrifying moment, Samantha wondered just whom she was marrying. The menacing man who'd seized her hand when she'd reached for his back? The one who'd just faced the door with all the readiness of a barbaric horde calling for blood.

Or the charming hedonist he pretended to be?

"English!" he greeted warmly, his wicked grin intensifying to devilish.

English? Samantha limped forward another step. Just who was he speaking to?

"Dear Thorne," a husky feminine voice greeted, matching him in warmth. "What a thorough pleasure. I know this is mostly a formality, but I simply couldn't miss your wedding day."

Samantha recognized that crisp, perfect British accent the split-second before Mena Mackenzie swept into view, draped in wine-red velvet, both her hands extended toward the apparently delighted Lord Thorne.

Gavin pulled the marchioness scandalously close, and lowered his head to plant a kiss on the woman's lush lips.

Samantha's unbidden sound of protest was covered by an equally inarticulate noise.

A growl, if she wasn't mistaken.

To her credit, Lady Ravencroft turned her head just in time to receive his kiss on her cheek. In doing so, she caught sight of Samantha, and quickly stepped out of Gavin's clutches.

"Oh, hello again, Miss Ross." She wiped at her cheek, looking a bit abashed, if not exactly guilty.

"Lady Ravencroft." The cold clip to her words surprised her as much as it did anyone else, Samantha figured. But sharp suspicion needled at her with surprising strength.

Gavin's head swiveled much like an owl's, and he speared

her with a look so bright with unidentifiable meaning, she swallowed and fought an instinctual step backward.

"You're not supposed to be down here," he said through his teeth, all pretense of charm slipping for the space of a dangerous moment.

Samantha had to pretend that his obvious displeasure at her presence didn't sting.

A dark brogue sounded from the doorway, thick with snide sarcasm. "If that's a sample of yer famous charm, Thorne, then 'tis a good thing ye're handsome."

"Liam, you told me you were going to behave," Mena said over her shoulder to the man still hidden behind the stones. She glided toward Samantha while pulling black kid gloves from her fingers. "Surely Gavin meant he wasn't supposed to see the bride before the wedding. Not only is it bad luck, it's rather wicked."

"See her in what? My mother's nightgown? That hardly counts, nor does it necessarily inspire wicked thoughts." Gavin made a dismissive gesture with his shoulders, his artificial smile reaffixed, though he swiftly overtook Mena in her quest to be at Samantha's side. "Besides, luck has nothing to do with why we're here today, so it's better we just get on with it."

Get on with it, Samantha thought glumly. His words would have hurt if she didn't entirely share the sentiment.

His gaze confused her, though. In direct contrast to his cold words, it lingered where her shawl revealed her clavicles and a few open buttons. For a moment his veneer slipped, and something a little like hunger tightened his features and fists.

"I'll have you know, I came in search of something *other* than your mother's nightgown to wear." She'd have planted her hands on her hips if she were able to let go of her cane. "I assume my entire trousseau was burned in the fire, and if you want to marry me in this getup while you're dressed like some French dandy then I'll need— *Oomph!*"

She didn't know he'd planned to scoop her off her feet until he'd done just that. Hell, he didn't even break stride. One moment she was on the ground, and the next she was draped over the swells of his biceps like a sandbag as he hauled her back up the spiral steps.

"Put me down," she demanded, a little breathlessly.

"Nay." His teeth had yet to separate, and Samantha knew somewhere back in that protective part of herself that a smarter woman would be afraid. But . . .

"Don't you fucking tell me *nay*." She mimicked his word rather terribly. "And while we're on the subject, where are my guns?"

"*Haud yer wheesht,* woman."

"Hold your own wished."

"Och, I like her." The Laird's chuckle followed them up the stairs and did exactly nothing for Gavin's dark mood.

"It's not like ye need a *real* wedding dress," he explained in the fashion of a parent running out of patience. Though how he could maintain his even breath while hauling her up three floors' worth of stairs was beyond her. "Alice was supposed to set one of my mother's pale frocks out for ye this morning and do the necessary alterations."

"Well, she didn't," Samantha spat, wriggling in his un-yielding grip. "I haven't seen a single soul but Eammon since yesterday. Including *you*," she added for good measure, painfully aware she sounded like a plaintive lover. "I've had nothing but a sponge bath since the fire. There's probably still soot in my hair, though you can't smell it over the aroma of the bog mud Eammon keeps slathering on my leg. And I'm not asking for a wedding dress or anything, but a clean pair of knickers would be nice as I'm currently not wearing any at all."

The sure-footed Highlander stumbled, paused, and glowered down at her with enough fire to set the stones ablaze.

"*Shite,*" he muttered under his breath, following that with a slew of words she'd never before heard but absolutely understood.

Samantha decided right then and there to learn Gaelic. It was apparently a lovely language for cussing, as he was able to fill the tower hall with blistering curses, all the way to his chamber door.

"Are you having an affair with the second Lady Ravencroft, as well?" As with many words, she regretted them the moment they'd escaped, and not only because he nearly dropped her a second time.

"With *Mena*?" The dubious curl of his lip went a long way toward soothing her pride that shouldn't have been ruffled in the first place. "Not that it's yer business, but why the hell would ye think that? Because she's my brother's wife?"

"Because the way you held and attempted to kiss her was the farthest thing from a show of brotherly affection."

"Not necessarily." He smirked. "As my doing so was entirely for my brother's benefit."

"Oh, you mean . . . you were merely antagonizing him?"

"And I didna mean for ye to see it." It wasn't an apology, but close enough. Samantha couldn't think of a time anyone had told her they were sorry, and it didn't seem that the thread was about to break.

Not that he owed her one, she reminded herself sternly.

"He sounded antagonized to me, if that means anything," she encouraged, summoning a half-smile for him. "He actually growled at you."

Thorne stopped in the middle of his vast chamber and tilted his chin to look down at her, the wisp of a genuine smile melting some of the sardonic ire in his smirk. She was beginning to tell when he was genuinely pleased with her, because a dimple appeared in his left cheek. "Aye, that he did."

Samantha's neck shook with strain from holding it aloft in this position, and she gave in to the instinct to rest it on his shoulder before she realized the affection the gesture might convey. "My neck," she explained quickly. Wondering why he hadn't put her down.

Wondering why she didn't want him to.

They stood like that for a silent moment. Well, *he* stood, and she nestled into the cradle of his arms feeling very small, and oddly safe.

It was queer to explore another's body with parts other than your fingertips.

His shoulder against her cheek was round and firm beneath the fine fabric of his jacket. His biceps swelled beneath her back and the crooks of her legs, taut with the strain of her weight. His lean torso pressed firmly against her sides, rippling with strength.

When she next glanced up at him, his eyes flashed with a ferocious and savage green storm that seemed to brand her with equal parts trepidation and titillation. "Ye gods, but do I wish this day were done with," he muttered fiercely.

This day. Their wedding day.

Something he apparently dreaded.

When she was alone, she'd have to have a good long talk with herself about allowing his flippant words to make her chest ache. This was Gavin *fucking* St. James, the most famous libertine since Caligula. He'd tuckered out more French whores than Benjamin Franklin.

Of course he didn't *want* to get married. Not really. He just wanted to sign a land deal that came with a passably beddable heiress whom he could stash wherever and go right back to being whatever the Gaelic word for Lothario was.

Which was fine with her. Really.

So why the hell wasn't he putting her *down*?

A soft knock sounded at the door, and Samantha grasped on to Gavin as he whirled around.

Lady Ravencroft tentatively pushed the door open, and Samantha was surprised to see a footman with a trunk lingering behind her.

"I hope I'm not intruding, but when I heard about what happened to Erradale yesterday, I very much worried that you might have lost your belongings in the fire." She ventured into the chamber, her jade gaze touching on everything and registering the same surprise at the simple, masculine contents as Samantha herself had shown.

Samantha couldn't say why, but it pleased her to note this was obviously the first time Mena Mackenzie had been in this room.

The marchioness motioned for the footman to set the trunk down.

"Of course, everything in my wardrobe would look as large as a circus tent on you, but my husband has a grown daughter, Rhianna, who inherited the Mackenzie height. I brought some of her skirts and blouses and such from before she . . . matured. She's not quite so lean as you are, but I have a few sashes and belts that would help ensure everything fits."

In a few long strides, Gavin took Samantha to the bed

and gingerly set her down before turning back to the expectant marchioness.

"Ye are an angel, English," he declared. "Much too good for the likes of the Demon Highlander."

"So they keep telling me," she replied with an impish wink. "Now do go away and leave us girls alone. I'll have your bride presentable within the half hour."

"I'll return to collect her when ye send for me," he vowed, and closed the door behind him.

Presentable. That's as good as she could ever hope for. Most especially in contrast to Mena's stunning and voluptuous beauty. The marchioness reminded her of some of the sensational paintings she'd seen at the opera house in Denver the one time she'd gone with Bennett. Lush and luxurious, with soft curves and a come-hither gaze, painted in vivid color from her vibrant red hair to her green eyes.

Even her ivory skin seemed illuminated by some inner light. What, Samantha wondered, created such an effect? Money, maybe? Expensive creams and haberdashery. Happiness?

Love?

"I'll leave her in your . . . capable hands." Gavin took one of those hands and kissed it before shutting the door behind him.

Christ, was she going to have to endure him flirting like this with all women?

Or just the uncommonly lovely ones with the impressive breasts?

The moment they were alone, Mena rushed to her, claiming a place on the mattress beside her, and taking her hand. "I've been worried sick about you ever since Thorne galloped to Ravencroft at dawn yesterday. He said you'd been shot! That Erradale burned to the ground. My God, are you all right?"

"I'm fine. The bullet grazed a bit into the muscle, but I was lucky."

"Thank heavens," Mena continued emphatically. "But *then,* Thorne announced that he was marrying you *today* and Liam had to be the one to perform the ceremony or he'd have to wait for a license from Glasgow. I could have fainted, I tell you. I almost did! Liam only agreed out of sheer stupefied curiosity."

"He's not the only one," Samantha muttered.

Mena gave her a probing look. "You can imagine my surprise at the news, especially after our previous visit not so very long ago."

Samantha considered how best to proceed. She didn't want to make the marchioness suspicious, but neither did she want to seem like she'd fallen under Gavin's spell like so many idiot ninnies before her. "A lot has happened since we talked last," she said carefully.

"If this is about money, or a place to stay, I'll have you know that I've gathered a great many men who are not only willing, but eager to help with your cattle. I was going to call upon you to give you the news. Likewise, you could always come to stay at Ravencroft until Erradale can be inhabited again. Indefinitely, if you need. I've already spoken to Liam about it and he's more than willing."

"To save me from marriage to his brother, you mean."

"I didn't say that." Mena looked away guiltily.

"You didn't have to."

"It's just that . . . I've seen marriages for the sake of land and legacy go very wrong, indeed. Thorne is a good man, but . . . troubled. There are rifts in this family that . . ."

"I know about Colleen," Samantha said softly. "Hell, Gavin's father killed mine. This situation couldn't get more complicated."

Would that were a lie. Things could get much, much messier in a hurry.

Some, if not all, of her jealous ire at Lady Ravencroft evaporated at the earnest look of concern on her face. Would she still make the same offer, Samantha wondered, once her belly began to swell? Or would she turn her out to the cold, as she'd seen so many do, including the Smiths with their own daughter, Clara. The fourteen-year-old pregnant girl had only been welcomed back into the fold when she'd married the reluctant father and "repented her sins."

Samantha had a feeling the Scots, the English, and the Americans were not so very different in their regard of unmarried mothers.

"This wedding is . . . to our mutual benefit," she reassured them both. "I need protection, and help with Erradale."

"But Liam would happily provide—"

"I need a husband," she said firmly. "And the annuity he promised. Inverthorne needs an heir. Frankly, I vowed to keep Erradale out of the hands of the Mackenzie Laird, your husband, which is where it will likely go if I let the court proceedings take place. So today I am marrying Gavin St. James."

"All right, dear." Mena squeezed her hand after anxiously searching her face and finding nothing but rote determination. "Then let's get you dressed."

CHAPTER SEVENTEEN

It occurred to Gavin that the first thought a groom had upon spying his bride shouldn't be to wonder whether or not she wore knickers. By his troth, it'd been all he'd thought about since the admission had left her mouth.

He'd felt like an utter shite for not considering such details before, and was then made a greater bastard for wondering how long he could keep his wee wife's nethers accessibly bare beneath her skirts.

In a room full of people, the knowledge was unbelievably erotic.

Mena preceded Alison into the study where a motley assortment of folks had gathered for the occasion.

Gavin stood to the right of his brother, in a sort of intimation of what an actual wedding would look like. Callum and Eammon in shabby, if clean, Irish colors gathered at his left elbow as witnesses.

His mother was down with a migraine, though he knew Liam's presence to be the true reason for her absence. Ravencroft had inherited the baritone growl of Hamish

Mackenzie, and the sound of it gave her heart dangerous palpitations.

"Ye were supposed to send for me to fetch my bride," Gavin scowled at Lady Ravencroft.

"We managed." Mena opened the door wider. "A woman is owed an entrance on her wedding day."

Gavin had always been rather derisive of any romantic clichés, but the sudden burn in his chest for lack of oxygen had him reassessing his position. For if his breath had been stolen, his bride was undoubtedly the reluctant thief.

The dress was simple, though the woman inside was anything but. A high-necked silk blouse the color of the velvet Highland mists was tucked into an indigo skirt adorned with so many layers, it resembled a waterfall. A wide belt accentuated her impossibly narrow waist, the pewter buckle adorned in the front with the emblem of the Scottish thistle. She wore no other jewelry, though Mena had worked some sort of magic with her luxuriant dark hair, pinning it beneath a simple triangle of long white lace that trailed down her back in place of a veil.

She needed no jewels, for her eyes shone more luminous than any sapphires. Her lips would have shamed rubies. A fresh, unfettered glow seemed to illuminate her sun-kissed skin from beneath.

She wasn't the most classically beautiful woman Gavin had ever seen. Nor was she the most elegant, seductive, nor flawless. She'd a cane instead of a bouquet. Calluses on her fingers instead of diamonds. More challenge in her eyes than seduction. And more sass than honey on her tongue.

But gods, he'd never wanted anyone more.

When she entered the study, her features lit with a brilliance he'd not expected, and for an incandescent moment, his entire being glowed with the pleasure of it.

Until he realized she *wasn't* looking at him.

"Calybrid!" she exclaimed, limping over to the left to where Locryn stood behind the wheelchair they'd once used for Gavin's mother. "You're not well enough to be out of bed."

Calybrid's pallid face split into an unrepentant grimace that *could* have passed for a grin. "If ye're well enough to be married, then I'm well enough to watch Locryn give ye away. Besides, I taught these two bog trotters to throw knives when they were wee lads, so that entitles me to a wedding invitation." He motioned to Gavin and Callum.

"Of course it does!" Her hand went to her mouth in a girlish gesture. "Really, Locryn? You'll give me away?"

"Only if ye keep hold on yer tears, lass," Locryn allowed gruffly, stabbing a commanding finger at her. "I'll not have ye blubbering all over me like some simpering waif. Ye keep yer chin up and *haud yer wheesht,* ye ken?"

"I promise."

"Well, then." Locryn adjusted his tam-o'-shanter cap and patted the little fluffy ball above it before taking her arm. "Let's get this done before Calybrid gives up the ghost and ruins the whole day."

"I'd not give ye the satisfaction of life without me, ye nanny goat," Calybrid wheezed, and then clutched his side for an alarming moment before finding a more comfortable position. "Ye're dying first and that's the end of it."

"We'll just see about that." Despite his blustery disposition, Locryn was surprisingly patient, allowing Alison to lean heavily upon him as he conducted her the few painstaking paces to the desk, whereupon he offered her to the Demon Highlander. "Well, Laird, here she be," he said by way of presentation. "I give her to this ne'er-do-well under protest."

"Canna say I blame ye," answered Liam from where he reluctantly towered over the bizarre congregation.

Gavin watched Alison intently as she noticed Laird Liam Mackenzie for the first time. His elder brother had always stood just a bit taller than him. A bit wider. His features more barbaric and blunt than the sharp blades of Gavin's own construction. His build bulkier and less elegant. His muscles larger, but less defined. His hair and eyes a midnight black.

Just like their father's.

Gavin hated to look at him, and was glad his mother didn't have to for she'd have lost what little composure she'd scraped together.

He wondered what his bride thought as she studied the Laird with unanticipated stoicism. This was the heir to the man who'd killed her father, after all, and she stood assessing him as though she felt nothing more than mild curiosity.

"'Tis a pleasure to finally be acquainted with ye, Miss Ross," the Demon Highlander said.

"And you," she replied shortly, inclining her head as Mena joined her husband. She darted a nervous glance at Gavin, though her gaze bounced away the moment she found him.

"Are ye . . . of sound mind and body, lass?" the Laird queried.

At this her head snapped up. "Are you?"

An audible gasp permeated the room, uttered by more than one person.

The Demon Highlander's lip merely twitched upward. "No offense intended, Miss Ross, but we were half afraid Thorne coerced ye into this against yer will. I'm here to rescue ye if need be."

"Ye're here to marry her to me, and that's the end of it," Gavin snarled.

Liam remained silent, his midnight eyes never leaving those of Gavin's intended's. "I'll have yer answer, lass."

Whatever breath left in Gavin deserted him as the one woman he'd never been able to tempt, and the one man he'd never been able to forgive stared at each other in silent congress.

In what dim light filtered through the storm, Gavin saw in Alison what he'd not noted before.

Not just defiance. Strength.

Smudges of exhaustion bruised her lapis eyes. A pinch of strain about her strawberry lips. The load of a thousand worries lifted by thin, rebellious shoulders. Yet here she stood against a man who'd withered legions with only a look.

And she never blinked.

Suddenly he wanted everyone to go away, most especially his brother. He wanted to take her in his arms and tell her everything. He wanted her to *know* him, to understand him, because no one did.

No one tried.

Every woman looked at him—stared at him—but none of them saw a fucking thing.

He wanted to promise her that he'd let her rest until those dark smudges beneath her eyes disappeared. To offer to shoulder the weight of her burdens. He would vow that he'd never make her afraid. Or hurt. Or betrayed. That she'd never go without. That he could not give her his love but, hunter that he was, he'd bring the corpse of anyone who dared threaten her and toss it beneath her feet. That he'd rid her of the shadows that haunted her eyes like tormented ghosts.

She didn't look at him. Not once.

Gavin's heart kicked behind his chest as she met the eyes of the man they called the Demon Highlander with as steady a gaze as he'd ever seen and said, "My will has *always* been my own, and I aim to be married today."

* * *

Samantha stared at her signature as the dark giant they called the Demon Highlander took the pen and scrawled his name on the marriage document. He was what Robert Smith, her foster father, would have called a "corn-fed side of beef." If Samantha thought he was handsome, it was because he resembled Gavin, but only like a shadow resembled the real thing. Sort of bigger, darker, and more unwieldy.

Lord love Mena for taking him on. She supposed someone had to.

Alison Ross, the signature said. It wasn't her name, and it wasn't her writing, either. Her hand had trembled so terribly, it looked like an illiterate child had signed for her. Which they probably suspected she was.

She might be brave, but she certainly wasn't fearless.

She could feel Gavin's intense regard, and for some reason couldn't bring herself to look at him, lest she lose her nerve. He was too beautiful to marry, wasn't he? Too selfish. Too experienced. Too damaged. Too old, probably.

How old was he?

Lord, that was almost certainly something one ought to know about her husband, as she was fairly certain he had at least a decade on her twenty and four years.

She had the sense she was making some terrible mistake, but every time the thunder roared above the stones of the keep, it was him she wanted to reach for.

Maybe she wasn't of sound mind, after all.

"Very well," Liam Mackenzie said. "This document means naught unless consent is exchanged."

"There's plenty of witnesses to be found here, who'd all appreciate it if ye'd refrain from stalling," Gavin snapped.

"All right, join hands if ye must," Liam commanded. To call his tone unamused would have been kind.

Only then did Samantha look over to her right, where her fiancé of little more than a day extended his hand toward her. Though his features remained stoic, his big frame vibrated with something Samantha couldn't begin to understand. It might have been rage, but it somehow went beyond that. There was desperation in the verdant lightning flashing from his eyes, and Samantha looked to everyone else, wondering if she was the only one who sensed it.

Did they not notice his smirk was just a little too grim? That beneath his placid perfection brewed a storm to match the one outside?

Right now Gavin St. James *was* the thunder, and it would take nothing to make him bring this castle down around their ears.

Impulsively, Samantha reached out, and pressed her palm to his.

His hand was rougher than hers, engulfing hers in a masculine grip so absolute, his fingers could have been shackles.

She'd never been clung to like that, and without thinking, she squeezed in a gesture of encouragement.

Their eyes locked and held, and suddenly Samantha breathed a little easier. She had the sense she pleased him, and that was never not a good feeling.

The Laird Mackenzie's expression revealed that he'd rather officiate over his own funeral than this wedding, but he took up an old book and began to read. "Alison Ross, have ye come here to enter into marriage *without coercion* freely and wholeheartedly?"

"Asked and answered," Gavin spat. "Inappropriately, might I add?"

"Ye have to say it as part of the ceremony, it's in the book." Liam pointed to the passage.

"I have," she said clearly.

"And ye?" the Laird asked his brother with obvious lack of aforementioned ceremony.

"I have." Gavin's lips didn't move, but the words escaped him all the same.

"Are ye prepared to accept children lovingly from God and bring them up according to his law?"

"Of course I am," Gavin stated with abject resolution.

Samantha glanced sharply up at him once more, if only to check for a mocking sneer or some evidence of a joke. So vehement was his reply, she thought he surely must be in jest. She could hardly believe it, but she'd never seen a look so serious before in her life.

"Ye have to answer, too," Liam prompted her.

A hand flew to her belted waist, her resolve renewed. "I—I am, yes."

"All right now." Liam turned to his brother and speared him with a disdainful glare. "Gavin St. James, do ye take this woman to be yer lawful wife? Do ye—"

"I do," Gavin cut in.

"Oh, lad . . . let me finish before ye say *aye,* there's a lot to carefully consider here, especially for ye." The Laird held the book up, advertising a certain kind of relish for the upcoming passage.

"There's really no need to—"

Liam raised his booming voice above Gavin's protests. "Do ye promise to be *faithful* to her in good times, and in bad, in sickness and in health, to *love her* and *honor her* and *cherish her* until yer inevitable untimely *death*?" His every emphasis was like a dagger that hit a bull's-eye, and by the time Liam had finished, Gavin was gripping her hand so hard she flinched.

To his credit, he relaxed.

Christ, Samantha thought. Her husband-to-be had been

the infamous lover of the officiator's—his own brother's—late wife. Samantha would have found the melodrama a bit funny if both men weren't glaring at each other like leviathans about to meet in battle, which made her the likely collateral damage.

"I do," Gavin growled.

"What about ye, lass? Knowing what ye do about the Lord Thorne's infamous value—or lack thereof—for wedding vows, do ye, Alison Ross, take this . . . *man* . . . to be yer lawful husband? To have and to hold from this day until his interest wanes, for better, or likely worse, for richer or until he squanders yer fortune, in syphilis—pardon me—sickness and in health, until his death blessedly parts ye?"

Gavin stepped forward. "You son of a—"

"I do." Samantha had to raise her voice above Gavin's enraged curses, Locryn and Calybrid's ill-concealed chortles, and Mena's sound of distress.

Only the Monahans remained silent, their identical golden eyes round with astonishment and not a little foreboding consternation.

"Think on this carefully, lass," the Laird admonished dramatically. "Are ye certain?"

"She said *aye,*" Gavin hissed, his bronze skin becoming mottled with barely leashed fury.

"If anyone can think of one or a multitude of reasons why this man doesna deserve a wife, speak now or forever hold yer—"

"If I didna need ye to pronounce us man and wife, I'd kill ye myself," Gavin snarled.

"Where's yer plaid and her sash?" the Demon Highlander remonstrated, apparently unconcerned with the threat of fratricide. "Did ye not plan to handfast her today?"

"Ye mean, where is yer plaid?" Gavin made a rude gesture to the Laird's kilt.

"*Our* plaid." All traces of mocking levity vanished from the Laird's features. "The Mackenzie plaid."

"We're wearing what we're wearing, Liam, so do yer duty and then get out of my keep."

"I'm not pronouncing ye married without the Mackenzie colors, Thorne, now where. Are. They?"

"Up yer own arse, ye sanctimonious fuck."

"Thorne!" Mena admonished. "Really!"

Samantha immediately realized why they called Liam Mackenzie the Demon Highlander. An unholy maelstrom of rage swirled in his black eyes and propelled him a step forward, blood his undeniable intent.

Samantha would not have thought Gavin a lesser man for stepping back in retreat, but he didn't. He stepped forward, as well, placing himself between her and the approaching mountain of wrath.

"In a few months' time, I'll not be a Mackenzie," he said with relish. "And ye'll hold no dominion over Inverthorne *or* Erradale."

The furious Highlanders stood face-to-face, nose to aristocratic nose, and Samantha noted dimly that their height wasn't all that dissimilar. Dear God, what if she was to become a widow *again* before she even became a wife?

"What. Did. Ye. Say?" The Demon Highlander's features were so hard, a well-placed thwack with a chisel might have shattered them.

"It's as good as done, Liam. I'm emancipating myself from the Mackenzie clan. I no longer want to be stained by the name."

"Not possible."

"Entirely possible. All I had to do was declare war on paper in a council of clans. I had to state crimes, cruelties, and indignities, against my person and others by Mackenzie Lairds past and present, which I did. And trust me, brother, I had plenty of witnesses to speak to it."

Samantha had seen a look of cruel arrogance on Gavin's face before, but now an unholy rage burned with a dark flame.

For the first time, he truly frightened her.

"But not against Liam, surely." A concerned Mena stepped forward. "Consider what you are doing, Thorne. You'll be without a clan."

"Maybe I'll become a Ross."

Samantha swallowed heavily. That would certainly mean the end of her charade. Lord, but this was getting problematical. Someone should stop this, stop them, before they ended up killing each other.

"I told ye before, Gavin, ye'd be a fool to go to war with me." The Laird's eyes flashed with obsidian fire.

Gavin merely grinned, revealing entirely too many teeth. It was the smile of a wolf. "What will ye do, Liam? How will ye punish me for my defiance? Whip me? Cut me? Burn me? Lock me out of my own keep to face the Highland winter naked and alone? Do I look afraid, brother? Do you think that's anything that hasna been done before?"

A fraught and potent silence blanketed the room. It screamed through the mere inches that separated brother from brother. They were two alpha wolves snarling in front of their pack, and any moment Samantha was certain one would go for the other's jugular and rip it out.

The only question was which?

"They call ye a demon," Gavin sneered. "But ye're nothing but one of those damned bulls out there, charging with your head down, unable to see what's stalking you from the bushes. Ye may be undefeated in open war, but life has many battlegrounds, brother, and I'm a man of patience, and strategy, and endless reserves of stamina. So if ye fight me on this, ye'll find yerself sorely outmatched."

"Ye'll lose the distillery," Ravencroft threatened. "What'll become of Inverthorne without income?"

"That isna a problem anymore." Gavin glanced down at her triumphantly.

"Ye selfish ingrate!" Ravencroft roared. "If ye think I'm pronouncing ye married now, ye can go straight to hell."

Here, panic roused Samantha from her openmouthed stupefaction. "No! Wait!"

Mena, possibly the bravest woman alive, stepped forward and took her husband's bulging arm, her jade eyes made brighter by a sheen of tears and regret. "Liam. If you don't marry them, they'll just find someone else . . . It's *Alison's* wedding, too. Do what must be done, and we can leave. We'll discuss all else later, when cooler heads prevail."

"Fine," the Laird barked. "Ye're man and wife." His inky glare found Samantha and she swallowed around an instant lump in her throat. "May God have mercy on your soul."

"Isna that what they say when they're about to condemn someone to death?" Calybrid remarked.

"A life with that bastard is the worst sort of sentence," the Laird growled.

"Our brother Dorian would have a thing or two to say about that." Gavin had regained some of his usual chill. "And once again, *I'm* the only other git who's *not* a bastard. Why do I keep having to reiterate that?"

"Aye, ye're legitimate. A legitimate *Mackenzie,* and ye'll leave my clan over my dead body."

"If that's what it takes," Gavin snarled back.

For the second time in as many hours, Samantha found

herself swept up into Gavin St. James's arms, and she clung to muscles cording and shaking with more fury than strain.

"Ye can see yerselves out," her husband called over his shoulder.

Alison found Mena, and they passed a wordless communiqué before Gavin kicked the study door closed with such force, Inverthorne shook with it.

Samantha only dimly heard Locryn's bemused query as the furious Highlander once again conveyed her up the stairs to his bedroom.

"So does it still count if he doesna kiss the bride?"

CHAPTER EIGHTEEN

If Samantha had learned anything from her short previous marriage, it was the wisdom of keeping her own counsel when she could see the whites of a man's eyes.

Her husband swept her into his chamber and bolted the door before striding over to the bed and plopping her onto it as gently as he was apparently capable.

Turning his back to her, he stalked to one of the windows and threw open the shutters with such strength, Samantha flinched at the splintering sound they made when they hit the wall. Thrusting the window open, he invited the storm into their bower, breathing it in with the gasp of a man who'd broken the surface after too long submerged underwater.

Lightning sheeted across the gray sky tinted with darker shades of evening, and Samantha caught one of the errant wispy bed curtains as the wind brought them to life.

After a few cavernous breaths he turned to face her, the glittering wrath in his eyes replaced by the customary languid calculation. The furious jut of his jaw relaxed enough for the sardonic smirk to return. Even the vein at his temple had disappeared.

But still the tempest raged, Samantha knew. He'd covered it with disingenuous sunshine and the imitation of calm.

They stood in the eye of the storm.

"I suppose ye're owed an apology, wife. That wasna much of a wedding."

Samantha shrugged and flashed him a counterfeit smirk to match his own. "Oh, I don't know about that. I'd say it was one hell of a wedding."

For an incredibly intense moment, he stared at her as if she were the queerest creature he'd ever seen. An unspoken cue rippled between them, and they both erupted into laughter, long and genuine and tinged with a bit of madness on both their parts.

"Ah, bonny." He sighed once they'd quieted. "Any other lass would be inconsolable with tears after all that."

"I'm not just any other lass."

His green eyes, so vivid against the gold of his skin, softened upon her, even as the wind continued to feather his hair against its shape now that he'd turned from the window.

"Nay, I've never met yer like."

Another vibration singed the air between them the moment before thunder crawled over the clouds, making its noisy way toward Inverthorne. What had started as a drizzle was fast becoming a gale to warn of winter.

Unable to stand his beauty, Samantha looked away, examining the fine stitching on the ripples of her skirts. There was only one thing left to do to make this little farce of a marriage complete.

Suddenly an extremity of exhilaration and anxiety stormed through her. She was no untried blushing bride . . . but this man had famously fucked more women than Casanova and Lord Byron combined.

She'd only ever had Bennett and, from her experience, sex, like everything else in her life, was a whole lot of work.

She thought back to her first wedding night with a distasteful wrinkle of her nose. They'd spent it drinking and carousing in the local inn which doubled as a saloon, and then Bennett had whisked her upstairs, much like Gavin had just done.

They'd been laughing, and her world had been spinning on its axis, more from whisky than Bennett's kisses. He'd dropped her on the bed and tossed up her skirts. She'd been giggling and willing when he'd climbed on top of her, confused when he licked his hand and reached between them. She'd been shocked when he'd shoved inside of her. He'd been done before she caught her breath, and asleep before she'd a chance to clean away the blood and such.

It had gotten better after that, but only because she'd been the one to take the reins, as it were.

You're such a good little horsewoman, Bennett would say as he stretched his sinuous, aroused body onto his back. *You can mount me, and gallop away. It's better for a girl, anyhow, if they're on top. Then I don't gotta figure out how to give you what you want, you can just take it.*

He'd been right, in a way. The handful of times he'd been in control of their lovemaking had been disappointing at best and catastrophic at worst. When she was on top, she could sometimes reach that peak that eased the deep ache of arousal.

Most of the time, the whole act just made her feel put upon and empty, and she'd climb off him burning and sweating and unspent.

Samantha puffed out her cheeks. She really didn't have that in her tonight, neither the energy nor the strength. It would hurt her leg too much. Maybe he'd take that into consideration and just let her lie there while he stood at the foot of the bed or something. Upon inspection, the bed seemed tall enough for a good tumble like that. Then neither of them would have to work that hard and her leg would remain unmolested, at least.

She glanced back up at him, ready to suggest just that, when all words died on her lips.

He was beautiful enough when applying his calculated charm. But like this, somber and dangerous and regarding her like a secret he was about to uncover . . .

She was in grave danger of forgetting that this marriage was a farce.

That he didn't care for her.

That she didn't want this. Want him.

Groping for something to break the sudden potency between them, she said, "I'm sorry your brother was such a horse's ass."

One shoulder lifted, and he prowled toward her, his chin dipped to his chest, low and lambent, like a stalking puma. "It matters not, he did what needed doing. The rest is up to us."

"Still, it had to hurt. The things he said, they had to have made you angry—"

"Liam doesna hurt me, and usually I doona get angry anymore."

"Bullshit," she scoffed. "You get angry at me plenty."

"Well," he rumbled, nearing her with infinite, patient steps. "Ye're a particular case, bonny, but believe it or not, I am a man who is usually difficult to infuriate. What does a temper get ye but enemies? What is anger but unfulfilled expectation? If ye need no one, ye fear no loss. No one truly angers ye. If ye expect nothing, no one disappoints ye."

"If you love no one, no one can hurt you," she whispered, her heart suddenly thumping to be free of its cage.

He stopped in front of where she sat, and Samantha did her best not to notice the ridge of his arousal against the seam of his trousers. Swallowing profusely, she arched her neck up to look at him.

"It seems we understand each other," he said gravely.

"It seems we do."

The flash in his eyes warned her of his hunger. Samantha knew exactly what he wanted, and how he wanted it. His lust had teeth. And darkness. The storm had made him wild. He was about to hammer her into something with his hips. Hard.

She tensed, readying herself for it. She was tough. She could take him.

Probably.

So when he turned from her, she almost allowed a sound of protestation to escape.

He whipped his suit coat off one arm at a time and threw it on the high back of the chair facing the fireplace. That finished, he went to work on the buttons of his vest.

Nearly panting with equal parts apprehension and an unexpected anticipation, Samantha lifted her fingers to her own blouse and began to do the same.

"Callum said they call ye Sam." He discarded his vest and grappled with his cuff links.

"They do." She undid her belt and peeled her blouse from her shoulders.

They were silent as he flicked open his cuff links and made short work of the buttons of his shirt. She, in turn, kicked away the slippers she'd been able to wear without stockings, as the pressure hurt her leg too much. She also unpinned the scrap of lace from her hair and set it next to her.

Pausing, he touched his chin to his shoulder. "Are ye afraid, Sam? Do ye have questions of me? About what I'm going to do to ye?"

"No," she lied. On all three counts. "I already told you, I'm no virgin. And everyone knows you've made love to most of the maidens in Europe, and half the married women, besides." She said this more to remind herself, than for his benefit.

"I *made love* to no one. I fuck. Love has nothing to do with it."

Then his shirt was gone.

Though his back was to her, he faced the fireplace so his scars were naught but shadows. Samantha wouldn't have noted them anyhow. In the firelight, the broad slopes of his shoulders seemed to be carved from pale pine and sanded to a perfect, smooth finish. His back was wide and long, roped with thick muscle that tapered into a lean waist.

Samantha gaped.

He was like a banquet to her eyes. She made an appeal to both the graces and the muses to grant a simple girl like her the words. Only the language of the angels could have done him justice.

All she could think was how lucky she was to have not met him *before*. Before her illusions about men had been shattered. When she still believed in silly, girlish things like romance, heroes, and happy endings.

She would have been counted among Lord Thorne's many, *many* casualties.

Now, she could merely appreciate his unparalleled physique and pretend that he elicited no instincts of covetous possession.

He turned back to her, and instead of divesting himself of his trousers, as she expected, he reached for her. Gently, he pushed her to her back, with her legs still dangling over the edge of the bed, and through some magic wrought of experience, he peeled away her skirt and corset. Leaving her bare but for the bandages on her leg.

When he leaned down, she expected him to crawl between her knees and open his pants.

Instead, he drove his hands beneath her, and lifted her once again.

"What—what are you doing? Are we not going to—"

"If ye think I'm not making this marriage completely legitimate, ye're mad. I want no one to be able to contest my claim."

He didn't say his claim to Erradale, though she knew that's what he meant.

"You don't really have to woo me, or anything. You can just—you know—get on."

"Get on?" He looked down at her, his perfect brow furrowed with confusion.

"Fuck. Like you said. The bed's right there and—"

Then she saw it, and gave a moan full of more erotic yearning than she'd ever expected to utter that night.

Samantha couldn't believe she'd not noticed it before. In her defense, the porcelain claw-footed tub had somehow blended with the marble of the fireplace. The steam rising from the water beckoned with a sinuous dance as cool air circulated around them from the partially opened window.

"I didna have time to get ye a proper ring or a wedding gift, bonny, but I thought—"

Overcome by a surge of gratitude, she threw her arms around his neck and planted her lips right on his in an enthusiastic kiss. Her exuberance in his arms drove him back a few steps in order to avoid landing on his ass, but he maintained his balance and returned her kiss through lips tight with a pleased smile.

Pulling back she said, "It's perfect." And wriggled a bit in his grip to get him walking in the right direction.

"Careful, lass," he warned, as a gleam of wickedness lurked beneath his playful grin. "If ye persist in moving like that whilst naked, the bath might be cold before I'm done ravishing ye."

"I promise to be good," she vowed instantly, curling around herself and modestly covering her notoriously unimpressive breasts by crossing her arms.

"That makes one of us." He strode to the tub and lowered her down, deftly positioning her injured leg upon a soft towel previously draped over the lip to keep it out of the water.

She gasped as her chilly limbs tingled with the sudden heat of the water. How strange and wondrous it felt to be submerged after so many weeks of heating just enough ice-cold river water over the fire at Erradale to rinse off the grit of the day with harsh charcoal soap.

With her calf draped over the ledge like it was, her split legs allowed the heat of the water to flow against her parted sex. The sensation was both delicious and alarming and brought every bit of her attention *there*. To that place suddenly swollen and throbbing and astoundingly hot.

Another moan escaped her before she could call it back.

Hovering to her left, still bent over the tub, her husband whispered in her ear. "I've given diamonds to a lass that elicited less effusive pleasure."

"What the hell would I do with diamonds?" she breathed, allowing her eyes to flutter closed as she luxuriated in the masculine scent of his soap and aftershave that lingered from the bath he'd taken prior to their wedding. "Oh, I know," she amended. "I'd buy a thousand of these baths."

Gavin said something against her ear in his native tongue that produced shivers along every inch of her bare skin. No mean feat for one submerged in warm water.

Turning toward him, she was struck by how dangerously close their lips were. How sweet his breath felt as it cooled the moisture beaded on her cheeks by the steam. "What did those words mean?" she whispered.

"I'm not sure, myself," he answered.

Suddenly it was all too much. The erotic golden glow of the fireplace burnishing his bare torso a celestial color. The appeal of his parted lips. The heat between her parted legs, some of which, she had to admit, had nothing to do with the water.

Samantha retreated the only way she could think of, sliding down to dunk her head.

Opening her eyes, she saw through the filter of the rippling surface that he'd stood and left her. Had she not been submerged, she'd have breathed a sigh of relief.

Resurfacing, she slicked her hair back and wiped her eyes, blinking them open to note that her husband was nowhere to be seen.

"Gavin?"

"I like it when ye say my name, bonny." The rumble came from behind her, but before she could maneuver for a look, his hands rested on her scalp. Strong fingers quickly produced a sudsy lather in a rhythmic massage that turned her bones to hot wax and her muscles to puddles of pleasure.

"I noticed ye were right this morning," he said conversationally, as he kneaded the tender hairline behind her ear. "Ye'd not been able to wash the soot from yer hair. Forgive me the oversight."

In this moment she'd forgive him just about anything,

and as soon as her tongue started working, she intended to tell him so.

He gently pushed her shoulders forward, so he could gather the length of her hair from behind her back and work the suds into it, as well. Then, he dipped an ewer into the water. "Look to the clouds, lass," he prompted.

Obediently, she looked up, and noticed for the first time that a skylight had been installed over the fireplace. Of course, in the storm, no stars were visible, but his hand cupped over her forehead to protect her eyes as he poured the water over her hair, and then dipped the ewer to repeat the action until all the soap had been washed away. She could think of nothing so luscious as the slide of the water and soap over her shoulders.

"What is the skylight for?" she asked, doing her best to dispel this strange, heavy sensation building between them. Nothing like a little small talk to do just that.

"Inverthorne is older than Ravencroft by a few hundred years," he murmured in a silken baritone, dipping the ewer a third time. "More a fortress than a manor, ye ken? They tend to be rather dreary and dark. But I like to study books here by day, and the stars at night, when I can see them."

"Oh," she said, rather idiotically, as he took an unbelievably fluffy towel and blotted her face with it.

Setting the ewer aside, he picked up a bar of white soap specked with what appeared to be tiny purple herbs.

Samantha reached for it, but he easily held it out of her grasp.

"Allow me," he said with a solicitous smile.

"No. I can do it myself. It's only my leg that's injured. My hands work just fine." Suddenly self-conscious, she once again covered herself as best she could, crossing one arm over her breasts, and cupping the other one between her legs.

A devious smile lifted the corners of his mouth. "Glad to hear it, bonny, and we'll test that claim in a moment, but I've just acquired a wife, and I believe I'd like to thoroughly inspect my acquisition."

"And you may," she retorted, holding out her hand for the soap. "Just as soon as she's clean and presentable."

"Ye might not know this about me . . ." He knelt by the bath, dipping the hand that held the soap dangerously beneath the calm, now opaque surface of the water. His skin was slightly flushed, even in shadow. "But I prefer my women . . . a wee bit dirty."

Three successive flashes of lightning broke the darkness in the room, illuminating eyes that burned above the crests of his cheeks a more startling green than usual. It distracted her enough that she didn't flinch when the hard surface of the soap slipped along her arm.

"I've imagined more than once what yer foul mouth could do to me." The soap slid up her arm to her shoulder, and then angled back down over her clavicle and down the expanse of her chest. "I doona care if ye're tarnished. Or filthy. All to the good, in my opinion."

He ran the soap along the arm that covered her breasts. "Experience should have taught ye by now that denying me what I want only makes me more relentless."

Lord, she might not know much about her new husband, but she certainly could attest to that.

"Give in to me, lass," he purred. "I promise ye willna regret it."

It wasn't that she didn't want to. She just was seized by last-minute nerves. Suddenly all she could hear was Locryn and Calybrid telling her how unimpressive her breasts were. And the buxom Mena asking about her nonexistent accomplishments. And the myriad other voices back through the years. The ones who'd mistaken her for a boy when she was little. The others who'd made her feel small, skinny, weak, awkward, and ungainly . . .

"You don't have to do this," she reiterated, hating that her lip had started to quiver. "I'm your wife now. I'm kind of a sure wager."

His other hand joined the first, gently prying her arm away from herself. "Something else ye'll learn about me, wife. I rarely do anything I doona want to."

Samantha swallowed loudly, but relaxed her arms to her sides.

With a triumphant rumble deep in his chest, he glided the soap first over one breast, then the other. His free hand followed, slipping playfully over the soap-slicked flesh. Caressing the small mound of her breast before sliding beneath to cradle first one, then the other. Gently, he touched her nipple with his thumb, sliding over and over it until it created a budded peak.

"I'm going to taste these," he vowed, eliciting another swallow. This one infinitely more difficult.

The soap slid lower, over the ridges of her ribs and across the plane of her belly. Her womb quivered when he reached it, but he didn't linger.

Why would he? He knew nothing of the secret she held inside.

His destination lay just below.

True to form, Gavin did what she least expected. His soap passed by the softness between her legs completely, sliding down her thigh, her knees, and her calf, washing every bit of her leg and foot with infuriating thoroughness.

Samantha narrowed her eyes at him, but he didn't look up at her once, though a sly little smirk toyed with the corners of his mouth.

Damned arrogant man. He knew exactly what he was doing to her. It was futile to hide it.

He lingered at her feet for a while, even washing the one left out of the tub. By the time he'd finished, she'd rested her neck against the ledge, gazing up at the rhythmic drops of the rain against the skylight and enjoying the capricious crackles of the thunder.

She'd relaxed so thoroughly that when the soap returned to caress her open inner thigh, she nearly jumped. His touch suddenly became liquid fire, sliding up and up and up until it seemingly wandered into the soft hairs between her legs, and then to the bare, delicate place past it.

Samantha tensed, but she remained passive, staring stubbornly up at the skylight, reminding herself to blink. To breathe.

He was her husband, this was his right.

And, she realized with astonishment, she wasn't the only one struggling to breathe.

The soap slipped and slid over her open sex, a hard but not unpleasant surface. It pressed against the throbbing little peak bared by her split legs in a way that caused her inner muscles to pulse and clench around emptiness.

Then the soap was gone, replaced by a wandering fingertip searching through the cushiony softness until he found slick, warm flesh.

Each of them made very soft, very different inarticulate sounds.

"Ye're wet," he groaned.

"I'm underwater," she told the skylight, more than a little anxiously.

"I ken that, bonny." He chuckled, his clever, elegant finger parting her inner folds to probe at the entrance of her body. "But this dampness has nothing to do with that."

She knew that. She felt it, even underwater. His finger

circled her opening, aided by a rush of desire somehow impossibly wetter than the water surrounding her.

"My dirty wife," he crooned darkly. "Let me wash ye. Let me clean the memory of any other man from this flesh, because after tonight, no other man will touch ye. After tonight, ye'll never want anyone else to."

That wasn't what they'd agreed to, was it?

His ruthless fingers drew upward, delicately brushing the little peak throbbing beneath the vulnerable hood of her sex.

Samantha's vision blurred as he began a gentle assault upon that place so excruciatingly sensitive, she couldn't keep her hips from flexing and twitching in time to his measured movements.

She tried to keep quiet. To keep control. To enjoy it, but not too much. She gritted her teeth against the pleasure, but the soft notes climbing her throat became harsh when they escaped her lips.

Dear God. It had never been like this. Not ever.

She moaned when he replaced his finger with his thumb, circling the pliant flesh with sweetly abrasive motions. She sobbed in an inhale when a finger slipped inside of her, rubbing and curling, eliciting unspeakable sensations that struck her mute.

The pace of his dual stroking increased, along with her heartbeats, until she was clutching the sides of the bath with white knuckles to keep from writhing or lashing from side to side.

He controlled his thrusts with absolute precision, his long fingers working together to create a wash of pulsating bliss that seemed to rise from somewhere deep, deep inside her, until suddenly every muscle in her body tensed and arched. It broke through her like a tidal wave, brimming over her veins and washing her flesh in a crescendo of effervescence. The peaks of the pulsing waves lingered, the valleys only a momentary respite before she was barraged again.

Samantha kept her neck arched, her eyes fixed on the sky above and, even through the heavy storm clouds . . .

She saw the stars.

CHAPTER NINETEEN

Gavin thought she looked like a water goddess, draped half out of the tub, arching in that lithe, sinuous way of hers. Riding his hand with that same rolling grace with which she rode a horse.

Even like this, spread open and helpless, she was a wild, unattainable thing.

God, but he wanted to train her to his hand. To respond only to him, ever.

When she began to tremble with a sudden and intense exhaustion, her movements more of an escape attempt than a come-hither, he reluctantly pulled his fingers away from her softness. She sank back down into the water, as though she'd become a part of it.

He couldn't describe this ferocious, possessive welling of instinct that had seized upon him. All he knew was that it began the moment she'd reached for him in front of Liam. The moment she'd chosen *him* in a room full of people who thought she ought not to.

A sensation of unprecedented wonder had seized upon him, and not let him go since.

It intensified with every steady, uncompromising answer she gave to the frightening Mackenzie Laird. In the past, Gavin was among a very small handful of people who'd stood against the Demon Highlander and lived.

His bonny was certainly the smallest.

In the innumerable empty nights he'd spent with countless empty women, he'd never wanted inside anyone with such desperate intensity.

Not even Colleen . . .

Surging to his feet, he gathered her up and tried not to enjoy the feel of her slick, thin arms around his neck as he retrieved a drying cloth woven for a man of his size. Lord, she felt like a scrap of nothing in his arms. He could carry her like this for a whole day and not tire of it.

For a lifetime, perhaps.

Shoving that disquieting thought aside, he set her on her foot and steadied her until she found her balance. "Hold fast to my shoulders," he directed gently as he wrapped the plush towel around her shoulders and bent to dry her.

Though she looked a bit dazed, she didn't stand passively beneath his attentions as he'd expected her to.

The hands on his shoulders slid up his neck, then seized his jaw and pulled his lips the rest of the way to meet hers.

She made a sound he'd never heard from a woman before. There was nothing coy or teasing in it. Nothing seductive or husky or practiced in the least.

It was pure. Honest. Need.

And he was lost.

Maybe he'd been losing himself slowly since the moment she'd barged into the Highlands, guns blazing, eyes snapping, and tongue lashing.

Now these were lashes he could give in kind.

He fastened his mouth to hers, pouring all his skill into the kiss, and greedily drinking all the pleasure he could.

She tasted like rain and sex. Like the storm bearing down upon them, wild and dangerous.

Dear gods, what was happening to him? He was Lord Thorne, the legendary lover. Sex with him was a blend of practiced, systematic technique and unparalleled performance.

Somehow, with this wee bit of a woman, he felt thrown to the mercy of something he'd promised never again to submit.

Passion.

Raw, unparalleled, unbridled desire. It stormed through him with all the bone-trembling strength of the thunder.

Before he realized what he'd done, he had her on her back on the floor, devouring her with a hunger he'd never before felt. He'd become a frighteningly insatiable beast with teeth and claws and a fathomless wellspring of desire. There was no time to get to the bed. They were going to consummate their marriage here.

Now.

In front of the fire and beneath the storm.

Their skin was still slick and slippery, and her back was only cushioned by the towel and the lamb's wool rug beneath it.

For a panicked moment, he had the absurd urge to jump to his feet and run. To escape the connection strengthening between them, to flee this surge of terrifying, warm emotion that glowed beneath the fire of his lust.

In the past, he'd have said something cruel and callous. He'd have done something provoking, anything to establish some distance . . .

But . . . that would mean he'd have to lift his mouth from hers.

And that just fucking wasn't going to happen.

In her embrace, he was barraged by sensations he'd not felt in twenty years. Helpless. Pathetic. Sentimental . . .

Powerful. Passionate. Predatory.

Wanted.

Not simply in the realm of the physical—he'd never been lacking on that score—but something in her eyes called out to him. To his soul. It was as though her gaze pleaded for what her pride would not allow.

She'd wrapped her arms around his neck and her long, long legs around his waist with surprising strength for one so injured. It was his only consolation. That her hunger—her desperation—seemed to match his own.

Their kiss spun out of control, their tongues sparring, their mouths clashing and releasing, only to go at each other from a different angle. He nipped at her lower lip as it slipped along the seam of his and she made a sound that vibrated into his throat, rippled along his spine, and spilled into his already full cock.

For a moment, he feared the worst . . . That with one moan, she'd unman him.

What kind of woman held such power?

Abruptly, he tore his mouth from hers and rose up on his arms to stare down at her with a wretched sort of bewilderment while he focused on bringing his lust under control, starting with his breath.

She really was nothing special. Right? Her hair wasn't artfully mussed or curled, but slicked to her head and mostly hidden behind the fluffy towel pooled around her. Her face wasn't delicate, pale, or painted. Her cheeks never rouged, her hands never softened with creams. Her long body nearly disappeared beneath his.

But those lips, a wide bow that could punish as well as

give pleasure had become the object of his most salacious introspections. He'd counted those freckles in his memories. He swam in the pools of her eyes, like some oasis of warmth in his cold, gray world.

Treacherous heat spilled through him as he gaped down at her, spreading entirely until he felt as though he might immolate.

"What have ye done to me?" he demanded roughly.

Her eyebrow lifted and she glanced around as though a bit baffled. "Nothing, yet . . . You've been doing all the . . . the doing." She winced rather adorably at her inability to articulate, and then gave a defeated sigh as she peered up at him with an exhausted sort of sadness permeating the haze of her artless passion. "Am I not . . . you want I should do more? Is it my turn to make you—"

"Nay, lass." He put his finger over her mouth. Momentarily wondering just who she'd been with before. This Grant fellow? Had that bastard caused the insecurity that hovered over her features?

No wife of *his* would feel thus. Not ever. "It's *always* my turn."

She melted under his next kiss, he made certain of it, filling her mouth with warm silk and soft strokes of his tongue. Once again, he drowned in the dizzying rush he experienced in the process. He hoped she didn't note how his fingers trembled when they shaped to her jaw and followed little droplets of water as they escaped down her neck, fleeing their demise against the warmth of the fire.

Unable to resist, his mouth reluctantly left hers to rescue a few. He caught some with his lips, others with his tongue. Kissing and laving down her graceful neck to her collarbone, and then below.

Her breasts were high and tight, her nipples deliciously

small and taut. He'd not thought she had much of a shape beneath her workshirts, but there was certainly enough here to feast upon.

Perfect. They were perfect.

She was perfect.

With a growl, he claimed her breasts with his mouth, raining a storm of worship upon them that had the exact desired effect. Her legs parted wider beneath him, and she pressed into him, pulling his hard body closer.

Without leaving her unattended, he swept away his trousers and settled in the cradle of her thighs.

His breath hitched when she reached between them and pulled his sex away from where it throbbed against his stomach and positioned it against her.

"Shit," she whispered.

He froze. "What?"

"Big," was all she said.

"Aye." He grinned.

His teeth ground together as he pushed slowly forward. He dropped his head to the side of hers, so he didn't lose himself in her body like he did in her eyes. She was small, snug, and oh, so deliciously wet. She writhed beneath him, doing her best to accommodate.

"I don't think . . ." she whispered. Then, "Oh!" as he curled his hips sharply, stinging into her, stretching her wide with one long powerful thrust.

An involuntary shudder overtook him, followed by waves and waves of impossible heat.

"Don't. Move," he ordered through his teeth. *Christ.* It was too much. She was too sweet. Too tight. Too soft.

The stars called his name too soon, and he answered them by throwing his head back and roaring his pleasure to the storm. He could feel them pulse behind the clouds, could nearly sense his place among them as pleasure pulled him from himself, tore him apart, and then reshaped him. Creating a creature of chaos where before there had been order, and Gavin knew as he crushed his wife to him, that he might never be who he once was.

Samantha bit down on her lip as she witnessed the splendid sight of her husband caught in the throes of bliss. His every muscle corded tight as his body went rigid above hers, his beautiful features locked in a grimace that looked like it might be pain, but she knew better. It was the exact pleasure he'd given her in the bath. The kind where you couldn't be sure your body still belonged to you anymore.

She closed her eyes, focusing on the hard, hot, spasming flesh inside of her. On the warm jets of seed bathing her occupied womb.

This was what she needed.

Now she could relax somewhat.

Though she didn't want to. For the first time in her life, she didn't want this act to be over. She wasn't ready for him to collapse upon her, then roll over to fall asleep.

She wanted more. More of this slippery, exquisite friction. More of his incomprehensively large sex, now that the fullness had finally stopped being uncomfortable. More of the magic his fingers had given her in the bath.

Oh well, she thought. If she pleased him this much, there would probably be a next time.

After an eternal moment, he dropped onto his elbows over her, his dark green eyes drowsy but still glittering with intensity as he pressed his forehead to hers. The gasps of his breath exploded against her cheek in hot bursts.

It was done. Now they were man and wife in every sense possible.

Now her child was safe.

She closed her eyes, and in doing so her awareness no longer resided behind her eyes . . . but inside her body.

Inside her body, where *he* still remained. Hard. And hot. And pulsing.

What?

Five breaths. Five breaths was all it took him to recover.

A hum of masculine satisfaction rumbled deep in his throat before he threaded his fingers through hers and slowly guided them above her head as he finally began to move.

Her eyes flew open and she gasped at the sight. Even though she'd seen him dozens of times, his beauty still had the power to startle her if she wasn't prepared.

Hadn't he just . . . ? How was he still . . . ? Oh God, that felt good . . .

"The only Mackenzie trait I'm glad of, lass," he said by way of arrogant explanation. "We spend ourselves more than once."

Jesus Jehosephat Christ.

Samantha's eyes fluttered closed again as each slick, slow glide branded her with unparalleled sensation. She concentrated on opening her legs wider, on taking him deeper, on trying not to lose herself in the lyrical nonsense he murmured against her ear.

He stretched her, filled her, opened her, with sleek, almost ruthlessly patient movements. His eyes burned down at her from features growing ever darker as night loomed.

The muscles in her back, in her buttocks, in her thighs couldn't help but respond to the whispers of pleasure that mounted into waves, and threatened to become pulses. She tried to call back the tiny mewls that were quickly becoming sobs.

What was this? She'd been beneath a man before . . . but

not like this. Not a man like him. This building pleasure wasn't just the alchemy of a man and a woman fulfilling a biological imperative or a marital contract. This was something deeper than that.

So much deeper.

And the depth of it shocked and terrified her.

His controlled breaths frayed and fractured into gasps, then jagged pants. "God," he bit out. "You're too lovely . . . I'm too deep."

She could attest to that.

The release that took her wasn't sudden as it had been in the bath. It built in slow waves, made more intense because she stood on the shore watching them come for her, knowing she'd be swept away. That she'd drown in it, become a willing victim of its awe-inspiring force. Suddenly she couldn't move at all. Her body became a prison of pleasure, arcing against it as he rode her through crashing peaks of unimaginable sensation.

Somewhere through the storm of bliss, she was dimly aware of his low sound of surprise when his body gave a great shudder and then several rhythmic spasms. She reveled in her body's sinuous clenches around the hard flesh buried inside of her. The pleasure noises he made harmonized with the melody of hers, and the thunder created the perfect percussion to their erotic crescendo.

A pleasant, heady exhaustion blurred the moments in which they remained tangled into incalculable measurements. Eventually, he lifted off her, took a cloth and dipped it into the bath, and returned to wash the remnants of their pleasure from them both.

She fought heavy eyelids as he used a separate towel to dry himself, and the rest of her with patient blots and long drags. She felt drunk, almost like she'd done upon waking in his arms half out of her mind with laudanum.

She was dimly aware of a dull ache in her leg, and was certain that so much flexing and straining couldn't have been helpful, but what did she care?

Lord, had her husband just quite literally fucked the wits out of her?

She glared at him through slits between lids that felt increasingly swollen with sleep. She'd be mad if she wasn't so damn content.

"Poor bonny," he crooned to her as he lifted her yet again and conducted her to the bed. "It's not many a lass who can survive me. Ye've done decently well."

"Decently well?" she huffed, a stab of indignation permeating her bliss.

"I told ye when a woman loses consciousness around me, it's either a swoon or exhaustion." He wiggled arrogant brows at her, and lifted her arms so he could pull her nightgown over her head.

"Oh, spare me." Her jaw cracked on a yawn as she passively allowed him to dress her. "I'm a cripple," she said with a scowl. "Just wait until all my parts are in working order, then I'll show you *decent,*" she muttered as he moved to his side of the bed and rummaged for something on the stand beside it.

"Trust me, lass. All yer parts work just fine." The bed compressed behind her, but still she sat staring at the fire, unwilling to be charmed by him just yet. "Better than fine." His breath tickled her neck from behind, as he gathered her still-wet hair from her ear. "In fact, I'd hazard to say yer parts are fast becoming my favorite parts. Even the crippled ones."

That elicited a bashful smile she was glad he couldn't see as he pressed a kiss to her jaw.

A slight tug on her hair brought her scowl back. "What are you doing?"

"I've got to work these snarls out, lass, or there'll be no fixing this in the morn."

He was . . . brushing her hair?

She turned to whisk the brush from him. "You don't have to—"

"But I'm going to." He used the leverage of her hair to gently but firmly direct her head back toward the fire.

Dumbfounded, almost horrified, Samantha sat, stiff shouldered, as he groomed her. She might not have been a virgin, hell, this was even her second marriage.

But tonight was definitely the night of a thousand firsts.

He obviously knew what he was doing, starting at the bottom of her thick mane, holding it away from her night-gown so as to not wring the water against it. Working the difficult tangles with deft and clever fingers instead of yanking on the brush. A green-tinged misery stole over her, ruining her enjoyment of the unexpected intimacy. Was this some kind of seductive ritual for him? Did he have a pro-clivity for hair?

"How many women have you played lady's maid to?" she asked with forced nonchalance.

"One," he answered blithely.

Oh God, that somehow made it worse.

"My mother."

Stunned, she froze. "Your . . . what?"

"My mother wasna always blind, ye ken. That was my father's doing."

Samantha pressed her lips together as her blood raced. She'd suspected as much, but it had never seemed her place to ask.

"When we first came to Inverthorne after she lost her sight, we had no money for staff. It was only Callum, Eam-mon, and I. And my mother, of course. There were many things she couldna do for herself like arrange her hair."

"I see," she murmured. This was not at all in keeping with the Earl of Thorne that she thought she knew.

"That's all I'll say about it."

She nodded, letting the rhythm of his brush strokes calm a mind that wanted to race. What an enigma her husband was. Ruthless, relentless, cunning, manipulative . . .

Generous, honorable, and . . . kind.

"Thank you," she whispered around a sudden lump in her throat. How could he know that no one had ever done anything like this for her? Had ever done anything for her. She'd never been bathed. Never been dressed, tended to, or groomed.

She came from a hard place where self-reliance was the primary virtue. She'd never considered that a bad thing.

But . . . neither was this.

Her husband was a hard man, a lethal hunter, they said. And somehow that made this moment that much more disarming and alarming at the exact same time. Somehow, it made him more dangerous, because in one night he'd melted her multiple times. Not just her body.

But her heart, too.

Once the brush ran smoothly through her hair, he plaited it expertly. That accomplished, he pulled back the covers, snaked a thick arm around her middle and dragged her down to the pillow.

"Don't husbands and wives sleep apart in this country?" she queried, trying not to appreciate that he slept naked. She'd been afraid he'd don one of those ridiculous nightshirts Bennett used to wear when it wasn't cold enough for the equally unimpressive long johns.

"Stop confusing Highlanders with the British," he mumbled, slumber already walking alongside the playful note in his voice.

"I'm just saying, you don't have to give up your bachelor's chamber for me, it's not like we're . . ." It had been a private worry of hers, that he'd resent sharing his space. That he'd push her out into a smaller, less comfortable room. It was within his right. And maybe he would eventually.

The longer he waited . . . the harder it would be.

"If ye think ye're escaping me now, bonny, ye've gone daft. Now go to sleep."

Samantha had never been one to obey, not really. But this once couldn't hurt.

He'd left the window cracked, she noticed, but it only served to pull the warmth of the fire closer, without making it stifling.

As she listened to the storm toss the forest about, and felt the lift and fall of the big chest behind her become slow and even, she allowed one tear to escape so as to hold back its multitude of threatening compatriots.

This. This was all she'd ever asked for. What she'd wanted since she could remember. It was what Bennett had promised for her, but had never delivered.

A home by the sea, surrounded by a lush forest. A warm fire by which to make love beneath the thunderstorms.

Okay, so it wasn't lovemaking, because Gavin St. James didn't make love.

He fucked.

She gave a lithe stretch and felt his arm tighten about her middle, pulling her deeper into the cradle of his body, until the hairs of his muscled thighs abraded the backs of hers even through her nightgown.

Well, she decided. He fucked. She lied. Either way, she was safe and warm and they were both pleased with each other.

For the moment, that was enough.

CHAPTER TWENTY

Finally, Gavin thought, as he checked Demetrius's saddle and adjusted the cinch. Finally he would set foot on Erradale for the first time this morn as its proprietor.

He glanced around the empty stables, noting the hastily discarded tack and what-not that bespoke an early mass exodus. He'd hired a few hands in Strathcarron, and they were to meet him and Callum here at dawn.

He grimaced. Then grinned. Morning had dawned maybe two hours ago.

Callum had left a hastily scrawled note saying they'd tired of waiting on him, and no one dared disturb the wedding bower, so they'd gone on ahead.

It amazed none more than he that he'd slept the dawn away with his wee wife tucked next to him.

Gavin never slept past dawn. Why would he?

Especially today when Erradale—*his Erradale*—awaited him.

Even after he'd roused, a disquieting reluctance to leave her had kept him abed longer than it should have. He'd convinced himself that it wouldn't have been so difficult had she not turned to him in the night, and clung to him in her sleep with all the desperate strength of a lass being chased by a nightmare.

Her arm still draped over him this morn, and her leg—the injured one—had been thrown over his thigh. When he'd moved, she'd gripped him fiercely, though she'd yet to wake, and suddenly he found he'd rather chew off his own limbs than disturb her.

She looked peaceful for once, and awfully young. The wrinkle of perpetual cynicism smoothed from her forehead. The parentheses caused by the determined set of her mouth disappeared. In the morning light, he'd had the absurd notion to wake her by kissing every freckle sprinkled like golden fae dust over her cheeks and across the adorable bridge of her nose.

He didn't, though, for if she'd awakened, he'd have been *much tardier* than he was now.

It was possible he'd not even have made it out of bed, and what would his men have to say about that?

Nothing. If they valued their jobs . . . and their limbs.

Everyone understood that theirs was a wedding of convenience, but that didn't mean two young, attractive people wouldn't thoroughly consummate such a contract.

There were heirs to beget, after all.

The thought summoned another pleased tilt to his lips. If he had his way, his wee wife would be pregnant by Christmas. And if not, he'd be happy to keep trying.

Gods, but he'd never—

"Just what the hell is this?" The furious feminine demand turned his secretly pleased smile into a broad smirk. Ye gods, he'd have to stop grinning like an idiot all day, or people might get the wrong idea . . . That he was actually falling for his wife.

"Bonny!" he greeted. "Ye're awake." A swift spurt of pleasure at seeing her framed in the stable doorway was followed by an unexpected bloom of heat.

"You're goddamn right I'm awake, no thanks to you." Had she not required the use of a cane, Gavin had no doubt she'd have made quite the entrance. She'd hastily donned a simple blouse, a dark woolen skirt, and the wide belt she'd been married in. Somehow, she'd gotten her hands on a weathered long coat that threatened to drown her. The fly-away tendrils of hair escaping the long plait revealed that she'd not even checked a mirror before coming after him. And still, she managed to look fresh as an early-summer bloom, even in the wan gray light of a winter morn.

"You left me asleep with nothing more than a note!" she accused.

"Ye're welcome, lass." He beamed at her. "Not so many newly wedded husbands would be so thoughtful. Had I had my way, ye'd have woken up with me inside of ye."

She blinked at him for a stunned moment, and then made the obvious decision to ignore him, brandishing the scrap of paper in her hand. Though he didn't miss the pink blush that crept above the collar of that ridiculous coat. "It says here you were going to Erradale without me."

"And I still am." He checked the saddle once again, more for effect this time than anything else. "Now give yer husband a farewell kiss to hold me over until I return for supper." He ducked around Demetrius just in time to catch a balled-up letter to the chest.

Och, but she had excellent aim on all accounts.

"If you think you're leaving me behind, you can think again. Erradale is still mine, too. Now saddle me a horse and let's be off." She limped over to the stalls, inspecting the few horses that were left, her cane making an audible *thunk* on the wide planks.

"It's a mighty cold day out there, bonny. It's like to start storming again any moment, and ye canna ride."

She whirled on him, almost upsetting herself, using the cane to catch her in time. "Don't think that just because we're married, you get to tell me what I can and *canna* do. Didn't you notice that your brother left the word 'obey' out of the wedding vows?"

Lord, but he loved it when her azure eyes flashed with temper.

"Och." He chuckled, scratching at his morning shadow-beard. "More than a slight oversight on his part. Tell ye what, if ye prove to me that ye can ride, then ye can go."

"Fine." She shot him a triumphant smirk. "I think that bay mare would do nicely."

"I find it charming, lass . . ." He let his thought trail away as he sidled closer to her, a wicked intent heating his blood and already pulsing in his loins.

"Find what charming?" She shied away, but not fast enough.

"That ye thought I meant for ye to ride a horse." He snaked an arm around her, pulling her full against him, letting her feel the press of his hard erection, even through her skirts.

"Let me go, you big, stupid ox!" she huffed, though a playful sparkle in her eyes belied her scowl. "Riding you doesn't just prove I'm capable, it proves *you're* lazy."

"All right, ye sharp-tongued banshee, ye talked me into it. I'll mount ye, instead." He cut off her protest with his lips, and reveled in masculine triumph when her outrage melted into something else, entirely.

Not surrender, not his bonny, but something like it.

Suddenly he couldn't wait another minute to be back inside of her. The memory of her silken flesh clamped around him seared along his veins until he was certain he was made of both hard steel and molten desire.

His tongue thrust past her lips, tasting, circling, *claiming* as he tossed her cane aside, ripped her coat off, spread it over a mound of straw, and pulled her down, trapping her beneath him. He kept her busy with his mouth as he split her legs with his knees and settled in between them, pressing his arousal against the beckoning heat he could feel even through the layers of their clothing.

Gavin tried to breathe, willed his galloping heart to slow. So much of his blood now raced to his cock, he was afraid there was none left for the rest of his bits. Christ, but a hundred thousand trained and perfumed courtesans couldn't hope to elicit such instantaneous, ferocious desire as his wounded, unkempt wife.

Later, when he was able to form a coherent thought, he'd let that fact trouble him.

She pulled back and their eyes locked. The force of her defiant, Baltic gaze hit him with the strength of last night's sea gale.

"I *can* ride," she declared. "I'll ride you witless, Gavin St. James."

Just when he'd thought he couldn't get any harder—she had to go and prove him wrong.

"By all fucking means," he growled. Seizing both her mouth and her lean hips, he controlled their roll, levering her above him even as he sucked her tongue deep into his mouth.

Bunching her skirts in his fists, he burrowed his hands beneath them, sliding his fingers over the silken flesh of her thighs until he found the soft hair between. Cleaving her folds apart, he found the slippery cove of her body already wet and ready for him.

They both sucked in a harsh breath. "I'm delighted to

see that ye never found undergarments, bonny," he purred against her lips.

"Hold your wished." She sealed her mouth over his threatening smile at her horrid mispronunciation of his native tongue, all the while fumbling with his trousers.

His breath deserted him completely as her hand closed around his pulsing shaft, freeing it to fit against her.

Holy Mother of God. He cursed—or prayed—as she lifted slightly, positioned him, and lowered her small, sweet sex down around the head of his cock.

She didn't make it very far, and had to sit tall, writhing and rolling her hips a bit to gain any ground. Gavin flushed with each wriggle and flex she made, every inch of his flesh prickling with ever-intensifying lust.

Unable to take it anymore, he put his hand to his mouth, licked the tips of his fingers, and brought them to where their bodies joined—to where he'd become a part of her—and slicked the moisture over both of them.

Quickly, he found the tight bud exposed by her position and thrummed it softly, delighting in the satisfied gasp she made just as much as the ground he gained within her.

"Aye," he breathed. "Take all of me." He stroked her again, and again, feeling the answering clench of her inner muscles with each sensitive glide of his fingertip, and the subsequent release that came in slow, wondrous gives until he was seated deep within her.

Bracing her hands on his shoulders, she began to roll her hips in careful, concentrated motions.

Ye gods, but she was exquisite, perched above him, her hair wild, her swollen lips parted, her eyes wide with equal parts wonder and determination.

Instantly, he could tell she was favoring her leg, and that her thighs trembled. Determined or no, her strength wasn't what she wanted it to be.

But he also knew his wee wife wouldn't forgive him if she lost this battle.

Gripping her hip with one hand, he anchored and supported her weight, using his strength to thrust up inside of her. His other hand remained trained on the throbbing little pearl above where they were joined, teasing it in time to his desperate, increasing rhythm.

He watched a pink flush overtake her golden skin as he surged up and up, increasing his penetration with such force, she bounced above him with shocked little *ohs* of pleasure.

Stroked and gripped by her tight, wet depths, Gavin bared his teeth as his breath began to hiss out of him, dragged from his struggling lungs by unbridled pleasure.

With any other woman, fucking had always been about one thing, the burning, throbbing, climax at the end.

But with her, with his wife, the climb was equally as satisfying as the peak. Even as he drilled into her, a single-minded beast, he marveled at the pleasure he found just being inside of her. At the tenderness she evoked that underscored the ferocious lust.

"Kiss me," he demanded in a guttural whisper, surging up to meet her as she fell against him, rocked by the relentless movements of his hips. Their kiss didn't last long. It was interrupted by her hoarse cry as a wet release flooded around his rock-hard shaft, her sex pulsing and milking at him, bearing down greedily, and then curling away.

She ripped his own orgasm from deep beneath his spine, her body clenching around him so tightly his shoulders dropped back to the hay. His fingers dug into her hips as though they'd save him from a long fall into the void. Holding her still as the voluptuous rhythmic pulls and grips of her own release were all that was needed for his sex to pulse liquid warmth inside of her in a few final, ecstatic jerks.

She collapsed on top of him, and his arms instinctively encircled her, his fingers toying with the long rope of hair he'd braided the night before. Their chests heaved against one another's with uncontrolled breaths, their bodies still joined beneath the spread pool of her skirts.

"All right, lass, ye win," he panted. "Ye can ride."

Her reply was muffled against his shoulder, but it sounded something like "You're goddamned right."

"Who knew being married was such fun," he panted, pressing a kiss to her temple and swatting her backside simultaneously.

She pulled back to look at him, one of her rare, reluctant smiles tugging at the corner of her kiss-reddened mouth. "You probably should have done it years ago."

"Nay, lass," he said, suddenly feeling very serious. "Then it wouldna have been ye."

Encouraged by the shy lashes that spread down across her cheek, he lifted his neck to kiss her, gently this time, and her response was unlike anything he'd ever experienced with her.

Soft. Tentative. Uncertain.

A protective tenderness bloomed inside of him, intensifying as she shaped her small fingers to his rough jaw, cupping his face in her hands.

He reversed their positions, settling above her with a possessive moan. How had he ever thought her a hard woman? All he'd first noticed of her was her sharp angles and even sharper tongue.

It wasn't sharp now, as it glided past her soft lips and into his mouth, hotly exploring him as her hips began to roll once more, coaxing his cock to twitch and swell.

Moved by a foreign, frightening emotion, Gavin clutched her to him. "I canna believe—"

The doors to the stables slammed open and Eammon's voice boomed through the causeway. "I've had it with you, you bloody daft ass! No one has all bloody day to wait on you!"

Chapter Twenty-One

Samantha's heart stopped for several incomprehensible seconds before she registered that Eammon Monahan was, in fact, addressing a mule.

With a low curse, Gavin leaped off her, turning his back to the stable doors while he fastened his trousers, tucked in his shirt, and adjusted his vest.

Watching the elder Monahan in horror as he grappled the stubborn animal into the barn, Samantha set her skirt to rights and then blindly groped around for her cane.

Her husband hauled her out of the straw pile and shoved her cane into her hand just in time for the grizzled Irishman to notice them, and narrow suspicious amber eyes.

"Eammon!" she greeted brightly. "We were just . . . I mean I tripped and . . ."

"I know just exactly how ye got in that pile of straw, lassie, and who put you there." A glower furrowed beneath his beard, but a twinkle of laughter in his eyes gave away his good humor. "You forget I've been around the Mackenzie for well nigh thirty years now."

"Ye know I'm no Mackenzie." Gavin plucked a few errant straws from her hair, and Samantha suppressed a self-conscious giggle.

"Aye, but what's in your trousers still is."

"Careful, old man," her husband growled, but there was no real heat in the warning.

Eammon crossed himself, thrice, and complained to the stubborn animal beside him. "Jesus, Mary, and Joseph, I forgot that with newlyweds about you have to check every shadow to be sure they're not tupping in it. Now this straw's not fit for good Catholic horses anymore."

"What we did was no sin," Samantha pointed out. "We're married."

"Was more than a wee bit wicked, though." Gavin pinched her bottom through her skirts and planted a kiss on her cheekbone before sauntering over to Demetrius with a loose, lanky stride.

Samantha tried, and failed, not to appreciate the view as he walked away from her.

"What are ye about, Eammon?" His voice retained a husky note that elicited a secret feminine pleasure to warm her middle.

All traces of levity vanished as the stable master cast her a speaking glance before answering his lord. "I'm after the cart, as we've some . . . rubbish to haul from Erradale."

"Corpses, you mean?" Samantha decided now was not the time to mince words.

"Aye. We're glad of the freeze on their account, I can tell you that."

A wave of nausea overtook a flare of anxiety, and Samantha swallowed a threatening flood of moisture. "What's to be done with them?"

What she really wanted to ask was, *What will happen to me?*

Gavin's eyes narrowed. "Throw them in the sea from the Dubh Gohrm Cliffs and let the Selkies feast on their bones for all I care."

Eammon's expression told Samantha that she wasn't the only one present astonished by the dark vehemence in her husband's tenor. "But Thorne, they're each of them Pinkertons. Not exactly agents of the American government, but . . . they'll be missed." He lent his words a regretful grimace.

"Do I look like I give a ripe shite?"

Indeed, he did *not*. Samantha checked to be sure.

In a powerful yet graceful motion, Gavin mounted his steed and danced around the mule to the tall stable doors. "I'll claim the pleasure of disposing of them, myself," he snarled, morphing from the languid lover of only a few moments ago, to a muscled mass of wrath and retribution. "I'll send the Pinkertons a message. I'll inform them that their men came to *my* land, injured and threatened the life of *my* woman. That I put holes in them, *myself*. And if I see one more of their so-called detectives set foot in the Highlands, I'll ship pieces of their butchered corpses back to their offices in crates full of their blood."

He gave a harsh *yah,* and spurred Demetrius into a leap, galloping from the stables and across the bridge without a backward glance.

Samantha stared after him, the sudden chill against her tongue telling her that her mouth had fallen open.

"And he says he's not a Mackenzie." Eammon snorted. "What utter horseshit."

His woman? He'd take the blame for her? A sense of emphatic relief threatened the strength of her knees. He'd said he'd protect her, that Inverthorne would be her sanctuary. But . . . she hadn't expected that in such a short time, and without being asked, he'd already begun to set the matter to rights.

Remembering himself, Eammon mumbled, "Do pardon the profanity, my lady."

"Oh," she breathed. "None of that is necessary. You can call me Sam."

"Nonsense. You're a countess now."

Oh. Right. "I may be a countess but I'm no lady." She pulled a face. "Are you still planning to take the cart to Erradale?"

"Aye." Leaving the harnessed mule where he stood, the stable master retrieved a length of leather with two brass rings on each side. "Several of the Mackenzie showed up this morn, claiming that ye hired them . . . I've a feeling we'll still need to haul away a few corpses once yer husband finds them."

Samantha squeezed her eyes shut, cursing the fact that she'd forgotten to amend her agreement with Mena to recruit men to help gather cattle. "Is there room for someone to ride shotgun, in that cart, Mr. Monahan?"

He eyed her cautiously. "Feeling more than a bit better, I wager."

"Much better." Instead of pressing her hands to heated cheeks, she retrieved the coat Locryn had lent her, as he was still loath to leave Calybrid's side. "My . . . husband agrees I'm fit to ride."

When she straightened, Eammon had turned back to secure the leather length to the animal's bridle and harness. "Apparently," the Irishman muttered under his breath.

"I heard that."

He flashed her a charming, conciliatory grin. "No offense meant, lassie, I've been known to profane a few haystacks, meself, back in my day."

She didn't doubt that for a moment. "Does your mule

have trouble with tossing his head?" Approaching the animal, she touched its withers, and then stroked the bristly neck and velvet ears as she watched Eammon adjust the strap.

"Good eye. To be fair, this daft animal has trouble with everything." Retrieving a sugar cube from his pocket, Eammon held it beneath the mule's nose, then turned his shoulder and strolled toward the cart in the courtyard as though he didn't care if he was followed. After a thoughtful moment, the mule sighed and turned to pursue.

"Useless beastie," the Irishman groused, but he stroked the blaze between the silver mule's eyes as he gave up the sweet rewards in his hand.

Mollified, the beast stood still as Eammon hooked the cart to his harness.

Samantha would have helped if she was able, but her tumble in the hay cost her leg more than she liked to admit. Not that she at all regretted it.

She allowed Eammon to boost her up onto the seat before he heaved in next to her, and she sank into the coat as they plodded down the lane in the winter's chill.

"Daft ass isn't half as smart as his mother," Eammon said conversationally as they crossed the bridge and turned north toward Erradale. "But he's young yet, and from the strongest stock in the empire."

"You're still breaking him?"

His mustache twitched with a frown. "Never liked that word, 'breaking' an animal. It means you've broken their spirit, doesn't it? That's not what I do."

"What do you call it, then?"

"Mhúineadh."

"That's a lovely word. What does it mean?"

"I'm their *teacher,* as Callum is their keeper. They call him the Mac Tíre. It means a Son of the Earth. It's an ancient privilege in my country, one the Monahans are proud of."

"Teacher," she echoed.

"Don't misunderstand, girl. There is discipline involved, but there is trust to be built, and affection. A broken animal will never be as good to you as a loyal one. I taught Lord Thorne this as a child. Lord knows, his father never did. My boy, Callum, was born with this awareness, instinctually. And I think you were, too."

"I don't know about that," she muttered, ever uncomfortable with compliments.

"Callum says you sit a horse like you were born on one, and you handle the cattle better than any Ross ever did. Did I not know better, I'd have thought him a bit sweet on you."

"But you do?" Samantha asked with alarm. "Know better, that is."

"Aye. His heart belongs to another."

"Who?" she asked, before it occurred to her that it wasn't her business.

His gaze skittered away from her. "Well . . . never you mind who."

Used to the impatient honesty of hardworking men, Samantha didn't allow his rebuff to dampen the moment. "You know, I never wanted to be a rancher," she confessed. "Or to be tied to one place, dependent on the variables of nature and a herd. I despised the very idea. And yet, I came to the Highlands—er—*back* to Erradale, and I found a new appreciation for it. I was—am content in a way I thought I'd never be."

"Maybe it wasn't the *vocation* that disagreed with you, lassie, but the *location*."

"What do you mean?"

"You were raised American, for all intents and purposes, but you've the blood—the soul—of a Celt. You are one of the People, now. Perhaps you just needed to find your clan. To find your way home."

Samantha suppressed a squirm, needled with remorse over her deception. This was not and never had been her home. Not that she really knew where her people came from.

"What about your clan?" she redirected. "Do you miss Ireland?"

Eammon looked to the west, where past the forest, the Hebrides, and the narrow sea, lay his emerald homeland. "Callum supposes that it's him and Gavin that's kept me at Inverthorne all these years, but it's not. Not completely."

"Eleanor?" Samantha guessed.

His Adam's apple bobbed beneath his collar as he swallowed, staring straight ahead at the ruts in the road, and the skeletons of lesser trees interspersed with evergreens and pine. "I've loved that woman for the better part of twenty years. But . . . what Hamish did . . . That broke her. Beyond repair, I fear."

She was almost too afraid to ask. "What did he do?"

"What a terrible night. A terrible night for almost everyone in Wester Ross."

It was always a startling sight, to watch such a masculine man's eyes redden with emotion. It affected Samantha so much, she had to look away.

"Hamish whipped Thorne within an inch of his life and threw him out the window, breaking his collarbone," Eammon revealed.

Samantha's hands turned to fists in her skirts. "The scars . . . his back?"

Eammon nodded woodenly, his eyes gazing into the past. "Poor lad had to listen to what his father did to Eleanor. She hit her temple on the edge of a trunk where he threw her, and lay for who knows how many hours when Hamish left her for dead. He went to the town and caused no end of trouble that night. Poor Thorne was left out in the cold, locked away from his own keep. When Callum brought him home to me that morn, I hied myself to Ravencroft, tore the door down, and brought poor Eleanor to Inverthorne. The surgeon did what he could, but head wounds are tricky, and when she opened her lovely eyes . . . her sight, and some of her faculties, were totally lost."

"My God." A tear froze on her cheek, and Eammon gave a suspicious sniff.

"Aye, well, when the current Laird Ravencroft finally did old Hamish in years later, I happily helped rid him of the body."

Samantha gaped. "You're saying Laird Mackenzie . . . *Liam Mackenzie* . . . killed his father? Gavin's father? Are you certain?"

"Poorly kept family secret, I'm afraid. Everyone suspects. And no one much minds. *Bealtaine a anam dhó i ifreann.*"

Samantha wanted to duck the fervent words, as though they were an ancient curse, and she stared at the man in silent inquiry.

"May his soul burn in hell," Eammon translated, spitting past his elbow onto the frostbitten dirt road.

Samantha added her spit to the ground, along with a curse. Seemed like the thing to do. If there was a hell, she'd give her own soul to see Hamish Mackenzie in it.

"So . . . Gavin knows what his brother did?"

"Aye. Thorne was barely older than a lad at the time, but already a lord. Inverthorne was not much more than a pile of rubble before Callum brought him limping home that morning, bleeding, broken, and flayed open. I was groundskeeper and stable master, which was master of nothing, all told. Hamish paid me a pittance out of the lad's own income to look after the place, and I took it, God save me, as I was battling the darkness caused by my own wife's death."

"Did folks know what Hamish did to his family? Did you know?"

"Aye." His heavy shoulders caught on a tired sigh. "He was scarce better to his clan than he was to his kin. Thorne used to romp about the forests with Callum as a wee lad, and I knew it was to escape his father's cruelty. Stitched the boy up more times than I should have allowed, to my ever-lasting shame. But Hamish Mackenzie was a mountain of a man, just like Liam, and a marquess besides. So many of us relied on him for a living. The distillery, the fields, and the forests. None of us knew what to do. That is to say, none of us were man enough to do what needed doing."

"We've all of us deeds that we're ashamed of." She put a hand on his shoulder. "And sometimes it's not what we made happen that haunts us, but what we allowed to happen."

"You're kind." He looked toward Gresham Peak, be-yond which lay Erradale. "The Mackenzie lads, they've more demons than most."

"I'm starting to understand that."

"'Tis why they've always been at each other's throats, I think. More's the pity. They're left a legacy that's more pain and indignity than pride or joy. It takes a rare and pa-tient lass to walk alongside their demons."

"It's strange. Gavin's all smiles and charm." Except when he wasn't. "I never would have guessed . . ."

"Some men hide their pain behind anger and blood-shed, others behind vice and levity."

Samantha nodded, understanding that he presented to her the different paths that Liam and Gavin walked.

"What happened after that night? After Gavin and Eleanor came to Inverthorne?"

"Hamish never came after Eleanor, though I know that Gavin had to pay for her freedom with blood. He planned on going after his father once he was old enough. Hated the bastard with single-minded vehemence. We all did."

"But Liam got to him first."

"Aye."

Now Eleanor's absence from the wedding made much more sense. She'd wondered if it could have been more than just a headache. And it was . . . so, so much more.

"How does it happen?" Samantha wondered aloud, lost in her own past as much as her husband's. "How do some men become such monsters?"

"There's no simple answer to that. Some are made so by circumstance. Others, like Hamish Mackenzie, are born to it. He was the type that tortured wee beasties as a lad. That took pleasure in both power and pain."

"I hope his death was slow," she said through clenched teeth.

"I wasn't part of that, unfortunately." Eammon looked at her as though she pleased him. "But I only regret that parts of him lingered with his sons, even after his death."

"Scars," she murmured.

"More like . . . open wounds. Ones that still fester, I think."

Like the shards of Gavin's heart that Eleanor had warned her about. Broken one too many times to ever give away.

Suddenly Eammon's gaze became penetrating, as though he could see her secrets and her deception. "You've granted him what he's always wanted, what he's always been denied. Independence from Inverthorne's reliance on the Ravencroft Distillery income. A family. A future. To him, Erradale represents salvation. And maybe ye do, too."

"I—I hope I can—"

"Sam." He said her name with absolute gravity and none of his usual respect. "I'd not see him wounded again."

This time it was Samantha's turn to look straight ahead as her heart began to pound. Guilt twisted and rotted in her gut, and she pressed her fist there.

"Neither would I," she whispered.

Samantha had a long cart ride to prepare herself for her husband's ire. So she resented that the sight of him bearing down on her at full gallop once she descended the gentle slope of Gresham Peak affected her nearly as much as the sight of Erradale in ashes.

Those pleasant white cottages were nothing but bits of char, and only the grand stone fireplace and chimney still stood in the rubble of the so-called manor house.

This place might not have meant much to Alison Ross, but for a short time, it had been everything to *her*. A sanctuary. A new beginning.

A home.

She surreptitiously surveyed the ruins for the bodies of the men who'd come for her, and found no one. Gavin had already taken care of them. Did he toss them in the sea, she wondered, as he'd threatened to do?

Had he found anything on their corpses? A new and frightening prospect lanced her with terror. What if they'd had documentation of some kind regarding her real identity? If they were hired by Boyd and Bradley.

That was certainly likely.

Perhaps it was her uncovered secret causing the furious set of her husband's perfect jaw as he pulled Demetrius up short and took five full seconds to unclench his teeth in order to speak to her.

Samantha didn't breathe the entire time.

"Ye. Hired. *Mackenzie* men." He gestured to the several or so riders inexpertly driving a handful of shaggy beasts toward the only pasture with part of a fence left. Another half-dozen Highlanders labored to rebuild the gate in order to keep them in place.

Oh, whew. She puffed her cheeks out with a storm of relieved breath. *This* she could handle. "Actually, *I* didn't hire them, Lady Ravencroft did. Though I bade her to."

Now it was Eammon's turn to hold his breath beside her, as Gavin's skin mottled a dangerous new shade.

"Ye have seconds to explain yerself, lass, or I'll—"

"You'll *what*?" she challenged.

His jaw clamped back together with an audible crack. For a moment, she feared for his teeth.

"You forget, husband, that up until two days ago, we were enemies," she said with just a touch of pointed melodrama. "You were trying to bully me off my family land, and I was the unwilling victim of circumstance—"

"That's not what—"

"The day I went to Ravencroft, Mena offered a few workers that the distillery wouldn't need until the spring who were glad of the work. Though now that my money is gone, I suppose *you'll* have to pay them."

"I'd rather roll in a mountain of cattle shite than accept anything from the Ravencroft house—"

"Oh, do be smart instead of stubborn, Gavin."

Eammon gripped her elbow, and she yanked it out of his hold, meeting her husband's enraged glare.

"You've led these men—albeit under duress—as the Ravencroft Distillery foremen for years, haven't you?" she continued when he seemed to have lost the ability to speak.

"They're used to working for you. I'll bet they even like it. What if these Mackenzie decide that they prefer a rancher's life to one of laboring in the Ravencroft fields or with machinery? There's certainly money in it, we could even offer a profit share like they do back in America."

Some of the rage on his features was replaced by calculation, and Eammon let go of her arm.

Encouraged, Samantha continued. "To turn a profit come the slaughter, it's imperative that we track down a herd that's been scattered for longer than ten years. That means we need men, doesn't it? Dipping into your brother's workforce is a fantastic thumb in the eye that will leave him shorthanded and scrambling. But he can't blame you because his own wife offered them before you and I united. So, either way, we win."

"Hah!" Eammon cackled. "You married a wee mercenary, Thorne! Leave it to an American to bring economic warfare to the Highlands."

Her husband peered across at her as though he'd never seen her before, but that self-sure half-smile slowly dimpled his cheek, and his shoulders had somewhat relaxed.

He looked almost as pleased with her as she was with herself.

An unkempt Highlander with long, wild hair, wrapped in layers of wool, galloped up on a pony that was almost comically small for him.

He spoke to Gavin in Scots Gaelic and, though Samantha could barely differentiate the vowels from the consonants, she gathered the news wasn't good.

Following the man's gesture off to the west, she noticed one of the cattle on its side in the distance. A few men had gathered around it, and no matter what they tried, they couldn't seem to get the beast on its feet.

"Another pregnancy?" she queried hopefully.

"I'm not sure," he answered.

"Take me over there." She reached for him to pull her aboard Demetrius. "I might be able to help."

Both men eyed her suspiciously.

"You forget what happened in the forest already?" she pushed, urging him to hurry. "I may not know how to be a wife or a countess and such, but I know cattle."

Gavin shook his head and regarded her with disbelief, though he did admit with a sly smile, "Ye ken more about being a wife than ye give yerself credit for, bonny."

"Don't be disgusting," Eammon groused, as her husband took her in a strong grip, lifting and settling her into the saddle in front of him.

She welcomed his warmth and the strength of his arms around her as they gripped Demetrius's reins. They moved together in the saddle just as well as they did in bed, she noted with delight as they made their way toward the distressed animal.

Several Highlanders eyed her with different expressions of wariness and curiosity as Gavin dismounted, and reached up to lift her to the ground.

"It's certainly not pregnancy this time." She gestured to the bull's anatomy as Gavin assisted her approach.

"Certainly not," he agreed. "What say ye, lass?"

A few of the men addressed Gavin, their words harsh and their tone mocking.

He had a few words for them, as well, and they shut their mouths in a hurry, though none too happily.

"What did they say?" she asked.

"Best ye didna know."

She sent them a withering look of her own, wondering if Gavin was right and she should just send them all packing. Pushing her ire aside for a moment, she knelt by the bull, his troubled, heaving breaths tugging at her heart.

Putting her ear to his distended belly, she diagnosed him instantly. "Hand me your knife." She held her hand behind her to her husband. When one didn't appear in her palm, she glanced back to see what the problem was.

A congregation of narrow-eyed Highlanders crossed their arms above her in a choreographed show of resistance.

"What?" Was it something she said?

"It's called a dirk, lass," Gavin stated seriously. "And a man doesna just *hand it over.*"

"Lest he find it in his back," another muttered.

Oh, so some of them *could* speak English, they just chose not to in front of the outsider. Lord, spare her from obstinate Highlanders.

Gavin put a hand on her shoulder. "If the beast's throat needs cut, let me—"

"Christ, you've been reading too much *Macbeth*," she huffed. "Just let me use your *dirk,* and I swear you'll have it back before you can say 'How'd eyre washed' or however that goes."

She got the sense that she'd amused her husband, but not many others.

The moment he handed it to her, she took it and quickly thrust it in the cow's belly, instantly removing it.

Gavin pulled her back to her feet with a foreign curse as a small spout of blood gave way to a rather comical flatulent noise as the bull's middle significantly deflated.

They all watched the beast in openmouthed wonder as Samantha stooped to clean Gavin's dirk on the grass and handed it back to him.

"Cows have four stomachs," she explained. "Sometimes if one of the middle ones becomes bloated, they can't do anything about it and it distresses their lungs."

The man who'd retrieved Gavin said something unintelligible to his comrades, and they all burst out laughing.

Scowling at them, she asked. "Is he laughing at me?"

"Nay, bonny." Gavin chuckled.

"Then what did he say?"

"Only that he wonders if that would work on his mother-in-law."

"Oh." She giggled, pleased to see the bull struggling to his feet. "Tell him that he'll never know until he tries."

A melody of masculine amusement was a welcome tune to her ears, as most of the men gave Gavin a few parting words before kicking their horses to return to their work.

"What did they say?" She was going to get tired of asking that before long.

Returning his dirk to its scabbard, he took her in his arms and regarded her with a soft, knee-weakening emotion. "They're saying, lass, that I picked a good wife."

Inordinately pleased with herself, she performed a triumphant little wriggle in his arms.

"I have to admit, bonny, they're not wrong." He took her mouth in a possessive kiss, and the rowdy whoops and hollers of the Highlanders barely registered above the rush of her own happiness.

CHAPTER TWENTY-TWO

"All this chaos in one fucking railcar," Gavin raged. "I vow I'm going to just hang everyone involved and be done with it."

A sheaf of papers landed on the table in front of Samantha, effectively paralyzing any life-sustaining functions of the organs protected by her rib cage. Her grip tightened on the handle of her pistol, though it was useless as a weapon with the parts all spread out before her for cleaning and oiling.

"H-hang who? Why?" She couldn't bring herself to look. Was she only going to be allowed two weeks to enjoy this marital arrangement? Because, dammit, she did enjoy it. Despite herself. Despite everything.

Even with her bad luck, it seemed excessively cruel of the fates to take this away from her so soon.

To take *him* away. Just when she was starting to . . .

"I'd give up my earldom if it meant I didna have to be magistrate anymore." Gavin cast himself into the chair beside her with a weary oath, then scooted the mahogany monstrosity closer to the one she occupied. "I've cut my time at the bench back one day a week, and I hate even taking that much time away from ye . . . I mean, from Erradale."

Relief washed her cold terror away in a sluice of warmth, and drew the most genuine smile to her lips she could remember.

She'd missed him today, too.

"What happened?" she asked.

"The Campbells of Kinross and the McCoys of Witherdale have been at each other's throats for . . . Och, I doona ken, probably five hundred years or so. One of the McCoy spinsters, fifty if she's a day, shared a railcar with the entire Campbell clan returning from—I forget where—but it all started when Kevin Campbell said . . ." He paused, his brow furrowing as her hands resumed brushing out the pistol's cylinder. "Are ye . . . cleaning yer pistols on the dining room table?"

"Complaining about your day and nagging me about cleaning my gun where I ought not to . . ." She leaned in her chair toward him, thinking that no one in the world had such a handsome husband. "When did you become the wife?"

"I suppose we've done even more profane deeds upon this table." His chuckle did dark things to her insides as their mouths met briefly.

To hide her blush at the salacious memory of her bent over this very table, she returned to her scrubbing with renewed vigor.

Even after such a brief kiss, her lips now tasted of the toffee he kept in strange little caches around the keep. Aside from the crystal dish on his study desk and another in the entry, she'd found a small bundle of them in his saddlebags, one in his closet by where he kept his cuff links, by the bedstand, in the library, and even the armory.

How his perfect teeth hadn't rotted from his head was a sin against the laws of God and nature.

It surprised her not at all that Gavin St. James was afflicted with a sweet tooth. The men in her previous life were known to tuck tobacco between their lips and gums. She'd always hated the smell and taste of it, let alone the mess.

Yet, every time she found another sack half full of toffee shards, it brought a smile to her mouth, and her heart.

She'd taken to pilfering a bite for herself just to see if he'd notice. They were sharp, jagged, hard, and surprisingly sweet.

Just like the man she'd married.

"I put an oilcloth down." She motioned to the cloth beneath the discarded components of her weapon. "The family dining table shall live to see another day."

"*Ye* might not if Mrs. McCabe finds out," he teased, capturing a tendril at her temple and running it through his fingers in an affectionate gesture. "I can save ye from many things, bonny, but not my housekeeper's wrath."

"You should sack that harpy," she groused, pretending that his tiny physical intimacies didn't threaten to melt her into puddles of sentimentality. "I think she's trying to put some kind of Gaelic curse on me."

"I would if I wasna so afraid of her." Leaning back, he loosened his cravat and let it hang limply from around his neck with a relaxed sigh. "But do inform me if ye break into boils or yer hair starts to fall out . . . so I can make certain to do what I can to remain on her good side."

Samantha swatted at him, but he caught her hand and brought it to his lips.

Trying to ignore the flutter in her chest, she snatched it back. "I can't believe you have a McCoy feud over here, too," she exclaimed. "Seems to me that family is trouble just everywhere. We've an epic one in America."

"That, there, is the record of it." He made a profane gesture at the sizable file of documents. "Seems to come down to the fact that Eloise McCoy was once jilted by Thomas Campbell, the cooper, and couldna stand to share a railcar with him, his wife, and their many wild and braw sons."

"Was blood spilt?" she asked, gorging on a bit of drama.

"Not this time, more's the pity." The appearance of his wicked grin threatened her breath again, but she didn't at all mind.

She loved this place, where clan arguments lasted longer than her entire country had been ratified. Samantha suddenly wanted a mirror, to see if she reflected the same inner luminescence she'd noted highlighting Mena Mackenzie's lovely countenance.

Because if one could feel luminescence rather than see it, Samantha did in this moment.

How was it a marriage of two weeks, one built on a bevy of dangerous falsehoods, could feel more real than the one she'd spent four unhappy years in?

"If I remember correctly, ye have two pistols in that set," Gavin noted.

"I lost one the night I was shot," she lamented. "I've looked for it everywhere."

"We'll do what we can to find it. I'm sorry for yer loss." When she put the lonely pistol down, he placed a hand over hers, as though unable to help himself.

"That's mighty kind, but it's not like the thing was a person to me."

His manner became sly as he rested his chin in his hand

and propped his elbow on the table. "I'd wager my fortune ye named that gun."

So as not to watch the flex of his muscled forearm beneath the rolled cuffs of his sleeve, she scowled down at her remaining pistol.

Probably an unbearable weight, propping up that big head of his.

"Come, bonny . . . we both ken that I'm right."

Pouting, she muttered, "Caesar and Antony."

"As in Julius Caesar and Mark Antony?"

"Yep."

He frowned. "Great men, surely, but werena they both defeated and slain?"

"Well, they wouldn't have been if they'd had a set of these."

Gavin barked out a sound so full of mirth it startled her. "Ah, bonny, ye never cease to surprise and delight me." Eyes sparkling like emeralds in the candelabra she'd lit to see to her work, he wrapped a hand around the arm of her chair and pulled it close enough to touch his.

Something about a show of strength, even one so benign as pulling an occupied chair with one arm, brought to life every part that made her a woman.

"Tell me about these troublesome McCoys in America," he requested, threading his fingers with hers on the table while scrubbing his free hand over his face, as though to wipe away exhaustion.

"It's kind of a long story," she warned.

"Just the interesting parts, then." His jaw cracked on a yawn. "The ones with the most blood and tears and such."

A gentleman barbarian, her Highlander husband.

"Well, the papers say the carnage began over a land dispute a century ago, but really heated up during the Civil War. You see, the McCoys fought for the Union, and the

Hatfields for the Confederacy. The pater, a man they called 'Devil Anse' Hatfield, supposedly ordered the death of the head of the McCoy family, Asa Harmon, but as it was wartime, no charges were filed. After that Floyd, Devil's cousin, took a hog from Randolph McCoy. But 'Preacher Anse' Hatfield—a cousin, I think—was the justice of the peace, and ruled in favor of Floyd. A couple people were murdered in the dead of night over that one pig."

"I'm beginning to regret asking ye to tell the story." He sighed.

"Oh, hold on. It's just about to get good," she promised, talking as fast as she could so as not to lose her audience for the tale that had kept her glued to the newspapers, gorging on the violence. "Last year, Devil's son Jonce took up with Roseanna McCoy and she lived with the Hatfields in sin for months. So, when the McCoys arrested Jonce for bootlegging, Roseanna rode all night to beg Devil to save him, and how do you think he thanked her?"

"I couldna begin to guess."

"He left her pregnant ass for her cousin Nancy, the slag."

His shoulders shook with a lazy chortle. "That's her title, Nancy the slag?"

"No, that's just what I call her. I learned that word yesterday from Douglass Mackenzie. Now don't interrupt me."

"My apologies."

"So, Roseanna's brothers, Tolbert, Pharmer, and Bud—"

"Now ye're just making up names."

"Hand to God." She lifted her free hand like a woman about to give testimony in court. Though her other hand wasn't on the Bible, but grasped in the warmth of his. A warmth she was beginning to consider sacred. "What did I say about interrupting me?"

"Do go on." He traced the small curved web between her thumb and fingers in a soft, rhythmic stroke.

Doing her best to ignore the disquieting glow gaining radiance in her chest she continued. "Roseanna's brothers allegedly murdered Devil's brother Ellison by stabbing him twenty-six times!"

"Allegedly?" His thumb massaged the inside of her palm in slow, delicious circles.

"It's a word Americans use when litigation is pending, which it will be in perpetuity, because Devil rounded up a mob and stole the McCoy brothers from custody, tied them to pawpaw bushes, where a bunch of Hatfields emptied a total of fifty bullets into their bodies."

"Are ye certain Hatfield isna yer real surname, bonny?" His lazy fingers drifted to her knuckles and her wrist, and tickled the very sensitive skin on the inside of her arm. "That sounds like a very *you* number of bullets." For the first time ever, he enunciated the word "you."

"Aren't you funny?" Her tone relayed sarcasm, but in her chest, her soul might as well be dancing. She loved this part of their budding relationship. They laughed all the time, teased, and dug, and bickered, but always with a smile.

Never in her life had she smiled so often as now.

"But get this . . . ," she continued, doing her best to keep her traitorous emotion out of her voice and focus on the job of entertaining her husband. "Before I left the States, I read in the papers that— Hey! What the hell you think you're doing?"

In a smooth, strong motion, he'd taken her hand captive, secured it around his neck, and scooped her out of her chair, careful of her still healing leg.

"I decided this tale would be much more interesting if ye were naked."

She always hated it when he was right, but she couldn't disagree in the least. "What about my pistol?" It was as close to a maidenly protestation as he would get. "I can't just leave it on the table, Mrs. McCabe will . . ."

"Let her curse it." He grinned. "I'll buy ye new ones."

CHAPTER TWENTY-THREE

Emotion was barely something Gavin had taught himself to identify, let alone trust. But if pressed to describe the general sense of what he'd experienced in the month he'd been married, he might be so bold as to give it a name.

Happiness.

Even as he thought the word, he wanted to shrink from it. Lest it bite him.

Lest it disappear.

If it did, he couldn't go chasing after it just now, as he was confined to the oversized tub by the weight of his wee wife settled between his legs, her shoulder blades resting against his torso. Her head was tucked against his neck as she gently scrubbed at some of the stubborn grit from the grooves surrounding his fingernails, and he reveled in the almost innocent intimacy of the act.

Most men would happily give their right eye for a quiet woman, but it seemed that his bonny was especially silent today. Pensive. He should ask her if aught was amiss, but every time he thought to do so, he decided against it.

In case the answer was *him*.

It occurred to him that in spite of the fact that he was immensely gratified by their arrangement, she might not be. He cast the net of his memory back through the days since their wedding, looking for a place where he might have given offense.

Their days had fallen into an immeasurably pleasant routine rather quickly. He was pleased to find they both had a tendency to wake early, eager to set out for Erradale. His wife, he discovered, was a different person upon waking than he was used to. A bit surly, pale, withdrawn, and without appetite. She'd slip out of bed and make for the water closet at dawn, which usually roused him. Upon her return, he'd tease and grope at her mercilessly, which did little for her mood as they dressed, but amused him to no end as he learned a helpful array of American West curse words. Eventually, his harassment seemed to draw her spirit out of her, and by the time they mounted their horses and made for Erradale, she was either smiling or spitting mad, and he enjoyed her either way.

The work was hard and bitter cold, but she never complained. She ordered braw Highlanders about with the gravity and indefinable authority of Napoleon.

His own little dictator.

The men listened to her, as did he, because time and time again she proved her knowledge and skill. Erradale was beginning to resemble a right proper cattle operation.

Gavin had offered to allow her to stay home in the relative comfort of Inverthorne and keep his mother company, or take up whatever matronly hobby she desired. She'd immediately informed him that no one but she had the sense or the know-how to keep Erradale running correctly, and come the evening, he could go fuck himself instead of her.

She'd only been right on one account.

Because, of course, no matter how vigorously she bickered with him during the day, she met him with a matching spirit in bed at night. Well, not *always* in bed, he amended with a fond smirk. A few times they'd fucked against a tree when they couldn't keep their hands off each other in time to make it home. Then there was that once in the study when she'd been too impatient to allow him to finish the payroll ledgers, and perhaps tonight in the bath if he could tempt her away from whatever distracted her at the moment.

"Did ye have an agreeable Christmas, bonny?" he ventured, smoothing his free hand down her long hair, and splaying it across the surface of the water in rippling, dark waves.

"I did," she answered sedately. "Though I still feel bad that your present hasn't yet arrived."

"Think nothing of it. Ye'd lost everything ye had, and ye didna get yer annuity in time to send away for gifts. Ye gave me Erradale, and my mother gets another woman in the house, which I can tell pleases her to no end."

"Still," she worried. "You both ordered me such thoughtful gifts." She motioned to the long sapphire silk robe his mother had commissioned for her, and the ornate box that held within it brand-new pearl-handled pistols ornately engraved with her initials, *A.S.J.*

Alison St. James.

The gift had delighted her, at first, and the kiss of uninhibited joy she'd gifted him with had kept him warm all the day long. So much so, in fact, that he'd barely been able to make it through Christmas dinner. He'd tried to take pleasure in Locryn and Calybrid's hilarious banter and ancient, bardic solstice stories. He usually enjoyed the lively music performed by Eammon's fiddle and Callum's bodhran drum. But tonight, all he wanted was his wife.

Later, he'd caught her running her fingertips over the inscription on his gift, a sheen of moisture darkening her eyes from cobalt to midnight blue.

Happy tears, he'd thought at first. But upon closer inspection of her features, he wasn't so sure. A bleakness bracketed full lips drawn tight, and a wrinkle of ever-present anxiety creased her forehead. Had she been more affected by recent events than she let on? She'd been so fond of her guns before, so proud of her skill, but perhaps getting shot put her off them.

But could that be? She wore her old pistol on her belt every day, was never without it, in fact.

Maybe the new ones displeased her, somehow, and she was loath to tell him.

He'd know if he could just scrape enough courage together to ask her, outright. Instead, he'd a bath drawn, as he knew of her fondness for them, and he'd intended to take his time undressing them both.

She'd refused to relax, and had avoided his touch, going so far as to undress herself and plop into the tub, drawing her knees into her chest.

The gesture made room for him, though, and he noticed that she hadn't been able to resist watching him strip until he joined her.

Once he'd pulled her in close and settled her soft posterior against his lap, their physical connection had done just what he'd thought it might and, as always, she'd melted against him. He'd washed her hair and her body, and now that she was returning the favor, it was becoming increasingly difficult to remember that they needed to talk. However, he could sense none of her usual heat or desire, and intrinsically knew that to take her to bed now would be folly.

"Are ye . . . Is there aught bothering ye, bonny?"

She stilled mid-scrub. The tiny bristles needled his flesh, but he didn't dare move, hoping his silence would draw her out.

"It's nothing," she said finally, resuming her ministrations with crisp efficiency.

"In my experience, if a lass says ' 'Tis nothing,' then 'tis most definitely something."

"I'm well aware of your infamously extensive experience with other women," she snapped. "But when I say it's nothing, it's nothing."

"Now ye've convinced me it's something," he murmured against her ear, licking at the delicate shell, hoping to disarm her a bit.

She plopped his hand back into the water. "Fine. It's something I just . . . cannot discuss at the moment, how's that?"

The words he'd harshly spoken to her on their wedding day came rushing back to him. He'd firmly locked the door on a few very specific topics, and perhaps one of them needled at her on a holiday that was supposed to be about family.

"Ye want to share secrets, bonny?" He enfolded the bulk of his arms around her.

She took a moment to think about it, and then deflated with a breathy sigh. "No. It's probably best we both keep our secrets for the time being."

An odd reply, he thought. Taking a deep breath, he prepared himself to do something he'd not done in longer than a decade.

Trust someone.

"I told ye I wouldna discuss my back, my father, my brother, or Colleen . . ."

She took in an expectant breath, and that confirmed his suspicions.

"But . . . I was wrong to do that. To shut that door forever, was I not?"

She shrugged. "We barely knew—know—each other. You're entitled to keep your past in the—"

"How will we get to know each other without personal revelations?" he interjected. "If ye have any questions about me, lass, ye can ask them. And no matter what they are, I promise I'll answer them honestly."

For a moment, they both didn't breathe, though he was sure she could hear the pounding of his heart against the bare flesh of her back.

She finally inhaled. "I heard something a while back . . ."

"I'm certain ye've heard a great many things about me," he murmured. "And since I've already proven that the rumors of my sexual prowess are all true, am I to assume this is something slanderous?"

"Yes?" She made a sound in her throat both reluctant and frustrated. "But not about you. Not really. I heard that . . . that Liam killed your father. Do you believe that to be true?"

Not-so-secret family secrets. Gavin grunted. It was time she learned what it was to be tied to Hamish Mackenzie. "I know it to be true," he answered honestly. "It's common knowledge, in fact." There was no reason to ask where she heard the rumor, as it'd persisted among the Mackenzie since the moment Liam had come home from accepting his commission just long enough to gain a wife and lose a father.

"Is that the reason you hate your brother?" Her voice held neither surprise nor censure, merely cautious curiosity.

"That's part of it. I wanted to do it, myself. Justice isna the only opportunity Liam robbed me of."

"Is that why . . . why you had an affair with his wife?"

"Nay. I was with Colleen in spite of my brother, not because of him."

"You . . . loved her?"

Here, Gavin paused. Would the truth hurt her? He wondered, because he was startled by the realization that if he heard of her love for another man . . . A strange ache pierced his chest, followed by flare of possessive fury.

"Aye." He kept his vow to answer her honestly, but felt compelled to explain in a way he never had before. "We were courting before my father signed a betrothal contract between her and Liam. I often suspected that Hamish did it because he knew I wanted her."

"Did Liam know you wanted her?"

"He claims not to have done." Gavin thought back to the horrid night of the wedding. He'd refused to attend the festivities, and when the lights of Ravencroft had dimmed, he'd lain awake brutally tortured by thoughts of his brother with the woman he loved.

"You don't believe him?" she asked quietly.

"Actually, I think I do," he said after a time. "Because I doona think he would have married her and fathered two children had he known what I knew."

"What do you mean?"

"Everyone in Colleen's household thought she was besotted with a demon, and she was, in a way. Just like we all are. But her demon was nothing more or less than madness. She heard voices, upon occasion, and sometimes it was impossible to break her of certain obsessions. When she was at her worst, she'd convince herself of the strangest things, like that her cook was trying to poison her, or her lady's maid was a spy."

"How awful."

"She'd already confided in me. I'd already seen evidence of her madness, and I told her it didna matter, that

I'd help guide her through the bad days so we could spend the good ones together. Because when she was young, it wasn't all that serious. When she was lucid, she was beautiful and softhearted and kind. And she loved me, too, as well as she could."

"Then . . . why did she agree to marry your brother?" His wife sounded puzzled. "It's not like this is the Dark Ages, can your father really still sign you away without your consent?"

"According to Colleen, she submitted because both she and her father feared what Hamish would do to their family if she defied his commands."

"Yet another reason to hate your father." His wife surprised him by threading her slim fingers through his beneath the water. "Did Liam love her, as well?"

Gavin shook his head, struck by how easy it was to unburden his past. For the first time, the gall of it didn't choke his throat. "Until Mena, Liam loved nothing so much as the shedding of blood. He married Colleen because he needed a marchioness and an heir, and she was the highest-born lass hereabouts who was anything to look at."

"Poor Colleen." Her compassion unstitched him, and he closed his eyes against the strange welling of vivid emotion. "Was Liam cruel to her?"

"Not on purpose, but neither did he ken what to do with her madness. He was gone to war more often than he was home, and his abandonment only caused her distress, though neither of them much desired each other's company. He thought that making her a mother would help, but it only seemed to exacerbate her condition. For years I did what I could. I spent a great deal of time at Ravencroft with her, but innocently, only to watch her deteriorate. One night, when things were particularly bad, she sent for me and . . ."

"And you went to her."

"It was the only night we spent together . . . in that way. After, I pleaded with her to leave him. To come away with me. I was sure that I could make her better, that our love would somehow withstand my brother's wrath and the confines of her mind. God, but I was young and eternally daft."

"She didn't run away with you."

"She sent me ahead to prepare, wrote a confession to my brother, and threw herself from the Ravencroft battlements."

"Holy God!" She gripped his hand tighter, and he squeezed back, feeling more unburdened than angry for the first time in more than a decade since the occurrence.

"Now ye see why there is a rift between Liam and me that will never mend." He brought their joined hands to his lips and kissed her knuckles.

"Never is a long time . . . ," she said hopefully.

"Not long enough." He made a short sound of melancholy amusement in his chest. "It's all ancient history, anyhow. I spent the next decade becoming the dissolute and debauched ne'er-do-well ye've come to know and lo—" His throat caught on the word.

Love.

They'd never spoken of it, except to deny it. He'd promised himself he was forever incapable of opening himself to the emotion again. That the best they could hope for was to put up with each other to their mutual benefit.

He already knew it had gone way beyond that.

At least on his part.

"Do ye feel better knowing that, lass? Or worse?" He kept the anxiety out of his voice as he asked, wondering if his honesty had earned him her condemnation.

"Better," she said instantly. "And worse."

"Ye canna ken the guilt I've carried," he confessed. "Ye canna know the regret."

She twisted to face him, her lithe body sliding along his, her lovely features pursed with a mirroring apprehension. "This may sound strange . . . but I think I can."

"Is that so?" He searched her face, suddenly struck by how little he knew about her. What sins could possibly haunt the past of a woman so young? "Confess yer sins, then, and I'll absolve ye as ye have me."

She pressed a soft kiss to his lips. "You didn't need absolution. You didn't mean to hurt anyone . . . Thank you for telling me." To his surprise, she pushed away from him and got out of the tub with rather jerky, ungainly movements for a woman with such usual grace. Remaining hunched over, she covered herself with a towel and padded across the room. Reaching for her robe, she hurriedly belted it around her.

Goddammit, he'd just gotten her naked, and laid himself bare. There was no way she was covering up now . . . nor was she avoiding his question.

Most especially now that he was certain she hid something from him. Something important.

The water nearly sloshed out of the tub as he swiftly rose and dried himself before stalking over to the bed upon which she attacked her hair with the brush.

Unabashedly nude, he gripped both of her wrists, putting a stop to her frenzied almost violent grooming, and pulled her to her feet.

"It's yer turn, lass," he said gently. "I know ye've been wounded, as well. And I want to know by whom." Was it Grant? God, he'd never forget that name.

The man she might have married if not for him. The man who'd taken her virginity?

"I'm not wounded," she said warily. "I—I'm broken. I'm ruined. And it's no fault but my own."

"Nay, lass," he argued, forcing her arms to wrap around his middle, drawing her close until he splayed her hands over the scars on his back. "I see wounds in your eyes when ye forget to hide them from me. We share them, I think. The kind of wounds that never heal. But we doona let them break us, do we? They scar, but those scars create us. They remind us of what we can survive. Of the strength we have. Ye're the strongest woman I've ever met. It's one of the reasons I—"

"I'm weak," she said, burying her crumpling face against his chest. "And I'm a coward."

"Tell me why ye think that."

"You don't want to know," she groaned.

"Ye're wrong. I want to know everything about ye. I want to know what makes you desperate. What makes you despair. I want to know what brings ye joy." The truth of his confession astounded them both, it seemed. But he meant it. Sliding a finger beneath her delicate chin, he gently forced her to look up at him. "I want to be yer husband, lass."

"Well . . . you *are* my—"

"Nay, not like this. Not in the way we initially agreed. I doona want to be *somewhat* faithful to ye, and I doona want ye to pine for another. Because, even though I've loved in the past, I never think on her when I'm with ye." This felt like a revelation, even to himself.

"I thought it was just Erradale that made me happy this last month, lass. But now I ken it's more than that. It's working alongside ye, sleeping beside ye, being inside ye. It's all of it. It's this life ye brought back and gifted me with."

His every word seemed to create a wellspring in her

eyes that overflowed her lashes in fat rivulets somewhere during his declaration.

"I want to return that happiness to ye. I want to keep the burden of yer secrets, as well. So tell me, lass . . . what are ye hiding from me that I—"

"I'm pregnant!"

Samantha *meant* to say more. She really did. Greater, more damning confessions sat poised on her tongue like shards of ice, caught in one place so long they'd begun to sting and burn. He'd find out eventually, and she knew it now. So why not confess?

She shook all over, balanced on the brink of admission. Her blood flushed hot, and then cold. Her heart pounded in her ears, behind her eyes, in the fingers pressed against the ridges of scars on Gavin's back.

I'm not who you think I am. I'm not Alison Ross. I'm an orphan. A thief. I'm a murderer. I'm a liar.

I'm a mother.

And the child isn't yours.

He pulled her away from his chest, cradling her face in both of his big hands.

Here it is, she thought. He wanted a confession, he was about to get one.

On his head be it.

The moment she opened her mouth, his tongue was inside it, his lips sealed to hers in a kiss so tender and evocative, it shook the foundations of the medieval stones beneath her. He tasted like loss, and happiness, and hope.

It was a kiss for the ages. One that broke every wall they'd erected, and rebuilt a few parts of them both that had previously shattered. Suddenly, the shadows of the night surrounding them blurred the lines of morality. Of sanity.

Of honesty.

He wanted this. He wanted her, and this baby. He wanted them both to be his.

He desired a life with her. This life. A life she'd grown to love. Something she yearned for more than anything she'd ever dreamed of in the past.

And he deserved those things. He was nothing like the worthless, selfish brigand Alison Ross had led her to believe. He deserved a woman who patiently stitched his broken heart back together. He deserved children who established a new legacy for his family. One of success and pride and decency.

But Samantha didn't deserve him. Not this ferocious, protective man who loved so fiercely, he piled sorrows and stress upon his wide shoulders in order to shelter those he cared about.

In a way, his lie was as big as hers. When he'd said he was incapable of feeling, she should have known right then that the opposite was true. Gavin St. James felt more deeply than perhaps anyone she'd ever met. He was a man of incomparable strength and wit and fathomless depths of passion and need. He'd done whatever he could to save his mother. His land. And Colleen. The only woman he'd ever loved.

Samantha closed her eyes against the pain of that.

She . . . *she* was the scoundrel here. One who should maybe end this charade before she became yet another of his tragedies. But where would she go? She had some money now, but she'd planned on staying at Inverthorne at least long enough to give birth. Long enough to truly and legally give him what he wanted.

Running and hiding as a pregnant woman would prove nigh to impossible. This wasn't supposed to happen. The plan was that they marry and tolerate each other for a short period of time. That he move on to his next conquest, and once he'd forgotten about her, she'd slip away. That was the bargain they'd struck. That she could go live elsewhere. That she could be both free and protected.

She'd never expected that the chains threatening her freedom would be made of velvet instead of steel. That the one place that truly never belonged to her was the one place she'd never want to let go of.

Covering his hands on her face with her own, she broke the kiss, but was unable to pry herself free of him.

It was his expression that sealed her mouth closed. She watched it carefully, guiltily, as a bloom of awestruck, marvelous wonderment transformed him into a stranger. Gone was the ever-present cynical twist to his lips, its place stolen by a blinding smile that was all teeth and masculine delight. A suspiciously damp gleam deepened the verdant depths of his eyes to that of a rain forest, the kind of green that fought for the nourishment of rare sunlight, and sparkled with abundant life once it was granted. He regarded her—*her*— as though she were a miracle unfolding in his arms.

"Gavin, I should tell you—"

Dipping his head down, he feathered soft, abundant kisses over her upturned face. "A month," he whispered. The silk of his lips trailing over her brow. Her temples. Her eyelids. "I've lain with ye for a *month*." Her nose. Her cheekbones. The tense muscle of her jaw. "And ye've never denied me for . . . feminine reasons." Her chin, her jaw, the corners of her mouth. "I should have suspected. I should have known."

"There's something you have to—"

"I'll do anything." His words hardened from a whisper to a vow. "*Anything* to prove that from now on, ye and this bairn are all that matters. There is no one else for me, lass.

Not in the past, and not in the future." He reached into the part of her dressing robe and spread his hand against her belly, only the slightest bit less flat than it had always been. The simple weight of his warm, work-roughened hand was heavier than any burden she'd ever carried. And sweeter than any touch she'd ever known.

Samantha knew she was the only one that felt the flutter beneath his palm, soft, like the wings of a butterfly.

"Ye doona ken what a gift this is." His other hand threaded into her hair, cupping her head so he could rest his forehead against hers. "Ye've given me more than just Erradale. Ye've given me a chance to be what I've always wanted to be. A good man. A good father. I need this, bonny. I need ye. *Us.* And even if ye doona feel the same, I'll do what it takes to make ye happy. I'll protect ye and this child from anything and everyone. I'll—"

She wrenched herself away from him, turning back to the bed in the futile hope that some distance would return some of her clarity. Her sanity. Was it possible, just this once, that things could go right? She pleaded with the heavens. Both the cruel palace of perfection that housed the vengeful God she'd been raised with, and the older, more human gods of this place. Could she be forgiven? Redeemed? Happy?

"It wasn't supposed to *be* like this," she sobbed.

"What do ye mean?"

She touched her chin to her shoulder, glancing back at the perfection that was his face and form. "I wasn't supposed to fall for you."

His arrogant smile returned, though with none of its previous cruelty. "Well, doona be too hard on yourself, bonny. It's an understandable mistake that thousands of ladies in your position have made—och!"

He ducked just in time for her hairbrush to sail harmlessly over his head and clatter against the far wall.

And then she was in his arms again. "But ye're the first woman I've ever felt this way about," he said seriously. "Ye're the last woman I'll ever want."

Well . . . shit, she lamented as more hot tears leaked over her cheekbones. She was done for.

His mouth took hers again, distracting her from what his hands were about until the chilly night air kissed her flesh and she realized that she was naked again.

Gavin left her no time to process that fact as he shaped his strong hands over her body, spanning her narrow hips, splaying over her ass, and lifting her against him.

Left with no choice, she wrapped her legs around his lean waist and her arms around his shoulders as their tongues speared and tangled with each other. He tasted of salt, but Samantha had the strange sense that the tears she licked from the seam of their mouths might not only belong to her. That the preponderance of them carried not sorrow, but joy.

Hope.

She let the next word skitter across her thoughts until it disappeared beneath the dense blanket of raw lust and incoherent need evoked by his touch. She dare not think that word.

Not yet.

Gavin walked them both to the bed, though instead of spreading her beneath him, he surprised her by turning and sitting on it, splitting her legs over his hips so their mouths could remain fused.

Samantha didn't mind one bit. After tonight, her man deserved a good ride.

The blunt pressure of his cock pressed intimately against her, impossibly hotter and harder than the rest of him. She reached between them, lifting herself in preparation to take into her body the one thing it wept for.

Lord, but with just a few kisses, her husband set her skin on fire, and released a wet flood of preparation all at once.

A fucking miracle of biblical proportions, *that* was sex with Gavin St. James.

In a sinuous motion of both unparalleled grace and strength, he stretched his magnificent body onto his back, all the while lifting her hips and dragging her up his torso and past his shoulders.

"What are you—"

His wicked mouth answered her, but not with words.

Knees split on either side of his head, she hadn't the time or the strength to fight him as he pulled her to his lips. The lick was little more than a pass, their wet flesh whispering against each other with the promise of more.

She felt it all the way to the roots of her hair. Tossing her head back, she arched her pelvis forward, offering him what he would ultimately take.

His tongue traced the slippery skin around the place where she twitched and throbbed for him. An iniquitous tease with wet consequences.

Samantha made a hoarse moan of pleading that she'd never in her life thought to utter. This wasn't her, this wild and needful woman. In his arms she was no longer skinny Samantha. She was lithe. She was supple. She was a twisting creature with long, tight limbs and endless desires and demands.

She wasn't just a wife, she was a woman.

Tired of his teasing, her fingers instantly found his hair and gripped it, pulling him closer, demanding satisfaction.

She'd expected him to comply, but she hadn't expected his moan of anticipation as he cleaved her sex open with the flat of his tongue. Nor the following one of appreciation at what he found.

"Holy fuck," she gasped, as his mouth sealed over her sex in earnest, and his clever tongue went to work.

His chuckle against her clitoris caused a flush of sensation to shock through her, and she gasped as his shameless, relentless tongue dipped into her body, curling around the resulting release of wet desire he found there.

He circled her most sensitive peak, nipped at it with his lips, tormenting her closer and closer to the climax she knew awaited her, but denying her each time her fist tightened in his hair.

"Please," she begged, both ashamed and uncaring. "Please . . . let me . . . I need."

He shook his head in denial, but with her sex in his mouth, the movement felt incredible.

Suddenly, she realized, two could play at that game.

Her mouth flooded with moisture at the thought as she lifted her hips away from him, and his mouth let her go with a lurid noise.

Ignoring his words of protest, she quickly levered her body around, split her legs over his head, and stretched her torso over his.

"Holy fuck," he echoed darkly, as she slowly slid her tongue around the weeping head of his cock.

"I can tease, too," she said as she slowly stroked his throbbing length. "And I bet I last longer."

"Och, lass," he gasped, his hips twitching and arching against her touch. "'Tis a wager we both win no matter who loses."

His arms clamped around her thighs and spread her open. Samantha had only a moment to sense the ultimate vulnerability this position put her in before another lick

stole her breath, and gave her back warm spills of building pleasure.

She realized she had some catching up to do, and she
took as much of him into her mouth as she possibly could.

He tasted of sex and the slightest hint of soap. She
swirled her tongue around the smooth heat of him, stopping to explore the subtle ridges of veins as she controlled
his withdrawal by tightening her lips.

She could feel his reactions to her ministrations not just
through the flexes and trembles of his thick limbs, but also
in the slips and catches of his own tongue. His attentions
to her sex became less skillful with every glide of her wet
lips on his cock. His mouth was less teasing and more demanding. His tongue less practiced and playful and more
desperate and overwhelming.

When she added her hand to the base of his shaft to
move in tandem against the flesh that she couldn't fit into
her mouth, she quickly realized that she'd never had a
chance.

His mouth ruthlessly latched onto the engorged peak of
her sex and centered all movement just below the tender
bud. The sensation overwhelmed her instantly, scorching
through her sex and burning through her veins with such
potency, she had to pull him out of her mouth lest she do
him damage.

She squirmed to escape, but his incomprehensible
strength kept her immobile as he devoured her core until she
only succeeded in surging against his mouth, riding it
until aching pleasure engulfed her in great, shuddering
spasms. Ecstasy flowed from his mouth into her body as
she bucked against his hold, squirming, arching to get
closer as it ebbed and flowed in erotic, torturous pulses.

Finally she collapsed, her forehead resting against his

thigh, very aware of the cockstand still gripped in her palm. She thought he'd give her a moment to catch her shuddering breath.

She thought wrong.

With an inarticulate curse, he tossed her onto her knees and rose behind her. Her eyes flew wide as he seized her hips in a brutal grip and buried himself to the root inside her still-pulsing depths.

He drilled into her, the hard planes of his hips pounding against her as a fresh storm of pleasure began to build deeper within her loins. She shivered and convulsed, gritting her teeth together to keep herself from screaming. She enjoyed the wicked, brutal sounds their bodies made, the growling breaths that exploded from him.

He pushed her to her elbows, his hands both rough and reverent. He took her like a stallion mounted his mare. This was not their usual encounter, she realized.

This was a claiming.

He was a hunter, a predator. And now, she'd become his mate.

A jolt of pleasure followed this revelation, screaming through her with the speed and awesome force of a lightning bolt. She bucked against him. Curling her back and fighting a little, making him work for his domination.

Suddenly his grip was tinged with a bit of pain, and the hand in her hair yanked her head back and anchored it as he made a desperate sound, and then another, until the night was filled with his roar of pleasure, just as her womb was filled with the warmth of his seed.

Their climax synchronized and became an ecstasy so complete, the earth that she knew fell away. Time, as she understood it, ceased to tick away her life. And every star she'd ever wished upon was close enough for her to reach out and pluck from the sky.

But she didn't need to, she thought dimly, as she allowed herself to float back to the bed with deep, exhausted breaths.

She'd already found heaven.

Gavin allowed her to lie there as he cleaned them, extinguished the lights, and crawled into bed next to her.

They were both silent a while, listening to the sounds of the winter night. Gentle snow drifted in flakes the size of dove feathers outside the casement, and though it made no sound, there was a melody to it. A muffled softness that seemed to blanket the entire Highlands.

"I was going to make love to ye tonight, lass," Gavin murmured finally as he pulled her close. "But ye drove me beyond all control."

Samantha smiled at the night, thinking about how she didn't mind one bit. "Next time," she whispered, patting the arm he'd draped protectively around her.

"Next time." He yawned, and promptly fell asleep.

Samantha lay quietly in the dark, her body still singing and her soul still a little troubled.

She could do this, couldn't she?

Gavin moaned when she shifted her position a little to ease a new ache in her back. His fingers found her belly, and he splayed his palm against it, making a dreamy sound.

That flutter startled her again. Had the child caused it? Or was it her own reaction to the man?

"Are . . . are you awake?" she whispered.

He replied with a soft, masculine snore.

Samantha's heart squeezed so powerfully, she thought for a moment that the ache might kill her.

Come hell or high water, she knew she'd steal every moment in Gavin's arms, in his bed, and in his life that fate would allow her. She wanted nothing more in the world than for this child to have him as a father. He'd teach a son how to be a man, a kind, honest, strong man, and he'd allow a daughter to feel cherished, appreciated, and protected. What a life a child would have at Inverthorne. Romping in the woods with Callum. Reading to Eleanor. Riding with Eammon. Laughing and teasing with Locryn and Calybrid. Working alongside parents who would do anything to secure a happy, prosperous future.

This was a family. The mutual desire that brought them together. The thing that could bind them despite whatever threatened to tear them apart.

Including her deception?

Perhaps . . . This wasn't just about her needing protection, anymore. He'd just admitted he needed her too, needed the child she carried.

For the first time, Samantha considered that her secret . . . might just be one worth keeping a little while longer.

CHAPTER TWENTY-FOUR

Eammon Monahan's sense of trepidation intensified as he lifted the saddle blanket from Lysander's back, and uncovered the mystery as to why the beast had thrown poor Sam from the saddle. He'd awoken this morning sensing trouble on the north wind. The Monahans had always sensed the wind, and this one blew alteration and revelations whispering through the winter trees.

"A thistle." He held it up for her inspection, though how Sam could see anything from eyes narrowed in fury confounded the blarney right out of him. "Right beneath the blanket. Left a proper scrape too, here on his back, poor lad."

"I *knew* it had to be something. I can count on one hand the times I've been unseated from a horse, and more than a few have tried." Sam plucked the sharp thistle from Eammon's outstretched hand and inspected it thoroughly. "Gavin thinks he can order me to stay home, does he? The high-and-mighty Lord of Inverthorne Keep. Ha! I'll saddle up, take this thistle to Erradale, and shove it up his—"

"Come now, lassie, don't be too hard on your husband."

"Someone has to be."

Eammon chuckled, even though he still felt a mite pale, and his palms were still slick with moisture. "He was worried about you, is all."

That morning, Eammon had aided in preparing a few horses for permanent transport to Erradale so the workers could have use of them, since they'd cobbled together a new stable of sorts on the land.

Lady Sam, Lord love her, had offered to prepare and saddle her own mount, and he'd allowed her to as he knew no one but Callum more adept with horses.

All was well until she led Lysander into the courtyard. The moment her wee arse plopped in the saddle, before her opposite foot had found its purchase, the beast had jumped, bucked, and reared, dumping her onto the stones.

Luckily, the girl knew how to fall, and had popped back up, quick as a fleet-footed cat, and subdued the animal.

That hadn't stopped Thorne from losing his Mackenzie mind over it.

Their resulting yelling match had revealed three very amusing facts.

First, the new Countess of Thorne was the bravest woman alive, to stand up to her husband in such a state.

Second, she was pregnant, a fact that had been snarled at her by her husband in front of God and everyone.

And third . . . Gavin St. James was in love with his wife.

Beneath all of Lord Thorne's brutish bluster lived a terror only understood by a man who'd survived a loss which he'd been helpless to avoid.

Well, the winds of alteration and revelation. They were never wrong . . .

After Thorne had ascertained that Sam—and the baby—was all right, he'd ordered her to stay at Inverthorne in a, granted, needlessly stern manner. Any sane man would have known a woman with spirit wouldn't have responded favorably.

But Eammon had noted that Thorne's usually golden skin had taken on a ghostly shade. His nostrils wouldn't cease flaring, and when he shoved his finger at his wife and ordered her to bed, his hands had trembled violently.

Sam seemed not to have noticed, because she'd resisted him up until the moment he'd threatened to decapitate any man who allowed her on a horse with a blunt sword before riding away fast enough for her curses not to blister his backside.

Aye, that was love for you.

Eammon studied Sam, and wondered if she knew it. If they'd said the words. If she realized that Thorne would ride harder, work longer, and suffer more physical labor because the demon inside him would be whispering what ifs in his ear all the day long.

"Lysander, here, threw you good and far," he ventured, patting the animal on the rump before shutting the stall door behind him. "Thorne was right to mention that such a topple puts you and your child in danger. I'd be wary of these beasts until the wee one's arrived."

"We weren't going to tell anyone about my condition for a few weeks yet . . . ," she groused. His new lady was in no great habit of capitulation, but she puffed out her cheeks in that way of hers and muttered, "But I suppose you're . . . not wrong."

"And that's almost like being right." He chuckled.

"Don't push it."

A sparkle of humor underscored her churlish scowl, before she bent to investigate the saddle blanket. "I just don't understand. I prepared and saddled Lysander, myself. I'm certain I'd have noticed a thistle of this size."

Eammon was fair certain of that, as well. Though he knew that pregnancy often took its toll on a woman's focus. He'd also lived long enough to know better than to mention it.

"Since you're home today, why don't you tell Lady Eleanor the good news? She'll probably be a bit hurt if she hears it from someone other than you, and word of these things tends to spread quickly through a castle."

In a gesture as old as time, Lady Thorne spread her fingers over her womb and nodded. "Thank you, Eammon," she said, and turned to drift through the courtyard, her dark braid almost catching in the iron gate to Inverthorne as she secured it behind her.

The thistle troubled Eammon well into the afternoon. It'd been chaos in the stables and the courtyard this morning. Nearly a score more carpenters, craftsmen, and laborers had shown up in search of work at Erradale. Between that and the men who'd arrived from the bustling ranch to escort the horses back over Gresham Peak, he'd lost track of everyone tramping in and out of Inverthorne lands.

Was it possible someone had deliberately placed the thistle beneath the countess's saddle blanket?

Barely more than a month had passed since Lady Sam's enemies had attacked Erradale, and all had been quiet in the Highlands since. Though her wound had healed, she and Thorne both comported themselves with a certain amount of wariness. Gates were locked at all times, the keep secured as though expecting a Viking siege at any moment.

No one had exactly been told why, but all the necessary precautions had been taken, in any case.

As Eammon finally set his stables to rights, he made up his mind. If a detail niggled at him this much then it was obviously important. He should hie himself to Errad-ale and talk to Thorne about—

He turned and froze. How in the world had he allowed himself to be caught unawares? He'd been so deep inside his own mind, he'd never even registered that he wasn't alone.

"M-my lady," he breathed.

The dowager tilted her graceful neck in his direction from where she stood stroking the neck of a kind mare who'd come to the stall door to greet her. Eleanor was a vision in lavender silk embroidered with small green leaves the color of her eyes.

Would her beauty never fade? He almost wished it would. Then maybe to look at her with the rare golden late-afternoon sunlight streaming in through the wide stable doors would not do the same thing to his lungs as did a horse's hoof to the chest.

"I didn't think to find any horses left in the stables today. It was my understanding that my son took them all to Erradale."

Eammon closed his eyes and prepared for another polite, nonsensical discussion with the woman he'd worshiped for the better part of two decades.

She was *here*, he told himself. She'd come to the stables without Thorne. Without Alice, even. And that was something. It wasn't hope. But . . . something.

"Hermia's a bit too old to be chasing cattle all over the moors of Erradale." He approached Eleanor like he would any skittish animal. With enough noise for her to always be aware of him, but an even voice and no sudden, loud movements. "So she gets to enjoy the comforts of home."

He stood behind Eleanor, patting Hermia's brindled neck, careful not to allow his fingers to touch the dainty ones rhythmically smoothing down the animal's glossy coat.

"She's lucky to have you. So many men would sell her to the slaughterhouse once she'd become useless to them."

"Well, she may be a bit older, but she's not useless at all. I still put her out in the pastures while I'm teaching Great Scot's Ghost to take to a rope. She helps remind him how to behave."

Slight twitches of Lady Eleanor's sightless eyes and a change in her posture told him how aware she was of his proximity. She knew he stood beside her, their shoulders almost touching. Though, for the first time, she didn't flinch away.

"Why come to the stable, my lady, if you didn't think to find any horses?" He swallowed his heart when she turned to him, her face lifted as though she would study him.

Christ, he burned.

He burned with the memory of holding her limp, bleeding body in his arms as he carried her from Ravencroft, vowing that Hamish would have to walk through his bones to get her back. He burned with a helpless, barbaric rage each time she looked up at him and saw nothing.

But he was grateful, too, in a dreadful way. That she couldn't discover what seared in his eyes when he looked at her.

For he was certain it would frighten her away. And he wanted nothing more than to be in her presence, for however long she could stand it.

"I did not properly present myself, Mr. Monahan," she noted. "Good afternoon." Reaching between them, she offered him her ungloved hand, high and bent in an obvious invitation to be kissed.

She'd been doing this quite a bit lately. In fact, every time he'd seen her since Sam had arrived and he'd dared to kiss her hand that first time.

"At your service, my lady." He rubbed his rough palm on the thigh of his trousers before taking her incomprehensibly small fingers and planting a lingering kiss on the backs of her knuckles.

He about fell over when she didn't let his hand go right away, but gave it a soft squeeze—one he'd wished to call reluctant—before she released him.

"I remember the first day the late Laird Ravencroft hired you to look after Inverthorne, Mr. Monahan. I remember thinking your eyes were the most extraordinary shade of dark gold."

She'd remembered the color of his eyes? All these years? He tried to swallow. To speak. But, it seemed, none of his faculties were in order at the moment.

"You were a recent widower, if memory serves. I didn't believe I'd ever seen anyone so sad before, except when I looked in the mirror." She was silent a moment, long enough for all the words he'd never said to her to spill into his mouth at once.

I love you. I love you. I love you.

Thankfully, she summoned an amused smile. "You . . . you didn't have a beard back then, but I recall a wealth of unruly hair the color of beechwood."

"There's more gray, and less hair these days." He croaked out an attempt at levity, his hand self-consciously finding a hairline that had retreated from where it had once been.

She lifted an elegant shoulder. "A great deal has changed since then, hasn't it?"

"Aye." He scratched at his whiskers. "You don't like my beard?" He'd shave it today. Right now.

Fluttering her lashes in a shy suggestion of delight erased decades of sorrow from her face. She could have been any unsure young lady experiencing her first flirt with a stable boy. "I like it very much," she whispered. "It tickles when you kiss me—*my hand*," she amended quickly.

Heart stalling, he cast about an empty head for a reply. "My late wife never let me have one. She thought it too bristly. Said it made her sneeze so I shaved every morning without fail." He winced with every bone he possessed. Should have said anything but that. Any green idiot knew you didn't speak to the woman you hadn't kissed about a woman you had. Christ, that'd been one of the first lessons he'd taught the boys about the fairer sex.

Suddenly, he wished the herd would return, so he could let one of them gallop over his head.

"Let you?" Her brow furrowed with bewilderment. "Did you not do as you please? Were you not her master?"

"Her master?" His bark of laughter shocked them both, and he sobered as quickly as he could. "Nay, my lady. My marriage . . . it was not anything like yours."

She nodded, as though accepting something she'd already suspected. "How was it?"

"I don't think you want to discuss—"

"How was it?" she repeated.

Reaching around to squeeze sudden tension from the back of his neck, he looked back through the decades. "Funny, mostly. Brigit loved to laugh, and if she wasn't laughing, I wasn't working hard enough. She had the patience of a banshee and was as stubborn as a fussy mule, but her laugh was my favorite sound on this earth."

"Was?" Eleanor whispered.

Driven by reckless instinct honed by a lifetime of working with fretful creatures, Eammon brushed a curl back from her jaw, allowing the very tips of his rough fingers contact with her precious skin. "Well, I've heard another voice since I lost her . . . one I listen for every day."

She stood stock-still, rapidly blinking those lovely green eyes as he trailed his finger up her jaw, tucking the curl neatly behind the shell of her ear. Emboldened, he traced the soft silver down at her hairline, finding the faded scar by her temple.

"Brigit," she whispered tightly. "What a lovely name." Then, to their mutual distress, she burst into tears.

Eammon panicked. He ached to hold her. Had she been any other woman, he'd have swept her into his arms. But he knew better than to imprison her against him. To show her his strength.

"What do you need, Eleanor?" he asked gently. "Should I get Alice? Or take you to her?"

"No!" Even through her tears, the word was strong. Decisive. "No, I found you on my *own,* and I left myself a path through the gate back to the castle. I'm not useless, you know. I may be blind . . . but I'm not broken. I'm still—still a—a woman."

"I know that," he soothed. Sweet Christ, he knew that. He'd been trying to forget for twenty bleeding years. "Tell me why you're here alone. Tell me what I can do. What you need." He pressed his handkerchief into her hand, and let her wipe her own tears and dab at her nose as she fought valiantly to compose herself.

"I—I found out I'm going to be a grandmother today," she said around delicate hiccups.

"Aye, but isn't that happy news?"

"The happiest." Her chin wobbled, but a moment of biting her lip harder than she should brought it to heel. "And all I could think while congratulating my daughter-in-law was that I'd have never—that Gavin and I wouldn't have survived that night if—I owe you my life, my son's life, and now my precious grandchild's life."

A fresh wave of sobs overtook her, and this time he couldn't stand it. He dragged her against him, and breathed a sigh of relief when she collapsed into his arms and clutched at his vest. The north wind blew . . . and he wished it to never stop.

"I think he makes her feel safe, Eammon," she cried. "When he speaks to her he smiles, I can hear it. And even if he is hard or angry, he does not make her afraid. He does not hurt her, not even with his words. He's a miracle, my boy. And after everything—" Emotion stole her words, and Eammon smoothed a hand over her silken curls, thinking that nothing ever was or would be sweeter than this woman in his arms.

"Whether he likes it or not, there is no mistaking his Mackenzie blood, but we've always known Gavin is not like his father." It was a miracle, Eammon agreed. He hoped the world never again saw the likes of Hamish Mackenzie.

"No," she said fervently against his chest. "He's like *you*."

His hand stalled in her hair. "What?"

"That's what I came to tell you." She sniffed as her sobs dwindled into little catches of breath. "Without you and dear Callum . . . Gavin might have been lost. After that night . . . well, I was certainly in no position to parent him. You've taught my son what it is to be a man. A decent man."

Eammon made a face, wondering if "decent" was a word that should be applied to Gavin St. James just yet.

"Well . . . perhaps I should say a kind man," she amended, and they both indulged in a breath of wry amusement at the thought of the Earl of Thorne's notoriety.

"You honor me, my lady." He pressed a chaste kiss to her temple.

She turned her head into the kiss. "Perhaps . . . you could call me Eleanor when we're alone."

"Oh?" Both his heart and his brows lifted at her words, and Eammon suddenly wondered if he might be trapped in a surreal dream. "Do you intend for us to be alone again?"

"Often," she breathed. Her skin tinged a lovely shade of peach that crept from beneath the high neckline of her dress. "If I may, that is . . . if you would . . ."

"Oh, I *would*," he said with relish. Maybe next time, he'd steal a kiss . . . see what she thought of his beard then—

Behind him, Hermia shifted restlessly, tossing her head. A swift shadow moved in his periphery.

Something Eleanor had said permeated the unbelievable bliss coursing through him with a lance of pure dread.

She'd found her way down to the stables alone. She'd left herself a path *back* to the keep. Glancing over her head, he peered through the stable doors out into the courtyard across which the iron gate to Inverthorne Keep stood open.

He might not have been so wary had the north wind not been blowing quite so hard. He might not have seen the shadow materialize from behind the gate, nor noted the pistol in time to cover Eleanor's body with his own.

CHAPTER TWENTY-FIVE

From behind her closed eyes, Samantha felt the shadow fall upon her like the specter of winter, stealing what warmth she'd found beneath the windows in the solarium.

"You're a crafty, double-dealin' bitch, I'll give you that much." Boyd Masters's Western drawl was an incongruous echo against stone walls used to more lyrical brogues than butchered, bastardized English.

For a ridiculous moment, Samantha kept her eyes squeezed firmly shut. This scenario played out often in her nightmares. Was she lucky enough to be dreaming this time, as well?

More exhausted than usual, she'd come to bask during a break in the clouds after pulling a chaise over to where a shaft of rare winter sunlight warmed the stones. Stretching out upon it like a lazy kitten, she'd dozed the day away.

That sunlight had disappeared now.

Maybe forever.

The residual ache in her leg and a few new bruises courtesy of her tumble from her horse this morning told her she was very much awake.

That her nightmare had become a reality.

Her eyes snapped open, revealing her unkempt brother-in-law's hostile leer as she instinctively reached for her hip.

Shit. She'd left her guns in their suite when she'd changed out of her work attire. Why would she need them within the safety of Inverthorne?

In a way, it was a blessing she didn't have them. Because if she'd laid her hand to a real pistol, Boyd would have squeezed the trigger of the Colt currently aimed right between her eyes.

"How did you manage to get to Scotland?" The question tumbled out of her on a gasp of disbelief.

Alison had said in her letter that the Masters brothers were hunted men, that their wanted posters were scattered from California to Ellis Island.

Right alongside hers.

With Boyd and Bradley's swarthy, almost exotic coloring and uncommon height, they weren't the kind of men to get lost in a crowd.

"Escaped south of the border, even though some would-be-hero marshal who started that whole fucking massacre winged me on that train. 'Course, we had to take the time to dig a grave for my brother first."

The back of his hand connected with her cheek with such force, little starbursts of darkness danced across her vision.

When she blinked her eyes open again, her head swam, but he'd moved to the foot of her chaise, continuing in his conversational manner.

"We set sail out of Puerto Cancún, Mexico, once we got word of what you did to them Pinkertons we sent after you." He made a short sound of reluctant mirth. "Fuckers should have listened. I done *told* them a skinny girl like you don't make no easy target, and could still shoot their eye out at fifty paces in the dark. That's what you count on, isn't it? Men underestimating your scrawny ass until you put a bullet in their heads?"

"No." She shook her head rapidly enough to dispel the sight of him and regain her equilibrium. "I didn't want any of this to happen . . . you *have* to believe that." A bolt of terror seized her muscles. "Boyd, who let you in the keep? Did you—did you hurt . . . anyone?"

"You mean that mountain of a man you went and married before my brother's corpse done gone cold in the ground?" His lips curled back in a terrible sneer. He'd lost another tooth since she'd seen him last. Even covered in grime and smelling like a peat bog, Boyd Masters was a passably handsome man until he smiled. She wondered if he lost that tooth to rot or tobacco. Probably both.

Hysteria threatened her consciousness. "Boyd, tell me you didn't—"

"Calm down, you simple slut, I ain't done him no harm. Been freezing our balls off in the forest tryin' for days to figure a way into this fortress. And wouldn't you know it, this mornin' luck was on our side. Every last workin' man rode north without you, for once, and then some blind old biddy left the gate wide open."

Samantha's heart leaped into her throat, and she had to swallow the bile threatening to escape her stomach as she pushed herself to her elbows. "Lady Eleanor? Where is she? Where's Bradley?"

"Stay right where you are, girl." He pushed the rim of his bronze cowboy hat up on his forehead to squint down from where he towered over her. "He's gatherin' up some folks. He'll be along directly."

"What have you done?" Gunshots would surely have roused her from her nap, but Bradley never had been much good with a gun.

He preferred to use knives.

The thought chilled her so completely, her soul shivered. What kind of hell had she brought to these people? How could she have been so stupid? She'd hoped that Boyd and Bradley would have to stay on the other side of the world. She'd hoped Boyd had been fatally wounded. That they'd forget about her in time.

She'd hoped . . . and that had been her gravest mistake.

"How *is* that little ass of yours, Sam? Quite a fall you took this mornin'."

A wave of helpless frustration almost knocked her over. *Of course.* She should have known. The stables were the only part of Inverthorne open to the small horse pastures and the forest beyond.

And a burr under the saddle was the oldest cowboy trick in the book.

"The thistle . . . that was you?"

"That was Bradley's doin'. I thought you were too good to let a horse dump you on your head." He snorted. "I only had two brothers in the whole world, and you kilt the smart one."

A scuffle and uneven footsteps disturbed the silence from the door behind her and she craned her neck in time to see Eammon with his arm around Eleanor leading a small procession into the solarium. Alice, a plain, bespectacled woman, stumbled on their heels, and Calybrid followed after, his hand pressed to his middle. It had been a month since he'd been shot, and he'd much improved, but gut shots were slow to heal, if they healed at all.

Bradley sauntered in behind them, his pistol trained on the little procession, his features too gaunt for his wide, dark eyes. He'd always been the ugly Masters brother. Opium and alcohol hadn't helped any.

"I locked the staff below stairs and barred the door," Bradley announced proudly.

"Sam?" Calybrid's reedy, befuddled voice broke her heart nearly as much as the sight of the wild tufts of fluff he called hair and his unsteady knees visible beneath his wrinkled nightshirt.

He'd been napping, too.

Emotion and regret stung behind her nose and filled her throat with woe.

"No chance ye got yer pistols on ye, Sam?" He blinked bleary, hopeful eyes at her, his shoulders slumping when she wordlessly shook her head. "Bugger."

"What's going on, Alison?" The tremble in Eleanor's voice defeated her completely.

"Please, Boyd, don't hurt them," Samantha croaked.

"Aww. Now we ain't here to hurt innocent folk, Sam." Boyd tugged the thighs of his denims so his long legs could squat down at the foot of the chaise. "You'll hurt 'em plenty by tellin' 'em the truth. That you're a lyin', murderin' whore." Though his voice remained deceptively mild, malevolence leaked from every syllable, as malodorous as the unrefined sludge they pulled out of the ground in Texas and New Mexico.

Samantha bit back a whimper as he rested the hand holding his pistol on the chaise. The barrel pointed between her parted feet. Were he to pull the trigger now, his bullet would land in her womb.

"When you've finished hurtin' them . . . *then* we'll hurt you." He cocked the pistol, and the familiar metallic clicks sent her hand to her belly. "We'll hurt you good for what you did to my little brother. And once they know the truth, they'll let us do it. Hell, they might even help."

"You don't want to do this—"

"Yes, I fuckin' do. It's all I've thought about for two months."

Breath sawed in and out of her as she fought to force the words past a throat quickly squeezing closed.

"The lassie's with child, man." Eammon blurted a plea. "Have some mercy."

"You think I fuckin' care that your master squirted some Highland brat into this worthless piece of—"

"Ye will when the son of a Mackenzie Laird comes for ye," Calybrid warned ominously. "Because he'll bring all the suffering hell can contain down upon ye."

"Not before I shoot her in the—"

"If you kill me, you murder your own kin." There. She'd done it. No going back now. The only mercy to be found was that she didn't have to look into Gavin's eyes the first time she revealed her deception. Boyd was a man without conscience or scruples, but family meant everything to him. Enough to risk crossing the Atlantic and storming a castle to take his revenge. "I've been pregnant since I left America. The baby belongs to Bennett."

The potent silence contained the individual astonishment of every person she'd come to care for.

And every person she'd come to hate.

Their thoughts, their fear, and their disbelief hurled through the space between them and battered at her with an inescapable dissonance.

Boyd stared at her blouse, as if he could see through it. "If you're lyin' to me . . ."

"I'm not. I'm more than two months along."

"You squirrely slut." Bradley's glee bounced around the room with a sickening chortle. "Is that why you married the first dupe who would look at you? So you could pass the baby off as his?"

"Fuck you, Bradley," she spat, her temper overcoming her fear, even her common sense. "That stunt you pulled in the stables this morning could have killed Bennett's child."

"You watch your whore mouth!" The butt of the pistol in Boyd's hand sailed toward her jaw, and Samantha braced for the blow. For the blood.

"Ye're already dead men." The voice from the doorway carried such arctic vehemence, it froze time.

The blow never landed, though pain still exploded through Samantha's entire body, caused by the undercurrent of fury burning beneath the ice in her husband's words.

"But whether yer death is mercifully swift or agonizingly unhurried depends . . ."

Samantha almost didn't recognize his voice. It was Gavin, but not. Gone were the silken tones of indolent sin, the leisurely indifferent confidence replaced by something as hard and unforgiving as the stones of his ancient keep. He sounded like a demon.

No. He sounded . . . like a Mackenzie.

"Depends on what?" Bradley could add impatience to his multitude of idiocies.

"On how she answers yer question."

Somehow, Gavin knew the second that Callum had ridden into Erradale and informed him of the evidence of a few outlanders' camps found in the forest that he'd have to kill someone today.

He hadn't realized until this moment, just how much he looked forward to it.

His grip tightened on both the pistol he had in his left hand and the dirk in his right. He trained the gun on the big, dirty fucker who'd almost hit his wife. Boyd, she'd called him. And the bastard had recovered his wits fast enough to aim his own weapon right back at Gavin.

The dirk he held in his off hand was poised to fly in the direction of the man to his right, but a knife was much slower than a bullet, and the slim, rat-faced cowboy had his gun pointed at Eammon and Gavin's mother.

Christ, he shouldn't have let Callum go back to the woods to track them. He'd thought Inverthorne impregnable, and still some instinct had sent him racing home. He'd expected to take his wife into his arms and warn her that her enemies might be close. To assure her that he would protect her and *his child* always. To tell her he was sorry for how he'd acted this morning. That fear had made him crazy.

That love had made him furious.

What he'd found was torment enough to turn his heart into an iron weight in his chest. An empty stable and an open gate. The signs of a scuffle and dragging footsteps.

He'd no time to go to the tower for the key to the armory. So he'd drawn his dirk and the sidearm he'd taken to wearing since the night Erradale burned, and searched his home for intruders.

He'd never have guessed one had lived among them all this time.

"Alison?" For some reason, her name from his lips sounded wrong, even to him. Only the back of her dark head was visible above the damask arm of the chaise.

She didn't look at him.

And in that moment, his heart turned from iron to ice as suspicion lanced him with a vengeance.

"Alison!" Boyd crowed the name as though it might be the most hilarious word he'd heard in his life. "You mean this poor bastard *still* don't know who you are?"

"Boyd . . ." It was the first time he'd heard actual terror in his wife's voice. She'd turned the man's terrible name into a plea. "Boyd, don't—"

Gavin itched to put a bullet right in the muddy brown eyes gleaming with the relish of a victorious predator about to rip out the throat of his opponent.

"You see, what we have here is what we call, back in the States, a Mexican standoff. You ever heard of that? It's where every party has an advantage, and a disadvantage. The moment you try to win one way . . ." Boyd gestured to his pistol, still pointed at Gavin, and then to his brother's gun, aimed at Gavin's family. "You lose another."

"Call it what ye like, ye still won't leave this room alive." No one entered a Highlander's house, terrorized their women, and left with their heads attached to their shoulders.

"I ain't so sure about that."

"Ye should be certain enough to make peace with yer Lord before I send yer screaming soul to hell. Or maybe I'll let ye live long enough to watch one more brother die."

"*Gavin.*" His mother's whispered gasp distracted him long enough for Boyd to strike out and drag his wife to her feet, turning her to use her slight body as a shield.

Her cry of pain still sliced through Gavin's fury and wrath to nick at his heart.

The control on his rage slipped, and he took a threatening step forward.

"Get your hands off me, Boyd," she spat, squirming in his one-armed grip.

Rat face made a startling noise. "If you're lucky, this bullet won't punch right through this Irish fuck and hit the old lady . . . You usually lucky, mister?"

The words caused Gavin uncharacteristic hesitation.

Nay. Fate and fortune had deserted him before he'd even been born. He'd a decidedly unlucky life. Unlucky in fealty. Unlucky in paternity.

Unlucky in love.

At Bradley's threat, Gavin's wife had gone limp in Boyd's hold.

The variable outcomes of this situation refused to process through one pulsing fact scratching at his rapidly unraveling humanity.

She wasn't denying her lie. These men weren't treating her like some woman who'd gotten in a lucky shot defending her life during a train robbery. At first, when she'd cried out that the child within her belonged to a dead man, he'd thought the worst of this Bennett.

Not of her.

Rape, possibly, for which he would take vengeance upon the entire Masters bloodline. Or dare he hope that she was lying to the man with the gun trained at her head? Using her wits to remain safe?

Look at me, he silently begged. *Let me see the truth in your eyes.*

She didn't.

Boyd's thick elbow tightened below her chin, and her fingers instinctively grasped at his arm. "Once you hear what I have to say, I think you'll let us walk out of here and take this lyin' bitch with us."

He could think again. "Ye will keep a civil tongue in yer head when you speak about my wife."

"That's the fuckin' thing, aint it? She *ain't* even your wife." Boyd sneered. "And seeing as how she murdered her last husband, *my brother,* in cold blood only two months ago, you'll be mighty glad of that."

"Her . . . husband." Gavin enunciated each syllable as though inspecting a word he'd never heard before.

"That's not true!" she cried.

Hope flared in Gavin for an awful moment, but Boyd shot it before it had a chance to take flight.

"Ain't it?" Boyd said through his teeth, tightening his

grip on her neck. "One lie comes out of your mouth, girl, and triggers start gettin' pulled, regardless of the consequences."

"Why would I believe the words ye forced out of a hostage woman?" Gavin changed tactics. "Ye're wanted men. Bandits. Thieves. Yer story means nothing to me."

Instead of panicking, or searching for another angle, a slow, victorious smile spread over Boyd's face. "Darlin'," he said against the tendrils of dark hair at her temple. "Reach into my pocket, would you? Don't pull out the biggest thing you find, but the folded piece of paper. That's it."

The revulsion on her face as she reached behind her and complied with his suggestion shot pure murder through Gavin's very skin and sinew. Had his mother not been in front of a bullet, he'd have emptied his barrel into the man's head right then and there.

Extracting a folded paper, she stared at it like it was a snake threatening to bite her.

"Go on." Boyd motioned with his pistol. "Don't keep everyone waitin'."

Trembling fingers opened what had been folded and unfolded time and time again, if the wear in the creases were aught to go by.

Even the deep groves of the substantial parchment couldn't hide her unmistakable likeness. The small, angular jaw. The pert nose smattered with freckles. The wide, shrewd eyes. In the rendering those eyes were more malicious than mischievous. The tilt of her full lips pursed in a hard, deviant way in an expression he couldn't imagine on her actual mouth.

The word WANTED bannered over the thick waves of hair he so loved to tangle his fingers into. A proclamation of her guilt.

The words beneath her picture that drove several daggers into him.

Train Robbery. A slice to his guts, ripping them open to spill on the stones.

Kidnapping. A puncture to his lungs, dragging the breath from his chest with such force he thought his ribs might crack.

Murder. His heart of ice shattered. Again.

"Samantha *Masters.*" He woodenly read the name aloud and slowly from beneath the damning list of charges, and finally. *Finally.* She met his gaze. The irony was, he wished she hadn't.

"Sam." He whispered her name.

"If you don't trust bandits," Boyd drawled. "You shouldn't have married one."

CHAPTER TWENTY-SIX

Samantha had always considered herself a strong woman. She had, indeed, shot her no-good husband just over two months ago, run away to a foreign country, and not only had she survived, she'd forged a life here. She'd thought she was sturdy. Resilient. Capable. If killing the father of her child hadn't broken her, nothing could.

How wrong she'd been.

Gavin stared at the wanted poster she still somehow brandished in front of her chest, but he'd long since ceased to see it. His was a blind gaze. One of a man who'd effectively retreated inside of himself.

But only for a moment.

He returned someone different when he blinked back up at her. His features were cold, unforgiving, and utterly bleak. She saw in him the thing he most feared. The same demon she'd sensed lurking in Liam Mackenzie.

The one they'd inherited from their father.

That demon regarded her from a masculine face more beautiful than that of an angel's. A face that, in spite of herself, she'd come to worship and covet as so many women had before her.

She hadn't fallen for him, she realized. Not like she had for Bennett, with the desperate need to escape a life of drudgery and oppression thrusting her into the arms of the first exciting man who'd offered her something more.

She'd stolen into love with Gavin St. James in small, imperceptible shifts of the cosmos.

Demons and all.

He was everything, she realized. He'd *become* everything to her. Her reason for waking so early, for working so hard, for upholding a lie. Somehow, she'd gone from doing whatever it took to keep Erradale from him, to doing whatever she could to give him what he wanted.

And the happiness he deserved.

From the moment he'd reached for her in the woods, when he'd kissed her against that tree. When he'd watched in boyish wonder with her as a new life entered the world. She'd seen in him not the man he was, but the one he tried his utmost to become.

Now, her deception had turned him into someone else. Someone ultimately and utterly dangerous.

"Deny it." His words were more dare than command. They both knew it.

"I can explain," she whispered.

"Are ye Samantha Masters?" His lips barely moved. The low register of his voice scarcely reached her over everyone's heavy, expectant breaths.

"No one was supposed to get hurt, and then the shooting started and I couldn't let—"

"Are. Ye. Samantha Masters?"

Whatever fire had thus far fueled her inner strength flickered, sputtered, and died. Extinguished by the pure frost in his voice.

The smoke tasted acrid as she exhaled. "Yes."

All the wildness drained from his eyes. Even the fury deserted him. Leaving nothing but a churning, empty darkness.

Samantha knew she wasn't the only one to sense it.

"Gavin . . ." Eleanor's voice broke on a tremble. "Gavin, don't."

"Quiet, Mother," he said without inflection.

Sam had to reach him. To bring him back. But in order to do that, she needed to get the family—her family—out of harm's way. She hadn't been able to look at them. Couldn't bring herself to face the confusion in Calybrid's rheumy eyes. The terror that seized poor Eleanor. Eammon's hurt and disbelief.

She faced it now. Though she did her utmost to disregard her shame. There would be time for that. Right now, her mind took in every detail it possibly could in that same, dispassionate way in which Gavin regarded her.

They made a macabre triangle. Gavin in the doorway, straight ahead of her, his gun trained at Boyd. *At her.* A dirk in his right hand poised to fly at Bradley, who stood to Gavin's extreme right against the wall. Bradley's pistol never wavered from the unarmed foursome in the middle of the room.

There had to be a way to fix this without someone getting hurt.

It was Bennett who gave her the idea. Rather, it was something he'd said to her before their first train heist. *Don't you be afraid. We're the wolves, darlin', we'll handle the wolves. You be the sheep and herd the rest of the sheep together. Unless they're hungry, wolves don't pay sheep no mind.*

Sheep. Huddled together. Eammon, Eleanor, Alice, and Calybrid. Were they not there, she'd be able to knock

Boyd's arm aside, providing Gavin a clear shot. But one wild bullet could hit any of them, and even if it didn't, Bradley would pull his trigger.

At this distance, even Bradley wouldn't likely miss should he pull the trigger.

"Here's what's going to happen," Boyd said, his drawl intensifying with the taste of impending victory.

"Ye doona dictate to me in my keep." The colder Gavin's voice became the more fear Samantha had to fight to keep her head.

"He does if you want your folks to live," Bradley hissed.

"Try something and I swear both of ye will die before I do."

Good, the wolves were snarling. Samantha stared hard at Calybrid, catching his eye. Today *she* would be a wolf, and he a wolf in sheep's clothing. She glanced down at the tall, delicate side table that had accompanied her chaise before she'd moved it into the sun. Upon the table rested an empty glass cobalt vase, a newspaper, spectacles, some of Alice's correspondence, and a letter opener.

Calybrid saw it, too, and inched in that direction without drawing Bradley's full attention, as the villain awaited his brother's signal and kept a wary eye on Gavin.

Excellent.

Next, she turned her focus back to Gavin, hoping he could fight his rage long enough to look at her.

"All right, that's fair," Boyd said, much friendlier now. "Look, I'm just here to get what's my due. My revenge and, apparently, my kin."

Samantha did her best not to flinch when he gestured his gun toward her belly again. She tried not to let the momentary slip of bleak grief on Gavin's hard features break her resolve.

He'd just lost what he thought was his child.

Finally he looked up at her, and she was glad she didn't have to meet the accusation in his eyes for long. It could have killed her right then and there. Meaningfully, she slid her gaze to Calybrid.

He didn't follow.

Dammit.

"I don't wish you or your people any harm, you know." Boyd was now gesturing with his pistol arm instead of aiming it at Gavin. The winch that had taken hold on Samantha's lungs loosened one degree. "It's obvious you didn't know you were harborin' a murderer. You look like you have a real nice family here, one who's been taken in by a fork-tongued she-devil, same as us."

At the mention of family, Gavin did spare a look in his mother's direction, and Samantha's heart released a little more when she saw that he noted Calybrid had already palmed the letter opener.

Calybrid tilted his head toward Bradley, and dipped his chin at Gavin in silent communiqué. Calybrid would act first, throwing the letter opener at Bradley. That would create enough distraction for Gavin to deal with Boyd.

"Tell you what," Boyd continued. "You all let us walk out with this here woman what done you wrong, and no one gets hurt. I swear it. You'll see hide nor hair from us again. I'm not a monster, you know."

Samantha's heart stalled as everyone stilled and looked to Gavin for his decision. Would he do it? If he gave her over, they wouldn't have to risk a coordinated maneuver. Gavin's mother, his family, would be safe.

"Can I trust you?" Though it appeared Gavin asked the question of Boyd, his eyes flicked to hers.

"Hand to God." Boyd actually lifted his pistol toward the ceiling in a show of good faith.

Samantha nodded back. *You can trust me.*

"Well, I believe ye doona consider yerself a monster, Boyd Masters." Gavin made a show of taking his pistol off Boyd and switching hands, pointing it at the floor. "But I am."

Calybrid acted first, hurling the letter opener with the ease of an expert. It sank into the crook of Bradley's shoulder.

Samantha had hoped it would fling Bradley's shot wide, but it did one better. Bradley dropped his pistol, unable to maintain a grip with the letter opener protruding from his muscle.

For her part, Samantha lifted her boots and kicked out, using the chaise as leverage to throw Boyd off balance, buying Gavin time to put Bradley down by filling his chest with bullets.

Boyd did pull his trigger, but the shattering of glass and crystal demonstrated that his shot landed in the chandelier.

Her weight wasn't enough to knock Boyd over, and if she didn't think of something quickly, he'd recover. She wildly threw her elbows back into his body, but he barely seemed to notice them.

No. This had to work. She couldn't be responsible for another tragedy. Not to this family who'd already been visited by multitudes of misfortune.

Boyd tightened his hold on her neck, and a dangerous pressure gathered in her head as she fought for oxygen. Her feet scraped against the floor, struggling to find purchase as, through vision becoming more blurred by the moment, she saw the hammer of Boyd's pistol pulled back and his arm stretched out. This shot would find its mark, of that she was certain.

An angel appeared in front of her just as shadows crept into her periphery. No. Not an angel. A demon. One with cold, green eyes.

Only a few details pierced her dimming consciousness now. The glint of a blade. The sickening plunge of steel against flesh. The harsh gurgle of a throat filling with blood.

The pressure around her neck released. She was falling.

And then she wasn't.

Air screamed into her with a sound she'd never thought herself capable of making, struggling through a throat bruised and raw, and filling desperate lungs with precious life.

Gavin held her aloft by the shoulders, as Boyd crumpled to the stones behind her.

It was over. Just like that.

Everyone was alive.

The splatters of Bradley's blood painted the feminine damask wallpaper of the solarium above where his sightless eyes stared at her from where he'd fallen.

Well, everyone that mattered was alive.

She dared not look back at Boyd. She knew she'd find Gavin's dirk buried deep in his neck.

Every event leading to this moment crushed in upon her then, and she collapsed against Gavin in a heap of quivering bones and broken breath.

"You saved us," she marveled. "You saved me." It dawned on her just how terrified she'd been that he wouldn't have done after learning the truth. That he'd let her go to whatever hellish future Boyd could devise, and be finished with her. She clutched at his work vest with desperate, numb fingers, burying her face into his unyielding chest. He smelled of winter and horses and Highland male dominance. He felt hard and solid when even the earth beneath her rolled and pitched, threatening to give way.

He felt like home.

"I'd not see yer child in the hands of such a man."

Your child.

He peeled her away from him like one would handle soiled, sticky refuse. "I told him he wouldna leave this keep with his life. That had nothing to do with ye."

Every word. Every explanation that leaped to her lips now seemed trite and terrible. He'd lost what he thought was his heir, and in turn, she'd lost him.

There was no excusing what she'd done, but *God* how she yearned to. She wanted to make him understand, that desperation made monsters of everyone.

Even her.

"I ought to have ye arrested. Deported," he stated drolly, "Ye're wanted for murder." He reached for her.

"Wait." She scurried back, placing Boyd's corpse between them. "Let me explain."

"Ye had my letter to Alison. All the correct papers. What did ye do, steal them from the real Alison Ross?" His eyes glinted with cruelty and suspicion. "Was she the one ye kidnapped? Did ye hurt her to take them? Did ye *murder* her?"

"No! I would never hurt anyone. Not unless I had to. Bennett forced my hand!" She held up that ineffectual hand against him. Against his suspicion and the violence gathering in his eyes.

"Who forced yer hand against me? Against us?"

His question landed like a cannonball in her gut. "Just listen," she begged.

"I've heard enough of yer lies. Ye'll be having that baby in a prison cell if I have anything to say about it." When he made it clear he would advance on her, she acted out of sheer desperation. Scooping down, Samantha snatched Boyd's pistol and levered it at the man she loved.

Again.

"I said *listen*," she cried. She knew he acted more out of hurt than hatred, and she prayed her words would reach him. Reach all of them.

"Sam," Calybrid wheezed. "Doona do this, lass. Put the gun down."

If Gavin had seemed furious before, there wasn't a word in Samantha's repertoire to describe the way he was looking at her now. Murderous, maybe.

But worse.

"I was a nobody. An orphan. Raised to do nothing but work on a desert ranch until my foster family informed me that they were forcing me to become the second wife of an old pervert." When Gavin's features didn't so much as flicker, she swallowed a growing sense of doom and forged ahead. "Bennett was my way out of that predicament. I was young, and desperate. I didn't know what I'd married into. What evil the Masters brothers were capable of until it was too late for me. You know something about that, don't you, Eleanor?"

"Aye," the lady whispered, as Eammon wiped tears from beneath her sightless eyes.

"Ye leave her out of this," Gavin warned.

"Alison and I made friends in a railcar that day. She was coming to see *you,* to stop *you* from stealing Erradale from under her."

"Don't ye fucking *dare* make me the villain here."

"I'm not. You aren't. *They* are." She gestured to the remains of the Masters brothers. "They were just after government payroll on that train. No one was supposed to get hurt in the robbery. No one had before . . . but then something happened, gunshots everywhere, and then Bennett . . ." She forced herself to sniff back tears and swallow bile, lest she humiliate herself further. "I told you the truth before. He burst into the car, shot a man, and put a gun to Alison's head. He was going to *kill* her. He said she'd seen too much. There was no talking him out of it so I—I—shot him." Here a ragged sob escaped her, and she forced herself to pull together once she noted that Gavin had inched closer. If he disarmed her, all hope was lost.

"Sending me to Erradale was all Alison's idea," she continued.

When he snorted his disbelief, Samantha truly fought hysterics.

"*She* gave me the papers. Your letter. She gave me her name and her blessing. She even wrote and told me that I could work Erradale indefinitely. That I could buy it from her if I wanted. All I had to do in return was to make certain that no kin of Laird Mackenzie ever took the land your father coveted."

"Horseshit!" Gavin snarled.

"She said she owed me her life. Because I'd saved her. She called it . . . She called it . . ." Samantha bit out a harsh sound of frustration as she desperately searched for the word, gasping it out when it finally came to her. "*Comraich*. She called it *comraich*. Sanctuary."

At this Eammon took a deep breath. "She knows the sacred word, lad. Not many do. Perhaps there's something to her story."

"She could have heard it somewhere. She's a liar, a con artist. Why the fuck would I believe you?"

"The letter," Calybrid suggested. "Ye could show us the letter from Alison."

The bottom dropped out of her stomach. "It's gone. It burned when Erradale did."

"We could hold the lass here," Eammon recommended. "Could summon Alison Ross to give her account."

"You could try," she said hopefully. "Though I don't know if you'd find her. Last I heard, she'd left on her honeymoon. And . . . I don't know where."

"Fucking convenient, wouldna ye say?" Gavin's vitriolic growl shivered over every hair on her body, lifting them painfully with pure, desperate anguish. "And here I am again, staring down the barrel of yer pistol, wondering if ye're worth the trouble."

"It's not like I planned this! I tried to stay away from you. To keep to myself."

"It's true," Calybrid sagely validated her. "She did her best to hate ye."

"When we married, we didn't even *like* each other. I thought—"

"Ye thought ye could pass off yer dead husband's child as mine."

There it was. Her greatest sin in all of this. The biggest lie she'd ever told. The reason he was entitled to never forgive her.

She couldn't stop the tears now as she looked from face to beloved face, knowing that her eyes pleaded for understanding. Even seeing that they wanted to give it to her . . .

But her offense was just too vast.

"I wanted to tell you. I was going to when—"

"Ye had every chance!" he roared. "Last night, for example."

A spear of guilt lanced her quickly shriveling heart.

"Ye deceived me. Ye deceived us all. Ye put my mother, my entire household, nay, every man in my employ in danger. Why? Why do that if your intentions were good? If ye were naught but a desperate, honest woman?"

As queries went, it was a valid one. And in that moment, Samantha promised she'd never again lie to this man. "I wanted my child . . . to have *you* for a father, instead of the terrible one I chose. You were offering to protect me, and I didn't think you would if I was already with child. I meant to tell you a million times. I really did. But I was a coward, because I wasn't sure you would keep me and . . . and . . . I was in love with you. With your family. And I wanted them to be mine, too. I didn't want my past any-more. I just wanted a future. With you. With all of you."

Eleanor made a soft, dare she hope, sympathetic sound, and Eammon let out a low curse. But Samantha didn't take her eyes from Gavin, lest he disappear.

Lest he strike.

What was he thinking behind that perfect façade? Was he forgiving her? Condemning her? Did he even believe her?

"As family melodrama goes, this is scintillating." A masculine, cultured, serpentine voice slithered into their midst and Samantha's pistol found a new target in the doorway.

The man filling the solarium archway could have been the villain of any novel. Swathed in black from head to toe to match his midnight hair, he seemed unaffected by the sight of a gun and two very dead bodies. A strange web of scars reached from beneath the high collar of his coat, tangled down a sharp jaw and up the side of his face.

"Who the hell are you?" Samantha demanded.

"I wish I knew." His devilish smile would have been handsome, had it reached his fathomless, dead eyes. "But people have taken to calling me the Rook."

At his odd reply, Samantha paused.

It took the length of the Rook's quick, calculating scan of the carnage for Callum to surge into the solarium behind him. "I was wrong about the tracks I found in the woods," he panted. "It wasn't the Americans. But agents of the crown."

Gavin snarled a string of Gaelic curses that even turned poor Calybrid's ears red. "How do ye know this?"

"After searching more thoroughly, I found more than two sets of boot prints, they don't belong to cowboys. They're military issue, Gavin. And they're looking for something."

"Agents of the crown?" Eammon echoed, and then addressed Callum and Gavin as though they were still witless young lads. "Just what the hell is going on, you two? Why is the most notorious pirate of modern history standing in the middle of our castle?"

Pirate? Samantha stepped forward, keeping her gun carefully trained at the Rook's substantial chest. The man was thick as a ship's mast and almost as tall.

His eyes snapped to her, and Samantha had the sense of staring into the abyss, and having it stare back. It chilled her to her very bones.

"Much as I love well-armed women, we haven't time to deal with . . . whatever this is." The Rook waved toward the dead Masters brothers as though they were as insubstantial as a pile of dirty laundry. "I'd a spy on my ship, and the matter has been summarily dealt with, but not before he'd spilled information about our . . . transaction to the authorities."

"We need to move everything," Callum hissed. *"Now."*

Eammon's face mottled beneath his beard, and if he hadn't been holding Eleanor, Samantha was certain he might have meted out a dire punishment to both the men he obviously considered his sons. "Tell me you're not smugglers!" he bellowed.

Gavin worked his jaw over a powerful emotion, one she'd never seen before and couldn't even begin to identify. "How do ye think I acquired the money to offer for Erradale?"

"Gavin," Eleanor whimpered. "No . . ."

"I suggest we hurry." The Rook turned and shouldered past Callum, who gaped rather dumbly at the gruesome tableau.

"We'll handle this," Gavin vowed, casting Samantha a

disgusted look before starting toward the door. "One disaster at a time."

Lowering her gun, Samantha reached out for him, catching at his sleeve. Her husband was a smuggler. Another outlaw. Lord, but it figured. "Let me come with you. Give me a chance to make amends." At least this was familiar ground. "Please, if I am *anything* to you."

He shrugged her off, whirling to tower over her, his eyes glinting with a verdant wrath. "Does Erradale rightfully belong to me?"

"No, but—"

"Does the child in yer belly belong to me?"

"You already know it doesn't."

"Are we even legally married, Samantha Masters?" He said her name as if it had turned to ashes in his mouth.

"I don't think so." By this time, her reply had become a broken whisper.

"Then ye are nothing to me."

"Gavin—" A punch to the stomach would have caused less devastation.

"If ye're not gone by the time I return, I'll arrest ye myself."

Perhaps she'd been right when she'd assumed she couldn't be broken by another man. Something broken could be fixed. The sight of Gavin St. James's wide, straight back walking away forever didn't merely break her.

It destroyed her.

CHAPTER TWENTY-SEVEN

Gavin had known many days of darkness in his lifetime, but the black hole in which he now found himself was un-equaled.

And not even wide enough to pace back and forth in.

Inveraray Jail wasn't as dismal a place as the infamous Barlinnie Prison, or even Newgate, but a Mackenzie earl and magistrate charged with smuggling and treason put the gaolers in an especially cruel mood.

He'd not seen the sun for what seemed like days, locked behind a steel door with only a small port though which he'd been fed five times. Whether that meant he'd been there two days or five, he couldn't tell.

Felt like an eternity, at least.

He slept some, and only in his dreams did he find light.

The light he'd begun to tease each morn from behind his bonny's blue eyes. Her thin arms would circle him, and she'd gift him with one of those brash, unrepentant smiles before pressing that foul, perfect mouth of hers against his own.

He'd loved her smile, the artless innocence with which she gave it. She never practiced it or posed in the fashion of coy or splendid ladies. It appeared as a smile did on a child, the genuine expression of joy. Of pleasure. And, at times, of victory over him.

A torment so excruciating would wrench him from his dream, as if even his subconscious violently rejected the memory of her.

Ye gods, had she been a good enough actress to counterfeit those almost ridiculously real smiles?

The thought made him sick. With rage. With loss.

With love.

Lovesickness. It was an affliction he'd never quite understood, until the moment he realized the constant lead weight in his stomach, the ache in his muscles—particularly his heart—had nothing to do with the meager food.

And everything to do with Samantha Masters.

Gavin brooded into the darkness of his cell. He slumped on the hard wood plank that was his bed and watched the ghosts of his past dance in the shadows.

Hellish, twisted things they were.

Hell. Surely his next destination. This place was a purgatory of sorts, a consign of reckoning before the swift and retributive justice of the crown was meted out.

Before another one of Hamish Mackenzie's sons swung from a rope for treason.

A bitter smile crooked across his lips. Even this distinction wasn't unprecedented. He didn't own it. He wasn't the most treasonous of the Mackenzie lads. That had been Hamish the Younger, who'd been hanged some years ago for war crimes against the Duke of Trenwyth and high treason against the crown.

Gavin wasn't the most monstrous Mackenzie son, either,

he realized. As Liam, the Demon Highlander, himself, laid claim to that title with twenty years of unparalleled blood-shed in service to Her Majesty.

In fact, he wasn't even the most criminal, as Dorian Blackwell, the Black Heart of Ben More, his father's youngest bastard, had ruled the London Underworld for the better part of fifteen years.

So where did that leave him? Nay, what did that make him?

He'd thought himself the clever one. The resilient one. And, aye, the handsome one.

What a fool he'd been. He was nothing more than a second-rate smuggler cursed by the fates with appalling taste in women.

Well, if he was going to die alone, at least it would be sooner than later.

His mother had Eammon, and Liam's son, Andrew, would inherit Inverthorne. He was a good lad, at least.

His hand pressed above his breastbone, at the place that seemed to seize with a very knifelike pain every time he thought of progeny. Of an heir.

Alison Ross, the real Alison Ross, had won the day after all. Erradale would remain her birthright. Empty. Un-claimed. Forever soiled by her father's death.

The world would go on. Perhaps it was best that he didn't . . .

The scrape of his door and a shaft of light brought him to his feet, the chains at his wrists—rather more redun-dant than necessary, in his opinion—dragging across the stones as Callum was shoved into the cell with him.

The Mac Tíre looked a bit worse for wear, even for him. His beard had grown out of control, his shrewd eyes wild, and his teeth bared as it took three gaolers to chain him to the wooden bed across from Gavin.

"Now stay still," the guard ordered them both. "We'll deal with ye soon enough."

He left the steel door ajar, confident the chains would keep the men in place, and Gavin was grateful for what little fresh air circulated into the dank cell.

"Are ye hurt?" Gavin asked his friend, unable to see the particulars of Callum's swarthy features now that he was no longer illuminated in the doorway.

"Nay," Callum answered shortly.

"Are ye . . . well?"

"Nay." The question seemed superfluous, but they both knew it was not. Callum wasn't able to abide small spaces for long, and judging by the growth of his beard, it had been closer to five days than two.

With a tight sigh, Gavin rested his head against the cold stones. "I suppose I should have seen this coming."

"You mean the sudden disappearance and abandonment of the world's most elusive and notorious pirate once the military showed up to seize the shipload of goods and weapons we smuggled for him?" Callum's voice could have turned the bogs into a desert. "Aye, we should have seen it coming."

"I mean all of it," Gavin ruminated. "For a moment there, everything was perfect . . . I should have known it wasna real."

"If they're coming to take us in front of the judge, Thorne, this might be the last time we see each other." A measured note returned to Callum's voice. "An Irish ex-patriot like me isn't like to be sent to the same place as an earl."

Sitting forward, Gavin swallowed a million regrets. "I'm sorry, brother. I'll do what I can for ye."

"Nay." Callum said the word so low, Gavin had to strain to hear it. "It is I who am sorry."

"Ye've done nothing. I asked ye if ye knew of black market work that would bring us a quick fortune. The Rook has never been caught out before and—"

"I knew Sam was not Alison Ross when you married her."

The moment carried that expectant silence between lightning and thunder.

Gavin exploded forward, meaning to drive his fists into the man who'd been his closest friend for decades.

His shackles brought him up short, and still he surged against them, violence pouring through him like a biblical flood.

"And ye said *nothing*? All this fucking time!" Were there no true souls left on this earth? No one to trust? "Ye let me marry her? Ye let me fall in—" He couldn't say the word. *"Why?"*

"Because I was hoping the wedding would bring Alison back!" Callum's snarl was just as vehement, stunning Gavin into stillness.

"What?" he breathed.

"Ye remember Alison was born not long after ye took up residence at Inverthorne. Mrs. Ross was never well after the birth, and Alison spent most of her childhood chasing me about the moors like a wild puppy."

"I remember," Gavin said warily. "Ye used to take refuge from her at Inverthorne, complaining of her being a pest."

"Aye. I did . . ."

"But?"

"She was still but a girl of thirteen by the time she left, and I was not only hiding from her at that point, but from tender feelings a lad should not have for a girl nine years his junior."

"Callum." Gavin reclaimed his seat, their past coming into sharp focus.

"I went to seek my fortune, and years later, when I thought I'd enough to win her, I went to America to find her." A bleakness crept into the hermit's voice.

"I presume ye succeeded."

"Aye."

"And?"

"And I've been living in a cave ever since," the man said darkly. "Trying to forget . . ."

"To forget what?

"Never you mind what."

It had been a mystery to Gavin, why a man as famous and well traveled an explorer as Callum Monahan had retreated from the world. He'd asked his friend a few times, but had always received the same answer.

Never you mind.

He'd not in a million lifetimes imagined it had anything to do with a woman.

"I am sorry that I kept Sam's secret from you," Callum continued drolly. "But when I read Alison's letter to Sam . . . I—"

Gavin leaned forward again. "Letter? What letter?"

"I'd know her writing anywhere . . . and I couldn't stop from steaming the letter open, if only to see the words written by her hand."

A commotion from out toward the sergeant's desk drew his attention. The authorities had probably come for them. They were running out of time.

"What did she *say,* Callum?" he demanded tersely.

"Alison sent documents from America along with a letter admonishing Sam to take up Erradale's claim against yours on her behalf. She thanked Sam for saving her life, and told her that she could take sanctuary on Erradale indefinitely, so long as she kept it out of Mackenzie hands."

The exhale Gavin expelled contained all the regret his body could summon.

She'd told the truth . . . about that, at least. "And when she broke her word to Alison and married me . . . ye still didna say anything?"

"I supported Alison's claim to Erradale all this time." Callum shifted in the darkness, his sinewy form still graceful in the shadows. "Like I said . . . I was hoping it would bring Alison back. That she'd fight for her homeland instead of marry that bastard, Grant . . . And then, when it seemed apparent that she would not return, I saw how happy you were with Sam. How happy she was with you. And I thought that if at least one of us could find love, it would all be worth it."

So many emotions eddied about in Gavin's body, they momentarily paralyzed him.

"Were we not about to hang, I'd not be so bold as to seek yer forgiveness," Callum confessed.

"Were we not about to hang, I'd not be so quick to give it to ye."

They exchanged smiles that neither of them saw, but both of them felt.

"Ye've been a like brother to me since—"

The door flung wide, and Gavin couldn't have been more shocked to find the towering, kilted form of his actual brother, the Demon Highlander, holding the chains imprisoning the absolute last person he'd expected to see again.

CHAPTER TWENTY-EIGHT

"You fucking son of a whore!" Gavin was on his feet again, surging toward the Rook, who somehow managed to look self-satisfied even with manacles securing his wrists in front of him.

"Careful, Gavin." Liam stepped out of the doorway to allow in the guards to unchain them. "The man permitted himself to be caught. Though ye'll forgive me for how many days it took me to track this one down. As it turns out, he's a hard man to find."

"Most wanted men are," the Rook stated blithely.

It occurred to Gavin that committing murder in a jail wasn't the cleverest path to freedom and so he waited with barely concealed impatience for the guards to finish with Callum's chains before they liberated him.

He turned to Liam. "I thought the next time I saw ye, ye'd be stretching my neck at the end of a rope, not saving it."

A look he'd never identified on the Demon Highlander's brutal features unsettled him enough to look away, even as the iron weights disappeared from his wrists. He'd have identified the expression as wounded, if he'd thought Liam capable of it.

"Ye are a Mackenzie, Gavin. And my brother. I'd not let ye hang."

"Didna stop ye before, when the Duke of Trenwyth hanged Hamish."

"Hamish was beyond saving, and ye knew it."

"So much blood on your hands, on your heads, on your name," the Rook remarked with only mild amusement. "And they say *I'm* the criminal."

As if sensing the tension between Gavin, Callum, and the Rook, three guards escorted the two men out of the cell, creating a line between Gavin and the pirate in the small, white hallway. They didn't move until the Rook had been pushed into the cell, the door shut, and the heavy key turned.

"I doona understand," Gavin marveled, rubbing at the places the manacles had chapped his skin. "By what miracle are we being released?"

"Due to a crisis of conscience, I confessed everything," the Rook stated through the port.

Gavin's eyes narrowed on his brother, then at the door separating him from the most dangerous criminal the seas had known since the days of Blackbeard and Sir Francis Drake. "'A crisis of conscience'?" he repeated dubiously. "What exactly did ye confess to?"

"Only the truth." The Rook's unaffected features were somehow more chilling from the confines of the dark room. "That I smuggled the goods and weapons onto your land without your knowledge, thereby victimizing a peer of the realm, and a magistrate besides. Look how contrite I am; do you think the High Court will have mercy upon me?" To say his voice was cheeky wouldn't be wrong, if someone could be both cheeky and menacing at the same time.

Gavin couldn't have been more stymied. "How?"

Liam addressed the guards. "If ye'd be so kind as to escort Mr. Monahan out, the magistrate and I would like a word with the criminal."

"Aye, Laird," they chorused, allowing a very relieved-looking Callum to lead their procession toward freedom.

"You've a very charming wife," the Rook observed casually. "With two very convincing pistols."

Samantha? What did she have to do with this? Was she here? Gavin wished his traitorous heart didn't thump against its cage at the prospect.

"Ye're joking," he gasped.

"Partly, yes." The Rook's chuckle made a devilish echo down the forlorn hall. "I was on my way to London, anyhow. Why not travel at the government's expense?"

Gavin wondered if it were possible to expire from astonishment. He stared down at his soiled, blackened hands and the once-white shirtsleeves he'd worn for too many days, before gathering the strength to look up at the brother who wore his hated father's features.

"Why are ye here, Liam?"

"I already told ye—"

"And I informed *ye* on my wedding day that I'm no longer a Mackenzie. Ye'll no longer be clan Laird of Inverthorne lands."

The rumble in Liam's chest truly was nothing less than demonic. "Do ye think papers in an English court decide yer blood, Gavin? Ye can have every trace of our clan erased from the annals of every record and history book from the beginning of recorded time if ye want. Ye'd still be my brother."

It distressed Gavin, a man used to discarding emotion

instead of facing it, to suddenly lose control over the muscles of his throat. He cleared the offending tightness with a rough sound.

Liam's dark eyes softened as they regarded him. "Ye know, for brothers with oddly comparable lives, ye'd think we'd understand each other better. That we'd have maintained a more . . . fraternal relationship over the years."

Gavin snorted. "Just because we had the same father doesna mean our lives are anything alike."

Instead of reacting as he would have once done, Liam merely quirked an eyebrow at him. "Just because ye're not the Demon Highlander, doesna mean ye doona have the Mackenzie temper. Ye've just hidden it behind vice and indifference. For example, I ken how angry ye are right now at yer wife."

"She's not my wife." Every muscle in Gavin's body tensed, and he darkly wondered what she'd done for the Rook to convince him to turn himself in.

"She loves ye."

"She lied," he said through clenched teeth. "Unforgivably lied."

"Yet another way our lives parallel one another. Or did ye forget that Mena also came to the Highlands under the guise of a spinster governess rather than the fugitive viscountess she was?"

"Samantha . . ." The name sounded foreign and bitter on his tongue. "She was married."

Liam lifted a shoulder. "As was Mena. If ye remember she was *still* married when I uncovered her deception. At least Samantha is already a widow."

"Because she *killed* her own husband."

"She just gets more and more fascinating." The Rook's smile only widened when the two brothers lanced him with their warning glares. "Oh come, I think we can al agree that not all deaths are the tragedies other people think they should be."

Gavin ignored him. "Let's not forget the child."

"Aye." Liam raised a hand to squeeze at the back of his neck. A gesture Gavin found himself doing often out of habit. "Under any other circumstance, her lie would be untenable. And maybe, to ye, it is. But consider this, Thorne. She was a lady who didna want her child to be a Masters. There is another lady I know who didna want her son to be a Mackenzie. If ye ask me . . . they both had good reason."

Again, Gavin struggled to swallow. The condition worsened when Liam laid a gentle hand on his shoulder.

"Maybe . . . we doona have to be our father's sons anymore. Perhaps we could just be brothers. Mackenzie brothers."

Gavin had to blink away a strange and foreign blur when he met the dark eyes he'd so often laughed into as a boy. "Ye think there's redemption, Liam? After that night . . . After everything we've done to each other?"

"I thought ye were safe at Inverthorne all those years ago. I didna ken he'd make ye pay for yer mother's freedom with yer own flesh."

"Because ye left, Liam. Ye always left."

"I didna just leave, I ran. And ken that each time I did, I took something away from ye. Yer brother. Yer name. The woman ye loved." Reaching into his sporran, he removed several papers with official wax seals. "This time, brother . . . let me give something back."

"What's this?" Gavin ran his thumb over the seal of the Queen's Records Office.

"She was planning on telling ye the truth the whole time."

"How do ye know?"

"Because once she gave ye this, all secrets would be revealed."

Breaking the seal, Gavin opened the document with trembling hands, pertinent words spilling forth in a whisper as his eyes devoured what they could barely process. "Bill of Sale . . . from Alison Ross to . . . Samantha Masters . . . all land and structures of Erradale Estate in perpetuity . . . in the amount of . . ." His jaw dropped at the same time his eyes lifted to meet those of his brother. "This is how much we settled on for her annuity, give or take twenty pounds." And a great deal less than he'd offered Alison Ross for Erradale only months prior.

"Aye." Liam nodded. "And she would have had to start this process at the time of your marriage, if not before."

Christ. No. She'd tried to tell him, she'd begged him to listen. And he'd not allowed her to speak.

He'd told her she was nothing.

She was not the only liar.

"There's a second paper," Liam said.

Gavin flipped the page and had to put a hand out to prop himself against the wall, lest he drop to his knees in the barren stone hallway. "The deed and transfer of Erradale Estate to Gavin St. James, Earl of Thorne . . ."

"Of clan Mackenzie." Liam finished what he could not. "She loves ye, Gavin. Despite anything else she may have said or not said, ye canna dispute the truth of that."

Gavin seized Liam's shirt, suddenly desperate to see her. "Is she at Ravencroft?"

Soberly, Liam shook his head. "She's gone to the Continent. Mena and I tried to convince her to stay, but she is worried about the extradition laws to America. She's still a woman wanted for murder, after all."

Gavin's mind raced faster than his heart, if that was possible. "Tell me, is Dorian at Ben More Castle?"

"Dorian?" An austere metal sound echoed down the hallway as both the Rook's hands landed against the door. "Do you mean Dorian Blackwell?"

"Aye."

"You have dealings with him?" This was the first bit of intensity Gavin had sensed from the Rook, and he had to admit he found it even more unsettling than the characteristic nonchalance. He shared a look with Liam. Neither of them had business dealings with the Blackheart of Ben More. They knew better.

He was, however, their bastard half brother.

"It doesna surprise me that ye're acquaintances," Gavin said carefully.

"On the contrary, we're not at all acquainted." The Rook seemed to have gathered some of his previous composure. "But Dorian Blackwell is a name that haunts me, and I'm taking this free ride to Newgate because that's where I know my past with him began."

Liam stepped forward. "I warn ye, Rook, he's our kin. We'd not see him harmed."

"Your kin?" The black gaze sharpened, and Gavin was struck not for the first time, at how much the Rook also resembled Dorian.

"Our brother." He scrutinized the pirate with new suspicion.

"Well," the villain marveled. "Say what you will about your father, he was rather indiscriminately prolific in creating notoriously dangerous men."

"Aye," Gavin said. "And Dorian will be looking for ye, Rook. We'll warn him ye're coming."

"Warn him all you like." The Rook's eyes glinted like obsidian glass as he melted away from the port. "He'll never see *this* coming."

CHAPTER TWENTY-NINE

Samantha had decided the sea was her favorite place to grieve. To weep. What were a few more drops of salty moisture into incalculable measurements of it?

Nothing.

It was nothing.

Just like she had become nothing to the only man she'd ever loved.

For she realized now that she'd never truly loved Bennett. She'd needed him at the time. She'd loved the way he'd made her feel, at first. But the grief she'd experienced at his loss didn't touch this hopeless sort of despair that threatened to drown her now.

It had proved impossible to properly nurse a broken heart while pitching the contents of her stomach over the side of yet another ship, as she crossed the choppy English Channel. She'd distracted herself from seasickness by studying maps and manuals of Europe to settle on where she would like to raise her child. She'd decided upon the Netherlands, and boarded a train toward Amsterdam the day after she'd

landed on the Continent. She'd needed the extra time to recover her land legs, even after such a short trip.

She tried to shove her pain aside. To focus on the child
inside her, on the future ahead of her. She was a fool to
allow a man so much control over her happiness. To let him
dictate her feelings with such a deft and cruel hand.

Especially *that* man.

She could add her heart to the legions of those he'd
broken.

The difference was, she'd deserved it.

She didn't believe it arrogant to assume she'd left a sizable wound on his heart, as well.

And would do anything to take it back.

She was glad, in a way, that she'd never see him again.
It would kill her to confront the accusation in his eyes, or
worse, indifference. To occupy the same space with his
beauty and be treated as a stranger. As an enemy.

She could survive so much, but not that.

It occurred to Samantha as the steam engine crawled
over the wintry border of Gelderland to Brabant that she
ought to consider avoiding trains in the foreseeable future.
They made her anxious, unsettled, and with good reason.

A private compartment had been an extravagance, but
grieving in a car packed with people was more than she
could bear at the moment.

She was glad she'd decided against settling in another
hot, arid climate. The Mediterranean seemed like the love-
liest place, but Samantha realized she'd grown fond of
green land and crisp, cool sea air.

If she couldn't stay in the Scottish Highlands, she could
at least find a comparable climate on the Continent.

The Dutch seemed like lovely people, and were famous
equestrians. It shouldn't at all be hard for her to find work
among them.

Looking down, she poised her quill and ink over the vellum paper and applied herself to the letter she promised to Mena.

She could think of nothing to say that wouldn't completely dishonor her. She wanted to ask how Gavin fared now that he'd been released from prison. She wanted to follow the post back to the shores of the only place that had ever truly felt like home. Wester Ross. Inverthorne. The happiest days of her life had been spent in a gray stone castle lording over a Highland forest that crawled down to a tempestuous sea. She'd lost her identity there.

And then she'd lost her heart.

A mist of tears stung her eyes, and blurred the plush golden felt of the seat opposite her. Would this ever stop hurting? Would she ever not be haunted by a gorgeous ghost with green eyes and a devastating smile?

The unmistakable clicks of a pistol's cylinder drove her to her feet, upsetting her lap desk and inkwell. She blinked the gather of tears from her lashes, and they coalesced into enough moisture to spill down her cheek.

"Ye forgot something important, bonny."

Her knees buckled and little spots of darkness gathered at her periphery as she half gasped, half sobbed his name.

Gavin.

He filled the doorway of her compartment with his beautiful broad shoulders, bedecked in a fine wool traveling suit that matched the darker tones in his thick, perfect hair.

For an absurd moment, she feared the pistol.

But then he'd dumped it, along with the wooden box containing the other, onto the empty seat, and went to her in three long strides.

There was nowhere for Samantha to retreat, so she just

whimpered when he pulled her against him, effectively helping her to avoid an uncharacteristic swoon.

He smelled glorious, like a cedar forest and soap. She tried not to notice. Tried not to process the bliss coursing through her at being in the circle of his arms once more.

Was this happening? Or had she fallen asleep, only to wake later from this dream, her grief fresh and crushing.

"Why?" she managed through a chest and throat flooded with too many emotions to safely allow the passage of air. "What are you doing here?

He cupped her face with gentle hands and pulled her back enough to look into his eyes. What she saw glimmering in the green irises, branching into the laugh lines, and furrowed in the brow, caused more tears to chase the others down her cheeks. That wasn't what forgiveness looked like, was it?

"I lied to ye, as well." The tender earnestness in his voice threatened to unstitch her, and Samantha held on to his wrists, ready for anything. "I kept from ye the fact that I was a smuggler."

"Your sin doesn't touch mine," she interjected quickly. "I kept from you the fact I was married, and a murderer. Also, my name and my—"

"Dammit, woman, let me apologize." His hands tightened on her face, but not painfully.

She swept her lashes down. Could they not even make up without fighting? she wondered through a budding smile.

"I'm sorry, do go on."

"I told ye that ye were nothing to me, and that was my biggest lie of all, bonny, because ye've become my reason for everything."

Behind her ribs, her heart thudded and swelled. And

still, she couldn't trust this moment. This declaration. This reason to hope.

"But I—"

"I've come to take ye home." His hands slid from her jaw, down the high neck of her gown, to clutch at her shoulders.

"But what about—"

"It's been decided, lass. By all of us. Mother, Eammon, Callum, Liam, Mena . . . even Locryn and Calybrid, who somehow now reside in my castle. Ye belong at Inverthorne. Ye belong to me, and I'm here to fetch what's mine."

Her eyebrows dropped into a scowl. "A Highland proposal, is it? One half conceit, and one half brute force?"

"If that's what it takes." He quirked that arrogant smile down at her, the one she used to despise. And then had come to crave. To love. "Ye know once I set my cap at something, I'm rather relentless. Ye might as well surrender now, bonny, and agree to marry me."

"Have you thought this through?" She wrenched out of his grip and turned to the window so as to gather her wits without his beauty and his brogue stealing them from her. "I'm still a wanted woman. I'm not safe in the Highlands anymore." Her hand went to her stomach. "And then there's the child I carry. The one that doesn't belong to you. I know what I did was wrong, but I'd still not have my child raised a bastard."

Even at her back, his charisma, height, and strength were undeniable. He moved closer, reaching around her stiff shoulders to place a document in her line of sight.

"Bonny Mackenzie?" she whispered, the official documents of birth and citizenship blurred as new tears threatened her vision. "You've given me a new identity?"

"My brother Dorian has a few men in his employ that are a deft hand at forgeries," he said against her ear. "I realized I never quite accepted ye as Alison Ross, and I doona know ye as Samantha Masters. But ye've always been Bonny to me. It's Bonny I fought and laughed with, and convinced to marry me, and bedded every night . . ."

He dropped his head to place a kiss in that vulnerable place behind her ear. The one that lifted all the hairs on her body, and created shivers of bliss that traveled all the way down to the apex of her thighs.

"It's Bonny I couldna get enough of. It's Bonny that I love."

The word she'd craved to hear landed like a lead weight in her gut. Turning back she pressed the point that he'd not yet addressed. "But this child—"

A long finger pressed against her mouth, quieting her words, but not quite her fears. "My father made at least as many bastards as he had legitimate children. I witnessed the agony of his unwanted children, and I swear by all the gods of my home and people, that I'll never see a child of yours, of ours, feel that kind of shame. If I love ye, I will love yer baby, and claim it as my own. And I vow this wee one will never know it isna of my body as much as it is of yours."

Processing his declaration, she stared at him mutely, waiting for the hammer to fall. Waiting for the next words that would crush the hope and love surging to the surface.

People didn't actually get happy endings, did they? Especially not people like her. The orphaned. The unwanted. The untruthful.

He took her mouth with his own, slanting his lips over hers, licking the salt of her tears from the seam with his velvety tongue.

She opened for him, accepted his possession, his love, and all the emotion he poured from his lips into hers. No longer was he the leisurely lover, the infamous rake. This time, his kiss conveyed a desperation she'd never felt from him before. A passion she'd not known him to be afflicted with.

Her response to it was instant and fierce. She threaded her fingers into his lush hair and turned her hands into fists, imprisoning him to the onslaught of her answering ardor. A lifetime of loneliness flared between them, fusing them to each other, offering what neither of them had ever been able to claim.

Belonging. He was hers. She was his. And neither of them would be alone again.

He groaned, then growled, crushing her to him, his hands everywhere, clutching and grabbing at the weight of her skirts.

She was so lost in his mouth, that she hadn't realized he'd pushed her onto the seat and pulled up her skirts until he was moving against her. Thrusting inside of her.

Her body was ready for his intrusion, wet and warm, open and needy.

His possession brought her to life, warming the blood from ice in her veins. Lifting the weight of guilt and sorrow, turning it into a taut and frantic lust.

Their mouths remained fused, as their bodies found a rhythm that matched the frenzy of their need. He filled her completely, gliding against her thighs in slick, graceful motions that increased in frenetic speed until he was pounding into her.

Raw sounds of animal pleasure crawled up her throat as her climax found her almost instantly.

Breaking the kiss, he pressed his palm over her mouth, muffling her screams as her body clenched tightly around his shaft in pulses of excruciating bliss.

The sounds of his own passion he stifled against her bodice as he jerked and kicked within her, filling her with the warmth of his release. Her name exploded from him, buried against her chest, against her heart. *Bonny.* Her new self. The woman he loved. The woman who loved him back.

After, they fought for their breath as the haze of lust became a glow of pleasure.

His wicked smile had returned when he lifted his head to look at her. "Ye know, Bonny, ye still havena accepted my proposal of marriage."

She met his wicked smile, and raised him one teasing crook of an eyebrow. "I thought my answer didn't matter. I was under the impression that you'd decided it was happening and no matter what I say, you'll still drag me home by the hair like a big dumb brute."

"Well, aye, but it's still nice to hear the words."

His answering impudence was so charming, her heart ached with the love it evoked. But she still rolled her eyes, more for effect than out of ire. "Well, obviously I'll marry you. I love you too much not to."

He rose up and kissed her, his breath still elevated. "Do ye know when I realized how much I loved ye?" he asked soberly.

She shook her head.

"When I had the deed to Erradale in my hand, and I realized that I'd give it away only to have ye back."

Her fingers pressed against her mouth, stemming a sob that had arisen there. "Truly?"

"Aye." He took her hand and kissed it. "Erradale is what I wanted most in my life, until ye came along. Ye were what taught me the difference between a desire, and a necessity. Ye are necessary to me, as I am not a whole man without ye by my side."

Unable to conjure words to properly express what she felt, she pulled him down to her, pressing her mouth and body against his. Using the language they'd always spoken so well.

The kiss lasted until they both broke it, more than a little breathless.

"Let me take ye home, and make ye my wife." He smoothed a hand over her heavy hair, disheveled now by their lovemaking. "Let me make ye my life. Let me make my keep the home of yer heart."

"Yes," she finally answered, beaming at her very own magnificent Highlander. "Take me home. To Inverthorne. Only . . . I have just one question . . ."

"What is that, my love?"

"Do we have to go by boat?"

He smirked down at her. "Unless ye've devised a way to fly over the Channel."

She winced, plopping her forehead against his hard shoulder. "I was afraid of that."

EPILOGUE

"It says here the press only just got wind of the Rook's escape from Newgate as the prison did its best to cover it up."

Gavin looked up from his ledgers to where his lovely wife read the paper while she nursed their baby girl in the plush chaise by the study fire.

"Canna say the news surprises me," he remarked. "He didna seem very worried about his status as a prisoner. Nor did he seem the kind to surrender his freedom for any altruistic purposes." He couldn't help but watch his wee family smile and coo at each other for a moment.

How precious they were.

It was as though an inner luminescence glowed through both of them, and beckoned to him to take part.

Pushing himself up from his desk, he went to them, lowering onto the chaise and pulling his wife toward him, enticing her to rest against his chest as he encircled them both with protective arms.

Eleanor Alison St. James, or Ellie, as her mother kept referring to her, took a precious moment away from her lunch to smile up at him with eyes that had become a deep, auburn brown.

Gavin offered her flailing hand his finger to clutch, as every time her wee fingers wrapped around his larger one, she gripped his heart, as well.

Had he not known better, he'd say she looked exactly like a Mackenzie.

And a Mackenzie she was, because a Mackenzie he remained.

A light knock on the door gave his Bonny a chance to adjust her blouse and shift Ellie to her shoulder to pat her vigorously on the back.

"Come in," Gavin called.

Eammon poked his head into the room, still wary of a newly wedded couple behind closed doors, even after all these months.

Gavin beckoned to the man who'd been like a father to him in more ways than he could count. Thinking that Eammon's own wedding would be upon them before long, as he'd engaged himself to Eleanor not two months ago.

"The post arrived," Eammon informed them, conveying a bundle of letters and such to the chaise. "There's one from America, addressed to you, my lady."

Bonny's eyes clashed with his. This was the letter she'd been waiting for. The response for her confession to Alison Ross.

Gavin took it, and with her permission, he broke the seal and ripped it open, tilting it so she could read over his shoulder.

Dearest Lady Thorne,
I confess I knew of your actions before word had reached me. I garnered this knowledge when apply-

ing for a marriage license, where I was denied for reasons of bigamy. The paperwork has subsequently been sorted, but not in time to retain my fiancé. It's all for the best, I suppose, as I realized that we are not suited to each other.

I have decided to return to the Highlands, and I believe that the enclosed pages from my late mother's journal will explain why.

It was preposterous to attempt to keep Erradale from Mackenzie hands, as it was owned by a Mackenzie all along.

I've sent word to Ravencroft, and will be arriving there in time for Christmas. I'd like to see you and your new husband as soon as possible.

All my love,
Alison Ross

"What a relief." His Bonny breathed out a great sigh. "She doesn't sound angry, does she? That's so good. It'll be lovely to see her again."

Gavin barely heard her, as his eyes scanned the subsequent journal entry with a growing sense of alarm and disbelief.

Erradale was owned by a Mackenzie all along.

That night . . . The night his mother was blinded. The night Liam conducted the unfortunate Tessa McGrath home. The night his father had gone to the village to claim a woman he'd had his eyes on for a long time.

The woman had been the delicately pretty Mrs. Ross. According to her journal, Hamish Mackenzie hadn't taken no for an answer that night. And nine months later, Mrs. Ross had given birth to a baby girl.

Alison.

Gavin thought about what Callum had said. That Mrs. Ross had never recovered, and Alison had grown up practically without a mother. James Ross had eventually called Hamish Mackenzie out, challenging him to a duel which he inevitably lost.

Then Mrs. Ross had dragged her daughter away. Far away. As far away from her rapist as she could possibly get.

San Francisco, California.

"Jesus Jehosephat Christ," his wife breathed, indicating that she'd read the journal page, as well. "You have a little sister."

"Aye," he breathed, unable to wrap his mind around the revelation. He looked up to Eammon, who blinked rapidly at them both. "We . . . we need to tell Callum that she's coming back. This is what he wanted."

"Agreed," Eammon said seriously.

Beside him his wife grunted, then snorted, then burst into laughter loud enough to startle poor Ellie to release the burp that Bonny had been trying to coax out of her.

Both men glanced at her as though she'd gone mad, which seemed to feed her hysterics until she was holding her child with one hand, and clutching Gavin's wrist with another.

"You know what this means?" she managed through chortles and giggles.

He scowled at her. "I know ye'd better tell me what's gotten into ye."

"For a month . . . last year . . . you were married to your sister!" She dissolved into fits of hilarity once again.

Gavin made a sound of distress and repulsion. Not for the first time, he thanked God that Samantha Masters, now Bonny St. James, had been the one in disguise. Because now, more than ever, her deception remained an utter blessing.

Alison Ross. His sister . . .

A sharp exhale of amusement escaped him, and then another, until he was laughing just as heartily as she.

"My old heart can't take many more of these revelations," Eammon muttered.

Wiping tears of mirth from her eyes, Bonny said, "We'll definitely have a lot to discuss with Liam and Mena when they arrive for dinner tonight."

Gavin blinked down at her. "Is that tonight?"

"Yes, it's our turn to host."

"So it is." He pressed his forehead to hers, needing her closeness and her strength in the wake of such information.

"It's a bit of magic ye found, me Bonny," he marveled. "How so?"

"That ye robbed the train carrying my half sister which no one knew at the time, that ye saved her life, that she offered ye her name, and sanctuary, here in the Highlands . . ."

"That I never actually shot you," she added with a tender smile. "That *is* a miracle."

"Aye, Bonny," he murmured, his heart so full he wondered if his chest would be able to contain it. "My family keeps growing because of ye. Ye gave me more than just a child, ye gave me back my brother, and now a sister I never knew I had."

"You'll have to tell Dorian," she said.

"Aye," he answered, thinking of all his bastard little brother had been through these past couple of months in regard to the Rook. "Aye, let's hope he can handle the news, as well. It seems, this year is one for the return of the lost."

"Whatever this season brings, know that I love you," his wife said with uncharacteristic sobriety. "We'll face it together."

"As we face life together." He nuzzled closer to her, brushing his lips across hers.

"Always," she whispered.

"Always," he vowed.

Read on for an excerpt from
Kerrigan Byrne's next book

THE DUKE WITH THE DRAGON TATTOO

Coming soon from St. Martin's Paperbacks

Lorelai's lantern trembled, turning shadows into sinister wraiths as she crept through the night, as best her foot would allow. Her heartbeats echoed off the walls of Southborne Grove's east wing. Her breaths like rapid-fire pistol shots in the consuming silence. Loud enough for the ghosts to hear, surely.

When the horrible sounds had first roused her, she'd thought maybe Cyrus and Joan were at it again. Howling and scuffling. The two hounds boasted only seven legs, three eyes, and one tail between them, but still they played like puppies. And sometimes their play turned serious.

Never this late, though.

The raw, animalistic cries beckoned her to *his* room.

Urgently, she pressed the door open, hurling herself into his room.

Lorelai didn't know whether to be more relieved or distressed that his great body seemed to battle naught but the darkness.

And whatever demons haunted his dreams.

His voice sounded younger than it did when he was awake. A note of terror thrummed beneath the bravado.

"Let me go," he threatened.

"Let me . . . go." This time, he begged.

Begged. And thrashed. Fighting a battle that it became more and more evident he was about to lose in some horrific way.

She had to stop this. Somehow.

A low groan decided it for her as she neared the bedside. His cheeks were wet with tears. His ebony hair matted with sweat.

Someone *was* hurting him. She couldn't bear it.

Knuckles narrowly missed her throat as she ducked around them, and tentatively splayed the fingers of one hand over his chest above his bandaged ribs. "Wake up," she admonished him, jostling him a little. "Come *back*."

Two monstrous hands shackled her arms like iron cuffs as he gasped awake, his entire body seizing, convulsing. He wrenched her hands away from his skin.

She'd underestimated his strength.

Fearing he might snap her bones in two, she couldn't contain her own sob of pain as it cut through her.

He stared up at her, his eyes two volcanic voids of unfocused wrath. His teeth bared, sharp and menacing. His breaths sawed in and out of him, as though he'd run a league at full tilt.

This was not the man to whom she'd fed soup only two days prior.

This man . . . might be a monster.

"It's me," she whimpered. "It's Lorelai."

As quickly as she'd been seized, she was released.

A low groan tore from him as he regarded his hands like they'd betrayed him. Like he would rip them from their wrists.

Ignoring her smarting arms, she ran tentative fingers over his fevered brow. It twitched with little shocks where they connected.

"It was just a dream," she crooned. "You're safe."

Though he said nothing, tears leaked from the corners of his eyes in an endless river, running down his temple and joining the beads of sweat glistening at his hairline.

His breath hitched and gasped. Deep grooves appeared between his brows, and his entire visage tightened.

"You are in pain," she realized aloud. Had he reinjured something? The bandages about his ribs were secure, as were the ones over his shoulder, neck, and right torso covering his rapidly healing burns. *Oh no.* Should she call the doctor? Did she dare check beneath the blanket twisted around his lean hips and tangled about his legs?

"What can I do?" she asked frantically.

He'd not wept the entire, agonizing time they'd treated him. Not once.

If he did so now, he must be in absolute anguish.

"Where does it hurt the most?"

Black eyes rimmed in red searched her face, as though he might find answers to a question he didn't know how to ask. The air shifted as threads of trust weaved through the space between them, adding a soft color to their tapestry.

Silently, cautiously, he took her hand, his thumb pressed against her palm, as he placed it over his heart and left it there.

His skin was warmer than she'd expected. Harder. His pulse kicked beneath her palm, the rhythm unsteady and frenzied, still waging the battle he'd carefully schooled out of his expression.

He was as stoic as ever, except for the moisture still gathering his sooty lashes into wet spikes.

She understood then.

His body, strong, young, and virile, healed with incredible alacrity. But, what remedy was there for a lonely and broken heart?

She could think of none.

His eyes fluttered closed, forcing more tears from between the lids. She had the sense that he hid whatever . . . *whomever* should stare out from the darkness at her. His hands clenched tightly, burrowing into the sheets. Shadows played across his jaw as he worked it to the side, battling to regain control of himself.

Instinct whispered that she must walk the line between compassion and pity most carefully here.

Struck by impulsive sentiment, she lifted her hand, bent over him, and pressed her lips to his heart.

He tensed. Froze. Not so much as drawing a breath until she pulled away.

"I'll heal that too," she promised. If it was the last thing she did, she'd figure out how to stitch his broken heart back together.

His eyes snapped open, regarding her like she'd taken his soul just then, or, maybe returned it to him.

Nervously, she licked her lips. They tasted of soap and salt and . . . him.

The air shifted again, dangerously this time, becoming heavy with the promise of something she couldn't identify and didn't understand.

Lorelai did her best to ignore it. "Someone was hurting you . . . in your dream . . . did you recognize who it was?"

He shook his head.

"Anything I can do?" Driven to touch him again, she bent to place a hand back on his chest. The cold night air prickled dangerously through her thin nightshift, reminding her of the untied ribbons hanging loose at the collar.

His tears had dried quite suddenly. His sweat had turned to salt. And the way he looked at her now . . .

Lorelai swallowed, thinking of how she had always considered black a cold color, until this very moment.

Banked obsidian fire danced in the meager light of her lantern.

"Go." The word seemed to strangle him as he plucked her hands away from him by her wrists, giving them back to her roughly.

"Pardon?" She hugged her hands to her body.

"Never visit me at night. *Never again.*"

She didn't understand. Wasn't she helping him? Hadn't she saved him from the assailants who hurt him in his sleep?

"What if you have another nightmare?" she contended. "I can't just let you—"

"Leave me to it. Let it take me." A feral, primitive warning lurked beneath the bleakness in his eyes.

"But I—"

"You can't control them!" he snarled. "And I can't control my—" His hands lifted toward her, then plunged into his hair, grabbing great handfuls of it. For some reason she couldn't look at the parts still covered by the sheets. She feared him like this, because he feared himself. But . . . she ached for him, too. Ached in ways she didn't yet comprehend.

"Just get out. *Please.*"

The plaintive note in his plea brooked no argument. Warned her away as sure as the hiss of a cornered cat.

Perplexed, dejected, Lorelai limped to the sideboard

as slowly as she could, waiting for him to call her back. To change his mind and realize he needed her company after all.

When he didn't, she lifted her lantern and shut the door behind her. Wishing with everything she had, that she could forget the bewitching taste of him lingering on her lips.

THE HIGHWAYMAN
by Kerrigan Byrne

is the first book in the stunning
Victorian Rebels series.

Take a sneak peek at the book that started it all!

Available from St. Martin's Paperbacks

Farah clutched the bodice of her dress, even though the buttons were still doing their job, and stared at the large, dark man in the chair.

He met her look with a level one of his own. "Second thoughts already, my dear?" The endearment was not meant as such, and they both knew it. His words were a challenge, an answer to one that she'd issued initially. She'd offered him her body, almost demanded that he take it, and now he'd come to collect.

It would be foolhardy to think that he might make this easy for her.

Farah lifted her chin. "No. I merely thought that you might want to take it off, yourself."

She was playing a dangerous game, and she saw that danger flash in his eyes. "If that were the case, I'd have ripped it off you immediately. Stop stalling and take. Off. Your. Dress."

Of course. He'd want to watch. It excited him. Aroused him.

Very well, Mr. Blackwell, Farah thought. *Watch this.*

Dorian could tell she pretended it wasn't the trembling of her fingers that stole the dexterity from her movements. She tried to keep his gaze locked on her challenging eyes, flashing with little gray storm clouds, but Dorian couldn't manage to stop from visually devouring every hint of skin each release of a button revealed. The slim column of her throat. The soft expanse of thin flesh stretched over her chest and collarbones, so rife with nerve endings.

She took her time, *damn her.*

The light from the candles kissed her silvery hair and her creamy ivory skin with gold as though King Midas had given in to temptation and touched her with his cursed fingers.

Regret tried to lick at him, to stir the humanity buried down deep beneath the layers of greed, self-loathing, violence, hatred, and anger he walled within that impenetrable casing of ice.

This was Farah. His wife. Should he objectify her like this?

Another button worked free, exposing the first hint of the swell of her bosom.

The question was: Could he stop himself if he wanted to?

Dorian already knew the answer.

Not for all the money and power in the empire.

As she exposed the valley of shadow in between her breasts, Dorian felt the intoxicating, almost chemical mixture of thrill and shame he imagined tortured the waifish opiate addicts that haunted the back alleys of the Chinese immigrant shops on the East End.

His body was going to get something it pined after. Burned for. Screamed with the intensity of its need.

And he'd hate himself in the morning.

Hell, she'd probably hate him, too. But she'd progressed

in getting the buttons undone to her navel, and Dorian spied one nipple outlined in pink-tipped perfection against the thin white silk of her chemise, presented to him by her tightly laced corset. All coherent thought dissipated like the mist before the sun's rays, and everything around him receded but for her. His next breath hinged on the next button being set free. The next expanse revealed for him to consume like a starving man.

He wanted to stop her. To demand that she continue. But for all his composure, words had become lost to him, communication beyond his ability. All he could do was sit helplessly and await her next move. Watching.

Farah found it strange that the more she revealed, the bolder she became. Perhaps it had something to do with the way Blackwell's gloved hands gripped the chair arms when she allowed her dress to slide down her curves and puddle at her feet. Or the flare of his nostrils as she reached up, aware of how the action lifted her breasts even higher beneath her sheer chemise, and took the pins from her hair, one by one.

She unraveled the heavy braid that fell over her shoulder, shaking the curls loose to fall to her elbows.

Farah could tell Blackwell fought it, but desire began to melt the ice in his stare, causing his lids to fall heavy over his eyes, and his lips to part in order to allow for the quickening of his breaths.

She hesitated only a moment before moving to untie her laces.

"Don't," he ordered. "Not yet."

Blackwell was a statue, but for the lift of his jacket in deep, heaving movements. His eyes traveled the expanse of her exposed flesh with all the tangible deftness of a caress, branding their way to the waist of her drawers.

"Get rid of them." His voice barely recognizable now, he filled his chest as though it would stop the little twitches of muscle she could see by his eye, below his collar, in his fingers.

Heart thudding wildly, Farah tucked her thumbs into the band of her drawers, preparing to draw them down.

"Wait," he clipped through gritted teeth.

Farah paused.

"Turn around."

Puzzled by the request, she silently complied, determined to follow his instruction. She somehow understood that if Blackwell felt in control, he'd be more likely to go through with this. Farah was prepared and unprepared. Afraid and yet not afraid. Embarrassed and emboldened. The need lurking beneath the chill in his eyes drove her to abandon her characteristic modesty. She was too old for virginal shyness, had seen too much of the horrors this world thrust upon others.

Men were visually stimulated creatures, and females were lovely. It seemed only natural that Blackwell would feel the desire to look upon what he found difficult to bring himself to touch. She understood that in order to conceive the family she wanted, she needed to entice him to do more than look, and that was her prerogative. To push him to a place where desire overcame fear, where the animal instinct to mate controlled the machinations of the body.

And so she faced the fire banked low in the hearth, closed her eyes, took a deep breath, and bent to push her drawers over her hips.

"Slowly." He hissed the command.

A hazard lurked in her plan, though, Farah realized as she languidly swept the lacy drawers over the swell of her rump and down the quivering muscles of her thighs. For a man such as Dorian Blackwell to be driven mad enough with lust to break the bonds of the past.

He might be driven to break her, as well.

Dorian had often studied the female form in every

modality from paintings to prostitutes. He'd seen them all. Appreciated a few, despite himself. But *nothing* could have prepared him for the vision of Farah's body, a dark and flawless silhouette against the backdrop of the flames.

His weak eye blurred detail in the direct contrast with the firelight, and so instinct drew him to lean closer. She flared out in all the places a woman should, dipping to create curves that were the soft answer to a man's hard angles.

Bent as she was, her ass was so exposed to him, the slight outline of her womanhood a dark secret in the low light.

Dorian's mouth went dry. His racing heart sped like a stallion on the last sprint toward the finish line. Impossibly faster. Pushed to the limit of its capacity. His breath sawed in and out of his chest in tight, painful bursts, burning like it did when he ran in the winter. Frost and heat. Ice in his blood and fire in his loins.

It had been almost twenty years since anyone had touched him in a way not meant to cause pain. To humiliate, incapacitate, and control. It had been just as long since he'd used his hands for a purpose other than defense, violence, or domination.

Farah's skin. Her flawless, unmarked skin. Free of scars, branded by no one, and belonging to *him*.

At last.